The Spy who Breathed Fear

An Augustus Benedict Cold War Spy Novel

P.J. Anderson

Nine Lives Original Books

First published 2023

ISBN: 978-1-8383410-5-3

Nine Lives Original Books

The Storey Building,
Meeting House Lane,
Lancaster, United Kingdom,
LA1 1TH.

CONTENTS

A selection of other books by P.J. Anderson available from Nine Lives Original Books (fuller details can be found at the end of this book):

The Spy with an Angel's Eyes: an Augustus Benedict Cold War spy novel

A Man Twice Dead: an almost perfect crime

The Ghost Fabler

ACKNOWLEDGEMENTS

Many, many thanks to Verity and Janet for reading and commenting on the first draft of this book, to Tim for commenting on Chapter One and to Anne for her consistently high editorial standards.

CHAPTER ONE

"A man with a bullet in the brain is a man who knows the answer to the ultimate question: is there life after death? Would you like to know the answer to that question Mr. Jacob?"

The gun was pressed hard against Jacob's skull and he had lost the ability to think about anything at all. The only thing that filled his mind was the panic induced by a terror so fierce that his fingernails cut deep into the flesh of his clenched fists. The chief interrogator, a bald, bull of a man whose biceps strained against the rolled-up sleeves of his grim, grey shirt, said,

"I'll ask you a second time Mr. Jacob. If there is a maker to be met, would you like to meet him?"

Jacob's wrists felt like they were bound with barbed wire and the thick blindfold over his eyes was so tight that it made his eyes ache. He had been forced to stand for hours in a variety of positions that had become impossibly painful, prodded repeatedly with the razor like tip of a butcher's knife and measured up for his coffin, just to rub in the potentially terminal nature of his predicament. He had almost passed the point where rational thought was still possible and the only wish that he had left was that they would get it over with and put him out of his agony.

Then everything changed. He heard the steel door of his cell burst open and the barking of orders in Russian. There was no longer a gun pressed against his head. He heard the scraping of chair legs across the cold, concrete floor as the furniture was hastily rearranged to accommodate the new arrivals. His sweating face was cooled by the welcome cold air that seeped in from the corridor outside. He heard his interrogators depart with a curse and the door slamming behind them and then the blindfold was pulled from his eyes.

Seated directly in front of him was a well-built man in an expensively cut thick woollen coat that only a KGB Colonel would be able to afford. He had a square, calm face and eyes that had seen life and death in equal measure. He smiled, his skin lightly wrinkling in the manner of someone in his early forties. There was neither warmth nor menace in the gesture, it seemed little more than a formality. He said, in perfect English,

"Mr. Jacob, how nice to meet you. Would you like a cup of tea?"

Jacob struggled to get to grips with the change in tone, the bizarre suddenness of the switch from barbarism to gentility. He thought it wise to play along and nodded feebly, wondering simultaneously if the offer was merely a game, a cruel mockery that would be the precursor to yet more suffering. The Colonel gestured to the lackey standing by the table at the back of the cell and the prisoner saw, to his disbelief, that a teapot and two cups had been assembled in readiness. The lackey poured a cup for each. The Colonel asked,

"Would you like milk and sugar and if so, how many lumps?"

Still struggling with the turnaround in tactics, Jacob nodded and said he would like two. The lackey brought the cups over. The Colonel said,

"Leonid, really, you can't expect Mr. Jacob to hold the cup between his teeth and drink it, can you? Untie the poor man and then give him his well-deserved refreshment. He has had a most exhausting morning. Is that not so Mr. Jacob?"

The razor-sharp twine that had been cutting into Jacob's wrists like a ring of nails was removed. He gasped with pain as the cold air bit into his suddenly exposed wounds. The Colonel said,

"Nothing broken, nothing that won't mend with a bit of medication and a bandage. You're a lucky man Mr. Jacob, I arrived just in time to save you. Your interrogator appears to be a man of yesterday's methods, a dinosaur in terms of his interrogation skills perhaps. I must have a word with him about how we do things now in these changing times. Give the man his cup Leonid. There's nothing like tea to resurrect the English, is there Mr. Jacob?"

Jacob felt considerably beyond resurrection. A previously fit and healthy thirty-nine-year-old, with a strikingly handsome face and the body of a sprinter, he now looked like a ragged battlefield casualty urgently in need of stretcher bearers. He raised his numb and shaking hands painfully and grasped the cup, almost spilling the tea all over his swollen knees. As parched as a desert rat, he gulped down the reviving brown liquid almost in one go. The Colonel smiled approvingly, cradling his own teacup in his hands as if it were a small animal that he was debating whether to cuddle or throttle. He said,

"What did I tell you Leonid? Quite miraculous. Look how our friend begins his return to the land of the living."

Observing that the Colonel hadn't yet touched his tea, Jacob began to worry that he might just have drunk from the proverbial poisoned chalice. Then the KGB man began to sip from his own cup and his fears subsided a little.

"How would you like a little walk Mr. Jacob, the chance to stretch your legs perhaps? You have been confined in such a small space and for so many days, I believe. It will do you good to get out and about again. There are things I would like to show you. I think you will find them extremely educational."

The Colonel took another sip and then handed his cup to the lackey. He stood up and gestured to the prisoner to do the same. He checked his watch and said,

"Come, let me show you something that few men get to see."

The lackey opened the door and Jacob shuffled out, following the Colonel down the ice-cold corridor that led past an interminably long line of cell doors. From behind several he could hear deep sobbing, desperate cries and the mumblings of those driven insane by their experiences at the hands of their captors. The Colonel moderated his pace to accommodate the painful struggle that Jacob was having with his swollen knees. He said,

"When Leonid and I arrived at your cell I heard your interrogator ask if you'd like to meet your maker. I apologise for your being asked such an un-communist question Mr. Jacob. I must really put in a recommendation for that man to be sent for re-education before he next interviews any of our prisoners. As all good Party members know, God is dead, or rather the idea of God is dead. There never was, nor ever can be such a being. He is a fantasy, a pure fantasy that must be eradicated from our culture, do you not agree?"

The point was lost on Jacob, whether the Colonel's pronouncement were true or false. His attention was entirely focussed on trying to avoid collapsing in a painful heap onto the concrete slabs that seemed to go on forever. He had the fear that he would be shot where he lay, like a dog that was too ill to be of any further use. The Colonel was quite happy to continue the conversation with or without any contributions from anyone else.

"That's what makes the life we have now, the here and now, so important. It is all we have Mr. Jacob and when it has gone, we have nothing, we are nothing. From nothing we came, to nothing we return. That's why it's so fortunate I've been able to save you. Only a minute or two later and you would have been history, another nameless corpse in an unmarked grave, remembered by no-one, as unmissed as a sparrow that falls out of the sky into a deep river on its last day on earth. Just like that

3

man there."

They had stopped at the entrance to a cavernous, white tiled room that looked in every respect like a mortuary. In the centre, a broken man knelt, his head bent forwards. A second man stood behind him, unmoving. Guards were stationed at the entrance and the exit to the room. The dull bells of the clock on the prison roof began to chime midday. The executioner raised his gun and fired a single shot into the back of the man's skull. He collapsed onto the floor, lifeless. The executioner stood over him and fired a second shot for good measure. A grey faced medic bent over the man, briefly examined him and pronounced him dead. The guards marched mechanically forwards and pulled the body onto a stretcher that had been laid on the floor in readiness and then carried their burden out of the room. A waiting cleaner waddled sullenly over to the pool of blood on the tiled floor and began mopping it up. It was all over in less than five minutes, a production line killing.

"I do like precision," the Colonel said. "The first shot was fired as soon as the bell chimed, dead on time, if you'll pardon the pun."

Jacob was consumed by the fear that he was the next in the queue. That any second now the guards and the executioner would march back into the room, seize him and put a bullet in the back of his brain. At the same time, he was having increasing difficulty just trying to remain standing. His legs and feet were struggling with deep cramps, on top of the other consequences of his being tortured, and his consciousness was beginning to spin like a Catherine wheel, his grip on reality decreasing with every passing second. The Colonel was saying something to him, but he could no longer hear his words as anything other than a blur of incomprehensible sound. A feeling like the onset of the deepest of sleeps suddenly swept through his brain and the lights in his mind went out simultaneously. He collapsed onto the floor like a puppet whose strings had been cut. The Colonel barked a command that echoed the length and breadth of the corridor and two guards came running within seconds. They brought a stretcher with them and lifted Jacob onto it, before carrying him off into the distance.

He regained consciousness briefly along the way. Finding himself being marched along on a stretcher in the manner of the executed prisoner, he feared that he too had been shot. That would explain the searing headache that burnt through his skull. He presumed that they must think him dead and that he was in imminent danger of being nailed into a coffin, or thrown into a pit of quicklime. If they found out that he was still in the land of the living, they would simply shoot him again and finish him off. If they didn't, he would be buried alive. There were no good options to hold onto. He didn't have much time to struggle with his predicament.

Almost as soon as it had begun to terrify him, he lost consciousness again. For the rest of his journey he lay as limp as a man dead four times over.

When he awoke, his grip on reality seemed finally to have gone completely. He was sitting up in a hospital bed. The expensively cut Savile Row suit that he had been wearing before the start of his nightmare – and of which he had been stripped after his arrest – was laid neatly over the top of a bedside chair, ready for him to wear. His knees were soothed by some form of medication and he could feel the reassuring grip of support bandages around them. His wrists also were bandaged where he had been bound with the razor-sharp twine. A man in a white coat was shining a physician's torch into his eyes and a nurse stood beside him, taking notes. Seemingly satisfied with what they saw, they left without saying a word to him.

Looking around the room he was surprised to see that his surroundings had more the appearance of a hotel than a prison hospital. The floor was carpeted and there were paintings of various striking rustic scenes on the walls. The window at the end of the room was without bars and looked out onto what seemed to be well manicured parkland. The only indication that he wasn't a free man was a chain round one of his ankles that was fixed to the bed frame. He had no idea how long he had been unconscious, but the clock on the wall told him that it was mid-morning, so he had been asleep for at least a day. There was a jug of iced water and a glass on a small table at the side of the bed and he reached over with still aching arms and poured himself a drink.

The cool liquid was a desperately needed antidote to the dry, burnt rawness of his throat. He lay back on the pillows that were supporting his still aching back and tried to recall everything that had happened during the nightmare that had brought him finally to this place. He remembered arriving in Paris, having travelled on the expertly forged passport that he had bought, via a middleman, in London. It had transformed him from being Gillow Elliott, British Foreign Office high flyer and inheritor of the extensive country estate of Sir Laidlow Elliott, into Carrington Wallace, a specialist investment broker. He couldn't work out why his captors kept calling him Jacob, although the name seemed to have a distinctive resonance in the parts of his memory that he still couldn't fully recover. He had dyed his blond hair black for his new passport photograph and shaved the beard and moustache that he had proudly sported since his early twenties. A pair of gold rimmed spectacles had completed the transformation. He had booked a room in a hotel that laid claim to hosting everyone from princes to Hollywood leading ladies and decided to road test his new identity in the casino. Everything had gone well. He'd enjoyed modest winnings and by the middle of the evening had even acquired the company of a glamorous young woman in an emerald green silk dress. They'd had a few drinks at the bar and then she'd invited him back to her apartment for a nightcap and maybe a little more. Jacob could never resist the prospect of 'a little more' and had swung out of the hotel with his bewitching new friend on his arm, ready to call a cab and head off into a night of many exotic and pleasurable delights. He'd got no further than the top of the steps that led down from the palatial revolving doors, however, when he froze as if his veins had been suddenly injected with ice. On the other side of the road was a black sedan and in the clear light of the streetlamp above it he could see two occupants who had the classic profile of KGB heavies. One of them was watching him as he came out. He had no doubt that he was the bee attracted by the smell of honey and about to be trapped. He would get in a taxi, be taken to a dark part of town where he would be dropped off and then seized by the two gorilla-sized goons who had been following behind. His oh so promising lady of the night would vanish into the shadows, ready for her next job.

He gave a lame excuse about having to go back to his room to get his hat and coat, but when he attempted to remove his arm from his escort's embrace, he found that she tightened her grip with the strength of a female wrestler and started to pull him down the steps towards an oh too conveniently waiting taxi that had just drawn up at the front of the hotel. With a sudden flash of inspiration he whipped the gold pin out of his tie and stuck it in her arm, causing her to scream and release her grip. He darted back up the steps and over to the hotel elevators, just managing to squeeze through the closing door of the nearest one. Leaping out at the seventh floor, he dashed over to his room, hurled everything into his suitcase and then hurtled to the end of the corridor, nearly playing ten pin bowling with a row of elderly guests lost in deep conversation as he did so. He flew down the fire escape to the basement and the hotel garage, where his hire car sat waiting for him.

He remembered driving like a madman out of Paris, careering down a succession of narrow country roads to try and avoid any pursuing vehicles that might have been sent after him. After a couple of hours, with no sign of any pursuers, he relaxed and began to drive at a normal speed. It was then, out of nowhere, that a black Citroen had appeared behind him, flashing its lights vigorously. He had started to accelerate, but the engine in the pursuing car was obviously souped up and his pursuers pulled out and drew level with him with ease. The two occupants of the vehicle were in police uniforms and one was gesturing angrily to him to slow down and pull in. Realising he couldn't outpace them, he did as instructed, presuming that his earlier wild driving must have been reported and that they intended booking him for whatever motoring offences they had in mind. The Citroen stopped in front of him and the driver got out, pulling his notebook out of his pocket as he did so. He gestured to Jacob to wind his window down and began taking his details. The second policeman examined the hired Mercedes while he did so, checking the tyres and doing all of the other things that a meticulous officer would be expected to do. It was a full minute into the proceedings when Jacob had felt the sharp stab in his arm. Looking up he saw the second man holding the syringe that had been jabbed into his flesh and it was then that he realised they were nothing to do with the police at all. He had tried to wrest his arm free, but his consciousness ebbed away so rapidly that his efforts were over before they had even begun. The next thing he remembered was waking up in the cell, handcuffed and wearing only his underwear.

All of that he could remember easily. What followed, his long, gruelling interrogation over several days of various degrees of discomfort, ranging from the disorienting to the screamingly painful, was rather foggy in his mind. The real problem, however, was in trying to remember why he had been in Paris in the first place and why he had needed to replace his normal passport with a fake one and a new identity. He had been fed a devastating diet of mind scrambling drugs during his interrogation, so it was hardly surprising that his memory had sprung a leak or two. He had a vague feeling that the Americans were in some way involved in his visit to Paris, but he couldn't recall how or why. The more he tried to remember, the thicker the blank wall became between him and the events he was trying to recall. As he was struggling with all of this the door opened and a now familiar figure entered.

"Ah, Mr. Jacob, you are looking so much better. You have some colour back in your cheeks I see. I must apologise for your little mishaps of the last few days, but we needed to get to the truth of things, very quickly. The methods used were a little crude and old fashioned for my taste and I have reprimanded the people concerned for the more painful parts of your experience, but they did the job nevertheless. You could even say that they saved your life. Had we not found the answers we needed before your usefulness to us ran out, then you would probably have been killed."

Jacob said nothing, eyeing the Colonel with a well justified mixture of fear and suspicion.

"Anyway, now we know why you did what you did we can give you a choice that otherwise you would not have had. You can either do what you were told to do prior to your little escapade and for which you were paid very handsomely, very handsomely indeed if I may say so, or you will be shot in the back of the head like the unfortunate young man whom we saw being despatched a couple of days ago. It was all over so quickly for him, wasn't it? One minute alive and breathing, full of those last despairing hopes for the reprieve that never came, and then nothing – the absolute, terrible nothingness that lasts forever when a man dies. You don't want that nothingness do you Mr. Jacob? You have so much to look forward to, if you do what we ask, that is."

He smiled and then strolled over to one of the paintings to see if he could find the artist's signature. He said,

"I must say, this is rather fine. I wonder if they'd let me borrow it do you think?"

The only things that Jacob was thinking were, "what on earth was it that I was told to do and why does everyone keep calling me Jacob?" He was afraid of revealing his ignorance about the first of these matters in case the Colonel took it as evidence that his brain was so far gone that he was no longer of use – and no longer of use would probably mean a bullet in the back of his skull. The KGB man turned round and smiled again, a mortician's smile. Perusing the tortured, despairing look on Jacob's face, he said,

"You look perplexed, Mr. Jacob. Tell me what it is that is troubling you."

Jacob's brain was still working on half power and he felt a sense of panic about being put on the spot in this way. He dare not say anything about his ignorance of what it was he was expected to do, so raised the matter of his name as the least bad of the only two options that consented to come into his weary mind.

"I don't understand why everyone's calling me Jacob all the time."

The Colonel raised his eyebrows.

"It is my standard practice to use the codename of someone in your position at all times. I insist all of my staff do the same. It is very basic safety-first Mr. Jacob. If I or one of our people were to become forgetful and use your real name in a communication that was intercepted, then our British friends would guess right away that you are one of our assets. So everyone is forbidden from using your real name at all times, unless, of course, they encounter you in a public context in the UK, in which case they will address you by your real name to avoid giving away your codename. It's complex I know, but it's a practice that is designed to protect you from discovery. Does that sound agreeable?"

Jacob nodded, inwardly deeply relieved that the Colonel hadn't realised that, prior to this helpful explanation, he didn't have a clue that he had a codename because he couldn't remember it. The KGB man was scrutinising his face carefully. He said,

"You still look like a lost soul Mr. Jacob. I hope you're not having doubts, wondering if you should do what you've never done before and play the hero, the man who unexpectedly regains his patriotic loyalty to the crumbling empire of the moth bitten British Crown? It's a difficult thing, this loyalty business, isn't it? It might depend on what you believe, what I believe. I might be utterly, totally loyal to the Soviet Union because I fervently believe in communism, the ideology that it has taken to its bosom. But I don't – not the monster that it has evolved into at least. Some of the people whom I work with don't either, but they say they do, as do I."

He smiled again and said, in a confiding manner,

"You see Mr. Jacob, I'm loyal to the Soviet Union for a variety of reasons other than its espousal of a particular form of communism. At the most basic level, I'm loyal because there are those who pay me well to be so, those upon whose power my own power depends. They represent the communist state for now, so, outwardly, it is the communist state that I uphold – as strongly as I did during the Stalin years. But the manner in which the powers that be of the Stalin era diluted and distorted the ideas and the values of Marxism-Leninism killed nearly all of my belief in the debased coinage that masquerades as Soviet communism today. Inwardly, I support it only because I believe it is still marginally better than capitalism. My superiors suspect that is what I think, they're intelligent people. But they'd never challenge me, because, under the skin, many of them are the same. In my country, it is not wise to say in public what you really believe if your belief is different from the official dogma, so we who think differently all pretend we are fervent Soviet style communists from the top of our heads to the tips of our toes. I can say that to you because nobody would believe you if you tried to tell them what I'd said. You have no credibility or status in such matters, you lost all of that as soon as you tried to run away. Now you have only your remaining usefulness to us, and that has an expiry date on it. So your mind must be focussed entirely on the loyalty you should be showing to us, not because we are communist or capitalist, but because we are the people who have the power to decide if you should die or live. That is the only kind of loyalty that is left for someone in your position. Be loyal and we will reward you. Be disloyal again and we will feed you to the rats. Do you want us to feed you to the rats Mr. Jacob?"

Jacob gulped and stared at the floor. He'd seen more than enough rats in his prison cell.

"I will take that as a no," the Colonel said. "It can be extremely tiresome when one party has to provide both sides of a conversation because the other refuses to speak, Mr. Jacob, but maybe I can understand why you're so lost for words, so ungrateful for me having saved your worthless little life. At the moment you hate us because of all the pain we have put you through – the moments when you thought you were about to

9

die and the moments when you wished dearly that you were already dead. I understand that Mr. Jacob. But you have to understand something as well – all of your pain was self-inflicted, none of it would have happened without your foolish little act of treachery. Do you believe in the devil, Mr. Jacob?"

The prisoner looked startled. He said,

"What?"

"The devil. I know I told you that I don't believe in God, but I did once upon a time, before my experiences during the Stalin years killed that belief. Paradoxical though it might seem, I do still believe in the devil though. When I was left with a massive hole in my world, where previously God had been, I found only the devil could fill it as the explanation for all of the evil I saw around me. You most probably think I am he. Perhaps I am, or perhaps I simply speak for him when I tempt you to continue betraying your country. But you also have your own satanic business Mr. Jacob, that one, fatal moment when you ran over a young man when you were drunk at the wheel of your car – and that defining moment when you chose to turn one crime into two. Do you remember it, when you paid that witness to keep her mouth shut? It is those two morally bankrupt moments in your life that have made us your masters and you were the sole author of both of them. So rather than hating us, you should perhaps hate yourself Mr. Jacob. Hate yourself and the devil who tempted you to pay off the witness, the corrupt civil servant who sold your vile little secret to us when she saw you rise up the ranks of the British Foreign Office. Hate the devil that has tempted you once again to save yourself by undermining your country – and hate yourself for being so weak and gutless in giving in to him. Let all of that hate rip through your system Mr. Jacob, purge it and purge it again. Then you will come to realise that this great act of betrayal that we are asking of you is in fact your escape route. You shouldn't hate us for asking you to do it, you should thank us for it. Do it and we will ask no more of you. Do it and you save your life. Do it and no one will find out that you killed an innocent young man in a cowardly hit and run accident all those years ago. Do it and you will not do the wrong that your government might accuse you of. It is our belief that what we will be asking of you will make the world a safer place."

The Colonel surveyed the broken, sunken wreck of an upper-class Englishman who lay strewn across the bed in front of him, a clever but spineless self-server with the morals of a delinquent banker. He had no doubt that he could crush and filter the prisoner's obduracy until only the required subservience ran out onto the carpet. The man was no hero. He had given up the information required of him and now the only way for him to save his worthless hide would be to do exactly as the Colonel wished. Now was the time to put the final squeeze on him, to put a stop to the sullen silences and get him to mouth the necessary words of contrition and re-commit to the vital task he had tried to run away from. He said,

"So, presuming you wish to stay alive, I'm assuming that we have your renewed consent to your meeting your obligations to us."

Jacob's brain was just not working at its normal pace. It was still clouded by intermittent fog and he was having enormous difficulty trying to fathom what to say, given that he couldn't remember anything of the detail of those obligations. He looked as though he was about to speak, but each time he tried the words froze on his lips. Watching him closely, the Colonel realised that something was amiss.

"Ah, so that's it, that's the cat that's got your tongue. I think I'm looking at a memory malfunction, is that correct Mr. Jacob? Are you having difficulties remembering what it is precisely that you're supposed to do for us?"

Jacob's mind went into meltdown. He couldn't bluff his way through this one. The Colonel was the kind of man who meant every threat and if he realised that Jacob had become useless to him, that may well be the end of the road. There was every reason imaginable to persuade the KGB man that everything was fine, but it would be no use if doing so resulted in Jacob being allowed to go free without having a clue what he was supposed to do to save his skin. That would simply result in a slightly delayed execution once it was realised that his brain was no longer functioning properly. To the Colonel, the desperate, terrified look on his face was familiar and told its own story. He said,

"I think what we are looking at are the continued after effects of Denetrylbe N9a, one of the experimental drugs that was used during your interrogation Mr. Jacob. Normally they should have worn off by now, but with some people it takes a little longer. With others, sadly, there is permanent brain damage. That is a side effect we haven't yet managed to eradicate. I can give you a bit more time to recall all that you need to remember within the short deadlines we're working to. There is no point in me giving you the details now because you may simply forget them again if you haven't first managed to recall them under your own steam, or you may not remember the fine detail of how you would normally conduct your relationships with the key players inside the Foreign Office. If you have lost the ability to do all of that and cannot get it back on your own, then your brain will have been damaged too much for us to risk using your services. You have two more days. I will assign a doctor to help you with some memory exercises. If you can't manage it, don't worry. We will supply the very best flowers for your funeral."

The Colonel looked again at the painting that had so interested him before. He said,

"I really must see if they will let me borrow this."

He smiled at Jacob, whose face was a mixture of panic and despair at this very short reprieve and then exited, mischievously humming the downbeat and slightly ominous opening to Tchaikovsky's fifth symphony.

As he marched down the marble tiled corridor, each step sounding like the distant crack of a pistol, the Colonel seemed to those in his path like a human projectile constantly looking for a target. Doctors and functionaries hardly dared look at him, nodding submissively and scrupulously avoiding eye contact. Wherever he went, his reputation froze the faces of the innocent even more than those of the guilty. The cold, raw fear of his presence cut deep into the minds of those who understood most clearly that he was a man with the power to cripple and the power to kill – a man who, in Stalin's time, had reputedly decided with the roll of a dice whether an underling who had annoyed him should live, or whether he should die. Some said that when he talked of the devil, he spoke of himself. A couple of years previously, in 1956, the Soviet leadership had announced a new gentler, post-Stalinist era. But, as was seen in Hungary shortly afterwards, some of the Stalin years' most terrifying figures still stalked the corridors of Soviet power – and Colonel Zaliatev was one of the most terrifying of all. He pretended to have altered his methods in the post-Stalin era and always blamed others for anything that smacked of the excesses of the past, but in reality, for him the ends justified the means. Precisely what philosophy now drove his zealousness, given his near total loss of faith in the path that Soviet communism had taken since the days when he had originally signed up as a true believer, one of the Party faithful, was a mystery to him. He could identify the vague outlines of the beliefs and half beliefs that together made up his view of the world and his place in it, but he couldn't quite combine them into a coherent ideological perspective. But in a way that was irrelevant. He didn't need such precise knowledge to continue functioning so vigorously, he just kept on doing what he knew he was good at, espionage in the name of the communist state and the maintenance of his power and position through his terrifying reputation.

It was said that in the Chinese intelligence service he was known as The Dragon, the spy who breathed fear.

CHAPTER TWO

The rain bounced off the pavement, saturating the shoes and ankles of those hurrying along Mayfair's golden trail of glittering shops and hotels. Among the teatime throng was a tall, elegantly groomed man in his late thirties. He was wearing a coat that cost more than the annual salaries of many of those toiling away in the corridors and offices of Claridge's Hotel and the other flagships of elite hospitality that he passed on the way to his five-thirty rendezvous. The storm was so fierce it was difficult to see clearly and he almost went past the entrance to the eye-wateringly expensive Crown Validorum Hotel, where his presence was awaited. After shaking his umbrella vigorously on the steps, he handed it to the doorman and hurried in, choosing to take the marble stairs rather than the lift. Once he had got to the third floor, he strode swiftly to the end of the long corridor and knocked softly on the door of Room 332. After a short delay, while those inside checked him out via the spyhole, the door was opened and he slipped inside.

Two dressing tables were rammed against the party wall, behind which the very sumptuous Room 333 sat. Every inch of their surfaces was filled with listening and recording devices, the most technically advanced that the late nineteen-fifties could offer. A young man with intense eyes and fiercely Brylcreemed hair was sitting monitoring the goings on in the room next door, via a set of headphones. The visitor asked to see the log and perused the summary of the main events so far. The subject was Sir Jeremy Wenstratton. He was a famously idle and unsavoury member of parliament whose one known talent was his ability to speak fluent Russian. He had played a useful role as an interpreter during the early post-war occupation of Berlin by the four powers. He was suspected of illegally accessing confidential information at the heart of government and selling it on to the

Soviets to fund his gambling debts. The purpose of today's exercise was to trick him into admitting his treachery. He had arrived in the room next door at three pm, with a MI5-briefed hostess on his arm. They had partaken of a few preliminary drinks and she had laced his with a drug that would remove many of his inhibitions and make him more inclined to let slip secrets that he would much rather have kept to himself. Unfortunately, despite her attempts to liberate the required information from him, he had so far retained enough of a grip on his mouth to avoid giving anything away. She would be aware, therefore, that as Plan A hadn't worked by five thirty, Plan B would very shortly come into play. If that should fail as well, then everything would depend on Plan C. That was very much the old honeytrap ploy, so beloved by the KGB. A camera hidden in the wardrobe would have caught enough compromising photos of the subject in flagrante delicto to hopefully persuade him to confess. The log keeper told the visitor that everything was now ready for Plan B. A second set of headphones was given to him and he sat down next to the equipment operator to listen in to the skilfully calibrated antics of the 'hostess' next door. He could hear much huffing and puffing and squeals, sighs and cries that sounded more like Saturday night around the back of a Soho pub than what might be expected within one of London's most refined hotels. The 'hostess' was leading her mark towards the climax of the afternoon, but not quite the one that he had in mind. She had taken the 'Grand Old Duke of York' very nearly to the top of the hill, but paused in a moment of carefully calculated deprivation of pleasurable release. It was then that the young man with the fierce hair struck. He dialled the number of the adjoining room. As the telephone rang out, the 'hostess' reached over to hook the receiver up off the bedside table. Her client gasped in despair, almost shouting,

"Oh for heaven's sake, this is hardly the moment Miss whatever your name is. Put the wretched thing down and let's get on with things. The train was just getting to the end of the line and now it's stuck at Clapham Junction."

"But I can't, Sir Jeremy, the caller wants to speak to you urgently. He sounds very important."

She passed the phone to him. He grabbed it angrily and barked,

"Who the devil are you and how did you get this number?"

Speaking to him in fluent Russian, the man with the fierce hair said,

"It's Vladimir from the embassy. Don't worry, this is a completely secure line. We haven't met, but I look after the paperwork relating to your case on behalf of Comrade Zhinomovsky. The Comrade has requested that I should ask you for just a little bit more information. I'm sorry to bother you with this now, but it is really most urgent. Comrade Zhinomovsky thought you might have left a crucial detail or two out from the intelligence you passed on most recently. Would you care to supply the missing parts of the jigsaw so that we can leave you to get on with things? We know all about your little weakness with the ladies and will be very happy to keep it to ourselves, should you be able to help us. We will be extremely discreet about today's, how shall I put it, 'exotic' rendezvous in Room 333 – and we will be very happy to lose the photograph we took of your glamorous lady friend entering your bedroom with your hand on her behind."

There was a frustrated gasp from Sir Jeremy, who was clearly no fan of coitus interruptus. Replying in Russian, he said,

"Look, I've told the man all I know. The US president is planning to reinstate the nuclear weapons collaboration with the British that was ended after the Second World War. Your people becoming the first to put a satellite into space so panicked the American Joe Public that the president needs some quick measures to show that the US is doing things to ensure the West wins the rockets and missiles race. Making NATO more effective by stopping the British wasting money doing research and development that the US has done already is part of that. With access to American nuclear expertise they can then spend more money on other military projects instead of duplicating research that has already been done. That is pretty common knowledge in diplomatic circles by now. The British are drawing up a shopping list of things they'd like to get out of the restored relationship and that list includes a variety of items that will never be publicly revealed, making information about them of premium value to Soviet intelligence. Those are the juicy bits that I can put on the table. As soon as I'm able to get hold of the details I'll pass them on, he can be sure of that. There is really nothing more that I can say until I get that additional information, which I will. Now please, don't call me on this line again and don't think for a minute that you can threaten me. There are lots of other governments who would pay just as well for the secrets I sell, so don't ever presume that Moscow is the only belle at the ball. I'm extremely busy at present and I don't have time to answer questions about information that doesn't yet exist. Good night!"

He slammed the phone down. Looking up at the nymph who sat astride him, he said,

"You should never have answered that. Now, can we please continue with the matter in hand – and no I didn't mean that as a pun, you can take that smile off your face. The good lady from whom I hired your services promised me an afternoon of unrivalled delight and I'm still waiting to be fully delighted."

The vigorous huffing, puffing, squealing and shouting resumed and the visitor ripped off his earphones hurriedly, saying,

"My God, I've never heard anything quite so deafening. You'd think they were murdering each other. She's extremely good at her job McTavish, but has Angus authorised all of this hanky-panky?"

McTavish, the log keeper, was a sharp-eyed, middle-aged man with a permanent smirk. He laughed and said,

"Angus made it very clear that he wants to know as little as possible about 'such lewd means of intelligence gathering'. He kept going on about how he would prefer us to keep to the moral high ground and not sink to the same lows as the KGB. But if he wants the benefits that Section D5 can provide for his operations then he has to take the rough with the smooth, I'm afraid. We're Henry's boys and girls. We don't belong to Angus and we don't always play quite by the rules. What I can say is that we didn't procure the exotic entertainer who is keeping Sir Jeremy so busy in there. He hired her from a madam whom he uses regularly to meet such needs and he did that all by himself. We merely paid her a little bit extra to, how shall I put it, use some of her many talents in the service of the national interest. I suspect all trace of the methods used will disappear from the official record anyway. That's the way of the world old man, and it keeps things nicely clean and tidy."

"Well, I can't say the ethics of the thing sit easily with me either, but we have at least got a result. My Russian is a little rusty, but from what I could make out the idiot has let slip pretty well everything he told Moscow's man. Whatever narcotic potions you fed him finally lubricated his tongue."

"Indeed. He was so anxious to get back to his lusty delights that he threw caution to the wind – a perfect sting. We'll be able to forget about the naughty pictures of their antics and the blackmail routine. He's done himself a favour and made them redundant."

The man with the fierce hair suddenly interjected,

"There's something going horribly wrong in there. I think the old fool's having a coronary."

The visitor grabbed the second set of headphones and listened intently. He said,

"Get the hotel to call an ambulance immediately and to check if there's by any chance a doctor in the building. Get the girl and all traces of her out of there and get this equipment packed up and out of the building pronto – and make sure you get the hidden camera out of there as well. I'll handle things from here on."

It was a full half hour before the outcome of the emergency was revealed. The visitor was by that time calmly seated in the hotel lobby, ostensibly awaiting the arrival of a fictional guest. He observed that the face of the patient on the stretcher that was carried out to the waiting ambulance was covered. He sighed, noted the time and wrote it down in his diary before quietly leaving. He nodded sombrely to the doorman, collected his umbrella and then disappeared back into the still heavy rain.

The following morning was even grimmer than before, with a storm so fierce that it flooded the gutters and turned the roads into shallow rivers. It was some of the worst weather that late nineteen-fifties London had seen. The 'visitor' of the night before hurried through the doorway of the imposing gothic revival building where his first business of the day awaited, unbeknown to him. After tipping the water from the rim of his hat onto the large, absorbent lobby mat that was the first line of defence against inclement weather, he squelched up the ornate oak staircase to his top floor office. It was graced by gold lettering on the thick, frosted glass window, proclaiming it to be the home of the Augustus Benedict Private Detective Agency, a claim which both the CIA and KGB took to be the lightest of covers for a MI5 funded operation. He opened the door to be greeted by a look of fierce annoyance. The look sat on the normally welcoming face of Alice Harding, Benedict's number two. She said, sotto voce,

"Gus, the dowager's here! I haven't been able to get a civil word out of her. The old firebrand marched straight into your inner sanctum and has been sitting there fuming for half an hour. I think she's gunning for you – she's got a frown on her face that would cause even the devil to scream and leap out of the window."

"I might well follow him if I go in there," Gus replied. "Tell her I've been delayed on a case and won't be in until tomorrow at the earliest. I'll be in my club – give me a ring when the coast's clear."

"Augustus!"

It appeared the great escape plan had been nipped in the bud. Despite the oak door to the inner sanctum being closed, his mother's ears – detection equipment that rivalled the best technology then available to secret services across the globe – had picked up his whisperings. She stood in the doorway of his private office with a look that, in popular parlance, would have said, "Gotcha!" She may have been only five feet tall, but she had the arms of a wrestler and a gaze that would have withered the fiercest of lions. She beckoned him forwards and pointed to a waiting chair in his office. He noted that it wasn't the comfortable leather swivel chair that sat behind his substantial Georgian desk, but a much humbler one, reserved for clients. He took off his hat and coat and seated himself gingerly. She was already in occupation of his own very grand chair, and occupation was most certainly the word. Gus had survived some of the most dangerous intelligence operations imaginable during the Second World War, so was not a man who might be described as easily scared. His mother, however, was one of the few opponents whom he truly feared. Her sense of humour was noticeable only by its complete absence, her tolerance of dissent was on a par with that of Attila the Hun and the clinical inquisitiveness of her mind would have made her a formidable interrogator for the KGB, had she not been as fiercely opposed to communism as a feline-averse Alsatian dog might be to a ginger tom. By the simple raising of her voice she had always had the power to stop all three of her children dead in their tracks, from the time of their first walking to the present day. She surveyed Gus over the top of her gold rimmed spectacles and said,

"Augustus, you've been avoiding me and it's not hard to see why. Would you care to explain yourself?"

"Avoiding you? No, of course not mother, I've merely been extremely busy, that's all. I'm delighted to see you, as always."

"Augustus, a mother can always tell when her children are lying and whilst lies may be the tools of your trade, they are completely wasted on me. When I ask a straight question, I expect a straight answer. Is that understood?"

"Well, yes, of course, as your thirty-seven-year-old child I always try to be straight with you."

"Stuff and nonsense! And don't try and be smart about your age – offspring are always a mother's children, no matter how old they might be. Now, I invested in your little business strictly on the understanding that it was to be no more than a private detective agency handling the most mundane and lucrative of cases – divorces, infidelities, that kind of thing. We had a clear understanding that you were to give up all of that dangerous undercover work for those unprincipled fools who run our intelligence services – you know very well I don't want to spend any more time worrying that the next unexplained death I read about in the Times will be that of my own child. I had enough of that during the war. Yet whom did I see going into this building when I was being driven past a couple of days ago but that wretched Angus creature, your old boss in MI5 – and the two of you were also in MI6 together during the war as well, if I remember correctly. And don't try telling me he was just popping in for cream cakes and a cup of tea. How could you lie to me Augustus? You should know by now there's nothing that can be hidden from your mother – your every skill as a wartime intelligence man was no more than a genetic inheritance from me, so don't waste your time trying to lie your way out of things now."

"There's nothing to hide mother – Angus is a client. I don't work for him anymore. Like everybody else, he has his own personal issues and, strictly between us, he's hired me to keep an eye on his wife."

"I didn't know he had a wife – he never struck me as the marrying kind.

He doesn't have the slightest idea how to talk properly to women, never mind marry one."

"Well he doesn't exactly shout about his marriage. He's a very private man."

The dowager scrutinised his face for evidence of duplicity, but Gus was a past master of the noble art of looking innocent when guilty. She said,

"I don't think I've heard a more unlikely tale of cock and bull in all my life, but I've no doubt that Angus will back you up, word for word."

"Well I'm sorry that I don't seem to be able to put your mind at rest, but that's the truth of the matter," Gus lied. "If that's all perhaps we can make you a cup of coffee with a …"

"No, that jolly well isn't all! I'd heard a rumour that you'd opened a second office under a nom de plume, in the East End of all places, so I hired a real private detective of my own to check things out."

"Yes, I know, I spotted him on his first outing and suggested we went for a cup of coffee and a chat. He's a very nice chap."

Ignoring the look of mischievous one-upmanship on his face, she said,

"He tells me that you're running it as some kind of free-of-charge social service for the poor of the district – a means of mothers finding runaways, or tearaway ex-husbands who've left them in the lurch, that kind of thing. And that's not all, it seems you're well known for using substantial parts of the profits from the respectable Mayfair part of the business to help down and outs and n'er-do-wells. I do believe, Augustus, that you're turning into a communist."

"I think you've got the wrong 'ist' dear. If you try philanthropist instead of communist you might be a little nearer the mark, although I've always regarded that as rather a self-aggrandising term for what those lucky enough to have wealth should do with at least some of it. I seem to remember that father had the same inclination."

"Indeed he did, wasting thousands of pounds of your future inheritance in the process – and now you seem determined to waste even more of his money. As soon as I give it you, you throw it away like confetti."

"Well, if you look at the balance sheets, you'll see that the business is doing rather splendidly and that the money that, as you put it, I'm throwing away comes entirely from my own salary. The money you've invested is not only safe, but it's earning interest every second that we speak, so there is really nothing whatsoever to worry about, mother dearest."

"You are as infuriating as your father Augustus – and look what happened to him."

Gus remembered very well what had happened. His father had felt so persecuted about the many aspects of his behaviour that didn't meet with his wife's approval that he'd signed up for an expedition to the Himalayas and had slipped over a mountain ledge while blind drunk. The dowager said,

"And then there's the little matter of the company you're keeping in the East End. My detective chappie tells me that you're bosom buddies with a man-gorilla who goes by the decidedly insalubrious nickname of Tasty Harry. Augustus, this man is a criminal and a racketeer. My detective tells me he breaks arms, legs and noses for a living. In the name of all that's holy and decent, how on earth do you explain such a thing?"

"Well, he's right about the arms and legs, but I don't think noses are really Harry's specialism."

"Augustus! This is not a matter to be taken lightly. I require an explanation."

"Well it's really very simple and straightforward mother and nothing to get alarmed about. Every detective agency needs contacts within the underworld, insiders who can provide information about the more underhand activities that some of the people we're asked to investigate become involved in. Harry is my main contact man for anything that has its roots in the East End – and it's surprising how much of our Mayfair business has links to that part of the world. He's completely trustworthy because I helped his sister rescue her daughter from a violent thug of a lover. We'd be much less successful as an agency without him, so I regard him as a rather good investment."

"Really! If I'd have known only half of this in advance, I wouldn't have invested a penny of your late father's hard-earned money in such a disreputable operation. If any of my circle were to hear of this, I would be barred from the bridge club for life."

There was a knock on the door and Alice entered, clutching a piece of paper. She said,

"I'm terribly sorry to interrupt, Lady Honoria, but there's an urgent message from one of our clients that Mr. Benedict needs to see."

The dowager sat glowering in silence while Gus read the note that was pushed under his nose. His heart missed three beats at once when he read that Mr. One, Alice's favourite nickname for Angus, was on his way and would be arriving in fifteen minutes time. The thought of a direct collision between his MI5 paymaster and the dowager was too much for any normal human being to contemplate. Calming his already frayed nerves he said,

"OK. I'll need to read the divorce file for Mr. Fallon before I see him. Perhaps you could take him to the teashop round the corner if he arrives early. He's a valuable client and it would be nice to show our appreciation of his custom."

Alice nodded with as straight a face as she could manage and said,

"Of course, will do."

The dowager's antennae were bristling. As soon as Alice had left the room she said,

"I know very well that the two of you were speaking in some kind of code. I wasn't born yesterday, Augustus, and I know you far too well. Heavens knows why you never married that young woman while you had the chance. She has twice the brain that's in your head and three times the one that sat between your father's ears – and she's very easy on the eye. I do hope that you behave yourself now that she's shown her good sense and married poor George instead. It's a bit of an odd arrangement to be employing one's former fiancée if you ask me, but then you and all of my children have been definitions of oddity."

Gus was quite used to such criticism, as were his siblings and he merely smiled beatifically. He said,

"Well, if that's all our business for today, perhaps I could show you out mother. I will be spending the rest of this morning working on a case that should more than justify your kind investment in the business. It's been a pleasure chatting with you, as always – indeed, we must do this more often."

As the dowager rose, wrapping her fur stole around her neck, she gave him the nearest she would ever manage to a smile and said,

"The one talent you have always had is the ability to charm the birds off the proverbial trees Augustus. But don't think you've seen the last of me. I'll be keeping a very close eye on you and how you run this extremely dubious business from now on. And be very careful how you use those charms with that young woman. She's married now, but she's still half in love with you and you with her I suspect. That kind of situation can be a recipe for disaster."

With that, she opened the door and made her traditional grand exit, nodding royally at Alice as she left.

Gus hurried over to his number two with a worried look on his face. He said,

"Angus must have come in through the front entrance when she spotted him. That's horribly bad luck in the extreme. He normally uses the tradesman's entrance at the rear so as not to be seen, so why on earth did he come in via the front door on the one day the dowager happened to be passing?"

"If it was last week, then I know the building managers had the decorators in. They were doing some work in the back offices on the ground floor. I saw them coming in and out of the service door at the rear of the foyer at various times when I was down there. They may well have locked the tradesman's entrance while they were at work, so that nobody coming through would end up with a paint pot on their head, or accidentally knock a painter off a ladder, who knows. It would be just like her ladyship to sail past at the precise moment poor old Mr. One was forced to take a detour."

A military style rapping on the door told them that Angus had arrived. As he walked in, every inch the former high ranking army commander, Gus said,

"Angus, little do you know it, but you have narrowly avoided a fate worse than death – you missed Lady Honoria by a cat's whisker."

Mr. One raised his eyebrows inquisitively and said,

"Well, not everyone is so lucky where death is concerned. I've come to discuss the rather embarrassing matter of Sir Jeremy and his unexpected transition into the afterlife. I have also identified the source of the information that our dearly departed friend was so cheerfully leaking to the Soviets. Shall we go into your office?"

CHAPTER THREE

The late September sunshine filled the large, eighteenth-century sitting room with a weak afternoon glow. A log fire burned sedately in the snug, ornately carved fireplace. The room, painted in faded green, with matching curtains, was a relic of an era when the old elites had lived in such vast houses, enjoying the hunting and shooting and other country pursuits that the surrounding woods and parkland facilitated. Jacob sat sleepily in an ancient but comfortable leather armchair, staring into the fire. His mind had been through so much during the past couple of weeks that it had very nearly collapsed into trauma-driven paralysis, but the rapid turnaround in his fortunes over the last few days had pulled him back from the brink. He could once again glimpse something of a future for himself, no matter how slight, uncertain and unpredictable it might be. Beside him, on a little circular table, a half full brandy bottle sat. He clutched a glass of the calming potion in his rapidly healing hands, taking a sip from it every now and again. He was in a kind of limbo, waiting for the next step in a drama over which he now had little control.

Gnawing at the back of his consciousness were the now fully restored memories of his life before his present nightmare had begun. The powerful combination of an agile mind and being born into a rich and well-connected family had sent him effortlessly through the elite training schools of Eton and Oxford, straight into the welcoming arms of the Foreign Office. It had been pleased to get its hands on a talented multilinguist with overseas family ties that were seen potentially as being of considerable benefit to British diplomacy. Apart from a period in the military during the Second World War, albeit in a relatively safe posting, his rise through the bureaucratic ranks had been inexorable. The income that came with the job had been a useful source of independence while he waited for his inheritance. He had never really had any moral compass other than his own self-interest and sense of privilege. He had fallen into a secret leisure-time lifestyle of multiple lovers, too much drink and inevitable catastrophe – his running over and killing of an innocent young man while so inebriated that he had been on the point of nodding off at the wheel.

He'd managed to cover up the killing for a while, but then he'd been betrayed into the hands of the KGB. They had used the information to turn him into their inside man in the British foreign service. The more they'd asked of him, the more he'd feared being found out by the British. Had he been caught and tried as a traitor he didn't fancy his chances of being let out of prison before he was old and very doddery. It was that which had led to his attempt to flee the country and begin a new life, with a new identity. But he had been found out and was now so firmly back in the clutches of his Soviet masters that, as far as he could see, he was theirs for life. The fact that he fully recognised the now deeply dire nature of his situation had enabled him reluctantly to accept it. From being the great escapee during his flight to Paris and beyond, he had become simply the prisoner. Things had improved, in so far as there were no longer any chains holding him to the spot, but he knew only too well that a heavily armed guard stood outside the room. His fate was in the hands of others and he would just have to wait until they decided what best to do with him.

Gradually, the brandy drew him into a calm numbness, with little other than the quietly flickering flames occupying his mind. He didn't hear the door open. The once colourful but now dull and threadbare carpet absorbed the sound of the visitor's footsteps as he walked over to the large sash window and looked down on the lush green parkland three floors below. He surveyed the view contemplatively. He, Colonel Zaliatev, could feel only contempt for the corrupt specimen that sat staring into the fire. He needed a few moments before he could resume the tedious business of restoring the Englishman to full usefulness. Life was much easier for those colleagues who handled willing agents, secret supporters of the Soviet Union within western governments and bureaucracies who passed intelligence to the KGB without the slightest need for coercion. The most difficult part of their task was establishing that these information donors were genuine and not double agents. His job was to try and double the number of intelligence providers via the coercion of those with access to classified information who would not otherwise even consider betraying their own countries. Jacob was a particularly valuable example of this kind of traitor, a man who had access to key figures in Washington as well as to crucial UK intelligence. The handling of such individuals was generally enormously time consuming and required a significant amount of digging into their deep backgrounds in order to find issues and scandals that could be used to exert the necessary leverage on them. It was work that made the Colonel a significant player within the KGB, but frequently it left him feeling that he had soiled his hands in dealing with individuals such as the Englishman.

There were some, but only some, similarities between the two men, but a far greater range of differences. Whereas Jacob had enjoyed a privileged, avowedly unreligious upbringing in which he was taught that wealth was the beginning and end of all things, the Colonel had been brought up in a poor, very traditional Russian Catholic family. With the Russian Orthodox Church as the dominant form of Christianity under the Tsars, Catholics had formed a small minority that frequently was barely tolerated by officialdom. Prior to the 1917 Revolution, his forebears had often pretended to follow the dominant Orthodox faith while privately practising their own beliefs.

With the family's poverty had come disease and Zaliatev had never recovered emotionally from losing his elder sister, Margarita, who was also his closest friend and confidante. She had died of tuberculosis when he was twelve years old. The day her eyes closed for the last time was the day that he felt the kinder part of him had died also. The family had had a tough and challenging life in which death was an ever-present shadow, but for him, this was one death too many.

Thereafter his own heart hardened and he developed a deep resentment that families like his should be forced to carry such a burden of death and disease. To him, communism seemed to offer an end to much of this suffering, should it be enacted with integrity and skill, and he became attracted to its promises of a new life for the poor. In the eyes of his devoutly religious family, however, the Soviet version of communism was a deeply flawed antidote to their predicament. For them it was a doctrine of the antichrist, being driven by fervent atheism. Because of this, he kept his views to himself, but was surprised by the advice that they decided to give him about this ideology that they despised so much. Observing what happened to people who dared express anti-communist views under Stalin, the family told their teenage son that he would have to develop a dual identity. In his heart, his mother had told him, he must always first and foremost be a Catholic. But in the views he professed in public, he must appear to be a fervent communist, just as his forebears had often pretended to belong to the Russian Orthodox faith. That would keep him out of prison – and even save his life – and allow him to prosper, while secretly keeping to his Christian beliefs.

He had indeed prospered. Like Jacob, he proved himself to be a virtuoso multilinguist and intellectually agile. He was talent spotted by a

Party official with links to the precursors of the KGB. He soon rose up the ranks of the intelligence services as a result of his ruthless efficiency, both as an investigator and a spy and, most particularly, his apparently unshakeable loyalty to Stalin and his every twist and turn of policy. At first, he had decided that he was prepared to live with the hard-line dictator and his version of communism because, in Zaliatev's view, it brought order to Russia and the various other components of the Soviet empire. The deadly purges and oppressions that preceded the Second World War were, to him, a deeply regrettable but necessary part of the price of that order. What Zaliatev feared most was the chaos that might result from the great dictator's iron grip slipping. He believed for a while that more people would have been killed should order have broken down than were executed during the Great Purge. At that moment in time he was prepared to give the dictator the benefit of the doubt and didn't question the regime's propaganda that all of those to be killed or exiled were a threat to the common good. He'd told himself also, for several years, that communism's loudly proclaimed goal of a society that would bring justice to the poor was in line with the New Testament's teaching on such matters, even if the violence that had been used to consolidate Stalin's power wasn't. While his survival instincts ensured that he kept his Christian beliefs to himself, he reasoned that whether or not Soviet leaders acknowledged the God that he had been taught to believe in was not important. What mattered were the promised results of the Soviet communist system in terms of freedom from poverty – and those results could only be delivered if there was order.

But, in 1939, everything he believed in was hit by a thunderbolt. The great dictator's signing of the German-Soviet Nonaggression Pact with Hitler was impossible for Zaliatev to stomach, although he was careful to keep this fact to himself. He found it hard to see any credible ethical basis for a Stalinist communism that saw fit to unite with a man who he viewed as the very devil himself, Adolf Hitler. Equally, in so far as, to him, the pact seemed to trample on all that was right and principled in a world that was already well on the way to a new Dark Age, he lost his faith in a God who was apparently prepared to allow such things to happen. As a teenager, Zaliatev had once asked a priest why, in a previous time, God had allowed Ivan the Terrible to inflict the murderous injustices that had killed so many of the Russian people. He was told that God's purposes are a divine mystery beyond human understanding. The priest also argued that too much divine intervention would remove the free will that had been given to humanity as a gift and that it was necessary for those opposed to evil and oppression to first take matters into their own hands and then ask God for help once they had done so. The evil and suffering that such tyrants occasioned was the devil taking advantage of a world in which humanity had free will and was not the fault of God. For a while he was satisfied with this reply. So deep was his disillusionment after the pact with Hitler, however, that all such arguments lost their force within his mind and his faith dissolved completely. He began also to doubt the veracity of the claim that all of those who had been executed in the Great Purge had been guilty of treason or other crimes ascribed to them – and to wonder, indeed, if the dictator was simply a variation on the theme of Ivan the Terrible. If he could reach an agreement with Hitler, how could he be trusted in anything he'd done or said?

The pact had been the moment when whatever remained of his belief in anything had nearly all evaporated.

He was driven thereafter by a curious mishmash of motives and values, at the centre of which sat his vague belief in the concept of the Soviet Union as an entity – and the need to preserve his own position and power. Should he lose them, there were too many enemies who would have him in their sights. His private judgment that, for all its faults, the communism that had evolved in the Soviet Union was still marginally preferable to the capitalism of the West, gave him just enough belief in the ideology he publicly subscribed to for him to feel that he was upholding something that was, at the very least, the lesser of several evils. But somewhere, at the deep centre of his being, he was looking for something substantial to replace his lost religious beliefs and his disillusionment with the way that Soviet communism had been blown off course – something that would be the new driving force behind his daily work for the flawed communist state. Almost without knowing it, he had become desperate to find someone, anyone, amongst all of the Soviet and foreign politicians, bureaucrats and intelligence officers that crossed his path, who he could believe was genuinely and solely motivated by the simple desire to do good: someone who would prove an antidote to everything that he had become and the deeply flawed political system that he served. Someone who would rekindle his hope in the prospects of justice for humanity and most particularly the poor, from whose stock he came. Hope was what he needed most, the hope that would persuade him that a better form of communism, or some other ideology promoting social justice, was still a future possibility within Russia. It was as if he were looking for gold in human form. All he seemed to find was fool's gold and the fools to go with it. He had no patience with those who failed the test when he sifted their beliefs and morals.

The Colonel regarded those who didn't measure up to this 'gold standard' as undeserving of his respect. Given that he was unconvinced that any of the people he encountered could meet his high expectations, he had contempt for pretty well everybody. To those with power that was equal to, or greater than, his own, he would pretend to give his respect because he had no choice. All others he would treat as he saw fit. Those who were within his power had a great deal to fear, for the Colonel's kinder side, as manifested in his desire for the just society, was counterbalanced by a ruthless cruelty that could be unleashed in the blink of an eye. Partially it had come from his own childhood experience of being viciously beaten by his father, whose drink problems had turned him into a terrifying variation on the theme of Jekyll and Hyde, and partially it had come from his early training as an intelligence officer under the supervision of a particularly brutal mentor. But that cruelty lay also in his own nature, something that his elder sister had been trying to change before her untimely death. For the Colonel, only those who were truly good, who truly cared for others, for people like the poor of his own village, were deserving of mercy, should they fall into his hands. For people such as Jacob, a man who had cared so little about killing an innocent man that he tried to buy the silence of a witness, Zaliatev had only contempt. The Colonel had ordered many killings in his time, but he did not regard any of those he executed as being innocent of what they were charged with. He liked to pride himself that he had been careful about that. People like Jacob were part of the problem, not the solution. He was a man with no regard for anything other than his own wealth and no discernible concern for the poor whatsoever, as far as the Colonel could see. Zaliatev regarded people like the privileged Englishman as mere tools to be used in the pursuit of the policies he was instructed to facilitate through his intelligence work. If they didn't function properly, they were to be thrown in the furnace and new ones found. Ironically, given his secret disillusionment with Stalin, it was in this single-minded attitude that those who had observed the Colonel most closely said they saw a parallel with the great dictator at his most ruthless and paranoiac. In that specific respect at least, it was said, Zaliatev saw the world through Stalin's eyes.

The Colonel looked at his watch and decided that he could no longer delay the dreary business of dealing with this principle-free Englishman. The acidic little play in which he was the writer and lead actor, with Jacob as the mere bit player, required simply to nod, agree and say yes when required, had once again to resume. He said,

"It is nearly time Mr. Jacob."

The prisoner jumped as the familiar, commanding voice cut into his calm reverie, like a knife pressed firmly into the flesh of an orange. The Colonel continued, without turning round,

"It has been very much a case of touch and go for you, but you have proved to be Lazarus twice over. First you achieved a resurrection of your broken body and now one of your mind. Well done – and I do mean that with the utmost sincerity. I know you had the assistance of the very best doctors that we have here, but regaining your memory after all that you have been through was no easy task and yet, that is precisely what you have done. So now I look once more at a living man. Had your memory remained in the land of the dead, then your body would have quickly joined it and you would be little more than fertiliser for the gardens below. You would have become a liability instead of an asset. Perhaps those of my colleagues who dispose of corpses might have named a new variant of rose after you, in recognition of your contribution to its growth? Or maybe not. Maybe they might have decided they had more than enough fertiliser and simply buried you in quicklime. It doesn't bear thinking about really, does it?"

The Colonel strolled over to the fire and warmed his hands for a few moments. It was not a particularly chilly autumn, but the high ceilings and cold stone walls of the old country house cooled the air in the manner of a refrigerator. He turned to face the prisoner and smiled in his familiar, emotionless way. He said,

"I hope that you've enjoyed your stay in this splendid building. You must feel quite at home – it's like a slightly larger version of your family house in England, is it not? People like you would have come to places like this when visiting those Russians whom they regarded as their social equals, no doubt. That was in the old days of course, before the revolution. Now we use this very grand pile of stones as a therapeutic and convalescent home for the most valued servants of the Soviet Union. You look surprised, but that is what you are, one of our most valued servants."

"Interrogating and bullying someone until they almost lose their mind seems a funny way of valuing them," Jacob said, almost to himself.

"Ah! The cat has got its tongue back! Very well done, Mr. Jacob, you are now in full working order. How very timely. I've come to give you your briefing before we put you back into the field and it is most reassuring to know that all of your faculties are present and correct."

Jacob took a final sip of the brandy and then put the glass down on the little table, deciding that it would be wise not to cloud his brain any further while receiving his instructions. He had escaped death by the narrowest of margins and could see clearly the hole in the ground into which he would fall, should he lose the plot again. The Colonel continued,

"It is fortunate that your attempt to flee from our grasp was made during your annual vacation. That and the fact that you left England in disguise and used a false passport has meant that nobody in your Foreign Office has noticed that you've been missing, as far as we can tell. Your moustache and your beard have grown back during your time in our custody and the hair dye that you used for your passport photograph has been successfully removed, so you look sufficiently like your old self for no one to realise that you so foolishly tried to change your appearance and your identity. That allows us to insert you back into your family home as if you'd never left the country, ready to resume your job as a mandarin next Monday – mandarin is the right word for a high-flying diplomat like yourself, isn't it?"

Jacob said nothing, but smiled grimly. The Colonel continued,

"Yes, I thought it was. Traces of your injuries are still visible, of course, so we have devised a little cover story about your having fallen while walking in the Scottish mountains. That should explain any remaining traces of swelling or bruising when you return. We've already arranged for a medical record of the event to be inserted into the filing system in a Glasgow hospital. It's a hospital where we're fortunate enough to have a longstanding sympathiser, a doctor who is a member of the Communist Party and a very loyal supporter of Moscow and all its doings – a useful idiot, as some of my more cynical colleagues would describe him. He has agreed to confirm the validity of the record, should that ever be necessary, and that he treated you. Traces of your wrist wounds will take a little while longer to completely disappear, so we have provided a dozen white shirts with specially tailored extra-long sleeves. They are already in your wardrobe back home and will ensure that your wrists are covered at all times. Just to be on the safe side, we have supplied also some cosmetic cream, which you will find on the dressing table in your bedroom. That will provide a waterproof, flesh coloured barrier that you can use to disguise the wounds as well. Use these little theatrical devices properly and all will be well, no one will be any the wiser as to what really happened to you during your little holiday."

The Colonel smiled ironically, saying,

"And what a holiday it was. Not many people I've known have spent their vacation being drugged and interrogated, Mr. Jacob. How privileged you are, a real trendsetter."

The hate and fear in Jacob's face spoke far more eloquently than any words could have done. The Colonel was well practised in reading both emotions and noted with some satisfaction that fear appeared to be the more dominant of the two. He said,

"For an intelligent man, I don't know how you ever thought you would get away with your little ruse – escaping our grasp by disappearing into a new identity in Switzerland, with the funds from the sale of your huge estate finding their way into your new bank account via a series of financial sleights of hand, little magic tricks that you thought would make it impossible to trace where the money had gone. What you forgot, Mr.

Jacob, was that we are past masters at the playing of such tricks. It was very easy for us to spot what was going on as soon as we realised that you were attempting to escape from our grasp and renege on our little agreement. So we forged a letter from you cancelling the sale of the estate before it could go through and provided all of the necessary confirmations that this was your most certain intention. We did this a fortnight ago, so when you return home, you will find that everything is as you left it. Not a single pound sterling managed to get into your Swiss bank account – which we have also closed."

The Colonel watched the last dregs of hope drain out of Jacob's face as he realised that he was now more firmly in the KGB's control than ever before. His lurch for freedom had simply been an illusion, tracked every step of the way by his Soviet masters. He and the Colonel both knew that, from now on, his role was simply that of a servant, a man who was bound to do whatever was asked of him. The Colonel said,

"The fact that the money we were paying you enabled you to restore your house to the extent that it was easily sellable was an error on our part and will not be repeated. From now on, our only payment will be our gift of your ability to stay alive, providing, of course, you do precisely as we say. The fact that your flight was entirely driven by the belief that you could break free from our grasp and live the life of Riley – that is the correct phrase isn't it – is what saved your bacon Mr. Jacob. You do not appear to have betrayed any details of our relationship with you prior to, or during your abortive flight. So, now that you are once more under our control, we can simply put you back on the table and use you as the pawn we had originally intended. Had we found, as we suspected initially, that you were involved in some kind of double dealing, then you would now be simply one more entry in our record of executions. If you had switched sides instead of attempting merely to escape, that would very definitely have been the end of your usefulness to us. We do, nevertheless, have to execute one person as a result of all this mess, Mr. Jacob."

Jacob looked startled, wondering whether the favourite lover he thought he'd managed to keep a secret from the KGB was about to pay the ultimate price for his folly. The Colonel, knowing very well what was going on in his mind, let him sweat for a few moments and then elaborated,

"Your latest alter ego, the investment broker Carrington Wallace, this little character you invented as your new identity before we caught up with you in Paris – the man who with one great leap would be free from our control and disappear into a new life in Switzerland, he must die Mr. Jacob."

The Colonel pulled Jacob's fake passport out of his inside pocket and waved it in its owner's face. He said,

"Not content with your own real name and the separate codename that we so kindly gave you, you wanted yet another name. How outrageous, how very greedy of you Mr. Jacob!"

Zaliatev tore the passport in two and then held the pieces in the palm of his hand, directly under the Englishman's nose. He continued, menacingly,

"Let us say goodbye to this new identity together. You have in England a little tradition of Guy Fawkes night, I believe, when effigies of a famous traitor are burned on bonfires. Well, today we will burn our own traitor, Mr. Jacob, this other you, the one we can't one hundred per cent trust, the one who would like to flee from our control. See, here he goes to his fiery end."

The Colonel threw the two halves of the passport onto the log fire with a theatrical gesture. He continued,

"Now all we are left with is the real you, the one henceforth we know we can trust to remain loyal, the one who has no desire whatsoever to follow his most recent alter ego into the flames."

He smiled at Jacob, an eagle watching its prey as its talons cut ever harder into its flesh. Then, he switched back to theatrical mode. Like a magician pulling an endless stream of surprises out of his inner jacket pocket, he produced an envelope, which he proceeded to open. He skimmed through the contents in silence, then said,

"There is just one more thing we need to say goodbye to, Mr. Jacob. When we realised that you were making a moonlight flit, our people thought it advisable to burgle your solicitor's office to see what instructions had been left – which is how we managed quickly to unravel your attempt to move your money in mysterious ways. We also found this, a letter to your Foreign Office bosses saying that you had resigned with immediate effect, which was to be sent three days after you'd left the country. As you can see, the letter was never sent and so I am pleased to say that you are still a most valued employee of Her Britannic Majesty's foreign service. Had the letter not been intercepted then, again, you would have ceased to be of use to us. You would have become a liability and you would now be mere fertiliser for one of the exotic rose bushes in the gardens below. So, once more, you have been such a lucky, lucky man Mr. Jacob. The Fates have smiled on you more than anyone I know, for no-one who has made so many mistakes has ever survived my wrath before. That must mean there is something incredibly important that I need you to do, something only a man with your particular contacts can achieve. You are familiar with the broad outlines of this, the great deception that you are to engineer for our benefit. I'm delighted that the doctors' hard work has enabled you to remember everything correctly. But there is a key detail of this task that I haven't yet told you, something that in itself will change the great game of international politics. Won't it be exciting to discover what that is, don't you think? The final, crucial ingredient of that one, special task that has saved you from the Furies and all the flames of hell, the flames that have just eaten whole your most recent alter ego."

Holding the near fatal letter between his finger and thumb, the Colonel waved it slowly in the air as if it were the carrier of a contagion. Jacob's eyes followed its movements in the manner of a man being hypnotised. The Colonel said,

"We'll leave the matter of the final details of your very special task until the right moment has arrived. Nothing must leak until then, either by accident or intent. What we need to do now is say goodbye to this letter of yours, Mr. Jacob, the one that so nearly cost you your life. Perhaps it should join your latest alter ego in the fire, do you think? That would make the chances of you reaching your next birthday much stronger, wouldn't it? Would you like to do the honours, or shall I?"

"Whatever you wish Colonel, you're the man in charge of my life now," Jacob said, acidly.

"How very kind. It must be the child still in the man, but I do so enjoy watching a good bonfire. Here we go – whoosh! All of your alter ego's follies have now gone up in smoke! Now we have only the sensible Mr. Jacob left, the one who is going to do exactly as we wish. May I have some of your brandy, do you think? I know it's one of your favourite tipples from all of our background research on you and its warming texture will be the perfect complement to the autumnal season."

"Like me, the brandy is all yours. Do with it whatever you would like. There is a second glass on the table, so I presume that it must be for you."

"How kind again, Mr. Jacob. You are a most convivial companion."

After pouring himself a drink, the Colonel went back over to the window and stood watching something that Jacob couldn't see from where he sat. After a few moments, the KGB man turned round, a deeply thoughtful look on his face. He said,

"When you go back to work there is a problem that we will need you to resolve, Mr Jacob. Immediately. One of your senior colleagues at the Foreign Office, Mr. Mallory Michaels, has deep suspicions about your links to us. He has not quite enough proof to act as yet, we are certain of that, so has not said anything to his superior. But he is on your trail in a very vigorous manner at a time when we need you to be free of all suspicion, given the importance of the task we will be setting you shortly. So what do you think you ought to do about Mr. Michaels?"

"The question, I assume, is rhetorical. What I should do is what you tell me, isn't that the way things will work from here on?"

"Well done Mr. Jacob, you are now passing every test I set you! Your answer is precisely right. I can see we are going to have a most fraternal and convivial relationship from this day forwards. So would you like to know what we require?"

"I have little choice in the matter, as you well know."

"Well, that is not entirely true. You could refuse to do what we want, that is your absolute right. The result of that would be very unfortunate for you, but at least your end would be swift. But it would be a shame to have to repair that lovely old chair that has survived intact through all the turmoil of the revolution and beyond. A bullet makes such a mess of the stuffing inside leather chairs I find, even after it has first passed between a man's eyes. So I'm rather hoping that, like me, you're a lover of venerable old furniture, Mr. Jacob and will agree to do all of the things that I ask of you to resolve the little matter of Mr. Michaels' suspicions."

"I'm exceedingly fond of old furniture," Jacob said, in a resigned, deadpan manner.

"Good, you are a man with a respect for history, Mr. Jacob. That is what I like to see. Now, the easiest way of saying goodbye to Mr. Michaels would be to slip something deadly into a cup of his favourite English tea. I'm sure, with a little instruction in the technicalities of the matter, that you could do that very capably. But given your recent adventures and your attempt at the great escape, I need to use a means of despatch that will increase still further our hold over you. So, I would like you to shoot your annoying colleague at a time and a place of our choosing, when we will be in attendance to photograph the killing. That photograph will free us from the need to track you down and execute you, should you ever try to slip your lead again, Mr. Jacob. We will simply ensure that your friendly British police get a copy and then leave the hunt to them. I believe hangings are very much a behind-closed-doors affair in England nowadays, Mr. Jacob, but we would at least be there in spirit to sincerely wish you ill as you plunged to your doom."

"You are such a jolly chap Colonel," Jacob said acidly. "I'm surprised that you have been given authorisation to eliminate such a senior member of the Foreign Office on British soil, particularly given the diplomatic and other consequences that would follow should you be found out."

He had been freed a little from his immediate terror of the man by his growing realisation that it was very much in the KGB's interests that he should be kept in one piece to conduct his highly important mission for them, whatever the final, as yet undisclosed details of that might be.

The Colonel smiled, an executioner's smile. He said,

"I am my own authorisation Mr. Jacob and in my judgment this assassination will be so well disguised as something else that my role in setting it up will remain forever invisible. Your role as the author of the act will be equally invisible if you cooperate fully with us in everything that we want you to do. Play the game and you will find that we are excellent custodians of your wellbeing. The gun that you will use is waiting for you in England, in a shoebox under your bed. It is a revolver that we have bought from London criminals. It has been used twice before in well-known murders, so when it is discovered, all prints removed, it will seem most likely that Mr. Michaels was the victim of a gangland killing, maybe as a result of mistaken identity perhaps. It will point in totally the opposite direction from you. But I am a great fan of what you English call the 'belt and braces' approach, so we will create a second option as a back-up. Our people will have burgled Mr. Michaels' house by the time the police arrive, so the whole affair will look also like a traditional robbery that has gone wrong, with the killers fleeing from the scene. This means that the authorities will be given two very full possible lines of enquiry to keep them busy, neither of which relate to you in the slightest. You will then not be inconvenienced by the police investigations that will follow and will be free to proceed with the most important task that shortly we will be setting you. You must applaud such great consideration for your interests, must you not, Mr. Jacob?"

Jacob simply raised his eyebrows, the most reaction that he could summon to his unasked-for role as a pantomime stooge. The Colonel continued,

"Yes, of course you must. I know your hands and wrists are still a little sore from your recent trials and tribulations, so let me do the clapping for you. There, you see, you will soon be able to do this for yourself again, once you are fully recovered. So, now the applause has died down, let me fill in some of the finer detail. Your target has a nice little house in the country, from which he travels to London every day. He lives on his own with an Alsatian dog, which his cleaner takes for a walk twice daily while he's at work. Our observations have shown that he arrives home by seven o'clock at the latest every evening. You will be waiting for him in the bushes. As soon as he gets out of his car, you will walk up behind him and shoot him in the back of the head. We will be present also. Don't be alarmed by the brilliant light that will explode all over you as you pull the trigger. It will merely be the flashbulb of our photographer's camera. And please don't even consider shooting him and trying to seize the negative. He will be accompanied by a marksman who will at all times have a weapon trained on you, to ensure your very best behaviour."

"What if I can't pull the trigger? I've never intentionally killed a man before, not even during the war. I was an officer in the Signals Corps, not a bloody sniper."

"Well, if you don't pull the trigger, our man will pull the trigger on you Mr. Jacob. If we can't trust you in this little matter, then clearly, we won't be able to trust you either in the much bigger task that we have waiting for you and we will simply have to cut our losses. So, my estimation is that you will do exactly as you have been told. Any other course of action would be suicide and whatever else you may be, Mr. Jacob, you do not strike me as a man of a suicidal inclination."

Somewhere outside, a string quartet began playing a stirring Soviet patriotic melody. A choir soon joined in and Zaliatev went over to the window to investigate. He said,

"How wonderful, Mr. Jacob, it is the weekly therapeutic music session. Those patients who have certain psychological problems are encouraged to join the hospital choir and a local string quartet gives its services free of charge so that events like this can be put on. There are about twenty patients today I think, a very good turnout. We must raise the window like everyone else so that they know their performance is being listened to and appreciated. Come Mr. Jacob, if you please, you must see this. The more people who are watching and listening the more appreciated these poor souls will feel. It all helps with their recovery."

He beckoned Jacob to join him. The Englishman did so with a pronounced lack of interest or enthusiasm. Looking down onto the large, semi-circular paved area immediately below, he saw an array of grey-faced patients in dressing gowns, singing heartily from sheet music held in often trembling hands. The quartet was highly professional and the choir well trained. Jacob wondered just who these people were. Were they KGB agents who had been injured or tortured in the field, who, like him, were here for therapy and recuperation before being sent back into service? The Colonel had said that this was a hospital for valued servants of the Soviet Union, so maybe anybody who the state decided was critical to its operation and survival could gain admittance, who knows. Beyond the choir, in the middle distance, he noticed a military truck coming down the central drive towards the hospital. It pulled up in front of the main entrance and the driver and his companion got out, opened the rear doors and then stood waiting. No-one was brought out of the vehicle, so clearly it had come to pick up someone from the hospital. The fact that it had two motorcycle escorts suggested the patient must be important and Jacob idly watched to see who that might be – an injured general perhaps, now able to return to his barracks to complete his recovery, or a senior politician?

The Colonel, meanwhile, was listening for a different kind of music to that of the choir. It duly rang out, the hospital clock chiming the hour with a graceful elegance. Looking over his shoulder, he saw that the door had opened on cue and that three medics in white coats were quietly advancing towards them. Jacob was still watching the truck with dull interest and saw none of it. The Colonel nodded to the head medic, who then crept up behind the Englishman and plunged a syringe into his arm. He yelped with surprise and attempted to turn round, but he was now being very firmly held by all three medics. His consciousness faded rapidly and he sank onto the wheelchair that they had brought with them.

The Colonel then returned to listening to the choir, which was working its way through one of the great songs of the revolution A couple of minutes later, he noticed Jacob being loaded into the back of the truck. Two of the medics got in with him and the rear doors were shut. The vehicle then drove back down the drive towards the road beyond, flanked by the motorcycle escorts. The Colonel closed the window, drank the remainder of his brandy and left, smiling.

No-one who passed him in the corridor dared smile back.

CHAPTER FOUR

Rain hammered on the window of Gus's office as Mr. One hung his dripping mac on the antique oak coatstand at the back of the room. The sky was so dark and glowering that it seemed as if all the light was being sucked out of it. Mr. One said,

"We've finally identified the source of all of the information Sir Jeremy Wenstratton passed to the Soviets before his unexpected demise. It was George Haigley-Smyth. Haigley-Smyth's family have bred race horses for years and that was enough of a connection with Sir Jeremy's love of betting on the gee-gees for the two of them to strike up a drinking relationship in the Commons' bars. Haigley-Smyth, of course, is one of the Cabinet members who has been in the inner circle on foreign affairs, which is extremely unfortunate when his famed over-consumption of alcohol is considered. It appears that Sir Jeremy became well practised in getting all sorts of secrets and gossip out of him when he was three sheets to the wind. One of the barmen who is in our employ remembers regularly hearing them discussing things that were so high above Sir Jeremy's paygrade that they were in danger of going through the roof. Well, that is exactly what appears to have happened in this case. The PM tells me that Haigley-Smyth is the only person from whom the deceased could hope to get the information that he was promising just before he died. He's moved him to a minor ministry where there are no secrets worthy of anyone's attention and thrown him out of all Cabinet inner circle discussions. With his demotion and Sir Jeremy's departure to the afterlife I think we can safely conclude that that particular leak in the government has been well and truly plugged."

"Well, that at least is a relief."

"Indeed. Given the Soviet Union's brutal attack on Hungary in fifty-six and their leader's lunatic statements about raining nuclear weapons down on Western Europe during the same year, our political masters have decreed that we need the most effective deterrent that we can get our hands on if we're going to give him a credible reason for not using the damn things – and that will be best constructed with American help. The last thing the PM wants is some drunken fool undermining Washington's trust in us again by leaking secrets right, left and centre. We've already had to sweat blood to undo the damage that the Suez debacle did to the Special Relationship."

The window suddenly rattled as an enormous clap of thunder detonated almost directly above. Lightning had been bouncing around in the sky for the past minute or so and this heavenly explosion seemed almost like a premonition of the kind of nuclear attack that was so worrying the government.

Gus said,

"It's ironic that the only sane purpose for nuclear weapons is using them as a deterrent to try and ensure that those same nuclear weapons are never used. However, I have more than a slight suspicion that the PM sees the deterrent as just as important in Conservative Party terms as it is in any strategic sense. I think he fears that any loss of the promised American assistance in its upgrading and modernisation would cause him considerable problems with those who might at some stage consider challenging his leadership."

"Indeed, although thankfully we have no need to dirty our hands in the murky waters of party politics and can focus entirely on the national security and public protection aspects of things. That is how the matter has been defined for our attention and to that we will stick. Anyway, as far as the Washington relationship goes, we've done our bit in catching Sir Jeremy red handed. Any punishment for his sins will have to be left to the Almighty, given that He is the one now most burdened with the cynical old traitor's company. Which leads me to the second item on this morning's little agenda. Our dearly departed friend seems to have been just the tip of the iceberg. There appears to be another traitor, one who is cheerfully walking the corridors of the Foreign Office."

A second, slightly less loud thunderclap interjected, making Mr. One noticeably edgy. Looking out of the window at the scowling sky, he said, whimsically,

"Speaking of the Almighty, it's almost as if He's trying to make some kind of a point with all these traitors and the possible disastrous consequences of their treachery, don't you think?"

"I think very little about the Almighty and if He does exist, I wouldn't be surprised if He thinks very little about me. My feet are firmly on the ground Angus."

"Well, be that as it may, as I say, it appears we might have another fish to haul in. I'm meeting one of the FO's top bods, Mallory Michaels, at my club on Thursday night. He contacted me yesterday to say that he has some lines of enquiry we might want to follow up urgently. He hasn't mentioned them to anyone above him because he's worried that, for fair reasons or foul, they'll try and brush the whole business under the carpet. I have to tell you, Augustus, that, on top of his anxieties, I'm not entirely certain of all of my own colleagues within MI5. Many are the best that one could ask for, but I have a gut feeling that somewhere or other within the various sections there is a very well concealed bad apple. For that reason, any work that we're engaged in is not to be divulged to anyone else – I will keep others below the levels of DG and DDG informed only to the extent that it is necessary and unavoidable and I would ask you to say nothing to any of my colleagues without my prior agreement that you do so. The closer we keep our work to ourselves the less likelihood there is of any of it leaking to the Soviets. I'll say no more than that on the matter, but would ask you to remember this guidance at all times. Anyway, as far as Michaels' specific allegations are concerned, if anyone can sniff out a mole in a hole it's you Augustus, so I'd rather like you to be in on this one. If you could join us at seven-thirty it would be much appreciated."

"Noted," Gus replied, "as is your advisory about dealings with others within the service. What alerted Mr. double M to the fact that something might be amiss?"

"Statements by a member of the Soviet Foreign Ministry that showed awareness of confidential FO information, for which there were only two possible sources. Mr. Michaels has the idea of baiting a trap by giving both suspects different juicy but false information and looking for evidence that it has found its way into Soviet hands. Whichever of the fibs is picked up by the Soviets will identify the mole who leaked it."

"OK, fair enough, that's what I'd do as a first step. The tricky bit, of course, is getting the evidence. It's not often that Soviet officials oblige by unintentionally providing it. We'd have to watch carefully for traceable behaviour that would give the game away – a KGB officer turning up at a time and place where he had been falsely led to believe he would see or hear something to his advantage, for example."

"Indeed."

"Has Mr double M given you the names of the suspects?"

"No, he's insistent that he'll only do that face-to-face, so that there's no chance of the information being intercepted. He doesn't want them to be given any advance notice that they are under investigation."

"Okey dokey, I shall wait to be enlightened on Thursday evening.

There does seem to be a proliferation of these furry little creatures scuttling about under the corridors of power at the moment – if that's not to mix metaphors, given that we were talking about hauling in another fish a minute or so ago."

"Quite," Mr. One replied, crisply. He was looking out of the window, watching the lightning display as it danced across the sky. He had an intense look in his eyes, as if he were debating something within his mind. He said,

"There's someone I've not been seeing, Augustus."

Gus wondered frivolously if One had just spotted him or her through the window, riding the crest of a thundercloud. He said,

"In what respect?"

"Behind all of this penetration, I think there's a single mind at work, one that's not really been on our radar until now."

"Have you any idea who he might be?"

"It's been like looking through a misty window into the fog. For some time I've been able to see his outline, sometimes the silhouette of his face. But until now he's never come clearly into view, he's never been quite in focus."

"And you think this someone is controlling the moles?"

"Indeed. Mastermind is not a word I use, normally, I've always associated it with the more fanciful thriller fiction. But I'm beginning to believe that, in this case, a mastermind is what we're actually looking at."

"Presumably we're talking about one of our Russian friends here?"

"There's a chap who keeps floating in and out of the country – he pops up in the United States quite regularly too from what our intelligence people there have told me. Zaliatev, a Colonel who is listed as a military attaché. Our friends in MI6 tell me he's KGB through and through, a shadowy individual whom they suspect has accrued significant power and influence, much more than one would have expected, even for a Colonel. I think he may be our man."

"Doing what precisely?"

"That's what I'd like you to help me find out, if you're amenable to the idea."

"It sounds interesting. Tell me more."

Mr. One hauled his lean, fifty-something-year-old frame out of his chair and paced around as he spoke, in a slightly agitated manner. There was something about Colonel Zaliatev that clearly had got to him. He said,

"Until recently we'd no real clues about what precisely he does when he's in London. He's been one of their most elusive and reclusive people, a bit of a ghost. I've placed a tail, parked within sight of his apartment block, during the last half-dozen times he's been in the country. The entire block is filled with Soviet embassy staff. Until recently he was never spotted leaving the building for anything other than a visit to the embassy or the ballet. Then yesterday, Albright, one of our cleverest new people, finally managed to work out what was going on. He cross-checked the surveillance logs for the last nine months and noticed that every time Zaliatev is in the UK a specially adapted van starts arriving at the entrance to the apartment block. As you might expect, there are several other chaps in the building whom we've been observing during all of that period, so we have the full day-by-day logs of comings and goings. On each occasion the vehicle reverses right up to the entrance door and then a chap in a wheelchair emerges from the building and is pushed up a ramp into the back of the van. Our people have simply noted what happens on previous occasions, wrongly presuming that the supposed wheelchair user is a relatively innocuous member of the embassy staff who is listed as being in a non-threatening occupation – he's simply a translator. Zaliatev is not disabled, has jet black hair and looks nothing like the chap in the wheelchair, who wears spectacles and has unkempt, longish blond hair. Albright was suspicious nevertheless and decided to follow the van. It drove for two miles and then pulled into a lock-up garage in Camberwell. Albright parked round the corner, nipped into a tobacconist so that he wasn't spotted and then watched through the window."

Another clap of thunder intervened, this time a little further away as the storm moved slowly over the city. Mr. One continued,

"The van driver tried to pull the garage doors shut behind him, but the strong wind caught one of them and, fortuitously, Albright was able to get a direct line of sight on the back of the vehicle. What he saw, Augustus, was a miracle that would have amazed even your sceptical eyes. The man in the back of the van set aside his wheelchair and hopped down onto the garage floor. Not only that, but a second miracle occurred. He who was half blind before could now see without spectacles. So amazed by these occurrences was this miracle man that his hair changed colour from blond to black, a transformation that was occasioned by the removal of a wig."

Mr. One, normally a stranger to wit, almost managed a half smile. He said,

"Albright recognised this miraculously cured individual as our good Colonel and realised that the supposed translator was simply a fictional member of the embassy staff created to provide Zaliatev with the cover necessary to foil our attempts at surveillance. The garage doors were locked shut after he departed and the burly driver hopped on a bus and disappeared. Our man followed the Colonel on foot to a pub just down the road. He observed that he sat down for a chat with a rather dodgy looking chap in a sharp suit and a somewhat outdated pork pie hat. He noticed that, while they were talking, envelopes were exchanged under the table."

"One of which contained a thick wedge of five-pound notes I assume?"

"Most likely so. After about ten minutes the meeting ended and Zaliatev headed for the nearest Underground station. The man from the pub got on a bus to Fleet Street. Our man slipped onboard as well. When the chap alighted, he went into a bookshop, where he bought a copy of an interesting little volume with the title, 'A History of English Names'. Our man then followed our dodgy looking friend to the favourite pub of Daily Mirror journalists, the rather aptly named The Stab in the Back. After a chinwag with his chums and a couple of pints of beer our friend went back to his flat in Islington. Albright did his homework and that's when things started to get very interesting. It turns out that our mystery chappie is Frank Chabler, a freelance tabloid investigative reporter with a nose for sniffing out scandals. He used to work full time at the Mirror and then the News of the World, but left both jobs under something of a cloud, so he lives entirely by what he can sell nowadays. My assumption, therefore, is that what was passed under the pub table to the Colonel was an envelope full of juicy information on a person of interest to him."

"For the purposes of blackmail."

"Precisely. The book is a bit of a puzzle, however. He might have bought it for other purposes, but the fact that he picked it up straight after his meeting with the Colonel at the very least raises the suspicion that it might in some way be significant."

Mr. One was so focussed on his train of thought that he didn't look where he was going and tripped over his own briefcase. He saved himself from an embarrassing forward roll onto the floor only by grabbing the coatstand and using it to pull himself upright again. Gus said,

"You make a lovely couple. If I put the radio on you could try a waltz or two together."

"Such wit, Augustus, such wit. You are in an unjustifiably jolly mood today. Now, to return to rather weightier matters, with everything we've got on our plate at the moment I need Albright for another job and I am decidedly short of replacements. I'm rather hoping you'll be prepared to fill the gap. I need to know on whom Chabler has been told to dig up dirt and whom he has investigated before on the Colonel's instructions. Then we need to know what the grand game behind it all is."

"Well, it's extremely kind of you to think of me Angus, but I did originally set this up as a genuine private detective agency and the balance between ordinary detective work and your intelligence stuff is becoming a little too much out of kilter. Lady Honoria is becoming increasingly convinced that her money is invested in what, in reality, is another cover story for MI5. She is never a happy bunny when she thinks the wool is being pulled over her eyes and she believes that is what is happening here."

"Of course she does, Augustus, and she's right, although you can never confirm that to her. In your heart of hearts you know that very well. The very justifiable soul searching that followed the Jennifer Marquis business aside, this is what you wanted from the start. MI5 on your terms – you're no longer a full-time employee, but you know very well that we still need your many talents, so you can pick and choose the jobs you take on. Mrs. Harding is doing an excellent job running the private detective agency side of things from what I understand and that is an extremely profitable part of your business. My information tells me that you now have two full-time employees to do most of that work for you and one of them runs your little free of charge missing persons operation for the poor of the East End during two and a half days a week as well. You now have more than enough time for our work in your personal schedule and we're paying you very well. Let Mrs. Harding do what she's clearly very good at and run the agency side of things for you. You're our man and we need you."

"It's not quite as simple as that, Angus. I need Alice for some of the intelligence work as well, given her wartime experience in Section Two of B Branch, and she gets pulled in too many directions at once if I take on too much of your work."

"That needn't be a problem, Augustus. You remember Marjorie Small, the woman who used to handle all the admin for our more intrusive operations? She retired six months ago, but she's not averse to some part-time work in a related field from what I hear. She's helping her daughter out with school fees and could do with a bit of a top up financially. She's vetted up to the hilt and would be the ideal person to fill in for Mrs. Harding when you need her for intelligence work. She's an invaluable asset, as indeed is Mrs. Harding of course. I can see if I can get you a little more money to cover the cost of employing her if you like."

Gus laughed. He said,

"Angus, you're mellowing a little. You're actually noticing the vital skills that women staff past and present bring to the job. Alice will be very impressed, not to say amazed, when I tell her."

"Me, mellowing, that's a thought. I do confess, I have noticed my outlook broadening a little of late. It may be the sight of my own retirement on the horizon, Augustus. I suspect at times that I'm beginning to think of life outside our closed little world, of how I might adjust to it, that sort of thing. Who knows? That's all for the future and today is for today, however. For the moment, I sorely need your services and trust that I can count on them."

"Alright, I'll give it a whirl Angus and see what I dig up. I'll try and keep Lady Honoria off my back. Presumably I'll be sharing Marjorie

Small's services if I employ her as you suggest?"

"Really, with whom?"

"The new tenants next door."

"Next door to where old man?"

"Here. We've had some new neighbours moving in during recent days, people who are taking up the entire remaining part of this floor."

"Who might they be and how are they relevant to Mrs. Small?"

Gus smiled while Angus retrieved his mac from the coatstand and began putting it on. He said,

"Angus, you really are the worst of actors. I'm referring, of course, to the accountants who aren't accountants."

"I'm sure I don't know what you mean Augustus."

"I'm sure you do, Angus. Your people have moved an entire cover operation slap bang next to my offices. They only do that when they can group like with like – and they and you are now assuming that we are the other 'like'."

"Well, to an extent your little business is pretty much a cover op Augustus, so that part of what you say is entirely accurate – and you're even more effective because you are also partially what your office door claims you are, a genuine, fully functional private detective agency. That makes your cover that extra bit convincing. But what makes you think these accountant chappies are our people?"

"Little snippets of conversation overheard in the corridor, one or two faces that look vaguely familiar, that kind of thing. But the biggest giveaway was the removal men's boxes when the stuff was brought in. I'd swear they were the same ones 5 used when I was working out of a cover op with them years ago."

"Really? We are getting a tad careless, aren't we? Well, I was going to tell you, but I thought it would be a useful test of how innocent our accountants looked if I waited to see if you'd notice what's really going on. Clearly, I need to tell them to up their game if you've rumbled them before they've got their feet under their desks. And if you really want to know why they've joined you, then it's quite simple. I prefer to know that a whole floor is secure when I'm leaving sensitive files on someone's desk, like the one I'm about to give you. So, when we needed a new home for one of our specialist units and I saw that the offices next door were vacant, I thought we could kill two birds with one stone, so to speak. I've had your agency's new private detectives vetted, by the way, just to make sure your side of things is absolutely watertight. Everyone you've recruited has been a former employee of 5 or 6 I see. Very sensible, very secure, just what I need. Well done."

Mr. One pulled a thick brown envelope file out of his briefcase and handed it to Gus. He said,

"This will give you a summary of everything we know so far about both the Colonel and the good Mr. Chabler. There's a list of mission objectives and a wodge of forms for your record keeping."

"I don't do forms anymore, Angus. I loathe forms. The only purpose I can think of for them is lining the litter tray of Lady Honoria's overfed cat. Writing out the damn things is not covered by your fee."

"It is now old man. I'm so short of time and men I can't cover that side of things for you at the moment. You'll soon get back into the swing of it. It's like riding a bicycle, learn to do it once and the knack is forever with you."

"Have you ever ridden a bicycle, Angus?"

"No, ridiculous things. Give me a horse any day. Right, that's all for now. Have a read of the file and then give this case your undivided attention, if you can. We need to know pretty damn quickly what our Colonel friend is up to and then get our response in place. We need all our ducks in a row on this one, Augustus."

"If you've already killed two birds with one stone you might be short of a duck or two, Angus."

"How amusing. Given that I seem to be famed for having no sense of humour whatsoever I fear that gem may be a little lost on me, Augustus. Oh, by the way, an old MI6 acquaintance of yours is interested in what Michaels will be telling us on Thursday evening and would like to liaise afterwards – a Major Cunnock."

"Cunnock? That under-brained irritant with all the diplomatic finesse of Vlad the Impaler?"

"That's the man. I had to inform MI6 of Michaels' approach to us, given that his suspicions have implications for them as well, and Cunnock was the man they chose to keep in touch over the matter. I thought that little bit of news would puncture your mood of unseasonal jollity, Augustus. Good morning."

The mere mention of Cunnock was enough to make Gus dive into his biscuit tin in search of comfort. He'd spent a considerable amount of time in the past keeping Cunnock away from anything he was involved with on the grounds of the man's incompetence. He'd never been able to work out quite how the major had held onto his job in MI6, concluding in the end that he either had something embarrassing on a superior, or was being protected simply by the old boys' network. Wiping crumbs off the top of the Zaliatev file, he opened it and began to read. He was interrupted by a knock on the door and Alice entered. She said,

"What on earth have you been putting in Mr. One's coffee, Gussie boots? He seems to be becoming recognisably human. That's the third time he's said good morning to me in a fortnight – a record. If this carries on, he'll be managing an occasional smile and who knows where things will go from there ..."

CHAPTER FIVE

The first thing that registered on Jacob's consciousness when he awoke was the sound of the dawn chorus floating into the room through a half open window. His vision was a little blurred at first, but soon returned to normal. The ornately decorated ceiling above his bed looked totally different to any he'd seen recently, yet strangely familiar. As he gradually came round, he realised that there was a good reason for this. He appeared to be back in his own bedroom, in the sprawling country house that was his inheritance. He had no idea how he'd got there and wondered for a moment whether the whole business of his capture and incarceration by the KGB had been simply a nightmare. Maybe he'd been ill, some kind of desperate fever from which he was finally beginning to recover. Perhaps he'd been confined to his bed for days, semi-comatose, while his brain went into fantasy-overdrive, concocting a stream of hallucinations with the terrifying Colonel Zaliatev at their core. He attempted to sit up, but was forced to desist immediately when this induced a fierce headache and a feeling of biliousness. Everything seemed to spin before his eyes for a minute or two before returning to normal. He lowered his ambitions in accordance with his current state and simply turned his head slowly from side to side to check out his surroundings in greater detail. What he saw confirmed his initial impression. On the far side of the large, palatial bedroom was the Dutch Master that his great-great-great-grandfather had bought from an Antwerp merchant in a year he could never remember. His mother had been incredibly fond of the painting, a vivid portrait of a richly attired young noblewoman from Amsterdam. She had arranged for it to be moved from the great hall into what was then her bedchamber, the room that was now his. Beneath the moody, atmospheric painting was his Chippendale dressing table. On the other side of the room he could see a gilded table, on which two large and highly expensive Meissen vases sat, both of which he'd been intending to sell. He made a second, more gradual attempt to pull himself up into a sitting position and this time was more successful. His head pounded less than it had done previously and soon calmed down once he had rearranged his pillows to prop himself up. At the far end of the room were the two large sash windows that looked out onto the formal gardens at the front of the house and the estate beyond, which he could see stretching into the grey-skied distance. Everything was as it had always been. He pinched himself a couple of times, just to be doubly sure that this was not simply some delirium inspired fantasy and the sharp pain provoked by his so doing confirmed that he was fully awake and in charge of his senses. He felt an itch and was about to scratch his arm to calm it when he noticed something that brought him down to earth with a jolt. Both of his wrists still bore fading scars. There was only one thing that could have caused them – the fierce, razor-sharp bonds that he remembered from his imprisonment. So that hadn't been a dream. The hard evidence in front of his eyes suggested that the memories of his time in the Colonel's company were as real as the room in which he now found himself.

The more he came round during the next few minutes, the more he remembered – and none of the memories were good. The last time he could recall seeing Zaliaev was at the hospital, convalescent home, whatever it was, watching the choir perform. Everything after that was a blank. He was totally baffled as to what had happened during the period between then and now. As he sat, wrestling frustratedly with this apparently unsolvable mystery, the bedroom door opened and a tall, muscular man in a dark suit entered silently and stood observing Jacob. He was in his early thirties, with cold, watchful eyes and the face of a bruiser. After a few moments he said, in a low key, matter of fact manner,

"How do."

Jacob, who had been unaware of his presence, started. He said,

"Who the devil are you?"

"I'm your butler, sir."

Jacob stared at him contemptuously.

"I sacked all the staff before my trip to France. I remember that well enough. So I don't have a butler."

"You do now, sir."

"Butlers do not tend to say 'How do' as a means of addressing their employer, not least in a thick Manchester accent."

"I'm very proud of my accent, sir."

The stranger walked confidently across the room and stood at the foot of the bed, staring Jacob straight in the eye. He said,

"Is there anything I can get you, sir – a cup of tea, this morning's newspaper, some scrambled egg, followed by marmalade and toast?"

"I'm sorry, I simply don't know you or how you came to be here. Who gave you the impression that I needed a butler and that you should just show up here, out of the blue?"

The man smiled in a coldly amused manner and said,

"A friend we have in common, sir."

"What? How could I have a friend in common with someone like you – or, should I say, a common man like you?"

The man smiled again. This time there was a look of smug satisfaction on his face when he said,

"The Colonel, sir. Colonel Zaliatev."

He watched contentedly while the impact of his words sank in. It was as if an all-encompassing dark cloud had settled over Jacob's bed.

"Oh. I see. Why does he think I need a butler?"

"Oh not just a butler – a cook, a cleaner, a chauffeur, a secretary and a security guard."

"Really? And where are all these people?"

"Standing right here, sir. I'm one and all of them. Quite a bargain in terms of salary costs don't you think?"

"And who is paying these salary costs?"

"You sir. The Colonel has arranged for your bank to start paying me from today. The bank is completely convinced that it's you who has made the necessary arrangements, so the money will find its way into my account without a hitch."

"And how much hitch-free money am I supposed to be paying you?"

"Oh, that's a matter between you and the Colonel I think, sir. I don't believe it's my place to discuss money matters. I'm just a dogsbody."

"Indeed. Well Dogsbody, you've clearly been given a brief, so what is it?"

"I'm to keep you in the manner to which you've been accustomed, sir."

"And?"

The man smiled so coldly that it seemed that every word froze as it left his mouth.

"I'm to be your master as well as your servant, sir. The Colonel was amused by the idea that an ordinary working-class bloke like me should be a toff's boss. He thought it might bring you down to earth a little, sir, make you feel a little less 'entitled', above yourself, up yourself, however you care to phrase it. So my job is to make sure you do exactly what he says. That's the stick side of the job. The carrot is that, providing you're a good boy, I'm to mollycoddle you, treat you just as a butler would. When you get callers, I'll be the ever so 'umble manservant, so that my presence

50

here looks perfectly innocent and natural. When you're on your tod I'm to treat you in accordance with your behaviour. The Colonel believes it's very important to keep someone like you fit and healthy and in good spirits, providing they're completely loyal. I'll feed and water you and drive you about on your missions. Be a bad boy and things change a little."

"In what way?"

"In a way that I wouldn't recommend you to wish on yourself, sir. If you step out of line, I'll give you a punch in the gut, or a karate chop, depending on the needs of the moment. If you're a really bad boy you'll get two chops or punches, and so on, depending on just how naughty you've been. I'm very well-trained, sir – I'll hit you where it won't show."

"You are a charmer, aren't you? How come he's using you and not a Russian?"

"A Russian butler might look a tad suspicious, sir, don't you think? I used to leak the odd secret or two to the Colonel's men when I was in the army you see. He was very grateful and has kept me in employment ever since, doing a little bit of this and a little bit of that. You're my little bit of that of the moment."

"So when I've had my scrambled egg, what am I supposed to do?"

"Oh, for now, take it easy until tomorrow, sir. You were drugged on the flight back to good old England and the after-effects will take another few hours to wear off fully. When you're back on your feet I need to go through our plan for dealing with Mr. Michaels. I'll be chauffeuring you to the hit and making sure that you don't make a mess of it."

Zaliatev's instructions on the matter came back into focus within Jacob's memory and as they did so the cloud hovering over his bed grew even darker. He said,

"I told the Colonel, I don't think I can kill a man in cold blood."

"He said you'd say that, sir and that I was to remind you that you had already killed a man when driving under the influence."

"That was different, I hadn't meant to do it."

"No, but you meant to cover it up, sir, you were quite ruthless about that. Ruthlessness is just what is needed in a killer, so you should be able to step up to the mark when the moment comes. You should be aware that if you refuse to send Mr. Michaels to meet his maker I have orders to shoot you – like a traitor, in the back of the head."

"How charming. How many people have you killed on the Colonel's behalf, Dogsbody?"

"Five to be precise, although one almost got away before succumbing to his injuries. That was nearly a very bad mistake. I won't make the same error with you, sir. It'll be a simple case of bang, bang, you're dead. Do you remember how we all used to play those games when we were young lads, sir? No, of course you don't, you'd be playing different games, rich kid's games. You'd be out watching how to shoot pheasants with your posh toff daddy, wouldn't you? Although I bet your lot would have rather preferred shooting peasants instead of pheasants, given half the chance, people like me perhaps?"

"There is a slight hole in the logic of what you're saying, Dogsbody. If the Colonel has this great secret mission for me that he keeps referring to, how is he going to be able to carry that out if I'm a piece of dead meat on a mortuary slab? I know your boss thinks that he has many powers over life and death, but I wouldn't have thought that they included resurrection. I can't do the stuff that he requires if I'm pushing up daisies. In short, you can't kill me."

"Your mission is only one of several that the Colonel has in play, sir. From what I understand it's highly useful but not indispensable. That means you also are not indispensable, sir. That's why I've been told to turn your lights out for good if you try and play silly beggars by not killing Mr. Michaels."

"I'm surprised that the KGB is prepared to risk a major diplomatic incident by murdering a senior Foreign Office mandarin like Michaels on British soil. Has the Colonel actually checked with his superiors on any of this?"

"In my experience the Colonel is his own man sir and he does things that no other KGB man would dare to. He doesn't check with the powers that be on anything that he's confident he can conceal and he's confident that he can make this killing look like the work of anyone but the KGB. So there's no way it's not going to happen old son. You're just going to have to get used to the idea that you've been chosen to be the man with the trigger finger, the man who terminates the big cheese. Terminates is a big word isn't it, sir? You must be rather surprised that someone as common as me would know that it even existed."

"I think I need some sleep, your common wit is boring me," Jacob said with a look of pronounced contempt for his unwanted companion. Dogsbody walked casually round to the side of the bed, smiling while saying,

"Indeed you do need a little bit of the old shut-eye, sir. As you've been so reluctant to do what the Colonel wants, it's my job to give you a sleeping pill. It might help you to see matters in a more positive light when you wake up."

With a movement so swift that the victim hardly saw it, he delivered an expertly placed blow to Jacob's head, knocking him out cold. Admiring his handiwork, he smiled sardonically and said,

"Sweet dreams, sir."

He rearranged his charge's pillows back into a sleeping position, made sure that he was properly tucked in, then left, locking the door behind him.

When Jacob eventually came round the room was in darkness. He had a thumping headache and felt distinctly groggy. The memory of what had happened, to the extent that he'd seen the blow that had smashed him into a sleep as deep as death, gradually came back. He shuddered with fear. It was as if he was back in the KGB interrogation cell, with a psychopathic madman waiting for the slightest excuse to inflict severe bodily harm on him. The terror that this realisation of his predicament induced reminded him that he was in urgent need of a pee. There was an ancient commode in the room, but that was very much a second preference to the bathroom two doors down the corridor. He managed to haul himself upright and walked unsteadily across to the door. When he found it to be locked, his heart sank. It emphasised that he was once more a prisoner, but this time even in his own house. He staggered over to the commode, but then noticed a cold breeze within the room, suggesting that a window was still half open. He decided that he would pee out of the window as he used to do on many occasions when a student at Oxford. It was the one small but symbolic act of personal freedom that he could manage in his currently constrained circumstances. As he shuffled towards the window, he remembered how he had once slithered down the drainpipe into the garden below when the room had first become his. He'd been drunk at the time and had done it as an act of inebriated derring-do. The room was only one storey from the ground and he'd managed it without breaking any limbs. The thought occurred to him that when he had regained a little of his strength it might be worth seeing if he could accomplish the feat a second time and make good his escape. He had little confidence that he'd be allowed to live once his usefulness to the KGB had expired, he was 'a man who knew too much' and a potential liability, so it was a serious option to consider.

He gasped with relief as he irrigated the rose garden a few feet below. Relief turned to shock when an outraged canine howl, followed by ferocious barking, suddenly ripped through the air. His long experience of hunting dogs and attack dogs told him that what he could hear was the largest of Rottweilers. Dogsbody clearly had stationed it directly below his window to ensure that the prisoner stayed put. His heart sank even further as his last possible escape route turned out to be another dead end. He shuffled back to bed and slumped down onto his pillows, exhausted and defeated. Sheer despair pushed all other thoughts out of his mind and within minutes he was fast asleep again, oblivious to the continuing disgruntled growling outside.

When he next awoke it was seven o'clock the following morning.

Dogsbody was standing at the side of his bed, watching him expressionlessly. Fear had been replaced by simple resignation and Jacob said,

"Here to give me another whack on the head, are you?"

"A new day is a new start, sir. If you're a good boy I won't need to give you another whack at all. I've laid today's shirt and an appropriate suit over the back of the armchair near the window. When you've washed and shaved you can get dressed and come downstairs for your breakfast. Porridge, scrambled egg and sausages, followed by toast and marmalade, are on today's menu, sir."

"Does that mean you're going to leave the bedroom door unlocked so that I can actually get to the bathroom?"

"Of course, sir. During the day you're as free to wander the house as you would be normally. I wouldn't try going outside unless I'm with you, though. Vladimir is guarding the front of the house and Leonid the rear. I believe that you and Vladimir became acquainted last night. He smelt pretty horrible this morning and I can only assume that you relieved yourself on him from a great height. I do hope that was an accident, sir."

"How was I to know that there was a bloody hound right under my window? I couldn't get to the bathroom so it was perfectly reasonable for me to use the window instead."

"I don't think Vladimir will understand such niceties, sir. I'd given him a sniff of one of your socks so that he'd know your scent, but he now knows it rather more than he would have liked. That makes it doubly important that you only go outside after I have restrained him, sir. He does have a bit of a vengeful nature."

Dogsbody strolled towards the doorway, saying,

"I'll be waiting downstairs. Breakfast is at seven-thirty, followed by your briefing at eight-fifteen."

"What briefing?"

"The briefing that I am to give you about the termination of Mr. Michaels, sir. You will be returning to your work at the Foreign Office on Monday and on Tuesday evening you will ensure that you leave your office in good time so that I can drive you down to the target's house in the country before he arrives back at his usual hour, seven pm. I'll advise you on all of the ins and outs of what's involved once you've finished your breakfast."

Dogsbody was in every inch and molecule of his being the military man, except with regard to his lack of loyalty to the state of which he was a national, despite having been trained in its army. Breakfast was at precisely seven-thirty, as promised, and the briefing that followed began the instant the first quarter hour chime of the mantle clock in the breakfast room rang out at eight-fifteen. By the time the briefing had concluded, twenty-five minutes later, Jacob was wondering whether he should save himself a lot of fear and trouble by simply running outside and baring his throat to the salivating fangs of a vengeful Vladimir. That at least would end things straight away and cut out the wait for what he felt to be an inevitable appointment with the hangman's noose at some indeterminate point in the future. He was sure that, one way or another, his killing of Michaels would lead to his own death.

Tuesday evening hurtled towards him so fast that its arrival came like a slap in the face, waking him from his remaining fantasies and hopes about different ways he might try and escape from the clutches of his KGB masters. Dogsbody had told him that if he wasn't in the back of the Bentley by five-fifteen sharp, then the Colonel had said that he was to be shot on sight. The knock-out blow he had received on the morning of his first acquaintance with the Colonel's enforcer had been all the persuasion he needed that this was a man who lived permanently on the edge of extreme violence and that it would be highly advisable to do exactly as he said. Accordingly, he was out of the Foreign Office and in the back of the limousine ten minutes before the deadline.

They arrived at Michaels' isolated country residence ninety minutes later. Dogsbody drove the car down a farm track opposite and parked out of sight, behind a large hedge. On the seat beside Jacob a pair of gloves and a shoebox awaited his attention. He had been ignoring both for as long as he could. Dogsbody turned round and said,

"Chop chop, sir, you should have the gloves on by now. We're later than planned thanks to the roadworks in Bayswater and the target will be here in twenty minutes."

Jacob picked up the said items distastefully and pulled them over his trembling fingers. Dogsbody had opened the door for him to get out. As he hauled himself from the vehicle, his body seeming to be twice its normal weight and devoid of all energy or strength, the 'chauffeur' said,

"Don't forget the gun, sir. You can't shoot a man by pointing your finger at him and shouting, 'Bang, bang, lie down, you're dead,' in the way that you did when you were at that posh preparatory school of yours."

Jacob bent over and opened the shoebox. He pulled the fully loaded revolver out and stuffed it into his coat pocket. The 'chauffeur' watched with a look of contemptuous amusement.

"Careful when you pull that out of your pocket, sir. It wouldn't do to shoot yourself in the foot."

Jacob, who was feeling closer to death than the man he was about to kill, didn't react. They crossed the road, with Dogsbody hurrying up the drive and the unwilling assassin trudging along behind him. While the thought that he might shoot the Colonel's man instead of Michaels crossed Jacob's mind, the fact that his Mancunian friend was keeping a weather eye on him as he led him towards the house made such a possibility a pointless ambition.

"Come on, sir, look lively, our man will be here before you're in position if you're not careful."

It was now fully dark with no sign of the moon. Their only illumination was the Colonel's man's torch. He avoided shining it above ground level in case the light was spotted by their quarry as he approached the house in his car. The outline of the generously proportioned Georgian house could just be made out thanks to a couple of ornamental coaching lanterns that mildly illuminated the entrance doorway. The drive opened out into a circular tarmacked area in front of the building, with an ornate stone fountain at its centre. There were large, neatly trimmed semi-circular hedges on either side of this area. Dogsbody beckoned to Jacob and led him behind the hedge on their immediate left. They stopped at a point where there was a gap in the foliage that was large enough to give them full sight of both the drive up which their quarry would be approaching and the area around the fountain, where they knew he would be parking. Dogsbody took a cigarette lighter out of his pocket and pushed it through the gap in the hedge, pressing it twice to send a signal. A matching signal quickly followed from the hedge on the other side of the drive. Jacob said,

"Your friend the photographer I presume?"

"Correct, sir – all ready and waiting to take a photo of Mr. Michaels' demise at the hands of your good self."

"And if I can't do it, I'll be the one to be sent to the mortuary slab?"

"Indeed, sir, but I have every confidence that you will do it."

In the distance a car's engine could he heard and a pair of approaching headlights came into view.

"Oh, looks like he's early. I'd get that gun out of your coat pocket and into your hand, sir. Remember everything I told you in the briefing and take three deep breaths before stepping out to shoot. Use four well placed bullets and hit him before he has time to turn round and look at you. You'll find it much easier that way."

Jacob's heart was beating so fast it seemed that at any moment it would burst through his ribcage. The car was being driven at some speed and soon turned into the drive. It swept past them and stopped a couple of yards away from the fountain, a large Humber Super Snipe black saloon. The driver's door opened and Michaels got out, a tall, lean moustachioed man in his early forties. Unseen and unheard in his soft-soled shoes, Jacob staggered towards him in the manner of a substandard ghoul from a low budget horror movie. His first shot was fired at the same time as he tripped on a large stone that he couldn't see in the dark and the bullet seared over his target's shoulder, shattering the glass in one of the front windows of the house. The photographer's flash went off within a millisecond, capturing perfectly the look of bemused shock on the faces of both the incompetent assassin and the intended victim. Instead of taking cover behind the large bulk of the car, or attempting to run away, Michaels turned to face his would-be killer. Horrified now by the realisation that his features were just about recognisable in the weak glow from the coaching lanterns, Jacob went into panic mode and fired twice. The first bullet hit Michaels in the shoulder and the second hit the cigarette case in his inside pocket. The photographer's flash went off a second time as the victim was knocked backwards by the impact of the bullets. He lay writhing on the ground, pleading for mercy. Jacob stood over him, frozen by the shock of what he'd done and was unable to fire the fatal shot. Dogsbody came up from behind and wrenched the gun from his hand. Without even a second's pause he shot the unfortunate Michaels between the eyes, extinguishing his life without even the slightest qualms of conscience. Surveying the trembling Jacob contemptuously, he said,

"I can see why they put you in the Signals Corps, you couldn't hit an elephant even if you were sitting on top of the damn thing. At least we've got the photo to make it look like you were the killer."

Any further conversation was precluded by the sound of shattering glass. Michaels' Alsatian dog had jumped through the remains of the window that already had been broken by Jacob's first shot and was bounding towards them. Dogsbody instantly aimed the gun at the enraged animal, but it jammed when he attempted to fire. The photographer, who had come out of the bushes now that the murder was complete, was scared of dogs at the best of times. He was so terrified by the sight of the snarling beast that he screamed something incomprehensible in Russian and fled for his life. Faced with a choice between the two individuals who were standing their ground and watching it, transfixed, and a third potential prey who was in full flight, the animal chose the option that offered it the maximum exercise and excitement and hurtled after the photographer. Dogsbody had pulled his personal revolver out of its holster, but by then the dog and the photographer were well out of range of his weak torch and he couldn't see the animal to try and shoot it. Jacob was aware that he had a very damp leg and felt as if his heart had now exploded. Even Dogsbody looked as if he'd just seen one ghost for every year of his life. He said,

"Come on, let's go back to the car and get the hell out of here before the hound changes its mind and comes after us. The props team will be here in a minute to do all of the theatricals and scene setting before the bluebottles arrive, they'll deal with the mutt."

They ran back down the drive and across the road to where the Bentley waited and then hurtled away from the scene of the crime at a speed that left Jacob holding onto the nearest armrest for dear life. He noticed a van waiting in a layby about half a mile from the house. It flashed its lights at them three times, evidently in response to a signal from Dogsbody. The Bentley stopped alongside and Dogsbody wound down his window to give the occupants the lowdown on the situation back at the house, most particularly with regard to the need to retrieve the photographer. As the Bentley moved off again, Jacob turned round to look through the back window and saw the van pull out and head towards the house. That evidently was the props team going into action. He wondered if there would be anything intact left of the photographer other than his camera.

Back in Michaels' car someone or something was stirring. Unnoticed amongst all the commotion with the dog was a female passenger in her early thirties. She'd fainted at the sound of the gunshots and only came round after Jacob and Dogsbody had departed. She opened the passenger door and hauled herself upright with some difficulty. She walked unsteadily round the front of the car and then saw Michaels' corpse staring up at her in the dim glow of the coach lights. She nearly fell backwards with the horror and the shock of what had happened. Hearing the dog barking in the distance, accompanied by several searing screams, she decided that the only safe option was to flee the scene and try and get to the nearest village, where she could summon help. She'd never learned to drive, so her only option was to run. Rather than risk heading straight into the hands of one of the perpetrators, should they still be around, she hurried over to the low wall at the side of the garden. Deciding that her high-heeled shoes would be a liability when trying to navigate her way across muddy countryside, she pulled them off. Climbing over the wall, she fled across the fields in the opposite direction to where the dog's barking seemed to be coming from and towards the lights of the little village that nestled quietly within the undulating countryside, just under a mile away.

Within a minute of her doing so, the prop team's van rolled up the drive and came to a halt beside the car. Four heavies got out, followed by a slimmer man with a hat that was tipped so far forwards it nearly touched his nose. He stood still for a few moments, listening to the violence being inflicted by the dog in the distance, then despatched one of the heavily armed crew to go and investigate. Noticing that the passenger door of Michaels' car was open, he hurried over to have a look inside. What he found did not please him. There was a woman's black leather handbag on the floor of the car, but no sign of its owner. She was a witness who had not been spotted and who clearly had escaped. He cursed the incompetence of the surveillance team who hadn't unearthed the fact that Michaels was in the habit of bringing a lover back to the house from time to time. He shone his torch around the front of the building in a circular fashion and then spotted the patent leather shoes that had been abandoned in front of the garden wall. He despatched a second heavy with a powerful torch to find the woman and bring her back. He then radioed for instructions as to what to do about her when she had been captured.

The escapee, meanwhile, was making good progress. She was familiar with the lay of the land from several country walks with her deceased secret lover and was no slouch when it came to running. There seemed to be every chance that she would outdistance her pursuer, whose torch she could see bobbing up and down in the distance behind her. Then her right foot went down a rabbit burrow and she hurtled forwards onto her face. Her knees were sore as a result of sharp stones that tore through her stockings and cut her flesh. Most problematic, however, was the fact that she had severely sprained her right ankle. She managed to haul herself to her feet, but could do little more than hobble. She was nowhere near a wall and in the pitch-dark was unable to see anywhere where she could hide.

All the time, the man with the torch was getting closer.

CHAPTER SIX

It was a busy Wednesday morning in the agency. Gus was sitting in the snug calm of his oak panelled inner office going through the accounts to check that Lady Honoria was still getting the return on her investment that she had originally anticipated. He wanted to ensure that he had the required hard evidence to hand when she came to look at the books, as she was now threatening to do, 'imminently'. She had a mind like a laser and would cut straight through any waffle he might try and offer in response to her detailed enquiries, so facts were the only riposte that would hold water. The tricky question was how to 'present' those facts in a way that would convincingly conceal the reality that a substantial part of the agency's work was for MI5. In the outer office, Alice was going through the particulars of a new assignment that she was in the process of giving to one of the agency's detectives. It was a potentially highly remunerative divorce case – the ideal kind of cover that Gus needed to divert attention away from his intelligence work. A loud knocking on the outer office door hardly registered on his mind, so engrossed was he in the finer details of the accounts. It was only when Alice entered that he looked up. She said,

"Mr. One has sent a car with an urgent request for you to join him. He says it's critically important."

The driver was tight lipped as to what was involved, saying that it was his job to drive and not to know. It was not until Gus stepped out of the car an hour and a half later that he discovered that he was at the very grand Georgian house of Mallory Michaels. Mr. One, in wellington boots and a thick navy duffle coat, was just coming back over the garden wall after an expedition into the surrounding fields in the company of the police and a couple of dogs. After a brief conversation with the bull-built, fierce-faced detective who was leading the murder investigation, Inspector George

Wallace, he strode over to where Gus was peering into Michaels' black Humber car.

"Morning Augustus, sorry to drag you out here at short notice, but it appears our Thursday meeting with Mallory Michaels has been cancelled by persons unknown. It's been clumsily dressed up to appear like a robbery gone wrong, but it rather looks like something else."

"I take it that Mr. double M is deceased?"

"What? Yes, of course. They took the body away about twenty minutes ago. Sorry, should have made that clear. What was most probably planned as a straightforward killing seems to have ended up as complete mayhem. Police dogs found evidence of someone fleeing from the scene and then being savaged by a large dog a third of a mile away. Part of a finger was found, which we presume to be male from the size of it, together with a lot of blood, but the victim has vanished. I assume that he was one of the perpetrators who fell foul of Michaels' dog. It appears to have leaped through the drawing room window and joined the melee – we've found some of its fur on one of the largest shards of glass."

They moved out of the way while a van reversed into the spot beside them so that the police dogs could be put in the back, ready to be returned to the kennels. The whole of the space in front of the house was busy with officers getting ready to leave the site. Mr. One continued,

"There seems to have been a second person in Michaels' car. They attempted to escape in the opposite direction to the individual who became a bit of a dog's dinner. We're pretty sure it was a woman. We found a couple of pieces of jewellery that we think she deliberately dropped as she was being dragged off. We gave the dogs a sniff of those items and the passenger seat of the car and they traced her trail out into the fields and then back again. As she wasn't found here, I assume that she's still alive and has been abducted. We've just conducted a search of the fields around the house to see if there's anything else to find, but there isn't, so the police are moving out."

"How was Michaels killed?"

"Very messily. It's almost as if there were two people involved – one who couldn't shoot straight and a coldly efficient executioner. The first shots were all over the shop and we found one bullet embedded in the drawing room wall, so that was a complete miss. The fatal shot was very precise, straight between the eyes. We found the gun on the other side of the garden wall. It was rather too easy to discover and I have the suspicion that we were expected to find it."

"So you think what happened here has the feel of some kind of set up?"

"Very much so. I think it would have been a lot better done had the dog not intervened and created chaos, as appears to have been the case. I suspect also that the perpetrators hadn't anticipated the woman being present. Having to hare after her threw things into further disarray."

"So, basically, you suspect that this was a hit designed to take out Mr. double M before we could talk to him. Everything else is just window dressing to try and throw us off the scent."

"Exactly."

"If you're right, as my instinct says you are, we do at least have confirmation that the mole Michaels was about to help us identify is up to something so important that his controllers will go to extraordinary lengths to protect him. We've also got a missing woman whom we need to identify and then rescue in the hope that she might be able to throw some light on whom Mr. double M suspected. On top of that, we've got a race against time to try and find whether or not there is anything in Michaels' office that might help us identify our elusive mole. He will probably be trying to get there before us. I assume that the killers have already thoroughly ransacked the house?"

"Indeed. The surface motive was, I'm sure, to make it look like a simple break in, during which they were disturbed by the owner's unexpected return home. But it's pretty inevitable they'll have been looking also for precisely what we would like to find. They seem to have gone through every drawer, desk and cupboard in the place. The police have done their fingerprinting work, so I've got a couple of men searching through everything now, just in case the killers missed anything. I've got a couple of other men going through Michaels' office while we speak."

"So what you want me to do is to find the mystery woman and get her back in the hope that Michaels might have mentioned his suspicions to her?"

"Got it in one Augustus. It's the kind of mission for which you are our first and last best hope. You have a nose for these things."

"OK. I presume that the killers removed all trace of her from the car?"

"Indeed. The jewellery she so cleverly dropped is quite distinctive, however, and should help us identify her pretty quickly. The boys in blue are holding onto it for evidence, as one might expect, but we've photographed it and the prints will be waiting for you in your office by the time you get back."

Mr. One looked uneasy. He said,

"The embarrassing thing is, Michaels told me over the phone that he suspected he'd been tailed last week. It came to a head when he'd gone to visit a relative in St. George's Hospital during Thursday evening and had parked in a deserted side-street. He'd noticed a car pull in about three hundred yards behind him and then two men get out and start to follow him. He'd broken into a slow run to test whether or not they really were on his tail and they started running as well in order to keep up. He'd nipped down a set of basement steps once he'd rounded the corner and the pursuers ran past without spotting him. He went straight back to his car and went home as a precaution. He said he hadn't seen them since then, but that's what persuaded him to contact me and arrange a meeting to share his suspicions about the presence of a mole this week."

"Didn't you put a man on him after that?"

"I did, but the decrepit old banger he was driving about in packed up yesterday afternoon and he wasn't able to get a replacement in time to follow Michaels home from work. By the time he got there the killers were long gone and all he was left with was the corpse and the debris. He hadn't seen Michaels picking a woman up on previous occasions, so has no idea who the missing lady might be. We've asked his cleaner if she knew that he had a lady friend and she told us that she was aware in the way that cleaners are that he occasionally had a female guest, but she'd never seen her and he'd never said anything about her. The really annoying thing is that I'd tried to persuade Michaels to move the meeting to last night to be on the safe side, but he said he'd got a clashing commitment – presumably the missing woman."

"Has anybody searched the inside of the car?"

"Well, yes, of course, as I said before, we've checked it out for anything that might identify Miss A.N. Other."

"I mean really checked it. Have you had the inner door panels off, looked under the carpets?"

"No, the police didn't see any need to go any further. Miss Other is hardly likely to have hidden a card with her name and address under the carpet. What do you think might be found?"

"Well, it's just an off chance, but Mr. double M was clearly a very careful chap. He was watching to see if he was being followed and he would only give you the name of the mole face-to-face, so he was clearly highly conscious of the need to protect both himself and the information that he had. Given that he suspected someone might be on to him, he would have stored his evidence in a safe place where only he would think of looking and the lining of his car might be just such a place. The car boot was still open following the police examination of the vehicle when I arrived and I noticed a very impressive do-it-yourself mechanic's toolkit, so Michaels clearly had all of the necessary skills to do something as simple as removing and replacing a door lining, for example."

"I don't wish to sound pedantic Augustus, but if you've thought of it as well, then clearly the lining couldn't be a place where only he would think of looking."

"Thank you for clarifying that point, Angus and I'm much too polite to call you pedantic. Shall we begin?"

Gus was well versed in the arts of vehicle engineering and dismantling as a result of his intelligence work in occupied Europe during the Second World War. It was when he was removing the panel on the inside of the rear passenger door that something fell out onto the tarmac. He picked it up and waved it in front of Mr. One's eyes with a triumphal smile.

"A locker key of some description by the looks of it," One observed. "You have a remarkable ability to read the minds of others Augustus, I must admit it would never have occurred to me that Michaels might have done such a thing."

"Now all we have to do is find out where the locker is to which it relates. It has the number forty-two on the fob and well, what do you know, St. Pancras. We have our good selves a station locker key Angus."

Mr. One called one of his men from the house, gave him the key and told him to go to St. Pancras and see what he found.

When they drove back to London, Gus asked to be dropped off at his office so that he could confer with an expert on women's jewellery, Alice. On his arrival, she handed him the sealed envelope containing the prints that Mr. One had promised. He opened it and dropped the photographs onto her desk with a mischievous look in his eye. She was transfixed by what she saw.

"Wow! For me?"

"As if, you cheeky monkey, Alice Harding. One spectacular necklace, one blindingly beautiful matching bracelet. Do you know who the most likely makers might be?"

"There's no most likely about it – they're both from the newest range at Cartier. I had one of my weekly ogles in their New Bond Street store last Saturday and I was bowled over by them. There are only four of each being made apparently and they're solely available from that store. It would set you back around ten thousand pounds for the two of them."

"You really do know how to make a chap's day."

He wrote down a name and telephone number on a scrap of paper from Alice's desk and gave it to her.

"If you could give this gentleman a ring and arrange to go with him to the said store, pronto, I'd very much appreciate it. I need to find precisely whom these items have been sold to. Given their value, Cartier won't divulge names and addresses to anyone other than the police, so Inspector Wallace is our passport to finding whoever the owner is."

"OK, no sooner said than done. Oh, by the way, someone's left you a present – it's in your office."

The present turned out to be a second telephone that was wired into a completely different socket to his original phone. Puzzled, Gus experimented with the new device by trying to ring his East End office. Nothing happened and the line seemed completely dead, so he assumed it mustn't yet have been connected properly. He went back into the main office to ask Alice who had fitted the phone and why, but she had already departed on her jewellery mission.

Gus didn't carry a weapon as a matter of course, but decided that the Michaels case was potentially dangerous enough to require the taking of appropriate precautionary measures. He went back into his inner office and opened the gun safe, choosing a standard British army service revolver. As he closed the safe door the phone rang. He picked up his normal receiver, but the ringing continued. He picked up the new phone and a familiar voice addressed him from the other end of the line,

"Augustus, I trust you like your new telephone. I forgot to mention it this morning with so many other things to think about."

"Very nice, but what's its purpose? There's only one of me, so I'm not quite sure why I need two devices."

"It's a dedicated direct line, Augustus. You may no longer be one of our full-time intelligence officers, but you now have so much of a foot back inside the door that I thought a secure line would be useful so we can chat over the phone when I need to get hold of you. It only works on this number and it's one way, so you can't use it for any other purpose."

"I wouldn't have thought someone as lowly in the pecking order as myself would merit such a privilege."

"As you very well know you're one of our best people Augustus and I had one of the things to spare, so you'll have to put up with it I'm afraid. Now, to rather more urgent matters. I put some pressure on the police and they've completed their checks on the origins of the murder weapon in double quick time. It's an unusual gun, a pre-war American manufactured one off that somehow found its ways onto these shores. There were less than five hundred made apparently, as a special edition. Nearly all of them stayed in the United States, mostly with collectors, so this one stands out like a sore thumb on this side of the ocean. The signature of the bullet is unique and there have been three previous murders in which it seems highly likely this weapon was used, all gangland killings."

"Which fits the narrative suggesting that Michaels' death was a result of him stumbling across big time burglars ransacking his house for treasure. It's certainly an imposing enough residence for crooks to suspect there might be lots of tasty valuables and maybe a safe full of cash inside, who knows. What's your view on the matter?"

"Well, that leads me on to my second bit of information. When our people checked the locker at St. Pancras, they found that it had been broken into and whatever had been inside had been taken. If the thieves didn't have the key, they must have been following Michaels closely enough to spot him putting a file or an envelope inside the locker and decided they needed to take a look. That fits with him spotting a tail when he went to the hospital and points away from the random burglary killing narrative."

"So let me guess, what you want me to do is use my criminal underworld contacts to try and find out if the gun was specially bought for the occasion and, if so, by whom?"

"As always, you are ahead of the game Augustus, yes that is precisely what I want you to do. That may give us much needed information on who these killers really were. You can try and find out via your good friend Tasty Harry no doubt, the man who breaks bones for a living."

"Oh I think Tasty's repertoire is rather more varied than that Angus. It will cost you though. If Tasty locates the right armourer, as I'm sure he will, the gentleman in question will want a substantial payment before he gives up that kind of information, even to Tasty."

"I'll reimburse you for however much it costs, with a bonus for Mr. Tasty, if he can get us the information by tomorrow. I'll send one of my men over in the next two hours with the precise details of the gun. How are you doing with regard to the identity of the missing woman?"

"We should have her name within the next hour or so if all goes well. Alice is following up a red-hot lead with the police in tow as we speak."

"Excellent, good work Augustus. I'll leave you to get on with things and await developments. My men are still interviewing people at the Foreign Office. There's a possibility that Michaels said something to somebody that might give us a clue as to who he suspected the mole might be."

"There must be a good chance that your chaps will speak to the mole as well, without knowing who he or she is, of course. That could be useful, in terms of panicking them into making mistakes, or just as easily warn them to be doubly careful in concealing their identity."

"Indeed, it's all a case of swings and roundabouts. There's no other way of hunting for the information we need, sadly. Good luck with the name, Augustus, we need to find this woman quickly if she's to stay alive."

Gus put the phone down and thought for a moment. From his long acquaintanceship with Tasty Harry he knew exactly where he would be at six pm – in the Lamb and Ferret public house in the East End. Harry was a creature of habit and rarely strayed from his regular locations. The two had formed an unlikely friendship after Gus had located Harry's missing niece, while refusing any payment or fee for doing so. His act of kindness had enabled Harry to rescue her from a violent thug of a man. Like Gus, Harry was a complex character. On the one hand, he would think nothing of breaking an arm or a leg of a villain who was unwise enough to try and double cross him, and he ran a protection racket that was quite ruthless in its pursuit of missing payments. On the other, he had a code of honour that he stuck to rigorously. He had no tolerance of violence towards or the mistreatment of women and would punish severely anybody whom he found to be breaking his unwritten rules on the matter. If anybody did him or his close family a genuine kindness, he would be their friend and protector for life. That was no small advantage to have on one's side. Harry had the build and the bulk of a wrestler and towered over anybody who came into his presence. In recognition of Gus's good deed for his niece, he would tap into the London underworld gossip networks on his behalf to find information that could be obtained through no other channel. He would be the best means of trying to find out what kind of organisation was behind the purchase of the murder weapon. Having decided to take the tube rather than a taxi, Gus made a note of the time he would have to leave by if he was to catch Harry while he was still sober and then turned his mind to other matters.

He took a large blank sheet of artists' paper out of his top drawer and unfolded it across the top of his desk. In characteristically methodical fashion he began to fill it in with all of the details they had so far concerning the Michaels case to see if he could spot anything of significance that they hadn't previously noticed. He became so engrossed he didn't notice the passage of time and was quite startled to find it was half past four by the time Alice returned, shortly after Mr. One's man had dropped off an envelope with the full technical details of the gun. She burst into the office excitedly,

"Got it!"

"And what precisely have you got Mrs. Harding?"

"Her name is Julia Emersly and she lives on the top floor of Wennington Towers in Chelsea. I've just been round to her flat with the police and none of her neighbours have seen her since Tuesday. One hawk-eyed old lady passed her leaving the building with a chap who the police say fits the description of a Mr. Mallory Michaels. She thinks it was around five-fifteen in the evening when she saw them."

Gus looked shellshocked. She said,

"Oh, that wasn't quite the reaction I was expecting. Is something wrong?"

"Well yes, actually there is – very well done and all that, excellent work Alice. It's just that I know the lady in question rather well, although I'd no idea she was going out with Mallory Michaels. She's my cousin."

"Oh good lord, how awful. I gathered from the police that she's been abducted. Do you have any idea by whom, they seemed to be pretty clueless?"

"At the moment I think I'm marginally less clueless than them. I'm setting something in motion via Tasty Harry tonight and if I'm lucky I might have a clearer idea by tomorrow afternoon."

By the time Gus had battled his way across London on the tube and got to the Lamb and Ferret, it was five past six and Tasty Harry was already ensconced at a table with two spare chairs that the other drinkers found it wise not to sit in. He was reading the evening newspaper while sipping a pint of best bitter. Gus pulled out a chair and sat down opposite him, causing everyone from the bartenders to the fiercest looking clients to stare in amazement. Harry lowered the newspaper a little and surveyed the intruder. The corners of his eyes lightly crinkled, betraying the grin that was hidden behind the front page. Then he laughed, a loud, deep-throated laugh that was almost enough to rattle the glasses on the vintage 1890s shelves beneath the ornately decorated bar.

"You always were a cheeky bastard Mr. Bendink-Benedict – you know very well you're the only one I'd let sit down there without even a how's your father."

He summoned the landlord,

"Alec! Bring this man a pint of your worst bitter."

"We don't have worst Tasty, we only do best and mild."

Harry laughed again, the rest of the pub joining in.

"There's no telling the difference between your best and your worst me old china, so get the good man one or the other and help him wipe that parched look off his boat race!"

Gus smiled warmly along with the general laughter. Now that it was clear they wouldn't have the entertaining sight of Harry ejecting his uninvited guest with one large hand on his collar and the other on his trouser belt, the other drinkers returned to their various conversations about dubious and dodgy matters.

"To what do I owe the honour?" Harry asked. "I haven't seen you anywhere near this manor for a month or more."

"Something that I thought was just another case, but which has come very close to home Tasty. Somebody's abducted one of my cousins after a murder and I need to find out where she is pretty damn urgently."

"Gordon Bennett, I'm sorry to hear that Gus me old mate, genuinely sorry, particularly after what you did helping me sister find her gal. What's this murder we're looking at then?"

"It was on Tuesday night, just outside a little village called Blea Frampton."

"Who was the geezer that bought it – I presume it was a geezer, not a gal?"

"Chap called Mallory Michaels. He worked for the Foreign Office."

"Oh, right, one of your hush-hush jobs then, eh? How does your cousin fit in?"

"She was with him in his car when he arrived home. It seems she managed to run off after the killers shot him, but they caught up with her and decided to take her with them. Nobody's got a clue about where she is at the moment, or precisely who's got her."

"So you want me to do a bit of asking about to see if anyone's heard any whispers?"

"I'd be extremely grateful if you could Tasty. I'm pretty sure it's a London based outfit because of the gun."

Gus described the weapon in precise detail to Harry, who scratched his head in puzzlement.

"I've never seen one of those Gus me old china, it sounds a rare old bird. But you're right, if it was sold anywhere it would have to be London. Nobody outside of this town would touch something as exotic as that."

"It's precisely the exotic nature of the weapon that gives us the best chance of finding out who took her. If you could gently or ungently prod your armourer chums and see if you can get any clues as to who might have bought it, then I'm three quarters way there to finding out where Julia is."

"That what she's called then? Nice, has a classy ring to it. Well, Gus me old mate, I'm not a grass, as you know, and I don't normally go as far as giving you names, but this is different. This is your flesh and blood, as my sister's gal is mine. Leave it with me, I'll see what I can do. You'll need an answer faster than a pig can fly if you're to stop anything happening to her. It'll take me a day to find everyone I need to speak to, but I'll make it my number one priority. Meet me here again tomorrow night, same time. One way or another, I'll have something for you me old china."

As he was speaking Gus's pint was delivered to the venerable old Victorian table with its well beaten copper top. Tasty said,

"Let's drink to your lady's very good health. If no one gives me a name, then they'll be in very bad health, you mark my words me old mate. I'll have something for you as sure as day follows night and dark follows light."

Harry laughed and said,

"Keeping the company of a posh toff like you is having a bad effect on me Bendink-Benedict, I'm turning into a poet ..."

CHAPTER SEVEN

Wednesday was one of the most stressful days of Jacob's life, rivalling even his time in KGB custody. He was one of the first to be questioned by MI5 about the killing during the previous evening. Exploding with fear inside, he somehow managed to maintain a calm exterior and kept faithfully to the carefully rehearsed story about his movements during Tuesday night, which could be backed up, of course, by his chauffeur. He told his questioners that the only direct dealings he had had with Michaels were all about standard Foreign Office matters and that there had never been any hint of concerns about a possible mole in anything that Michaels had said. Seemingly satisfied with what he'd told them, his questioners thanked him for his time and moved on to the next person on their list. So great was his nervous exhaustion that he nearly collapsed into the back of the Bentley when Dogsbody came to take him home in the evening. His 'chauffeur' observed him carefully in his rear-view mirror as they sat at a set of traffic lights, surrounded by all the hustle and bustle of rush hour London. He said,

"Looks like sir had a bad day. Did you manage to stick to the script or do we have a problem?"

"No problem, it all went fine. It was just so damned exhausting."

"Well, that's a relief, I'm glad something went well after all of the hoo-ha last night. You shooting in every direction but the right one was only half of the problem. I had the Colonel's little helper come round while you were out at work and she was not a happy bunny. Apparently, that bloody dog bit a chunk out of the photographer and then they found that there'd been a woman in the car with Mr. Michaels, God rest his merry little soul. Nearly got clean away she did. So one of the crew had to leg it in one direction to rescue the snapper and another had to leg it after the woman.

It beggared up the whole operation and the Colonel's little helper's not convinced that the hurried burglary theatricals will fool the bluebottles. The surveillance mob who failed to clock the fact that the deceased had a lady friend were sent back to Moscow on the first available flight this morning, on the Colonel's orders apparently. I'd think their next ten years will be spent cleaning latrines in a camp in Siberia. That's if they're lucky. The helper didn't know about your cock-up, so she was relatively happy with us. She just wanted to know if we had any idea who the woman is. I said I'd ask you seeing as you knew Michaels better than me. I only killed him, so we didn't have a lot to say to each other really, although I thought it better not to mention that to her. So, do you have any idea who she is?"

Jacob shuddered a little at the faux bonhomie of his psychopathic companion and the way this was mixed in with his casual references to a very brutal murder. Trying to sound unfazed, he said,

"I haven't a clue. I didn't know Michaels well enough to discuss his love life with him. Is this woman dead as well?"

"Doesn't sound like it. I think they've got her holed up somewhere. I didn't ask any questions. The Colonel's little helper told me more than she normally would because she was so hopping mad at the incompetence of those bits of the operation that weren't our responsibility. It's never advisable to ask more than these guys are willing to offer, that's my key to survival you see, sir. I just do what I'm told – and you should just do what you're told. That way we all stay alive and healthy. Oh, they got the camera back when they rescued the photographer, by the way, so the piccies of you are all safe and sound, ready to be used if you try and do another runner."

Jacob sank further into the soft, comforting red leather of the Bentley rear seat, hoping that it would swallow him whole, thereby making him invisible and safe from his deadly minder.

Thirty miles away, in a dimly lit upper room of a nineteenth century gentleman farmer's residence, Julia Emersly sat, with her chin hanging low on her chest. She had reached a point where fear had wiped nearly all thoughts out of her head, leaving only despondency and a feeling that her fate was completely out of her hands. The blindfold over her eyes was so thick she might just as well have been in the dark. Her wrists and ankles were firmly bound to the heavy old oak chair that she sat on and she was incapable of movement. She could hear muffled voices coming from downstairs, but she had no idea who her captors were, or what further violence they intended inflicting on her. She wasn't particularly religious, but she contemplated the usefulness or otherwise of praying to the invisible God that she part believed in on some days, and presumed to be a fiction on others. She managed a few short words, begging for help and then gave up half way through, telling herself she was probably speaking only to the walls.

She might have fainted at the sound of the gunshots the night before and she might be terrified now, but she was no coward. She decided that she would inevitably follow her dead lover into the grave at the hands of her captors and that she might as well face up to that fact. She felt deep burning anger towards the people who had taken him away from her and when they came to do their worst, as she had no doubt they would, she wouldn't give them the satisfaction of thinking that she was afraid of them, as in reality she would be. She'd give as good as she got verbally and go down fighting. That was the family tradition. Two of her brothers had won posthumous medals during the war for their outstanding bravery and they wouldn't want her to let the side down.

Then she heard the creak of a door as it opened downstairs, followed by what sounded like the precise and regular footsteps of a military man coming upstairs. The bedroom door opened and the bare floorboards in front of her creaked as her visitor entered. He placed a hand under her chin and gently but firmly pushed it upwards, saying,

"That's better. One should always maintain a good posture, even when in captivity. It's good for the morale."

The speaker's English was excellent, but his accent was difficult to place. He continued,

"I'm sorry that you had such an unpleasant experience. The loss of loved ones is always difficult to bear, particularly when they die in such a violent manner. I'm told that you've refused food and even a drink. That's a natural first reaction to such a shock, but you really must partake of a little refreshment if you are to keep body and soul together. It's also good for the morale. You'll find your spirits will much improve once you've had a nice cup of tea."

"Who are you, why did you kill my friend?"

"Friend? Oh I think Mr. Mallory Michaels was rather more than that, wasn't he? Lover, shall we say? I've had a look at the contents of your handbag and you keep several photographs of him tucked away in the back of your diary. There are also several of your letters to him in the batch of papers that we removed from his house. They are most definitely the tunes of a songbird singing to its mate, are they not?"

"I asked who are you."

"So you did Miss Emersly. You see, I now know who you are, courtesy of your handbag and its many and varied contents. But if I were to tell you who I am I'd have to kill you and at the moment I'd rather prefer not to have to do that. What I want most is information and if you cooperate by giving it to me, I'll be happy to let you go."

"Like you let Mallory go? The only place he's gone is kingdom come."

The interrogator was surprised by her defiance. He sat down on a rickety old chair opposite and mulled over how best to manipulate his prisoner into giving up the information that he needed. He found her an interesting challenge. Even with her eyes invisible as a result of being heavily blindfolded, she was an attractive woman. He'd been told that she put up an impressive fight as she was dragged back to the van. Ultimately, the large goon who had seized her became so fed up by being scratched, bitten and kicked that he'd knocked her out. Her face was badly bruised in consequence. Her right ankle was swollen from when she'd caught her foot in the rabbit burrow and she must clearly be in pain and frightened for her life. Her expensive beige jacket and matching skirt were covered in mud which was still damp and she must be feeling cold and utterly miserable. He might have expected her to beg for her life, given her now desperate circumstances, a prisoner who was completely at his mercy, but she was simply angry and seemingly resigned to whatever fate he had in store for her. He didn't particularly want to hurt her any more than she already had been. He didn't see the point, unless she refused to cooperate and he was left with no other choice. He would first engage her in a battle of wits, the kind that interested him. He would have to try and persuade her of a genuine chance of being allowed to go free if she told him what he needed to know. He said,

"If I intended killing you, I'd have taken your blindfold off. Then you'd see my face and be able to identify me. My men told me that you didn't see any of them because, obviously, it was so dark and you were knocked out just before you reached the van. You don't know where you are because you were brought here blindfolded and didn't come round until mid-morning. So, you know nothing of us and for that reason you are not a danger. You are only a problem if you refuse to help us. Then our attitude might change. We would need to get a little violent and that would not be an experience I would wish on you."

"You've already been violent. Your thug hit me so hard that for all I know my skull might be cracked. My head hurts like hell so you can go to hell, all of you. I don't know what you think it is I can tell you."

"I need you to tell me what you know about your lover's work."

"What I know? All I know is that he worked for the Foreign Office. He was high up. That's it. He wasn't going to babble on to me about great secrets of state, he wasn't allowed to. I'm not even interested in anything foreign."

"I wish I could believe all of that. You see, in my experience, powerful men often like to impress beautiful women, particularly when they're lovers. One of the ways that they do that is to tell them a little bit about the importance and the excitement of their work."

"Yes, well, weird men might do, but I don't go out with weird men. Mallory wasn't weird and he knew he didn't need to do things to impress me, I liked him for who he was. I really don't understand your logic – is that the way you behave with women? Do you feel it necessary to tell them about 'the importance and excitement' of what you do? For heaven's sake, you must be desperate old chum."

The interrogator did not appreciate these comments. His own track record with women had not been good. He'd been too monastic in many ways, dedicated to his work to the extent that there was little room in his head for anything else. A woman who was interested in what he did might indeed be someone who appealed to him, but the very nature of 'what he did' meant that he would never be able to tell her anything. Most of all, he was aware that he didn't really know how to talk to a woman as a potential wife or lover. He'd somehow or other never really developed the skills. All of his dealings with women were business-like and that kept them firmly within his comfort zone. Attractive though she might be physically, his only interest in this woman was getting the information he needed. He decided to make one final effort to persuade her to tell him what he believed she knew before bringing the gorilla-sized goon upstairs to give her a working over.

"I'm afraid that I've got a very busy schedule today and I simply don't have the time to play games. I'll try once more and then I'll deliver you into hands that you may find rather more persuasive. What did Mallory Michaels tell you about people whom he suspected to be traitors working in the Foreign Office? It was a big concern for him, a big worry, something that he would be likely to tell the person with whom he was the most intimate, someone he trusted as much as himself."

"Why? Why on earth would he do that? What would be the point? There would have been nothing I could have done about any traitor or whatever, I know nothing about foreign affairs. We were lovers pure and simple old chum. Rumpy-pumpy is my name, rumpy-pumpy is my game. Mallory was very good at rumpy-pumpy, end of story."

Her questioner was more than a little bemused by her final comments. He'd been hoping that, in passing, the interrogation would unearth a variety of useful small snippets about British thinking on foreign policy matters, valuable crumbs that Michaels might have tossed to her to add to his image as a man of some influence and standing, a powerful man, someone to be admired and desired. But there was clearly no use asking about any of those. Without the gorilla's arm round her neck she simply wasn't going to spill any beans. His most immediate need was to find out if Michaels had let slip any clues as to the identity of the mole and whether

Julia had passed them on to others in conversation. If she hadn't, then the mole remained safe and she could be painlessly reunited with her recently deceased lover. To let her go free would be to destroy the cover story of a burglary gone wrong at Michaels' house. Once she told the police about the questions he'd just asked her, they and MI5 would realise that something more sinister was involved. As far as he was concerned, her imminent death was her own fault. She'd chosen to become close to someone whom he regarded as a form of combatant in the Cold War between east and west. In doing so, in his eyes, she had made herself a legitimate target. He decided to go back downstairs and tell the gorilla-sized goon to do his work. He said,

"Very well, I'm sorry that you've chosen not to help me. I'll leave you in the hands of someone who will use rather more persuasive means."

As he opened the creaking door she said,

"It won't do you any good. I've got nothing to tell you. When you kill me, my cousin will come after you. He's a detective and he was in the intelligence services during the war. He'll trace a bunch of amateurs like you in no time. You'll just be gallows fodder old chum."

Being called an amateur did not sit well with the interrogator, but his ears pricked up when she mentioned her cousin. He stopped in his tracks and said,

"Really? So who is this great detective, the man who used to work for intelligence?"

"That's for me to know and you to find out. He'll be coming for you old chum."

"We're not talking about a Mr. Augustus Benedict by any chance, are we?"

Julia said nothing.

"By your silence I take it we are. How very interesting. You might just have saved your life young woman."

With that, Colonel Zaliatev returned downstairs. He opened the battered old oak front door and went outside. He stood contemplatively under the fierce looking thunder sky, lighting one of his favourite Cuban cigars while he did so. Above him, a death black crow flew onto the roof of the house and sat there cawing morosely, as if it were the devil offering advice in some secret language. The devil was someone the Colonel felt he knew well.

He considered what might best be done with his prisoner in light of her information about Benedict. On reflection, his instinct told him that she was most probably telling the truth when she said Michaels had mentioned nothing about the mole. As he'd been about to leave the bedroom, she had been completely resigned to death. She sounded authentic, someone who really had nothing to trade for her life, not an individual who was simply protecting secret information in order to be patriotic. There didn't seem any point in setting the gorilla on her, especially now that she had become of potential use. Keeping her alive now made much more sense than killing her. He could spare one man for extended guard duty and hold her in the house for as long as was needed. She was someone who could be bartered, given her importance to Benedict. Precisely what she might be bartered for was something he hadn't yet decided. One thing was clear though – she couldn't be released until Jacob had completed the crucial task that the Colonel was to set him shortly. He didn't want the mole's high importance confirmed to MI5 by her revealing the questions he'd asked her.

He re-entered the house and went into the kitchen, where two of the team that had abducted Julia the night before were sitting, drinking vodka. He said,

"Leonid, you are to remain here. Take good care of the woman, she might be valuable to us. Untie her and replace the ropes with a chain round her good ankle, nailed to the floor. There's one in the outhouse as far as I remember from the last time we kept someone here. Remove her blindfold and then wear a hood at all times when entering her room, or when in sight from her window outside. If she shows any sign of deteriorating as a result of that head injury let me know immediately and I'll have the embassy doctor sent down to have a look at her. I need her kept alive and in good health."

The Colonel had followed an elaborate routine involving the switching of vehicles and the use of decoys to make sure that he hadn't been followed to the remote house. As he climbed into the back of the van that would return him to London unseen, he mulled over the possibilities that Julia's revelation might open up to him. Augustus Benedict was someone of whom he was well aware, not as a 'detective', but as one of the most able of the counter-espionage people that MI5 had at its disposal: and he had something that he knew Benedict would desperately want to get back in one piece.

Jacob, meanwhile, had just arrived home. He had fallen asleep during the journey and was shaken awake by Dogsbody, who said,

"Time sir woke up; we're back at the ranch. I'll get us a tasty dinner on the boil while sir has his usual whisky or two and then I'll get him a nice glass of warm milk at bedtime, before I tuck him in, how does that sound?"

"It sounds like you're taking the mickey."

"Now why would I ever do that, sir? I am but a humble servant, doing my duties as one would expect when in the service of the landed gentry. May I help you with your hat and briefcase, sir, or would you prefer to propel yourself into the residence without the benefit of my assistance?"

Jacob said nothing. He yawned involuntarily and started to ease himself out of the car. Dogsbody suddenly grabbed his arm and hauled him fast-forwards as if he were the weight of an ant, nearly causing him to overbalance and fall face-first onto the gravel. His unwanted helper pulled him back just as he was about to topple over, saying,

"Dear, dear, we're a little unsteady on our pins tonight aren't we, sir? I'd go easy on those whiskies before dinner if I were you."

Jacob didn't say a word, sensing that the psychopath beside him was trying to provoke a reaction that would justify his punching his lord and master a second time. There was no doubt that Dogsbody liked hitting people and he clearly was in the mood for doing so at that moment. As Jacob stumbled sleepily up the imposing stone steps to the front door, he caught sight of a woman's face watching from behind a curtain in the drawing room. At the point their eyes met she pulled back, out of sight. He wondered if he had imagined her and didn't say anything to his companion.

Once inside the house Jacob went straight to the window where he thought he had seen a face to see if there actually was anyone there. When he found the room empty, he scratched his head in puzzlement and then made a beeline for the whisky decanter and poured himself a double. He was glad to see that Dogsbody had earlier lit a large fire in the ornately sculpted Georgian drawing room fireplace and went over to warm himself by it. The sound of a cough behind him made him jump and he turned round to see an intense looking young woman in a tight-fitting white dress. She sat down in his favourite armchair, watching him with a predator's eyes. She was beautiful yet somehow menacing, her hands clasped in her lap and the oils in her short dark hair glistening in the firelight. Dogsbody was standing in the doorway. He said,

"I forgot to mention, the Colonel's number two is staying the night, sir."

She said,

"We haven't met. I'm Irina Lashkanocova. The Colonel asked me to drop by to check that you were still holding up under the pressure of your duties. It must be so difficult, working for two governments at once."

Her words were a question mark that Jacob felt hanging over him heavily. There was something about the woman that terrified him, although he couldn't as yet quite put his finger on what it was. He said,

"I manage. I've got no choice."

"No, you haven't, I'm glad that you still recognise that. How was your day in the office? It must have been quite tricky with MI5 swarming all over the place and you having killed a British mandarin the night before.

The Colonel told me that's what your people call such men, mandarins. How strange."

"I stuck to the script. No one seemed to suspect me."

"Good. We will be giving you your very special task soon and we don't want anything getting in the way of it, do we?"

Jacob shook his head, so nervously it seemed more like a twitch. He had the feeling that the number of psychopaths in his house had just doubled. She said,

"Until then we need you to keep doing what you've been doing so well for us, giving us all the news you have on the current secret dealings between Britain and the United States. Do you think you can be a good little boy and do all of that for me? Perhaps you could give me a summary of your most recent news as a little diversion before dinner?"

She smiled, a gesture so without warmth that it registered on his mind as being more threatening than encouraging. She nodded to Dogsbody to leave the room and he went off to the kitchen to prepare the evening meal. She said,

"Before we do that, I need to know what the name of Michaels' woman friend is. He must have mentioned it to somebody in your grand, imperial monstrosity of a Foreign Office."

"If he did mention it to anyone it wasn't me. I never had the opportunity to discuss the details of his private life with him."

She nodded and said,

"Pity. Still there is other information you can give me. Entertain me with a summary of your latest revelations from the great British Foreign Office."

She took a notebook and pen out of her white handbag and began taking notes while Jacob summarised everything relevant that he'd heard or observed since his return from the KGB 'holiday camp'. When he'd finished, she closed the notebook and placed it back in her handbag. She smiled again and said,

"Very good, what a helpful little boy you are. Now go on, shoo, shoo, off to your bedroom or some other little hidey hole where you can play to your heart's content in this ridiculously large monument to wealth and decadence. I want to be alone this evening. Tell your butler where you will be and he will bring your dinner to you. I'll ask him to give you an extra cake for being so good. Now go on, away with you."

As Jacob trudged off to his study at the back of the house, he felt as if all the remaining hope and dignity within him had just been sucked out and replaced by a vacuum. He was now owner of his historic stately home in name only, with his Soviet masters and their servants ruling his life as surely as if he were a mere footman back in the grand old days of his family's aristocratic pre-eminence.

Back in the drawing room, Irina was examining a small piece of expensive looking modern art hanging in a gilt frame over the fireplace. She loathed what she felt to be its pretentiousness. Unlike the Colonel, she still had the flame of Marxism-Leninism burning within her breast, albeit in a way that was subordinate to her fiercely driven personal ambition. As such, she felt that she was standing in the beating heart of the enemy, one of the most grotesque and opulent symbols of its ill-gotten wealth and decadence, the English stately home. To her, people like Jacob were little more than reptiles to be tamed, used and disposed of as necessary. She had two goals in life. First, to help the Soviet Union win the moral and ideological battle against the west and establish its system of government as the dominant model for the civilised world. Second, she wanted to become like Zaliatev, a Colonel in the KGB. In that respect, her motives were less ideologically pure. She wanted the power and the privilege that went with the role. She wanted to be feared in the way that Zaliatev was, a formidable human sword in the armoury of Soviet power. She enjoyed controlling people, playing with them, making them dance to her tune. She had no need or desire to be loved. She had come from a loveless family and the men that she had encountered had been mainly misogynistic in nature. She admired the Colonel's almost monastic devotion to duty, the way in which he was so self-contained, a man with no need for love. She could use her physical attractiveness in all kinds of ways to lure unwitting men and women into compromising positions via which she could extract information from them. But her only genuine wish in intimate social dealings with men was that they might provide her with an hour or two of sexual pleasure, after which she would routinely toss them aside as if they were empty ice cream cartons. Like the psychopath she was, she could imitate the deepest and kindest of emotions of which, in reality, she could feel either little or nothing. She was the perfect actress in a theatre macabre. She admired also the Colonel's apparent devotion to the cause of Marxism-Leninism, being completely taken in by his constantly declared loyalty to the ideological gospel of the state. It was through the lens of her own, rather more genuine devotion, tainted by personal ambition though it was, that she now viewed the monstrous little painting on the wall and it was that same lens that gave her an idea. She strode out into the Adamesque grand entrance hall and bellowed for Jacob to return. He came scrabbling back as fast as he could, fearful of what she might have in store for him. She ushered him back into the drawing room.

"That painting, over the fireplace, it looks very expensive."

"My father bought it. It's by a disciple of Picasso."

"What is its value?"

"Roughly thirty thousand pounds, if I remember correctly."

"How very interesting. Take it down and let me have a look at it more closely."

He did as instructed. She smiled mockingly and walked over to the fireplace, throwing the frame into the vigorously dancing flames with a triumphant flourish. He tried to say, "No, please don't," but the words froze on his lips stillborn as the painting was consumed.

She smiled again and said,

"That's one of the many things the Colonel has taught me, the usefulness of throwing much valued objects onto fires to make a point. You wasted so much of my time when you tried to run away. I spent hours and hours helping trace you and had to miss out on one of the finest opportunities that I will ever get to steal one of your miserable little country's best kept naval secrets. So that is my price for every minute that I lost when I could have been doing other things, thirty thousand of your filthy rich pounds. And there's another lesson for you, speaking to you from deep within those flames. It is of the uselessness of wealth that doesn't belong to you, wealth that you have stolen from the people through your class based, capitalist system. One day the people of England will rise as did the people of the Soviet Union. They'll trample their way through your fine rooms and burn or sell everything that you have stolen, everything, until you are left with nothing but the shoes on your feet and the wind that blows through your hair."

Jacob was looking decidedly ill, wondering what humiliation or loss might next be inflicted on him by one or other of his unwanted guests. Irina said,

"Dear, dear, you look so white in the face little boy, you'd better sit down. Yes, sit down while you recover from your terrible shock. I'm tired of this room, I shall leave it to you for this evening, as my gift."

With that she exited grandly, in the manner of her role model, the Colonel, humming an ironic tune. For some reason it annoyed Vladimir the Rottweiler outside, who began to howl, reminding Jacob that he had no escape in any direction from the pure hell that his life had become.

CHAPTER EIGHT

Gus was the first to arrive for the follow-up meeting with Tasty Harry at the Lamb and Ferret. Seeing that Harry's table was empty and that the eyes of all the extremely dodgy clientele zeroed in on him as soon as he put his head through the door, he decided to wait outside until the big man arrived to guarantee a safe entrance. He didn't have to wait long. A taxi soon drew up and Harry's substantial bulk emerged from it with a grin as large as the man. The taxi driver refused to take any money for the fare and Gus wondered what 'little difficulty' Harry had sorted out for him in the past to give him the privilege of free travel.

"Evenin' me old china, sorry to keep you waiting, today's little errands took a bit longer than expected. Let's go in and wet the old lips with a pint of this and a pint of that."

Once they were seated with their drinks at Harry's usual table he said,

"Now then me old mate, I've bent a few ears and arms today and I'm pleased to say we've got a result, which makes you a lucky duck, as me old Aunty Hilda used to say."

"That's great Tasty, what have you got for me?"

"Well, I paid a little visit to Earache Arthur first of all. He'll get you all kinds of things that go bang, but the snag with him is he goes on for so long about the good old days and everyone he's known in the East End since Jesus was a little lad that anyone who listens to him loses the will to live. Anyways, it turns out he wouldn't touch anything as exotic as your gun with a barge pole, but he did have a punter who came looking for something just like it the week before your Foreign Office toff ended up brown bread. He gave the punter the names of a couple of other armourers who specialise in the more unusual end of the trade and he went off to see them. But what is useful is that Earache is a walking memory man and not just about the days when Flipover Fred ruled the roost at the old tea warehouse. He remembered that the punter was from Manchester. He had a northern accent and a blue MG roadster – Glacier Blue according to the punter, who was most particular about getting the name of the colour right. He doesn't mince his words does Earache and when he saw the car he said what a bloomin' 'orrible colour it was. The punter said it was his favourite shade of blue – and it's the nearest he could get to the colours of his footie team, Man City. Well, Earache's a big Arsenal fan, so he nearly threw him out at that point, but he did note a few things about him before he left. He said he had the look of a bruiser, about six feet two, with short cropped dark hair and eyes like a dead bloke. He said there was something weird about him, as if anything normal in his head had been sucked out and replaced with some kind of killing machine. He said he was all best mates one minute, but then his mood flipped and he could imagine him killing someone who sneezed just for the hell of it. A very dangerous bloke. Earache said he kept his finger on the trigger of the gun in his pocket all the time he was speaking to him, just in case."

"Did you find out where he went next?"

"I'm coming to that," Tasty said, sipping his pint. "The names of the armourers Earache gave him were not familiar, so I had to introduce myself before I got some cooperation out of the gents in question."

"Introduce yourself as get them in double headlocks?"

Tasty laughed.

"Yeah, something like that. The second geezer was about as friendly as a Doberman that hasn't had its dinner for a week. When I started asking him questions, he pulled a shotgun on me and told me to get out before he blew a hole in me head that would be big enough to put a fist through. So that's when I gave him a blast of me old George Henry."

"Who or what on earth is George Henry?"

"He's the little feller I keep in me pocket – your face, Gus me old mate, you look as though you've just laid an egg. Old George is the gun I nicked when I was in the war, I named it after the officer who kept putting me on a charge for anything he could think of. I always like to imagine shooting him in the backside with it. I thought it would come in handy back on civvy street and handy it has been. Don't get me wrong, it's not for killing, except in self-defence, but it ain't half useful for dealing with trigger happy geezers who look like they're mad enough to try and kill me. Anyways, I shot him in his foot and he started to do the finest one-legged highland fling I've ever seen. When I pointed out I was in the mood to shoot his other foot he became suddenly very helpful. He told me that he'd sold exactly the gun you described to a punter who fitted the description Earache gave me down to a tee. He said the geezer wanted something that had a bit of form, something that had been used in bank robberies and murders. He wanted it to be unusual, something that would really stand out as a gangland weapon. Those were his exact words apparently, a gangland weapon. Is that the kind of stuff you needed to know Gus me old mate?"

"That is really brilliant Tasty, gold as you would say. Did any of these people know where this character lives or who his associates are?"

"Now that's where our luck runs out, I'm afraid. I asked around and there's a few geezers who've seen this punter here and there, but nobody knows very much about him. He's not attached to any mob that anyone knows, but there's a feeling that he works for someone posh and dodgy. The notes he buys things with are all kosher and clean, in fact very clean – one bloke told me they always look as though they've come fresh out of the mint."

"What you've told me fits the picture we have of things very well Tasty. The information about the car is really useful – I don't suppose Mr. Earache noticed its registration number by any chance?"

"Didn't I mention that? Sorry, Gus me old mate, me thinking cap must have fallen off. He didn't make a note of it as such, but he did remember that it had the number eighty-three in it. He said that was how old Fractious Frannie was when she kicked the bucket and it reminded him of her."

"Tasty, you are wonderful, thank you. We'll get those details circulated to every police station in the country so that beat constables can keep an eye out for anything that fits the description you've given me. I don't suppose any of your contacts had heard a whisper or two about Julia's abduction and where she might be being held?"

Tasty shook his head sadly.

"No, sorry me old china. I did ask those geezers most likely to be in the know, but they hadn't heard a dicky bird. Your best chance of finding her is to sniff out where Mr. Manchester is holed up. If your lot nab him and need a little help persuading him to talk, just say the word and I'll have a friendly little chinwag with him. I generally find geezers are much chattier when they're hanging from the rafters by their feet."

Within thirty minutes of leaving his meeting with Tasty, Gus was seated in the plush surroundings of one of the oldest gentlemen's clubs in London, a place where he knew Angus could nearly always be found at this time of night. The oak panelled walls, lined with gilt framed portraits of famous old members, the comforting ancient leather armchairs and the roaring fire were as far away from the fist-battered tables and bare wooden floorboards of the Lamb and Ferret as it was possible to get. As soon as he had been told of the fruits of Tasty's research Mr. One retired to a private room and rang Scotland Yard to make sure that details of the Glacier Blue

MG roadster and its owner were circulated to every police force in England as soon as possible. When he re-joined Gus he was looking pensive.

"Your man Tasty has done extraordinarily well Augustus."

"I don't think Tasty is anybody's man but his own."

"Well, that's as maybe, but this information is extremely useful. That gun was very deliberately left behind to help draw us to all the wrong conclusions. The fact that Mr. Unknown from Manchester specifically wanted a firearm that would stand out from the crowd as a gangland weapon gives us as much confirmation that we could wish for that all the theatricals about a criminal gang's upmarket burglary gone wrong were just a cover. They were meant to conceal the fact that Michaels was murdered for other reasons."

"The other reasons most likely being the need to kill him before he could talk to us."

"Indeed."

"Which suggests that just as Michaels was watching the suspected mole, the KGB was watching him."

"Indeed. When Michaels told me about the time he'd realised that he was being tailed I asked him if he'd been doing anything that might have alerted the KGB to the fact that he was onto the mole. He confessed that he'd been conducting his own little after-hours surveillance operation with regard to each of the suspects when he had both the time and opportunity. I suspect that he was spotted by one of Zaliatev's men, checked out and identified. He must have done something that really alarmed them concerning his intentions, but obviously he's no longer around to confirm what that was. It may well have been revealed by the file that was stolen from the station locker at St. Pancras, which presumably was a detailed dossier of his evidence and suspicions. He didn't spot that he was being watched when he deposited it there for safekeeping and the KGB was anxious and suspicious enough to want to take a look at its contents. I've no doubt that they were responsible for the theft. Their reading of the file probably sealed his fate. Whatever they found, it was serious enough for them to conclude that they would have to get rid of him. That's the trouble when amateurs go solo, it nearly always ends badly."

"Indeed. If all of your suppositions are correct, Angus, then the fact that our KGB friends crossed a line and killed such a high ranking official on UK soil at least tells us just how important the job that their Foreign Office mole is doing for them is."

"Absolutely, which is why we need to catch him asap. There is at least one ray of hope within all the gloom in so far as the loss of Michaels doesn't leave us completely in the dark about the identity of the mole.

There's still the link between our friend Colonel Zaliatev and Frank Chabler, his muckraking tabloid journalist contact. That's now our best chance of unmasking the traitor that Michaels had been hunting. Zaliatev's clearly been busy amassing compromising information for the purposes of blackmailing as many of our less careful people as possible into becoming traitors and leakers. Once we've established just who Chabler has been investigating, we should be able to use that information to work out who is most probably Zaliatev's man in the Foreign Office. I know you've got other immediate priorities in terms of locating your cousin, Augustus, and the revelations about the gun are primarily a result of your hunt for her, a spin-off almost. But as soon as we've found Miss Emersly, hopefully alive and well, I need your unique talents focussed on the job I gave you prior to Michaels' killing. I need you to unearth everything the hack journalist has been up to on behalf of his KGB paymaster."

"As you say, my number one priority remains finding Julia and getting her back in one piece, Angus. But as long as that's understood I'm happy to help as soon as we've found her. At the moment locating her seems to be dependent on us first finding Manchester Man."

"Yes, of course. Finding the people who abducted her and getting them to talk may also be the quickest route to confirming Zaliatev as the grand controller of all of the jiggery pokery that's been going on. I'm convinced that he was the mastermind behind Michaels' murder."

"It's interesting that Mr. Unknown is clearly a British citizen by virtue of his accent and his devotion to one of the Manchester football teams. It's interesting also that it looks like Zaliatev is using another Englishman, a freelance journalist, to dig up dirt on whomever he intends to force into his network. There seem to be the beginnings of a pattern, with the Colonel making use of local talent for a whole range of purposes. It could be that he's used a local team for Michaels' murder and Julia's abduction."

"Indeed. These people are the potential weak links in the chain, of course, given the fact that we can disrupt them much more easily than is the case with people who can hide themselves away in their country's embassy, should the going get rough. It also sounds rather as if our Manchester friend is a little naïve with regard to his choice of such a distinctive vehicle. If he's still driving around in that we should have an excellent chance of catching up with him."

"The sooner the better from Julia's point of view. As she was presumably a witness to the murder the danger is that they'll only keep her alive long enough to interrogate her. They'll want to see just what she knows that might be helpful to them. She is a very unusual and very resourceful woman. If anyone can find a way of stalling them long enough for us to find her, she can, and it's that which gives me hope for her, but we need the police to move like greased lightning to find that car."

"I've told them exactly that. The search has been given the highest priority and I've every anticipation that we'll get a quick result."

Gus was not prone to dwell on the dark side of situations like Julia's and preferred to concentrate on the more optimistic potential outcomes. He'd seen too much of a barbaric and horrific nature during the war and had developed coping mechanisms for dealing with any potentially deadly or disastrous circumstances. They had been the only means by which he could keep functioning on terrifying, high-risk operations and in Julia's case, they had kicked in again shortly after he'd learnt of her abduction. Almost without any command from himself his brain moved all of the potentially tragic outcomes of her plight into a 'virtual box' at the back of his consciousness and closed the door as far as was possible. There was still a small opening that allowed enough of the dangers to seep into his thoughts to keep him focussed, but most of his mind was able to concentrate on those things that had the best chance of leading to her rescue. Mr. One understood what was going on in his head without asking, because he'd had to develop similar mechanisms for the same reason. If One hadn't been able to do this, he would have frozen at particularly crucial moments during the war and would not have survived.

At precisely ten o'clock the following morning Gus's new direct line rang. Mr One said,

"Augustus, we've had a bit of luck. A local constable with a beady eye thinks he's seen the MG. He's based in Maldon and says he spotted the car when it was very badly parked in the town centre, about ten days ago he thinks. The owner wasn't around so he took its registration number and kept an eye out for him to have a word when he returned to the car. Unfortunately, he got called across the road by a shopkeeper who'd caught a light-fingered child stealing and he wasn't able to collar the MG man when he appeared. He'd driven off before he could get to him. However, the registration number in his notebook does contain the number eighty-three and the owner fitted the description that your friend Tasty Harry had been given. Do you want me to send a car to get you over there?"

"No, I'll go straight home and pick up my own vehicle. Do you have the policeman's name?"

Once he'd set off in his Daimler convertible it took Gus just over an hour to find his way to the Maldon police station where Constable Hythe was already waiting for him on the steps, while talking to one of his colleagues. The policeman was the avuncular embodiment of everything that the small-town British bobby was supposed to be in popular mythology. Six foot two, with lightly greying hair and a moustache that was as precisely tailored as his uniform, Constable Hythe shook Gus's hand as if he were an old friend and lowered his substantial frame into the passenger seat.

"Good morning, sir, my sergeant says I'm to give you every assistance, so consider me at your disposal for as long as you need me. I can show you the shop that I saw him coming out of if that's a useful starting point."

Gus smiled to himself. He'd anticipated being lumbered with some officious time server with a surly disposition, as had been his experience several times previously when bringing in police collaboration. Constable Hythe was an unexpected breath of fresh air on a day when he needed the search for the Manchester man to deliver rapid results.

They drove round to Higson's general store, where the owner was able not only to remember the man in the MG, but also the fact that he'd stocked up from the shop on another occasion since.

"He was a northerner, sir, I remember that very well. Funny sort of bloke, quite amiable part of the time but then he seemed to be on another planet. His eyes seemed to be looking right through me, and he'd speak to me as though I were some kind of serf. Then he'd snap out of it and be back to the smiley chap. It was a bit disconcerting really, you don't easily forget a man like that."

"What did he buy as a matter of interest?" Gus asked.

"Mostly foodstuffs. He had a list – I don't know whether his wife had written it for him or whether it was his own – that's if he had a wife. He didn't say. He bought a lot of staple things like eggs and cheese, but there were also quite a few items that generally we only get the richer kind of customers buying. Expensive wines, the priciest cuts of meat. They were the kind of supplies we used to get the housekeepers from the old country houses buying years ago. Oh, and the dog food, sir, loads and loads of dogfood. The kind of meat you'd need if you were feeding really big hounds."

"Did he pay by cash or cheque?"

"Cash, sir, I do remember that, crisp five-pound notes that felt like they'd just come off the press. Very clean, that's what struck me. Most of the money we get round here is pretty dirty, so his stood out."

"And you've not seen him around since?"

"I've not noticed him around the town when I've been out and about and he certainly won't need to come back here for a while. He bought enough to stock up a reasonable sized house for a couple of weeks or more last time he was in the shop. The only regular items he'd need would be bread and milk. I assume he must get those from other suppliers, he didn't buy any from me as far as I remember."

"He didn't by any chance say anything that might provide a clue as to where he's living?"

"No, I'm sorry, sir, but the amount of food he was buying would suggest that wherever he lives it must be a pretty big house."

Gus was interested to see that Constable Hythe had copied down all of the useful information about the Manchester man, including the indications of an unstable personality and the likelihood that he would be found in a house of significant size with large dogs, probably either hunting dogs or guard dogs. He wondered how Hythe had never made it beyond constable and concluded that his genial personality had probably allowed those of a more ruthless disposition to leapfrog over him up the career ladder. As they walked out the shop he said,

"Our Manchester friend has probably bought some petrol in or near Maldon during his time in the area and there's a chance that he's paid by cheque, in which case we can trace him via his bank. Can you show me where all the garages serving petrol are located so that we can see if any of the staff remember him?"

After a fruitless three quarters of an hour, during which nobody they spoke to had seen the suspect, they finally struck lucky. Molly Henshaw, a petrol pump attendant at a garage just outside the town, remembered serving someone who fitted his description.

"He was definitely a bit strange, the way he looked at me, as if he wasn't quite right. I wouldn't like to meet a bloke like him on a dark night. The only thing is, he wasn't driving a blue car. I don't have much interest in cars other than filling them with petrol, so I didn't notice the make or anything. But it was a big posh thing, either dark red or black, I can't remember exactly, but it was one or the other."

As far as she could remember he'd paid by cash. Her conviction that he was driving a large expensive vehicle struck both Gus and Hythe as interesting, fitting in with the amount and type of food supplies the suspect had been buying. Gus said,

"Can you remember what he was wearing when you saw him Mrs. Henshaw?"

"Yeah, I don't think he owned the car. He was in a kind of chauffeur's outfit, as though he was somebody's driver."

As they drove away from the garage Gus asked Hythe if he could make a quick list of the places in and around Maldon that would be most likely to employ a chauffeur. They then began scouting around the various houses that Hythe had identified, trying to see if they could spot either a Glacier Blue MG roadster or a large black or red limousine within their grounds. After a fruitless couple of hours searching, they finally arrived at the firmly shut gates of a magnificent Georgian country house, which could be seen in the distance. Hythe said,

"It's a long time since I've done the country beat, but that's the biggest of the houses in the county. It used to belong to Sir Laidlow Elliott, but his son took it over after he died. The officer who covers this area told me a week or so ago that the son had paid off all the staff. Seems to be the way things are going nowadays, with all the costs of death duties and things. A lot of the gentry simply can't afford to pay the wages that people want for doing serving jobs nowadays."

"So we're unlikely to find a chauffeur here then," Gus said frustratedly. "I'll have a quick look anyway, just in case a driver was the one thing this gentleman decided to hold onto. If so, there just might be a blue MG parked somewhere around the front or the back of the house, you never know your luck."

They got out of the car and examined the main gate, but found it to be securely padlocked. Gus took a pair of field binoculars out of the glove compartment of the Daimler and began scanning the area around the front and side of the house for any evidence of cars. They then walked briskly round the crumbling perimeter wall until they could see the rear of the house and stables. Gus climbed on top of an old tree stump so that he could get a better view over the wall and scanned the buildings again with his powerful binoculars.

"Any luck?" Hythe asked.

"No, not a sausage I'm afraid. There are a couple of guard dogs outside, but there are no visible signs of life and no cars to be seen. The padlock on the gate doesn't make it look like there's anyone at home. It looks like we've drawn a blank for today. I'd appreciate it if you could ask the local constable to keep an eye on the place when he's passing, just in case any vehicles of interest do appear."

Hythe suggested that they return to the police station and ask his colleagues if anyone could think of a large house that still employed staff which he might have missed. Having run out of other immediate options, Gus agreed and they returned to Maldon.

Dogsbody, meanwhile, was driving through the streets of London on his way to do some shopping and then pick up Jacob from the Foreign Office later on. When they returned home in the early evening, Dogsbody stopped at the imposing iron gates and undid the padlock. After dropping Jacob at the front entrance, he drove the car into the stable at the rear, parking it next to his Glacier Blue MG roadster. He shut and locked the stable door and returned to the house.

As he sat discussing a couple of extra possible country house options with the police in Maldon, Gus's gut instinct told him that somewhere along the line during his fruitless search in the afternoon, he had been very close to the suspect. If only he could guess where that might have been.

So near and yet so far.

CHAPTER NINE

When Jacob appeared for breakfast the following morning Dogsbody, the deliberately imperfect imitation of a perfect servant, smiled disconcertingly as he poured a cup of coffee for the man who was simultaneously subservient and his supposed master.

"I have a nice surprise for you, sir. Would you like to hear about your nice surprise?"

"I'm sure you're dying to tell me," Jacob replied, with a mouth half full of scrambled egg.

Dogsbody sat down in the chair opposite him and clasped his hands excitedly on the creaseless tablecloth. Jacob tried to ignore his slightly unhinged grin.

"Well, when I pick you up from work tonight, we're going on a little mystery tour. I always used to like going on mystery tours when I was a kid. You know, the ones where families would hop on a coach, which would then take them to a secret destination and back again. Sometimes we went to the seaside, to Southport or Blackpool. If we were really lucky, we went to the Lake District. We'd go for a ride on a steamer from Windermere, then have fish and chips and an ice cream before setting off back home again. Lovely."

"How nice."

"Well yes, it was for those of us who didn't have very much in terms of pennies to rub together. I suppose it would be very different for you. Your daddy could tell your chauffeur to take you and your nanny wherever you wanted to go, whenever you wanted to go. With a big limo at your disposal you didn't need to hop on a coach and then get the bus home afterwards. You wouldn't need to rub shoulders with the hoi polloi in a chippy either, would you? Cook would make you a nice picnic which you could have in the back of the car without ever having to come into contact with the grubby likes of me when I was a kid. How nice for you, sir, how very you."

"Why don't you just cut to the chase and tell me why we're going on this delightful tour, even if you can't or won't tell me where? I have to do whatever you say, so I might as well know in advance what I'm expected to do."

"Oh you are a tease, sir, trying to get me to tell you things I shouldn't. Let's just say we're off to meet an old friend, have a drinky poo or two and chew the fat. It will be a nice trip out – you'll enjoy it. We've been spending too much time cooped up in this suffocating old pile of a house. It'll do us both good."

"I'll look forward to it."

"That's the spirit. I knew you'd come round to my point of view and realise what fun we're going to have. You like having fun don't you, sir?"

"I shall imagine we're going on a steamer ride, just like you used to."

"Oh very witty, sir, that is droll. Now if you'd like to go upstairs and get yourself ready smartish I'll take you to work. It wouldn't do to be late – you don't want to do anything that might draw unwanted attention to yourself."

Once Dogsbody had dropped him off at the Foreign Office, Jacob's day proved to be one of constant stress. As a matter of course he needed to not only read, evaluate and advise on a constant stream of incoming top-secret reports from Britain's embassy in the United States, but also memorise the key points of any that might be of interest to his KGB masters. He was aware that if it became apparent subsequently that the Soviets had become familiar with any of those key points, he would be one of only two or three primary suspects who would be interrogated about the leaks. However, since Michaels' murder there was a new ingredient in his daily working routine that raised his existing anxiety levels to fever pitch, the feeling that he was under constant surveillance. He couldn't quite place his finger on where the unwanted scrutiny was coming from and that made it all the more worrying. Several new faces had appeared within the section of the building where his office sat and as far as he could tell they all had convincing reasons for being there. That, however, was no consolation, given his knowledge that MI5 always had credible cover stories to hide behind. Any one of the faces could be watching him, waiting for him to make a slip that would reveal that he was the mole they were looking for. His only protection was the fact that he was a competent actor. To anyone casually observing him, he was on the surface a man of a calm and reflective nature, diligently working his way through the various demanding tasks of his day as he always did. But underneath the well-practised act there was turmoil and fear. He could feel it seeping through into his shirt in the form of anxiety-induced sweat and it made him constantly on edge, an elastic band waiting to snap. At home, he hadn't been sleeping well with the knowledge that there was a psychopathic maniac living on the premises. That gave him an extra level of stress because, from what past lovers had told him, he knew that he talked in his sleep. He was terrified that the exhaustion resulting from his long hours awake at night might cause him to nod off in a particularly soporific meeting and then start to babble about the fact that he had been one of the murderers of Mallory Michaels. On top of all this there was the worry as to just what Dogsbody's promised mystery tour might involve. He had the constant fear that his KGB masters might find a more trustworthy mole to replace him and that on such a day, an outing in the Bentley with Dogsbody would turn out to be his final journey, a surprise trip to a shallow grave. Once his usefulness was over, there were too many ways in which he would seem to be a serious liability to someone as ruthless as Zaliatev. He had the feeling that his murderous chauffeur had already measured him up for the plot of ground that had been earmarked for him and was just waiting for the order to be given from above.

With all of these fears and worries swimming around in his head Jacob slid into the back of the Bentley at five fifteen prompt and sank into the sumptuous comfort of his seat. He tried to drop below the level where Dogsbody could watch him via the rear-view mirror, but, with a wry smile, his ever-resourceful chauffeur simply adjusted the angle of the mirror so that he kept him in sight.

"Sir seems to have shrunk a bit. If you get any smaller, I'll be able to pop you in my top pocket where I can really keep an eye on you. I hope you've brought your bucket and spade in case we're going to the seaside, by the way. But there again, it could be the top of a hill or a thundering great waterfall. That's the thing with mystery tours, you never really know where you're going until you get there."

As the car moved off, Jacob noticed what appeared to be a thick black hood beside him on the seat. Picking it up, he said nervously,

"What's this for?"

"That's for you, sir. Your new hat. You'll be the most fashionable toff in the town when you put that on."

"Why would I need to wear a hood?"

"Well, a hood has many purposes, sir, that's for sure. You could pop it on if you had a bank robbery in mind, for example, or you could wear it if you were doing a burglary or two and didn't want to risk anyone seeing your face should they wake up before you'd got out of the house. But I would imagine those would be unlikely ways to earn a living for a gentleman like yourself. So, the only use I can think of is for when we get within ten miles of where we're going. I'll need you to put it on when I tell you, sir and for you to tighten the little elastic cord around your chin so that you can't easily pull it up when you think I'm not looking."

Jacob felt a cold sweat coming on and his heart started to race with terror. It seemed his worst fears about the possible purposes of the 'mystery tour' were about to be realised. He wondered if there was a shovel in the boot ready to dig his grave in some godforsaken patch of woodland. Dogsbody burst into a rasping laugh,

"Your face, sir, you look as though you've just given birth to a rat! Do you think I'm going to put a bullet in your head or something – you do, don't you? Dearie, dearie me, what a pessimistic bloke you are. You need to look on the bright side, sir. I'll only need to shoot you if you take the hood off before you're told. See? There really is a silver lining to every cloud. It's just that we're going somewhere that you mustn't see or be able to remember how to get there. It's got to stay secret, very, very indeed, totally secret. That's why I called this a mystery tour."

Jacob, whose face had gone completely white, started to calm down. He said,

"Who is it we're supposed to be meeting at this so very secret place?"

"Now that would be telling, sir. If I were to reveal all now it would spoil the fun completely. Why don't you play a little game? Just with yourself that is, I can't stand games. Why don't you spend the rest of the trip trying to work out who it might be? Then, when we get there and I pull the hood off, you can see if you were right. What fun, sir. By the time this is all over you'll understand just why I always used to love mystery tours when I was a lad."

Jacob was so exhausted from his accumulation of sleepless nights that before long he dozed off, slumping sideways on the seat. He suddenly found himself being rudely awakened. The car had pulled up at the side of a quiet rural lane and Dogsbody was leaning in through the rear passenger door, pulling and twisting both of his ears.

"Ow! What the ... what's going on? Owwww! Why are you pulling my ears?"

"Oh, you're awake, sir. I tried shouting at you to wake up, but you were so deep in the land of nod that I wondered if your ears had stopped working. I was just testing them to see if they needed a new battery, or winding up or something."

"What you mean is you were just having more sadistic fun at my expense, owwww!"

"Oh, sorry, sir, my hand slipped a little as I was removing it from your aural orifice. I read that once in a book you know – aural orifice. There were words like that on almost every page and I kept having to look them up in a dictionary. I got fed up in the end and threw the book on the fire so that it could at least be doing something useful by keeping me warm. Now, what we need to do before we go any further is for you to put that great big hood on your bonce, that way you won't see anything that you shouldn't and I won't have to shoot you. I really don't want to have to go and dig a grave tonight if I can help it, it's a bit nippy and I'll get these nice trousers covered in mud. Come on, sir, pick it up and put it on if you please."

Jacob did as instructed and Dogsbody pulled the elastic chin cord tight enough to make him gasp.

"There we are, sir, all fine and dandy. I must say the hood suits you really well. If there are any women round here whose inclination causes them to take a shine to a posh bloke in a hood, then I think you're in with a chance of a really fun evening."

Jacob muttered something unintelligible from within the hood. Dogsbody got back in the driver's seat and they cruised on down a series of narrow country roads for another ten miles or so before the car finally pulled into the grounds of a former Victorian gentleman farmer's residence. Dogsbody took hold of Jacob's arm as he slid out of the Bentley and then marched him into the house. Once inside, Dogsbody said,

"Now, sir, time to end all the suspense and see if you made the right guess as to who you would be seeing."

He pulled the hood off and Jacob found himself standing in the middle of a large, comfortably furnished drawing room. Ornately patterned Queen Anne armchairs were arranged in a semi-circle, with a coffee table positioned half way between them and the carved wooden fireplace. A coal fire was blazing in the grate.

"If sir would care to seat himself in the nice comfy chair on the far right-hand side of the fireplace his host will join him shortly."

Jacob did as instructed. He heard the creaking of floorboards in the room above, followed by the sound of footsteps coming down the polished wooden staircase. He noticed that Dogsbody was looking fidgety and nervous, something he had never seen in him before. More footsteps followed, crashing down the corridor that led to the drawing room. Then the door opened and Irina entered. She checked around the room with her very bright eyes, then nodded to someone behind her. A familiar face entered: Colonel Zaliatev.

Irina beckoned to Dogsbody and he followed her out of the room, nodding respectfully to the Colonel as he did so. Once the door was closed, Zaliatev sat down on the chair next to his guest and smiled with his customary emptiness. He said,

"Good evening, Mr. Jacob, we meet again. I'm delighted that you and my employee are rubbing along so well. Whoever would have thought it, given your very different backgrounds. But Irina tells me you are virtually brothers now and she never lies."

He smiled emptily for a second time, savouring the look on Jacob's face in reaction to this satirical characterisation of his relationship with Dogsbody.

"I have to tell you that you've gone up in my estimation, Mr. Jacob. Your heroic despatching of Mr. Michaels was so very impressive and a great relief to all of us. Had he stayed alive and exposed you as a traitor your use to me would have been at an end. But now that he has been taken out of the picture, we can safely move on to the next stage of our plans for you. We are going to give you a job that will make you a hero of the Soviet Union if you are successful. That means that if your British masters unmask you afterwards, we will spirit you away to Moscow before you can be arrested. You will be greeted warmly, be given a very decent apartment and a medal. Oh, and a weekly delivery of the very best brandy. Speaking of which, you'll notice that there is a bottle of your favourite cognac and a couple of glasses on the coffee table. Shall I be mother and pour us both a drink?"

Jacob nodded. The Colonel handed him a generous measure and then returned to his seat, saying,

"Your good health, Mr. Jacob, your very good health. Now, let me tell you a little story. You will remember how much your British masters and their American friends fell out over the Suez invasion a couple of years ago. As you can imagine, we were very delighted by that, particularly as it provided such a helpful distraction from our little difficulty with the Hungarians. We were rather hoping that this highly desirable dissonance would continue for as long as possible. It is, after all, very much in our interests that key NATO players should fall out with each other. Well, there is a danger that our hopes will be disappointed in a most inconvenient way. Our great success in putting the Sputnik satellite into space has had some consequences we didn't anticipate. Having seen our impressive feat of rocket technology as evidence of our growing power to rain down nuclear missiles on American soil, President Eisenhower has been running around doing all sorts of things to quell the concerns of the American public and make it look like he has this supposed threat under control. One of those many things is his intention to restore nuclear weapons cooperation with the British, giving your political masters access to American nuclear secrets and boosting the overall nuclear arsenal of NATO. The purpose of this, we have discovered, is to stop the British wasting money duplicating expensive nuclear weapons research and development costs so that they will have more to spend on conventional weaponry like planes and tanks. This again is a potential strengthening of NATO that we find most unwelcome. So, what do you think we should do about it, Mr. Jacob?"

The Colonel noted that the Englishman had drunk all of his large brandy at one go. Jacob was clearly a man in need of comfort at the end of a day that had been stressful from beginning to end. He said,

"I have no opinions on such questions, Colonel. I do what I'm told. You've told me many times that that's the only way I'll survive, so clearly, I have no choice in the matter."

"Right answer! My, how you have progressed since that unfortunate episode when you attempted to escape our grasp. It's amazing what a few days in a KGB holiday camp can do to reinvigorate the soul. So, let me tell you what your role in all of this is. On the coffee table you'll see there is an envelope. Inside it are several skilfully forged documents. They have been produced by a team we have used before with great success. Together, these documents appear to provide conclusive evidence of plans by the British government to do a number of things that are highly detrimental to American interests. Most particularly, they provide evidence of an intention to deceive Washington, to carry out these plans in such a way that they will be completely concealed from American eyes. The proposed actions are so damaging to United States' interests that they will cause a major row in which British denials will simply not be believed. I'd like to think the row will be so calamitous as to completely derail the plans to re-admit the British to the nuclear partnership that began and ended with World War Two. While the documents are excellent forgeries, the key to their being believed will be the route through which they are delivered into American hands."

"And that route is to be me," Jacob said dispiritedly.

"Indeed. Congratulations Mr. Jacob, you're running ahead of me. Yes, your status as a most trusted contact with a couple of those Americans who matter most in the inner power circle in Washington is the golden link that will give these documents true credibility. It's your family ties to these people that are the icing on the cake. They will simply not expect you to lie. You are scheduled to go to the United States next week. You will take the documents with you and arrange a meeting with your American family friends, where you will pass these most impeccable forgeries to them, together with your earnest concerns that the United States is about to be taken for a ride again. You will insist that your identity as the supplier of the documents be kept absolutely secret. Then you return to London and continue your very valuable normal work for us. If we get the slightest hint that you have been betrayed by the Americans, we will whisk you out of the country and into the safety of a nice Moscow flat before the British have time to arrest you. Have you any questions?"

"Could I have another drop of this rather lovely cognac please?"

"Most certainly, please help yourself. But I was rather hoping that you might have a question or two about your instructions. It would show a keen desire to make sure that nothing goes wrong."

As he poured himself another very large measure of cognac, Jacob said,

"Oh my desire is very keen, but I'm sure nothing will go wrong Colonel, I'm sure you'll have planned everything down to the very last detail. I will simply follow your instructions like a good little traitor and then pack my bags ready to become a happy Muscovite if everything goes down the pan."

He downed the brandy in one go and then smiled beatifically at Zaliatev, who chose not to return the gesture. The Colonel looked at his watch and said,

"Well, if you have nothing to ask that is the end of our meeting. My employee will take you back home. Don't forget to put the hood back on before you leave."

The Colonel left the room, clapping his hands twice to summon his underlings. As they joined him at the foot of the stairs, he told Dogsbody to take Jacob home. He waited until the Bentley had departed and then said to Irina,

"I have a bad feeling about our Mr. Jacob. I think that he is about to crack under the pressure, just at the point where I need him to deliver. I want you to return to that enormous monument to capitalism that he lives in first thing tomorrow morning and to keep an eye on him prior to his departure to America. He was drinking like a fish tonight, so I want you to dilute all the whisky and brandy that you can find around his place. Remind him constantly that if he tries to escape from our grasp a second time he will be found and executed on the spot. We can't afford to have this plan ruined by a morally depraved weakling prone to second thoughts. His family links to Washington make him our first choice for the job, if he can hold it together, but if not, I have a plan B that may work without him. It would be a shame to waste all the effort that we have put into getting him to this moment, but I now have a direct route into Washington, an American mole who will still be able to get the documents in front of the eyes that need to see them. It's just that Jacob provides the credible British source that we will lose without him, but things are what they are. If he is not up to the job, he will need to be eliminated in case he spills the beans and sabotages the whole plan. If you have to kill him, make sure that you bring the documents straight back to me so that I can reallocate them immediately."

As the Bentley hurtled back the way it had come, Jacob sat enclosed within the suffocating confines of the hood. He felt an oppressive darkness all around and within him, as if he had been sucked into the kind of black hole that had been predicted by Einstein and from which there could be no escape. He began to ruminate on the meeting he had just endured. He was certain that, should a major row break out as a result of the false information he'd been told to give the Americans, somebody or other would very quickly betray his identity as the source of the forged documents. That would enable the British to put two and two together and work out that he was the mole they had been looking for since Michaels' death. If the Soviets didn't move like lightning to rescue him, he would be taken into custody and a very long stretch in prison would follow. By the time he was released he would be an old man. None of this appealed to him in the slightest. However, if he tried to escape from the KGB's clutches a second time, they would very definitely kill him, if they caught him. The Colonel had promised him that. An escape plan that just might work was beginning to hatch in his inebriated mind, however. Behind the Dutch Old Master in his bedroom was a well-concealed safe that they didn't know about. He'd checked a couple of days ago and the five hundred pounds inside it was still there. That would give him sufficient travelling money. There were times during the day when he was allowed to visit the kitchen to make himself snacks when Dogsbody couldn't be bothered. That gave him the opportunity to remove some meat from the fridge and poison it, ready for throwing to the two ferocious dogs. He would lie in wait behind his bedroom door for when Dogsbody unlocked it in the morning, prior to his entering to make sure that the Foreign Office man rose on time. He would then try to hit him over the head with the substantial silver candlestick that sat innocently on his bedside table. If he failed, he would probably be as good as dead, but if he succeeded then he could throw the poisoned meat to the dogs and make his escape to the south coast. He would pay a fishing boat to take him across the channel and then make his way to Sweden, where his family had a small house that only he now knew about and which traditionally had been used as a secret location for extra-marital affairs by his great-grandfather. Once there, he would again shave off his beard and moustache, change the colour of his hair and use his well-honed skills of leading a double life to try and generate a new identity and a new way of earning a living. It would be nothing like the lifestyle that he had planned via his failed escape to Switzerland, but it could hardly be worse than the fate that awaited him if he remained under KGB control.

He began to doze intermittently as the journey wore on, but each time he awoke the escape plan seemed to have increased in attractiveness. By the time they arrived back at the house he was convinced that it was his only chance of something resembling a future that was worth living for, and quite possibly his only chance of staying alive long term. He was becoming increasingly worried about the unhinged bully whom Zaliatev had chosen to keep an eye on him. Dogsbody had refused to allow him to take the hood off during the journey back, purely out of sadism, and had marched him in through the front entrance in the same way that he had done for the meeting with the Colonel. Ripping the hood off, he'd said,

"Da da! All is revealed for a second time. This time it's me you're meeting. What a nice surprise for sir!"

He'd looked as though he were about to punch Jacob in the face, just for the fun of it, but changed his mind and let him go. The Foreign Office man feared that at any moment the mercurial Mancunian might suddenly step over the line from this kind of harassment to an act of violence that would cause him serious and lasting damage. Equally, he had little faith in the Colonel's promise to rescue him should he get into severe difficulties with the British. He suspected that he would either be abandoned or eliminated before he could talk, with the chances of each dire fate being roughly equal. Pouring himself an additional brandy once Dogsbody had disappeared into the kitchen, he decided that it would be now or never. Once he'd sobered up, he might well lose the alcohol-fuelled resolve. About an hour after they'd finished their evening meal in the oak panelled dining room, he told Dogsbody he was going to make himself a small sandwich to take up to his room for his bedtime supper. His unpredictable companion said,

"Do what you like, eat what you like and how much you like. It's your house as they say, in theory at least. I'm going to watch the telly. I'll be locking you in your room at ten sharp, so if you want to use the bathroom make sure you've done so by then. If sir has another widdle out of his bedroom window and soaks poor old Vladimir a second time, I wouldn't fancy his chances of getting as far as the car without a large bite in his leg tomorrow morning."

Searching through the kitchen cupboards he found that Dogsbody had removed and hidden anything that could be used as a weapon or a poison, most particularly bleach and other acidic or corrosive substances. Together with kitchen knives and all things sharp and pointed, they had been re-located to a padlocked cupboard in the pantry, to which only Dogsbody had the key. The only thing he could find that might be of use was a packet of sleeping tablets that had somehow slipped through the net. He decided that they would have to do and began working the drugs into the two substantial pieces of meat that he had liberated from the fridge, ready to use as bait for the dogs. He then hid the meat behind the fridge. He slapped a couple of slices of bread onto a plate as if they were his fictional sandwich in order to satisfy Dogsbody's curiosity as to what he'd been up to and carried the plate upstairs to bed with him.

Once in his room, he packed a suitcase ready for a swift departure, should his venture be successful. After hiding it under his bed, he set his alarm for an hour earlier than normal so that he would be ready and waiting long before Dogsbody came into his room for his usual sadistic early morning banter. As he heard the key turning in the lock on his door at ten pm sharp, he collapsed into bed fully clothed and rapidly descended into a deep, alcohol-fuelled sleep.

At five o'clock in the morning his alarm went off, an hour earlier than normal, as planned. His head still throbbing from his over consumption of brandy the night before, he clawed his way out of bed and sat rubbing his sore eyes for a couple of minutes. Then, gut wrenching fear set in and he remembered the enormity of what he was planning to do. Trembling, he went over to the wall safe that the KGB had somehow missed and removed the passport that was actually in his real name, together with the envelope containing five hundred pounds. He pulled his jacket on and slipped the money and passport into his two inside pockets. He then grabbed the silver candlestick that was going to be his one and only chance of dealing with Dogsbody and practised swinging it at the imaginary head of his foe. It was heavier than he thought and he almost dislocated his shoulder with the second attempt. He decided that the next time he risked swinging it, it would have to be for real. He pulled up a chair beside the door and sat down to wait for his intended victim.

It was nearly an hour later when Dogsbody announced his impending arrival with his usual cheerful whistling as he approached along the corridor. By then Jacob had dropped off to sleep again and it was only the fierce rattling of the key in the lock that woke him in time. Reacting so fast that he hardly knew what he was doing, he hauled himself up and let fly with the candlestick, just in time to deal a heavy blow to the back of Dogsbody's head as he entered the room. His victim stopped in his tracks, swayed slightly and then hit the floor like a bag full of rocks.

Jacob stood shaking and terrified for a couple of minutes, waiting to see if Dogsbody would come round and exact his revenge. The only thing that moved was a trickle of blood that seeped down the side of his victim's head onto the carpet. It seemed that his tormentor was either deeply unconscious or dead. Snapping out of his frozen state, Jacob rushed over to his main wardrobe and pulled out a thick woollen tie. He then used it to bind Dogsbody's wrists behind his back. Finally having the courage to check, he found that the felled giant was still breathing. He had no appetite for further violence and wondered whether his victim would survive anyway, given the great weight of the candlestick that he'd been hit with. He searched through Dogsbody's pockets and found the keys to the garage and to the two cars. Suitcase in hand, he hurried downstairs to the kitchen and retrieved the two large cuts of meat. He opened the kitchen window, called the dog outside by its name and threw the meat out. He then hurried into the drawing room at the front of the house, opened another window, shouted at Vladimir, who was loitering outside and threw him the second piece of meat. He collapsed into an armchair, exhausted, and waited for the sleeping tablets to do their work on the attack dogs. After about twenty minutes he checked the situation at both the front and the rear of the house and saw that the two dogs were, like their master, completely unconscious. He hurried out to the old stables, unlocked the door and then put his suitcase in the boot of the Bentley. Fearing that Dogsbody might yet wake up and manage somehow to wrestle free of his bonds, he deflated both of the rear tyres of his gleaming Glacier Blue MG. Once this had been done, he jumped in the Bentley and drove carefully out of the stables. His heart then skipped three beats at once. Driving directly towards him was a black Rover saloon that he'd seen once before when Irina had visited. On the Colonel's instructions she had driven down to the house first thing in the morning and she had arrived at precisely the wrong moment. Seeing no sign of Dogsbody in the Bentley she swung her vehicle in front of it to block its way and then jumped out. Pointing her gun directly at Jacob, she motioned to him to get out. Given that his only alternative option was to be shot on the spot, he did as instructed.

"Where is your chauffeur?"

"He's not well this morning, a dose of the runs I'm afraid. I said I'd drive myself into work."

"Uh-huh. Well let's just go and check your story with him. Put your hands over your head and lead the way."

They marched towards the house, with Jacob's thoughts swirling in panic. Seeing Vladimir flat out on the ground Irina said,

"What's the matter with the dog?"

"Same ailment that your associate's got, I think. He had some of the meat that his master ate for his tea last night and it seems to have had the same effect on him. Food poisoning I would think. I don't like beef, so I didn't have any."

She said nothing in reply. Once in the grandiose entrance hall she told him to stop while she called to Dogsbody. Her voice echoed as if she were shouting into a deep mountain valley, but there was no response.

"He's probably in one of the toilets," Jacob volunteered.

"Yes, probably. But just in case, I'll have a little check around the house. Take off your tie and give it to me."

He did as instructed. She bound his hands tightly behind his back with one half of the tie and then bound him to the slim gilded post at the foot of the staircase with the other.

"You wait here."

She was gone for a full quarter of an hour, during which Jacob struggled desperately to free himself. Finally, she returned, a grim smile on her face. She walked right up to him and hit him hard on his left cheek with the butt of her pistol. She then strode out of the house, leaving the door open behind her. Jacob tried again to free himself, but she was back within a few minutes, carrying his suitcase. She opened it in front of him and let its contents fall at his feet. She said,

"Oops. Looks like we were going on our holidays again Mr. Jacob. Your chauffeur definitely won't be able to take you, he's been hit so hard that I doubt he will ever wake up. Perhaps a chandelier fell off one of your fine ceilings and flattened him, while one of the goblins from the frescos on the walls above us jumped down and tied his arms behind his back?"

"We had burglars in the night and he tried to stop them. I hid in a cupboard until they'd gone. I was frightened that you'd think I'd hit him so was running to a place of safety for a couple of days, that's all. I was going to an hotel in Hampshire, so I wouldn't even have been very far away. I was going to ring the Colonel from there and if he'd have believed my story would have come straight back. That's all it was, I promise, I had no intention of trying to escape again. That would have been madness."

"Madness indeed."

She rifled through his jacket pockets, discovering his passport in the process. She waved it in front of his eyes.

"Just going to stay in a hotel in Hampshire? Since when has a passport been needed to get into Hampshire Mr. Jacob?"

"I always carry that with me in case they need to send me overseas at short notice. It's part of the job."

"The dogs have been poisoned with adulterated meat. There is still part of a slice hanging out of the mouth of one of the animals. I have an excellent sense of smell. Let me smell your hands."

She pushed him sideways and sniffed his hands. Then she examined his fingers. She said,

"Very careless. The smell of the beef is still on your hands, as is some of the dried blood from the same meat. I know these things, my father was a butcher. You have failed every test to see whether you are telling the truth Mr. Jacob and you know what the Colonel warned would be the penalty for a second attempt to escape. I have my orders and it is now time to carry them out."

She untied the knot holding him to the stair post.

"We're going on a little journey. It's to a place that we use for dealing with matters like this. You will lead the way back to the stables. There were no keys in the pockets of our man so you must have them, I think."

She rifled through his left-hand pocket and found a MG keyring with a Glacier Blue fob.

"Ah yes, here we have them. Walk please, we'll go in the sports car."

A small glimmer of hope rose within Jacob's mind as they returned to the stables with Irina's gun pressed firmly in his back. If she raced off at speed, without realising that the two rear tyres were flat, she just might lose control of the car. Hitting a tree or a wall would not be good news for either of them, but if the end result of the accident was that she was knocked out or killed and he survived relatively unscathed, then that was a far better outcome than he might otherwise expect. He kept his mouth firmly shut about the tyres and his captor did indeed press the accelerator down to the floor as they moved off. Unfortunately for him, the car's erratic handling and lumpy ride alerted her to the fact that something was badly wrong before they reached the estate gates and she brought it to a halt. She got out to see what the problem was and shook her head annoyedly when she saw the two flats.

"Your handiwork I presume?"

She pulled open the passenger door and told him to get out. He was then frogmarched back to the stables and installed in the passenger seat of the Bentley. They hurtled off for a second time, spraying dust all over the gleaming MG that sat abandoned near the gate as they went past. This time all hope had drained out of Jacob and his mind was filled instead with a dull resignation to the fact that the mere shadow that his life had become was about to be wiped from the face of the earth.

After an hour and a half's drive Irina stopped the car by the side of a deserted country lane and pulled a road atlas out of her shoulder bag. Having worked out where she needed to make a turn, she drove off again and about three hundred yards down the sunlit leafy lane turned left onto a rough track leading up the side of a hill. She stopped the car at the point where the track petered out, went round to open the passenger door and then instructed Jacob to get out. She marched him further up the hill until they came to a small group of barren trees. She told him to stay exactly where he was while she went into the centre of the little grove and clawed away a camouflaged covering which concealed a heavy wooden lid. She said,

"Come."

He walked over to her and she undid the bonds on his wrists, all the time managing to keep the gun pressed into his back. She said,

"This is a disused mine shaft and it is to be your grand tomb. Like the

Pharaohs, you will have a burial chamber with a long passageway leading to it. You will have some friends down there as well, people we have previously said goodbye to. Now, I need you to get down on your hands and knees and pull the lid away so that you can make your final journey."

"What if I refuse?"

"Then you will have even less life remaining than is already the case. I would have thought some extra moments to reconcile yourself to death, to pray to a god if that is what you believe in, would be worth the effort. I can shoot you now and do the work myself if you like, but you do have the option of a few extra minutes, with this brilliant winter sun shining down on you, saying its own goodbyes."

Jacob's eyes hid knives deep within them that he would have liked to hurl into her heart, but he eased himself down as instructed, trying to think of some way of attacking her before she could shoot, but no ideas were forthcoming. Once he'd pulled the heavy cover fully clear from the opening to the mineshaft below it, she told him to get up. He turned to face her, standing inches from the edge. She smiled with the satisfaction of a connoisseur of executions and advanced to within a yard of him. She decided to aim straight between his eyes for an instant result. As she was about to fire the shot that was intended to kill him, he managed to lunge forwards and take firm hold of her wrist, jerking it upwards as she fired the gun. Having knocked her slightly off balance, he pulled her with him as he stepped backwards over the edge of the shaft. His spur of the moment action was based on the knowledge that she would have martial arts training and would be likely to win any struggle between the two of them, which would simply mean that his death was postponed for a minute or two. If they fell down the shaft however, with her arm in his grip, he could try and manoeuvre her into a position where she hit the ground first, breaking his fall. It was an ultra-high-risk strategy with only a small chance of success, but it was better than all of the alternatives that he could think of. She was taken completely by surprise. They plunged down in a deep dive into darkness, a hurtling descent that ended far below with a loud splash as they fell into the groundwater lake that had accumulated at the bottom of the shaft.

In the branches of the dead trees above, sparrows and blackbirds chattered and fluttered. In the mineshaft, all was silence.

CHAPTER TEN

Jacob's house and grounds were swarming with police. The rural patrolman who'd been asked to keep an eye out for the blue MG had spotted it near the estate gates when passing on his early morning rounds and had immediately gone to investigate. Within half an hour of him calling in the details Gus and Constable Hythe had arrived. Gus's car had broken down during the previous evening and he'd been told that it would be in the garage for a couple of days before the parts necessary for its repair could be obtained, so he hitched a lift in a police car with Hythe. Things had moved quickly after they'd found the front door to the house unlocked and had searched the building. They'd discovered the deeply unconscious Dogsbody and he had been quickly taken to hospital. At that point Hythe had rung his superiors to let them know what had happened and the cavalry then arrived, with forensics, search teams and the dour but efficient Chief Inspector Hurley, a portly middle-aged man with a permanent worried frown. It was soon established that Gillow Elliott, as Jacob was known outside of KGB circles, worked for the Foreign Office and that he wasn't to be found at his desk in Whitehall or anywhere else. A tenant farmer in the estate grounds revealed that his landlord had a Bentley. For Chief Inspector Hurley, its absence suggested that he'd either fled the scene or been abducted in his own vehicle and the farmer's description of the car was rapidly circulated to neighbouring police forces. By late morning Mr. One had arrived.

Kneeling at the foot of the staircase in the grand entrance hall, Gus and Mr. One sifted through the contents of Jacob's suitcase, which had been left where Irina had tipped them, along with the suitcase itself. Gus said,

"This is but one of several mysteries around the house. Elliott's passport is here and he seems to have packed for a journey abroad, yet his office say he was due to be at work in Whitehall today. He was scheduled to go on high level official business to Washington next week, but didn't need his passport until then. Ultimately, he's vanished without any of this stuff, which rather suggests that he was abducted as he was trying to make some kind of escape. The chap we found upstairs fits Tasty Harry's description of the purchaser of the Michaels' murder weapon and the MG car numberplate contains the numbers that Harry gave us. The chap appears to have been the owner's chauffeur – he was wearing part of a chauffeur's uniform when we found him. That would explain why he'd been seen picking up groceries in the town. His own car was abandoned just before the exit gates with two flat tyres. They've not been hit by gunshots or slashed, so it looks like someone let them down manually to immobilise the vehicle. He was hit hard on the back of the head with a blunt instrument and from what the ambulance crew said when they examined him, he'll be lucky to survive."

"Which is very bad news from your point of view, given that he was our best potential lead on what might have happened to your cousin."

"Indeed. The police have sent a man to the hospital to guard him when he comes out of surgery and have promised to let us know if and when he comes round and is able to talk."

"So what's your theory as to what's been going on here?"

"Well, as with Michaels' murder, there's how it looks and how it was. What it looks like is somebody coming hunting for Elliott, who's been forewarned and is in the process of trying to escape from the house when his pursuers arrive. His chauffeur is a big beefy type whom he probably used as a minder and the two of them are upstairs when their attackers burst in. They surprise the chauffeur, knock him out and tie him up. Elliott manages to elude them initially and succeeds in getting as far as the bottom of the staircase before they catch him. He drops his suitcase in the struggle and it bursts open. They then drive off in the Bentley with him, just as someone drove off with Julia."

"So, if that's how it 'looks', what was it that really happened do you think?"

"There are too many things that don't fit the first version of events. For a start, the information from Tasty Harry made it pretty clear that the chauffeur was deeply involved in the killing of Michaels. He bought the gun and knew precisely what he was looking for. So why was someone like that working for a Foreign Office high flier as a chauffeur? I searched his room with Hurley before you arrived and we found this."

Gus handed a large envelope to Mr. One who opened it and began to read the contents with a deep frown, which became deeper as he progressed from one page to the next. After a couple of minutes he said,

"Good God. If these documents were genuine, they would be dynamite."

"The big question is 'if'."

"Indeed. I know two of the alleged signatories extremely well, we were all in the same regiment. They were pretty damn angry with the previous PM for wrecking our relations with Washington over the Suez subterfuge, so there's zero chance of them sanctioning actions that would wreck them a second time. The documents are expertly forged, but that's all. What on earth were they doing in the chauffeur's room?"

"Indeed. But that's not the only odd thing we noticed. Constable Hythe and I found the chauffeur flat out in what we've discovered is Elliott's bedroom. His positioning suggested that he'd been attacked just after he'd entered the room. We found a key in the lock of the bedroom door, but not where you'd expect it to be. It was on the outside, suggesting that the chauffeur might have just unlocked the door to enter."

"So he could have locked Elliott in his room overnight?"

"It's a possibility. Elliott could then have been the person who thwacked the chauffeur and attempted to escape with his suitcase and passport, although why he would want to flee the country when he could have simply gone to the police is a mystery. Unfortunately for him, there was a second person in the house and they intercepted him at the foot of the staircase, causing his suitcase to burst open in the struggle. The second person theory fits with the mystery Rover saloon we found in front of the stables. The tenant farmer who told us about the Bentley knew nothing about the Rover, although he had noticed the blue MG round and about."

"But if the second person was in cahoots with the chauffeur, why did they abandon him when they abducted Elliott?"

Gus said,

"It's quite possible they thought he was a goner, as indeed he might be."

Angus said,

"So it looks like Elliott may have been trying to escape from one or both of these people. There's an obvious Foreign Office link in so far as both Elliott and Michaels worked for the same shop."

"And another obvious link between the two of them in the form of the chauffeur's involvement with both. There's a possible clue as to what might have been going on in the form of another link, that between the probably forged documents and Elliott's schedule. The papers are obviously potential dynamite in UK-US relations, so maybe he was being blackmailed into taking them with him next week for passing to people he knew in the US administration."

Angus said,

"And prior to his US trip, he was to be kept under constant supervision by minders such as the chauffeur to make sure he didn't try and abscond without doing what he was being told to do. He was instructed to go into work every day, as normal, so that he would get to go on this high-level trip, but during every hour outside his office he was being watched. If all of this is true, they must have had something big on him to use for blackmailing purposes."

"Which could make him our long-lost mole, the person Michaels was anxious to tell us about."

"Indeed, Elliott could well have been Zaliatev's man in the Foreign Office. I think all roads merge into one with the Colonel. If we want to find Elliott and your cousin then we need to follow him and his known cronies everywhere they go in the hope that they will lead us to one or both of our missing persons. If Elliott has been taken away for interrogation following the events that happened here, then the Colonel is bound to be present. The people we've had following him are excellent, but even they have twice lost him during the past few days, so I replaced them with our most experienced trackers this morning. Unless our chauffeur friend wakes up and does a deal to unseal his lips, these people are the best chance we have of locating both Elliott and your cousin."

Back in the mineshaft, something was stirring. Irina was flailing around in the near-darkness, trying to find Jacob in order to stab him with the knife that lived in a sheath strapped to her thigh. Other than the obvious fact that the groundwater into which they'd dropped seemed to be very deep, she'd no idea how far down it actually went or whether her target had survived the fall. She'd wrenched her wrist free of his grip as they'd plummeted downwards, so she didn't know precisely where he'd landed. The light from the entrance hole above was far away and there were various side chambers that were in complete darkness, making it impossible for her to see if he was hiding in any of them. She swam around and around, trying to locate him without success. After a short while the coldness of the water forced her to stop and she pulled herself up out of the mini lake and onto a ledge. She kept completely still for five minutes, just listening for any tell-tale splash, cough or sneeze, but there was nothing. Finally, she concluded that her prisoner must have lost consciousness when he hit the water and drowned, or possibly even hit his head on one of the many jagged bits of rock that she could feel sticking out from the walls of the old and crudely engineered shaft.

Those irregular, roughly hewn bits of rock were her one and only chance of escape. She had come top of the class in the rock climbing exercises that had formed part of her training years ago and she now put her skills to full use. Slowly and painfully, she hauled herself upwards, grabbing one cold and slippery rock protuberance after another with her bare hands, while using her feet to find substantial enough 'stepping stones' to help take some of the strain off her arms and propel herself upwards. She didn't dare try and calculate how many yards separated her from the top of the shaft for fear that doing so might cause her to panic at the scale of the task and lose her grip. She ploughed on determinedly, resting every now and again to conserve her strength, before returning to the task in hand. After what seemed like an eternity of hard labour and several slips that had nearly led to disaster, she finally made it to the surface. With one final, massive effort she hauled herself up and onto the cold ground in the centre of the little circle of barren trees and lay there exhausted for a full ten minutes.

Soaked to the skin, she couldn't stop shivering and began to worry about the dangers of hypothermia. The brilliant winter sun had by now been swallowed within a bank of dull cloud and a cold wind had started to blow around the hill. She eased herself up into a kneeling position and began to pull the heavy lid back over the mineshaft. Her arms ached badly from the effort of having hauled herself up the steep rock walls and she found it impossible to heave the cover over the last foot of the shaft entrance hole. She collected a large broken branch and a couple of dozen substantial twigs and pieces of small but thickish dead branches and laid them across the remaining gap in a diagonal fashion. She then pulled the camouflage back over everything. There was something entangled within it that she didn't notice – her gun. When Jacob had grabbed her wrist and she had overbalanced and fallen into the mineshaft with him, she had lost her grip on her weapon. She had assumed that it had fallen with them and was at the bottom of the deep mini lake of groundwater. However, almost fully loaded and ready for use, it remained hidden from view only inches from where she knelt.

Her task complete, and still shivering continuously, she dragged herself upright and retraced her steps down the hill to the car.

Once inside the vehicle, she switched the engine on, together with the heater and sat for five minutes or so just trying to get warm. She'd left her own car back at Jacob's in case anybody spotted the vehicle in the vicinity of the KGB 'burial ground'. There was always a random possibility that somebody out for a ramble might stumble across the camouflaged shaft, pull back the cover and shine a torch down. If the first thing they saw was Jacob's body hanging over a rock, then an unwelcome investigation would follow and she'd have to get rid of a car she rather liked in case anybody had seen it near the scene of the crime. It was this ability to think through all of the possibilities of a situation that had gained Irina such rapid promotion by the age of thirty-three – together with her utter ruthlessness and ability to switch from being a sensual female charmer at one end of the spectrum of her personas to a manipulative murderous bully at the other, as circumstances demanded. Her decision to come in the Bentley, however, meant that she must now return to the estate to swap it for her own car. She remembered that she needed also to pick up the forged documents that were so important to the Colonel and take them back with her to London. She could also change into one of Jacob's shirts and a set of his trousers and then conceal them beneath her coat, which lay on the back seat of her Rover. Then, very much as an afterthought within her empathy-free mind, she remembered that she would need to check on the chauffeur to see whether he had regained consciousness or not. If he hadn't, she needed to bring in a specialist KGB team to deal with the situation and remove any traces of blood, etc. She turned the Bentley round and headed back down the track, towards the road.

When, finally, the long stone walls of Jacob's historic estate came into view, Irina felt a sense of deep relief at having survived an unexpected attack by her prisoner and at now being able to return in one piece to collect the car that, in some ways, was the nearest substitute for a genuine friend that she possessed. All of that changed as she approached the entrance gates and saw that the grounds were crawling with police officers. She presumed that somebody must have found the felled Dogsbody and raised the alarm, but had no idea as to who that somebody might be. She swung the car quickly away from the estate entrance and accelerated down the road, into the distance. As she did so, she wondered how she was going to be able to tell the Colonel that his prized forged documents, the means by which he was hoping to derail improving Anglo-American relations, were now in enemy hands. She also needed to reconcile herself to the loss of her favourite car of all time. It could only be traced to her if she was actually in it, given that the number plates, like the ill-fated documents, were excellent forgeries. The sad thing was, she reflected, that she could never drive it again. She had also lost her favourite winter coat. There was nothing in her pockets that could link it with her, she was always careful about such things. But like the car, on whose back seat it languished, in her strangely limited sociopathic relationships with the world around her, the affection she felt for it substituted for the liking she didn't have for the people who inhabited that world. Beautiful and bright eyed as she was, she now had nothing on which to focus her very limited capacity for affection and felt both bereft and depressed.

Oblivious to the fact that one of the key players in their various lines of enquiry had been close enough to hit with a cricket ball, as Mr One would have said, he and Gus were in the process of concluding their examination of the house and grounds. Gus said,

"You know, even though we haven't had the luck to catch one of the Colonel's people in a conscious and ready to interrogate state, this has been an extraordinarily productive set of discoveries, all within the four walls of this enormous pile of stone. We're now pretty certain who the Foreign Office mole is, even though we don't know where he is at the moment. We've located the chap who bought the gun that killed Michaels and we now know that he's a key minor functionary in Zaliatev's set up in the UK. There's a chance that he might make it through surgery with his marbles intact and if he does, he could be a crucial means of getting information about Julia's location. We've unearthed and disrupted a Soviet forged document operation that was intended to destabilise Anglo-American relations and can now warn the government about what Zaliatev is up to – and it's all down to Constable Hythe!"

The policeman was just walking past with Chief Inspector Hurley and Gus took the opportunity to thank him profusely in front of his superior for first having spotted the MG in the town and then diligently making sure that the local patrolman kept an eye on Jacob's estate, enabling them to locate both the car and its owner. Hythe beamed with appreciation as he did so. As he and Hurley bade their goodbyes and the two MI5 men headed towards Mr. One's car, Gus said,

"I couldn't resist that. People like Hythe spend a lifetime doing crucial donkey work and never get promoted or more than a nod of appreciation."

Mr. One came dangerously near to a half smile, saying,

"You're a big softie at heart Augustus, but you're quite right. I suspect I'm one of the people who have overlooked and taken for granted the Constable Hythes of this world You make a good point. I must also say that, as always, I admire your professionalism. I know how much your cousin's predicament is preying on your mind, but you've kept your focus on the whole job and not just personal concerns, as I knew you would. Spotting those documents was absolutely crucial to UK interests and that was your excellent work. It must now be my excellent work to ensure that our people stick like limpets to Zaliatev and his cronies. As I said before, if his man in the hospital doesn't wake up, tailing our KGB friends is going to give us the best chance of finding where they've got your cousin holed up."

Mr. One's driver opened the rear passenger door of the car and they climbed into the back. Gus had arranged for his own car to be delivered back to London when it had been repaired. As the vehicle drove off the MG and the black Rover were in the process of being towed away. Gazing back at the now desolate looking Georgian pile that was Jacob's country house, Gus said,

"To tell you the truth Angus, the more I know about our friend Colonel

Zaliatev the less worried I am about Julia's well-being. She's extremely feisty and if he's interrogated her, she's very likely to have warned him that I'll be on his trail. Once he realises her connection to me, I think he'll see her as someone he can trade. He'll know at least as much about you and me as we do about him, and he'll be in the process of thinking what he can demand from us in exchange for her safe return. Assuming that Michaels was killed to protect the identity of the Foreign Office traitor, then as soon as Zaliatev realises that Mr. Mole's cover has been blown he no longer has a reason to hang on to her. My anticipation is that if we don't manage to locate her within the next few days a go-between will be in touch with an offer of talks."

"That's interesting Augustus, although I have several reservations. Our priority must indeed be to get her back safe and well, but if we can avoid having to pay a price then we must do so. By definition, trades always mean that we lose something in return. I'll be putting every available resource into getting her back free of charge if we can. I know you're trying to remain as optimistic as possible about your cousin's prospects of a safe return and I admire that, but you know as well as I do that there are some prices that we cannot pay for one reason or another. It may be that Zaliatev asks for such a price, which he might be inclined to do as a payback for us having disrupted his plans to destabilise Anglo-American relations. If he does and we have no alternative but to refuse, then your cousin will be in grave danger. New intelligence shows that the Colonel has ordered the deaths of a great many people during his long career. If we don't pay what he demands and we can't find where he is holding her in time, then there is a strong possibility that this young woman might simply disappear on a permanent basis with all further knowledge of her denied. You need to prepare for that also Augustus."

"Well, be that as it may, no-one knows the outcome of a race until the runners have gone over the line, Angus. If we keep on doing what we're doing there's a chance we'll get her back, one way or another."

"I hope so Augustus, I really do. If we can sort out her situation that'll free the resources to follow up other matters of concern connected with our Colonel friend. In particular, we need to get back to the business of finding out on whom that grubby little tabloid journalist Chabler has been digging up dirt recently. We need to find out what he's been up to in the past as well. The sooner we unearth what Chabler has been up to the sooner we can stop Zaliatev getting his hands on any more secrets."

"Fret not Angus, as I've said before, that will be my first priority as soon as we've rescued Julia. Talking of secrets, I wonder just how many our presumed Foreign Office mole has given to the Soviets prior to today's falling out."

Angus raised his eyebrows and said,

"Indeed. At least he's now out of action in that respect. If he's double crossed the Colonel he could well be at the bottom of a lake by now."

The mole in question had not had a good day. His escape attempt had not gone to plan and his one piece of good luck was that Irina didn't manage to shoot him and he survived the plunge down the mineshaft into the lake. He'd managed to swim quietly away into the shadows while she flailed around looking for him. He then hid inside a miniature cavern created by an abandoned attempt to dig out one of several side shafts many years previously. In order to try and reduce the danger of hypothermia, he'd hauled himself up out of the water and onto a ledge. He then kept perfectly still to avoid detection. When she'd finally decided that he must have drowned and started her ascent back up to the surface, he was careful to observe both her route and how she managed to climb it, as far as the small amount of light seeping in from the shaft entrance far above allowed. He had a very limited experience of climbing from his university days, but that, combined with his close observation of an expert at work, gave him just enough knowhow to be able to make his own ascent half an hour after she'd disappeared from view and closed the lid. The fact that she hadn't managed to pull the cover fully over meant that there was just enough light seeping through the camouflage for him to attempt his climb. It had taken him twice as long as her due to his extreme caution, occasioned by his relative lack of experience, together with the fact that he was nowhere near as fit as she was. Each yard he climbed had increased his terror of falling, because he feared that he would bounce repeatedly off the jagged rock wall that he'd been ascending and end up too injured to make a second attempt, or maybe even to swim. The slimy nature of the damp rock and the very limited light made every attempt to gain a secure foothold or handhold heart-stoppingly perilous. Then, when he'd finally made it to the top, he'd had to hold his balance while pushing out of the way the twigs and branches that Irina had used to cover the gap between the lid and the edge of the shaft. He'd had to rest for ten minutes to regain the energy to haul himself up the last foot or so and then clamber out back onto the ground above. But, through sheer determination and willpower, he had finally managed to break out of his watery tomb and re-join the land of the living.

After half an hour lying flat on his back to recover, Jacob decided that he'd better head back down to the road and see if he could hitch a lift in the general direction of the southern fishing ports. He no longer had his passport, but he'd no doubt that he could bluff his way through that little problem as long as he avoided all the places where it would be likely to be required. What he did have was the five hundred pounds that he'd retrieved from the wall safe. Like him, it was extremely wet, but other than that was still perfectly usable. He hauled himself upright and repositioned the twigs and branches so that it would not be apparent that he'd escaped. He pulled the camouflage back over and in doing so noticed that Irina's gun was entangled within it. Picking it out from within the knotted strands, he examined it contemplatively for a few moments. He had been a pretty useless shot during the murder of Mallory Michaels, but he did at least vaguely know how to use a gun. He decided that it might be useful should his luck continue to be as unreliable as had been the case so far and slid it into his right-hand jacket pocket. If the Soviets caught up with him again, he would not be completely defenceless. He then hurried back down the track after having carefully checked that the Bentley and its KGB driver had departed. Once he got to the road, shivering violently in his soaking wet clothes, he started walking along the narrow verge in the hope of being able to flag down a passing vehicle for a lift. The problem was that there were no vehicles to be seen or heard. The road did not lead to anywhere significant and appeared to have the linking of several farms as its only current function. Coming to a roadside farmhouse, where a stone over the door proudly proclaimed that it had been built in 1676, Jacob noticed a lady's bicycle propped up against an outhouse. It occurred to him that he could use the bike to cycle to the nearest bus stop, abandon it there and then continue his journey to the south coast via bus and train. Seeing no-one about, he crept over to where the bicycle stood and then pushed it quickly out onto the road. What he hadn't spotted was the pair of eyes that had been watching him from behind the parlour curtains. As he hopped onto the seat and began to pedal off down the road, the front door flew open and the farmer's wife ran out, shotgun in hand, shouting at him to stop and return the bike immediately. When he ignored her and pedalled furiously away, she fired a couple of warning shots to the left and the right of him, nearly causing him to wobble over into the ditch running alongside the verge. He managed to recover and veered round onto a track on the other side of the road and disappeared into a clump of trees that obscured her view of him. Mrs. McNorton was not someone to be easily defeated however. She rushed back inside the house and rang the police.

Jacob had not planned for a rookie local patrolman who regarded the catching of a bicycle thief as his first step up a ladder that would eventually lead towards a chief inspector's job in a major crimes team. He was caught completely by surprise, therefore, when he rounded a bend in the track two miles further on to find his way blocked by a police car. As he braked hard and attempted to turn round, he felt suddenly the firm grip of two strong hands on his upper arms. He was hauled off the bike as if he weighed nothing at all and found himself being handcuffed by a smiling young constable who was six inches taller than him with the build of a boxer and the strength of an ox. Constable Haggerty, originally from Northern Ireland, was a rigorously thorough officer who had taken the trouble to familiarise himself with every road, lane and country track on his beat. He was also an acute observer of people. He knew just by the appearance of Jacob that he had arrested a man who was running away from something far bigger than a bicycle theft. His expensive, if soaking wet, city suit and the five hundred pounds the constable found in his inside jacket pocket made it extremely odd that he should find it necessary to steal a bicycle belonging to a farmer's wife in the middle of nowhere. But the gun was something else. Haggerty examined it closely and then said,

"So, what have we here? If you were hoping to play a British version of cops and robbers you've got the wrong weapon for the territory. This splendid little toy is made in Russia. How did you come to acquire a Russian gun Mr. Whoever You Are?"

Jacob said nothing, knowing that now was the time when he needed a solicitor. Haggerty said,

"The cat got your tongue then, now that's a shame. Into the back of the car you go, we're going to have a nice little ride down to the police station where we can have a proper chat and a cup of tea. The tea's for me and not for you by the way, I'm as thirsty as a dog in the desert."

As he slid his non-communicative prisoner into the back of the vehicle he said,

"It's no wonder you're inclined to keep your gob shut my thieving friend, I can tell just by the sight of you that you've been up to something very big somewhere or other. So you're the very big fish that I'm going to stick in a cell until we've done a thorough check to see who it is that matches your description and just what it is he's wanted for. How's that for a very fine prospect on an afternoon that up until now had been looking duller than dull and bereft of all hope of me ever nicking a major villain like yourself?"

Jacob's face was completely expressionless and his mind had sunk to a place that was even deeper and darker than the mineshaft he'd just escaped from. It seemed that, for all his efforts, he'd merely swapped one nemesis for another. He'd no idea as to precisely which can of worms the meddlesome investigations of this over-enthusiastic young officer would open, but he was as certain as he could be that the consequences for him would be severe.

Haggerty stopped the car at the farmhouse and after returning the bicycle to its owner, opened the rear passenger door and asked her to formally identify the thief, which she did. She then spat in Jacob's face. Initially startled, he looked up at her in his despair and said, ironically,

"Thank you. Relatively speaking, that's the nicest thing anyone's done to me today."

CHAPTER ELEVEN

Colonel Zaliatev did not like the office he was given to work from in the Soviet embassy. It had been chosen with respect not just for his rank but for his fearsome reputation and was one of the finest rooms within the most impressive of the embassy buildings, with an imposing desk and a pleasant leafy view that was the envy of many less privileged officials. Having come from an impoverished background he always felt uneasy in the presence of anything that reeked of grandeur. Grandeur, he believed, was built on the backs of the poor and his original reasons for joining the Communist Party had been to build a new society in which poverty was banished into history. While his disillusionment following Stalin's deal with the Nazis had long since killed most of his faith in communism, he still had a desperate need to hope that its original aims might be achieved via other means. Deep within his inner self, he still wanted to end privilege and replace it with equality of wealth and equality of opportunity. That yearning, so deep within him that he often almost forgot its existence, was the hidden cause of his distrust of the symbols and trappings of power and wealth. Paradoxically, he had no wish to lose his own power, yet simultaneously he felt uneasy about the temptations that came with it.

There were some tasks, however, for which his grand office was tailor made. He was well aware of the ambition of Irina Lashkanocova. He had no doubt that, at some stage, the idea would occur to her that he was not so much a role model but someone she should aspire and quite probably conspire to replace. Her ruthlessness was of use to him as long as it was entirely under his control. Should it break free and begin to work against him, then he would be faced with a dangerous opponent. So, while the abrupt failure of the planned Jacob-centred disinformation operation was a considerable setback in his attempts to complicate and destabilise Anglo-

American relations, it did at least have some valuable spin offs in his management of Irina. He had entrusted key parts of the operation to her and she had underperformed. He would make it clear to her that the mishaps that had occurred would be going on her record and that her continued position in the KGB in London was very much on the line. He had summoned her to a three o'clock meeting with him to discuss the various operational failures and give her a general dressing down. For this specific purpose, the grandeur of his office was perfectly suited. It provided a theatrical backdrop, a symbol of the power he held over her. It was really only on occasions such as this that the Colonel and the office were in harmony.

She arrived precisely on time, but he had arranged for her to be kept waiting for half an hour. The only reason for the delay was to emphasise that the price of underperformance was the loss of privileged, immediate access to her superior officer. When, finally, she was allowed to enter his office the atmosphere within the room was so cold even a polar bear would have turned into ice. He motioned to her to sit down in a chair that was noticeably set back from his gargantuan desk and returned to reading a file that he had laid out in front of him. She started to ask a question but he immediately and extremely formally requested her to be silent and the words died on her lips. After five minutes precisely he closed the file, sat back in his chair and gave her a long, hard look that would have shrivelled a tiger had it been in her place. He said,

"If you were sitting in this chair, looking at your record during this operation, what do you think you would have said about your performance?"

"I would say that mistakes had been made Colonel and that I placed too much trust in people who did not merit it."

"Mistakes had been made. How many mistakes were there do you think? I would like you to list them."

Irina's cool exterior hid the panic inside her head. With a man like Zaliatev there was no playing around. She could try and lay the blame on others where she could, but there was no point whatsoever in trying to cover up those errors that had been entirely hers. How well she handled herself in the next few minutes would determine whether she continued to work for him or was demoted to a junior office job back in Moscow. She said,

"Mistakes were made by the surveillance team that failed to notice that Michaels had a lover and that she might be with him on the night that was set up for the kill."

"The surveillance team that you chose and briefed."

"That is correct, Colonel, but they had good recommendations from other comrades who had used them previously and I was thorough in my briefing. They did not fully comply with my instructions."

"If they had performed well for others, why did they not perform well for you?"

"Because I am a woman, I think. I've been told since that two members of that team do not respect female superiors."

"You've been told 'since'. This is something you should have found out about beforehand. It is the first task of a senior intelligence officer to find out everything he or she can about those upon whom they rely. It was your failure as well as theirs Lashkanocova."

"Yes, Colonel, I will follow your guidance on this matter in all future team selection."

"I have yet to decide whether you will be selecting any future teams. Continue with your listing of mistakes."

"Your man chosen to manage Jacob, to be his chauffer and everything else besides, I should have kept a much shorter leash on him. It is only his carelessness that can have given British Counter-Espionage the clues that enabled them to turn up at Jacob's mansion and find the forged documents. It was only his carelessness that allowed a much weaker man to neutralise him. It is only that carelessness that has allowed him to fall into the hands of the British authorities, should he ever wake from his coma."

"As you say, another example of your underperformance. Keeping a short leash on such a man was imperative and you failed to do it. You have other failures you want to tell me about I think. I believe that you arrived back in London with very wet feet on a day when there had been no rain anywhere in England and that you had somehow lost your gun. How very, very curious don't you think? How did all of that happen?"

There were no failures that Irina could think of that she 'wanted' to tell the Colonel about, but there were certainly ones that she knew she would have to confess to.

"I was taken a little by surprise when disposing of Jacob. We both fell into the shaft, where he drowned in the deep groundwater at the bottom. I lost my weapon in the struggle."

"You were taken by surprise? You seem to be surprised far too often Irina Lashkanocova. I want you to reflect on all of these failures and write a report on how you are going to avoid similar errors in the future. The fate of your career will depend on how convinced I am by your efforts. I want the report on my desk within three days and it will then form part of your record. For the moment I am issuing you with a formal reprimand, which will also go on your record. Do you understand?"

"Yes Colonel. I am sorry for my failings and will ensure that they are never repeated."

"Moscow is extremely disappointed that the Jacob project did not come to fruition. I have placated them a little with the news about our captive in the safe house and the possibilities that she opens for a trade with the British. They want the results of that trade to be immense and exceptional, those were the words used. They want full compensation for the failure of the Jacob project. Part of my decision about whether your career survives will depend on how effectively you help me obtain those immense and exceptional results."

"I understand Colonel. What do you want me to do?"

"Our captive is a close relative of one of London's key counter-espionage operatives, Augustus Benedict, of whom you will be aware. Potentially, that gives us all kinds of opportunities for leverage. It is my intention to meet with Mr. Benedict, one-to-one, to discuss the price that will need to be paid for his cousin's release. I need those discussions to be free of all surveillance from his counter-espionage colleagues and for him to be aware that any prior mention of our meeting to his superiors will result in an unfortunate outcome for the captive. In the first instance, I need you to be the go-between that sets up the meeting. You have in the past shown a considerable range of skills in comparable situations elsewhere within Europe, so I will expect that you use them to the full in this instance also. There will be other crucial things that I will need you to do and you would be advised to ensure that they are all successfully delivered. There must be no failures in the execution of this project."

"I understand Colonel."

Irina understood her position very well. She had been set up as the scapegoat for the failure of the Jacob project and was being kept in place primarily so that she could be the scapegoat also if the Benedict operation went pear shaped. She was therefore determined to make sure that the trade went precisely as the Colonel intended and by so doing to preserve her career. She also was making a note of everything the Colonel did in managing her so that she could have similar tactics in reserve when ultimately she rose to his rank, as she had no doubt that she would. She knew that she would have to control and manipulate people who were after her job as she climbed up the ladder and she regarded the Colonel as a valuable teacher of the required arts. Irina was always calculating, always planning for the future. Now she had to plan how best to deal with Benedict.

When she got back to her own office, a much smaller affair than the Colonel's, she found a surveillance report on Benedict waiting on her modest formica desk. Reading it with a well-practised eye she concluded that he not only was constantly aware of his surveillance tails, but was in the habit of deliberately leading them up the garden path and having small jokes at their expense. On one occasion, for example, he'd led them into the lingerie section of a large department store and spoken to the departmental manager, pointing to his shadows while so doing. They had then been stopped by store detectives on suspicion of shoplifting underwear when trying to follow him out of the store and had yet again lost him. Irina wondered at the woodenness of the surveillance operative who had been so literal in his interpretation of his instructions to 'record everything' that he'd freely admitted to having been made a fool of. One of the few bits of useful information that she got from the file was that her target was in the habit of going for a mid-morning coffee in an Italian establishment just around the corner from his office. That, she decided, would be where they would meet.

There was also a deep background report on everything that was known about the man. When she read it she found him distinctly confusing. The upper-class schooling and Oxford University education were what she expected to see in the profile of a British intelligence operative of his kind. What she couldn't quite get to grips with was his habit of spending significant amounts of his own money and his scarce free time helping the poor of the East End. For her there were only capitalists and communists, with the first devoted to the promotion of the individual interest and the second committed to the advancement of the common interest. Someone like Benedict, who seemed to straddle both of these commitments and yet worked to protect the interests of an archetypal capitalist state against threats from communist states, did not fit in with any logic that she understood. What she also didn't understand was the fact that some of her own motives for being a 'soldier of communism' contradicted the core essence of what the ideology was supposed to be about. While, intellectually, she did agree with key tenets of communist doctrine and felt repulsed by the inherited wealth of Jacob and his like, the main reason she supported its theoretical commitment to egalitarianism was because this was the best means of advancing her own career. For her, communism was primarily the vehicle by which she could advance her individual interests and become a high-ranking, well-paid official within the Soviet state. So, in this sense and extremely ironically, like Benedict she straddled the ideological divide, although she lacked entirely his altruistic motives for doing so.

As she thumbed further through the document, she found a list of his known successes in counter-espionage operations of various kinds and that was disconcertingly long. The more she read about the man, the more she began to worry that her earlier confidence that she could ensure the trade went exactly as the Colonel intended was misplaced.

The third file that had been left on her desk contained her detailed instructions from Zaliatev. He hadn't put them in writing in relation to other operations in the past. On this occasion he clearly intended that there should be a documentary record of the precise orders that she had been given. Its purpose, in addition to telling her what to do, was to provide something that could be used in evidence against her should she fail in her mission. There would be a copy already placed with her records, ready to be pulled out if necessary and sent with a detailed report on her failings to Moscow Centre. She realised all of this and could feel the sweat on her palms as she began to read the document. There were details of how she should dress for the encounter with her target and how she should behave. He was known to like strong and sensuous women, so she should play up to that. She was at no stage to confirm that the Soviets actually held his cousin, but should, following appropriate small talk, intimate that she knew someone who might be able to help secure her release – and so on and so on. That was her brief for the preliminary stage of the operation. It was all well within her capabilities. It was the later stages that would be tricky and that was where she knew she was most in danger of coming seriously unstuck. Her target was slippery, extremely experienced, highly intelligent and in every way formidable – just like the Colonel. Being herself extremely bright she could see that what was being set up here was a game of chess between two grandmasters, with her in the role of fall guy should the Englishman win. Her confidence that she could continue to ascend the career ladder to the rank of Colonel was becoming shakier by the minute. When she'd asked Zaliatev what would happen to the captive woman should Benedict refuse to play ball, he'd said she'd probably either be 'disappeared' into the same mineshaft that Jacob had gone, or moved to a Soviet prison, where she could be held as an 'asset in waiting' in case another chance to trade her arose in the future. But he'd also said that Irina shouldn't so much wonder what would happen to the captive woman if Benedict couldn't be persuaded to trade, but what might happen to her.

Irina spent the rest of the day thinking carefully about how best to approach the target. Being bereft of the gentler sentiments, such as empathy for other people or love of anyone other than herself, she always had to mimic relevant emotions she'd seen in others when engaging in social interactions that required them. That ability had helped her navigate her way through school, university and relationships where she needed to imitate affection in order to get access to sex. It also made her an accomplished actor in other contexts, an invaluable talent for many of the KGB jobs that she had been given during her climb up the career ladder. Like the Colonel, her English was excellent and she was also an avid reader. During her tours of duty in Washington and London she'd spent a considerable amount of time consuming novels with strong British and

American women characters. She'd read everything from 'Jane Eyre' to 'Middlemarch' and 'The Portrait of a Lady' in classic English language novels and had become particularly fixated on the femmes fatales in Raymond Chandler's twentieth century crime fiction. She also spent much of her leisure time in the cinema, absorbing the different ways that women were played in British and American films. She had made detailed notes about each of the characterisations that she'd read or watched. In effect, she'd compiled a 'wardrobe' of characters that she could pull off a hanger and play wholly, or in part, often mixing and matching bits of one character with bits of another in order to try and achieve the effect that she thought would most likely gain the desired result in espionage situations. Had she chosen a career as a professional actress she would have been a queen of the stage. Or maybe not.

It was Henry James who decided the colour of her dress for her encounter with Benedict. She chose a close-fitting black number that she'd bought a couple of months earlier. In her imagination she hoped to emulate the impact achieved by Isabel in a black dress at the beginning of 'The Portrait of a Lady'. That, she thought, would most fit with the Colonel's instructions. She kept in her office a range of six wigs and three reversible coats. They were part of her camouflage when going in and out of the building. She would enter wearing one wig and change to an entirely different one when she left. Equally, she would frequently change coats, and the fact that the three coats were reversible in effect gave her six to play with. She would make it even more difficult for surveillance teams trying to monitor her movements by timing her departures from the building so that she was mixed in with a small group of office workers going out for their lunchtime break, or going home in the evening. For her meeting with Benedict, she decided that a closely cropped auburn wig would be most appropriate. She would wear also the reversible coat that was black on one side so that it would match her dress. She was still working on the persona she would adopt right up until the last minute during the following morning, when she saw her target going into the Italian coffee shop at his usual time. From her vantage point deep inside an office doorway across the road, she watched him take his coat off, sit down, order a coffee and then start reading his newspaper. As soon as his coffee was served, she crossed the road and went in to join him.

What she didn't know was that Gus had already spotted her. He was a master of the art of noting everything while appearing to look at nothing other than the road ahead, or in this case, a newspaper. He'd noticed someone in the shadows of the office building entrance where normally nobody stood. He'd noticed her crossing the road once he was firmly ensconced in his chair and he'd noticed the way that she pretended not to notice him when she came in. He always chose a window seat so that he could spot anybody who might be taking an unwanted interest in him.

The coffee shop was only moderately busy and there were two completely empty tables. Irina sat down at one and then complained to a waiter that it hadn't been cleaned properly. When he offered to rectify the situation, she said she'd prefer simply to go to another table. Conveniently, an elderly couple took the other empty table while she was talking to the waiter. She then gravitated towards Gus, who pretended to have noticed nothing and affected surprise when she addressed him. She said,

"Excuse me, would you mind terribly if I sat here? I always like a window seat and the first table I sat at was rather dirty."

"No, please, be my guest. I'll only be here as long as it takes to drink my coffee. Then you can have the table to yourself. I've got a busy day ahead of me."

He smiled and went back to reading his newspaper. Irina took her coat off and draped it over the back of her chair, being careful to bend over while doing so, making full advantage of the close-fitting dress. As she sat down, he noticed a particularly strong and extremely fragrant perfume. The same unfortunate waiter whom she had just upbraided about the supposedly dirty table approached again and she ordered coffee and cake. While she was waiting for them, she took a packet of up-market British cigarettes out of her handbag and started to hunt for the lighter that she could see very well at the bottom, but pretended wasn't there. Without looking up from his newspaper, Gus said,

"You're going to ask me for a light."

He took a lighter out of his pocket and held it out for her. He said,

"I oblige. You light your cigarette, sensuously, holding my hand gently as it grips the lighter. You then thank me with come-to-bed eyes. I go back to reading my newspaper, like this, but my interest is aroused. There is a pause of a second or two and then you begin the small talk. That makes me a ready audience for the main business of our chance encounter, when you think the moment is right to introduce it. How am I doing?"

Irina looked as though she had just been slapped across the face with a wet fish. She could do a, "How dare you, I never meant anything of the sort, I had no intention of asking you for a light," routine, but that would simply destroy the meeting and any chance she might have of achieving the objectives set for her by the Colonel. Alternatively, she could recognise that her act was maybe not the best one to have chosen for someone as savvy as Benedict and cut to the chase. She decided that the second option was the better one. The come-to-bed eyes had been replaced by her normal hunter-killer alpha female eyes, the ones that told those who viewed them exactly who she really was and that she very much meant business. She smiled ironically and then let him light her cigarette without holding his hand. She said,

"You are, shall we say, very direct. I like that."

She blew a puff of smoke into the air and offered her vacuous thanks to the waiter as he delivered her order. She said,

"I believe you've lost something that you want to get back very badly."

"I might have done. It depends what it is."

"A cousin perhaps?"

"Perhaps. Now you're going to tell me you might be able to help me get her back."

"I might. Are you interested?"

"Possibly. Who exactly do you represent?"

"Let's just say I know the people who have inherited her as she has been passed from one party to another."

"Which is shorthand for a denial of all involvement in a serious crime, during which she was abducted – whether or not that denial is true?"

"That would seem a not unreasonable way of interpreting things."

"And what precisely are these people you know offering that might interest me?"

"A meeting, just you and someone who will be a go-between, someone who can tell you what they are looking for and convey your reaction back to them."

"I see. When and where is this meeting to be?"

"Two o'clock in the afternoon, on the day after tomorrow. The meeting will be at Lesnes Abbey. It's about half an hour by train. There are some ruined walls that are still about nine feet high. You will find the go-between behind one of them. Are you interested?"

"I might be. Does this person have a name?"

"He does, but you will have to ask him what it is for yourself."

She stubbed the cigarette out in the ashtray, a prop that was no longer needed now that the routine with the lighter had failed. She didn't enjoy smoking and only did so as part of the theatre of her job. She said,

"There are conditions for the meeting and they must be adhered to strictly. Any failure to do so could have severe consequences for the missing party."

"There are always conditions. What are the conditions that apply to this meeting?"

"That you tell no-one prior to the event and you come entirely alone. Even the most discreet surveillance people will be spotted as easily as you spotted me and the meeting then will not take place. There will be no further contact and you will not see your cousin again. Are these conditions acceptable to you?"

"They sound to be pretty standard. You can tell your friends I'll be there. If you'll excuse me, I need to get back to my office now – things to do, people to meet, you know the kind of thing. Your English accent is excellent by the way, it's only the occasional wrong note that tells me you're Russian. Tell the Colonel I'll look forward to seeing him."

He smiled, paid his bill and left.

When outside, Gus crossed to the opposite side of the road, walked one hundred yards further down, then slipped inside a small jewellers, where he could watch the coffee shop doorway through the window. The staff were already busy with customers, but should they ask him what he wanted he would just tell them that he was waiting for his wife to arrive so that they could view some necklaces. He intended following the ice-eyed woman he'd just met so that he could see where she went and who she talked to next. While he waited for her to appear, he reflected on his tête-à-tête with her. It had proved him exactly right. Julia would reveal her connection to him, the relevant cogs would whirr in the Colonel's brain, then he'd set up a meeting to try and extract something of high value to the Soviets in return for her release. He was clearly determined to create the fiction that the KGB were not the people who had originally abducted her and that they'd acquired her in some kind of trade, but that was par for the course. Disinformation and enormous fibs were everyday tools of the KGB's trade. Julia would no doubt have a very different story when she was released. He'd no idea whether Zaliatev had originally intended to be the 'go-between' at the proposed meeting, but he'd delivered a clear message that he only intended negotiating with someone of his rank. It would be interesting to see who actually turned up. The woman in the coffee bar spoke with an authority that suggested she wasn't a mere minion who'd been tasked with making the initial contact. He assumed that she would be someone quite senior within the Colonel's set up, so, if she was the initial contact person, presumably the negotiator would be at least one or two ranks more senior than her and that did indeed begin to sound like the Colonel himself. He'd noted that she didn't look in the slightest bit surprised by his suggestion that it would be.

His mind switched back to the coffee shop when a small group of people came out and started walking slowly down the road in the opposite direction to him. There was no woman in black with auburn hair among them. When, after fifteen minutes, there was still no sign of her, he walked cautiously back down the road and slipped into the same doorway from which originally she had observed him. A middle-aged couple were sitting at the table they had occupied and there was no sign of her. He cast his mind back to the small group of people he'd seen leaving earlier. A young woman who'd looked about the same height as Irina had been with them,

126

or at least appeared to be so, but she had different colour hair and was wearing a dark green coat, not the black one that the woman he'd spoken to had arrived in. Then he remembered the lining of the coat. He'd thought it a little unusual – dark green. He smiled to himself and started to walk back to his office. He'd fallen for one of the oldest tricks in the book – the visit to the ladies', the wig switch and the reversible coat, then wait until a small group leaves and mingle with them. She might have made a dog's breakfast of the first part of her act, but her grand finale had been absolutely perfect and she had made a monkey out of him. She was most definitely one of the Colonel's leading ladies.

CHAPTER TWELVE

When Gus got back to his office, he did what the Colonel knew very well he would do, which was tell Mr. One everything that had happened in the coffee shop encounter. The prohibition on telling anybody else was an unenforceable formality. What was crucial was that Gus kept to his promise to go to the meeting at Lesnes Abbey alone.

They spoke over the secure dedicated line so that there was no visible evidence of them having discussed the matter straight after the event. When Gus had finished, Mr. One had news of his own.

"That's all extremely interesting Augustus, but I'm delighted to say that Zaliatev is not the only game in town. The fact that he's opened a negotiating channel is undoubtedly good news, in so far as it confirms that your cousin is still alive and well. But the price he'll try and extract is not necessarily one I will be able to pay, as you know. We do now have a potentially cheaper alternative. Our missing Foreign Office man has turned up in a police station, believe it or not and he very much wants to talk to MI5, which is extremely convenient, because we, of course, would very much like to talk to him."

"What is it that's making him so chatty and where precisely has he been?"

"Now there's a long story. Our friend is in a spot of bother it seems, he's being held on a charge of bicycle theft."

"A charge of what?"

"Precisely. He seems to be a man of many calamities and this is perhaps the unlikeliest of all. I think he hopes that if he talks to us, we might be able to make the charge go away. There is also the little matter of another potential charge of grievous bodily harm relating to the gentleman that you found on his bedroom floor. I think he might prefer to tell us how all of that happened rather than the police."

"Interesting. If his involvement with Zaliatev's people has given him some useful information about the whereabouts of Julia that will give us the breakthrough that we desperately need. Presumably he'll also ask a pretty big price for that kind of information."

"I've no doubt, but his bargaining position is rather weaker than the Colonel's. I think we may get a lead out of him for a much more manageable price than Zaliatev is likely to ask. I'd like us to go down to Hampshire this afternoon to interview him. He was moved to a police station there this morning."

"OK, at the very least it will make an interesting parallel line of enquiry to that we've now opened with our Soviet counterparts."

They arrived at the police station where the Foreign Office man was being held in the early afternoon. Mr. One had taken elaborate precautions to make sure that nobody followed them, which included two changes of vehicle en route. They were shown into a dark and dingy interview room, into which a dishevelled looking Jacob was brought ten minutes later. After his handcuffs were removed and he sat down, the accompanying police officer left the room and they were alone. Mr. One addressed him using his real name,

"Good afternoon, Mr. Elliott. You asked to speak to MI5, so here we are. What is it that you would like to tell us?"

On arrival in the room the Foreign Office man's eyes had been glazed and he had every appearance of someone who had been severely traumatised. The fact that his demand had been met and MI5 really had come to see him seemed to wake him out of a bad dream. He looked suddenly alert, his eyes scanning his two visitors as his brain kicked into gear. As an experienced diplomat, his negotiating skills were well honed and he was now in a position to make the most of them to try and dig his way out of the latest hole he'd fallen into. He said,

"What would I like to tell you? That depends."

"On what precisely?"

"On what you can do for me."

"I see. What is it that you would like us to do for you?"

"I need immunity from all charges – and to vanish into a new identity."

"That's an interesting wish list. My past experience is as an army officer not a lawyer, but I'll do my best to assess the legal ins and outs of your position. Let's start with the first of your not inconsiderable demands. What charges are you thinking of?"

"Major and minor. The minor one is the easy bit. I borrowed a bicycle to get to the nearest bus stop, I didn't steal it in any meaningful sense, I hadn't the intent. It would have been left at the bus stop for the owner to collect."

"Did the owner agree to this arrangement?"

"I didn't think there was anyone about and I didn't have time to investigate. My life was still in danger."

"I see, so we are indeed quite possibly looking at a theft charge, albeit of a rather minor nature. I'm sure something can be arranged if you have things to tell us that are of value. May I enquire why you wanted to get to a bus stop and why you thought your life was in danger? I understood that you left your estate in your Bentley, so presumably you mislaid that somewhere along the way?"

"I was abducted in my car by the KGB, by a woman, Irina Lashkanocova. She left me for dead at the bottom of a disused mineshaft but I had a miraculous resurrection, as you might say. She took the car after she thought she'd killed me."

Gus said,

"So you were trying to get to a bus stop to complete your escape?"

"That's correct. One doesn't tend to worry too much about whether someone has consented to lend one a bicycle if one's life is at stake."

A random mischievous thought entered Gus's mind that with all the references to "one" it could be said that Mr. One was interviewing another Mr. One. He said,

"To return to my colleague's question, why was the KGB trying to kill you?"

"A very good question and one I'll be happy to answer, along with many more, once I have my guarantees of immunity from prosecution and a new identity."

"I see. But you can tell me about this woman, Irina Lashkanocova. What did she look like and how would you describe her as an operator?"

"Attractive woman on the surface, but her eyes are as cold as death. Absolutely ruthless, a bully, someone who regards other human beings simply as tools to be used or disposed of. She's the kind of spy that would shoot her own grandmother if it helped her career."

"I think I might have met her."

"Sorry to keep repeating myself, but if you want to know anything more about her I'll need the guarantees of immunity, etc."

Mr. One said,

"We'll need rather more information before we can begin to discuss an overall guarantee of immunity. You've told us about the minor charge you're facing, perhaps you could tell us about the major charge you would like to avoid?"

"Grievous bodily harm. The police have been questioning me about the psychopath they say I tried to kill with a candlestick. If I wanted to escape from the KGB, I had no choice but to knock him out, but knock him out was all I intended. I was being held against my will by agents of a foreign power and I simply used as much violence as was necessary to recover my freedom. If I'd wanted to do him grievous bodily harm or kill him, I'd have hit him a great many times more than once. They don't understand what I'm talking about. I'm not certain that the thicker of the two detectives is absolutely sure what the KGB is. That's why I said I needed to speak to you."

"I see – and how did you come to be a prisoner of the KGB, if prisoner you were? I'm very unclear at the moment as to precisely what your relationship with them was."

"That's another thing I'll tell you if I get my guarantees."

"We don't buy anything unseen. You're going to have to put a sample of your wares on the table if you want us to buy anything from you," Gus said.

"Such as?"

"You could explain a little about the secrets that you leaked to the Soviets during your relationship with them, whatever the precise nature of that relationship was. Perhaps you could give us an example or two, together with an estimate of how many betrayals you engaged in overall."

"Oh, I see. Your intention is to frighten me into giving everything I know for free, otherwise you'll try and put me in the frame for a variety of espionage crimes that I didn't commit. That's not going to be very helpful to any of us and it will just mean that I will not tell you anything. I didn't leak any secrets, full stop. You'll need to think of another sample."

"But we know that you had become a mole Mr. Elliott, Mallory Michaels contacted my colleague here before he was murdered."

"He may have contacted him, I've no reason to doubt your word, but if he did, he didn't have any proof because there isn't any. There's no point in trying to pressure me with such evidence-free rubbish. I just want the guarantees of immunity that I asked for, so please, let's stop wasting time."

Mr. One looked at Gus, his expression saying more than words could about his lack of belief in the Foreign Office man's reply. He said,

"We're busy people Mr. Elliott, as I'm sure you're aware and at the moment you're not giving us much of an incentive to stick around. Unless you can give us some reason to stay, we're going to have to say goodbye."

Elliott's eyes darted from Gus to Mr. One and back again. There was clearly some rapid recalculating of the strength of his bargaining position going on. He said,

"Tell me one thing that you want to know that isn't connected to the nonsense about my supposedly being a mole."

"The woman who was abducted when Michaels was murdered," Mr.

One said. "Tell us about her."

"OK. There's not a lot to tell. The psychopath told me that they hadn't expected anyone to be with Michaels when they ambushed him. She was a complete surprise. He could be quite indiscreet at times. I assume they've got her stashed away in one of their safe houses. It didn't sound like they'd killed her."

"And where exactly are these safe houses?"

"I've been to one when they were trying to force me into doing something I wouldn't. She may have been there, I don't know. They were upstairs when I arrived, so they may have been interrogating her up there before they came downstairs to speak to me. There was more than enough room to hold prisoners in that house."

"Where was this safe house?"

"No idea – I was blindfolded on the journey there and the journey back."

"What did your ears hear?"

"What?"

"Your ears Mr. Elliott, think hard about the sounds you heard en route. They could provide valuable clues as to what kinds of things were going on in the locality and that then gives us a starting point for a search."

"I see what you mean. Yes, I did notice something."

"Go on."

"Sorry gentlemen, that is premium information. You will need to pay the full price."

"Mr. Elliott, in the matter of a criminal abduction you are as much withholding information from the police as us. If you do not help us, we will inform them of that fact and that will add an additional charge to those already facing you. Do you want to spend the remaining best years of your life in jail?"

"You won't tell them any such thing – you have no choice but to pay the price I ask. You want to find this lady too badly. I can tell – don't forget, I'm an experienced negotiator."

"Well, I'm afraid that in this case you've misread the situation Mr. Elliott. Good afternoon."

Mr. One rose and indicated to Gus that he should follow suit. As they left the room Mr. One told the constable sitting outside that the prisoner could now be taken back to his cell. They stayed by the side of the door, pretending to discuss something in the file that they had taken for reference into the interrogation. The Foreign Office man was led past them and they studiously pretended not to notice or be interested in him. He didn't bat an eyelid or say a word and disappeared down the corridor in handcuffs, ready to be put back in his cell. Mr. One said,

"I didn't handle that as well as I could have done Augustus. I should have contrived to put the request for information about your cousin into a wider context, as a mere aside. He wouldn't then have realised how high a priority she is for us, perhaps. Now the cards are in his favour and he knows it. My little bit of psychological warfare, the goodbye and off we go into the sunset routine, didn't work. He's playing the same game and trying to pretend he's happy to leave things as they are."

"We could up the ante a little bit more yet, just to be sure that he's not going to give us that information without his shopping list of demands being met. I suspect he's extremely anxious that the KGB don't find out he's still alive. If you look closely at his wrists, you'll notice faint tell-tale marks of his having been tightly bound with wire that has cut deeply into the skin. Somewhere along the line he's been interrogated in a less than gentle manner by our Soviet friends and only kept alive for the purpose of some significant act of great potential advantage to them. He's done something that has suddenly ended his usefulness and they now see him as a dangerous liability and want him dead. Maybe we should threaten to let his former friends know that he's still in the land of the living and see how he reacts."

Mr. One nodded and began to pace up and down, very slowly, with a look of deep thoughtfulness on his face, a habit with which Gus was well familiar. After a couple of minutes he said,

"My mess old man, I need to sort it out. We'll do what you say, but leave the initial questioning to me. If it doesn't work out, I have a back-up strategy that will not come without cost, but we have a moral obligation to do all we can to free your cousin and that's that. We also need to know precisely what he's been up to with the Soviets and whether there's a need to put some patches over any holes that have been knocked through national security. There's no doubt he was the mole Michaels was looking for – from what he's told us, it's very clear that the KGB had him completely under their thumb prior to his escape."

Gus said,

"That all sounds good to me. Shall we go and ask the nice policeman if we can have our playmate back?"

Ten minutes later the little gathering was reassembled in the depressingly dingy interview room. The Foreign Office man said,

"Changed your minds then? I thought you would. I'll be happy to tell you what you want to know about the woman who's clearly of such high value to MI5, but only in return for the guarantees I requested."

Mr. One said,

"The only thing we have changed our minds about Mr. Elliott is whether or not we should give you a second chance. We know that at some stage you have been aggressively interrogated by your KGB friends – we can see the marks on your wrists – and we know that you are terrified that they will come after you if they discover that you are still alive. That is why part of the deal you were offering included our help in enabling you to vanish into a new identity. So, here's the deal we're prepared to offer you. Tell us everything we want to know, other than about your role as a mole, which you refuse to admit to, and we will not let the KGB know that their hit failed. As things stand, we won't even consider helping you with your demands for immunity from prosecution and a new identity because you're not prepared to tell us anything about the secrets you passed on to the Soviets. We could come to an arrangement over your role as a mole if you can demonstrate that you were put in a position where you felt you had absolutely no choice but to do what you were told. However, it seems that you're not prepared to admit to the slightest degree that you were a mole and that refusal rules such an arrangement out. So the deal we can give you is much smaller than the one we would offer if you were fully cooperative, but it does at least mean that we will not let the Soviets know that you are still very much alive and kicking. Reject the deal and we will pass on the news of your continuing good health to your former friends in the KGB."

Elliott laughed, a hollow, mirthless, frightened laugh. He said,

"Frankly, that's a worthless offer and you know it. It is irrelevant whether you tell the KGB or not. With my family name my face will be all over the newspapers if I go to trial and that in itself will sign my death warrant, irrespective of what you do or do not tell the Soviets. The people in the Soviet embassy whose job it is to read the UK press will pass on the news to all the wrong people and I will be pushing up daisies before the year is out. They'll get somebody into the prison to do the dirty work. I've seen at first hand how these people operate."

"We should be able to do something via a D-notice to prevent the trial details being published, particularly any that would identify you – we could do this because of your involvement in matters of national security – and, if you're convicted, we may be able to ensure that you're put in a safe cell in the most secure of prisons."

"And you may not. I'm sorry gentlemen but, if you'll pardon my French, you can shove your so-called deal up your proverbials."

"Well, on the basis of what you've just said, if you elect not to tell us you'll be sentencing yourself to death. You'll go to trial with no gagging measures in place – no D-notice or anything – and your face will be all over the news for the KGB to see. Just in case they don't see it, we'll pass them the word for good measure."

"So be it. I'd rather keep everything to myself than submit to such a mockery of a deal. If just one newspaper ignored a D-notice I'd be finished. I may be a dead duck walking, but I do at least have my pride. I think your interview, interrogation, whatever you choose to call it, is well and truly over. I'll just have to take my chances and see what happens. Death comes to us all at some stage, doesn't it? I'll just have to accept that mine will be arriving rather earlier than I'd anticipated."

Mr. One nodded grimly to Gus and they got up and walked out. As the constable handcuffed the prisoner and marched him out of the room, the two interrogators hid behind the open door of the room opposite, listening for any comments that the Foreign Office man might make when it appeared that they had left the building. They heard him say,

"Going back to London, are they? What an utter waste of time that was."

Gus said,

"That went well."

Angus grimaced and said,

"Had we more time we could break this fellow, but time is very much at a premium. My primary objective is getting your cousin back in one piece without having to pay the enormous price that Zaliatev will demand – and to do that as quickly as possible. If we bring our Foreign Office friend back for a third session, he'll know that we can't afford to wait more than a day and he'll just continue to try and sit it out until we give him what he wants. I said I had a fallback option with a considerable cost attached and I'll have to resort to that now. I'm not going to give the blighter everything he wants at one go though. He'll have to fight for every bit of his deal and deliver everything we want, otherwise I'll pull the plug on the whole thing and let him sink into the pit he belongs in. Let's go and tell them to bring the wretch back and get this thing over and done with."

When the Foreign Office man was brought back into the room, he had a wry grin on his face. From the dishevelled, depressed specimen that they'd encountered at the beginning of the interrogation, he had been transformed into a man who was beginning to think he could sense victory. He said,

"Let's cut to the chase and get this over with. You either grant my request for immunity and a vanishing act straight away or I ask to be taken back to the cells and that's the end of the matter entirely. All of my professional instincts tell me that you need the information about the woman immediately, so there's no point in trying to pretend otherwise gentlemen. If it helps matters along, I have a piece of truly big information to give you on another deeply serious matter, one that you will get from no other source and I will make the disclosure of that part of my side of the deal."

The Foreign Office man held his breath. He had made his play and it was a bluff that he hoped wouldn't be called. He couldn't afford to walk away entirely from the two people who were his only keys for getting out of his cell.

Mr. One said nothing for a full minute and sat there staring at him. Then he said,

"I need you to be absolutely clear about this. If anything you tell us this afternoon or on any other occasion turns out to be demonstrably false, we will consider ourselves released from any agreement we make with you. Is that understood?"

"That sounds perfectly reasonable."

"Good. In order to get the deal that you want you are going to have to deliver on a truly major scale and that deal will not be guaranteed until we are satisfied that you have done so. Do you understand that also?"

The Foreign Office man's heart was beating so fast it seemed that it was about to explode. The impossible was actually happening and it looked like he might be able to get part or all of the deal he was demanding. Despite his calm outward exterior, he was a bundle of nerves inside, terrified about the leap he was going to have to take in terms of confessing the information that he had passed on to the KGB. He was sure they would be demanding full disclosure of all of that and, if they promised that they were prepared to forego pursuit of a prosecution, he would have to take a risk, trust them and give them what they wanted. As long as the KGB's photograph of him participating in Michaels' murder didn't come to light, he was confident he could keep his involvement in that sorry episode to himself. He didn't want it to complicate his attempts to get a deal. If MI5 did discover that he had been present at the killing, however, his position could become very difficult and that possibility caused him some considerable anxiety. He could try and argue that he hadn't fired the fatal shots and had been forced to take part, but he had no idea how they would react to the news that he had been involved in the assassination of a superior. He was scared also that his trump card, a disclosure of 'truly big' information, may either turn out not to be big enough in their eyes, or something they already knew. He was terrified more than anything else by the possibility that, having promised him everything he'd asked for, they'd simply renege on the deal once he had given them what they needed. There was nothing he could do about the risk of this and he knew it. He had a gut feeling that, as an ex-army officer, Mr. One was someone who believed in the idea of a 'gentleman's code' and that he could appeal to that in order to make him stick to his side of the deal. He assumed that Gus was cut from the same cloth. He would just have to hope that his instincts were correct and keep up the super-confident act in order to try and carry the whole thing through. It was a strategy that at least offered him some hope of survival and a future, whereas before he could have hoped for neither of these things. Ever since he'd attempted to cover up his drunken killing of an innocent pedestrian years before, he'd been trying to avoid the consequences of his actions and now was no exception. He said,

"Yes, I understand that.

"In that case we will ensure that you are not prosecuted for either the bicycle theft or the attack on the gentleman currently in a coma under police guard. We can smooth the matter over regarding the theft by telling the police that you were pursuing a matter of national security at the time. That will also explain the gun that was found in your possession, something you forgot to mention. We will use the same explanation to ensure that assault and grievous bodily harm charges are not laid against you. We will make the charitable assumption that your spying activities for the Soviets were occasioned by severe pressure that you felt unable to resist. You will not be in a position to leak any further secrets because you will never again be employed by the British state in any capacity. With considerable reluctance we will take the rather unusual step of foregoing any pursuit of a prosecution for those activities. In return, we do expect you to give us the information we need concerning the KGB's method of recruitment, the pressures that it exerted on you and who your handlers were. We need you to abandon your pretence that you weren't a mole – something that it is now safe for you to do in light of my promise not to pursue a prosecution – and to provide us with the details of any information that you passed on to the KGB. We also need full details of what you say is 'truly big information' – and it had better be 'truly big' if we are to give you everything that you ask. Finally, if you cooperate fully in the way we require, we will furnish you with an alternative identity and arrange for your financial assets to transfer into the name of that identity via untraceable routes. We would suggest that you re-locate to a country where you are least likely to be noticed by KGB personnel."

"What guarantee do I have that all of these promises will be honoured?"

"The sensitive nature of what we are offering you means that nothing can be put in writing. I give you my personal guarantee as an officer and a gentleman."

The Foreign Office man was more relieved to hear those words than his interrogators could ever imagine, but he decided to press Mr. One a little more on his promise. He said,

"If you break your word and I end up being prosecuted I shall make a statement to the court about the way in which a deal was promised by MI5 but not delivered."

"I'm sure you would Mr. Elliott, but as my word is my bond you will not have to do that. But do remember the deal is two-way and you will have to make a very substantial delivery of information to us if we are to honour it – you have to deliver on your part before we will deliver on ours. Do you agree to the terms I am offering you?"

The Foreign Office man paused for a moment, a little frightened by the scale and risks of his part of the deal, but concluded that he would get nothing better. He said,

"I do."

Mr. One said,

"Good, now we are getting somewhere. If we could start with the information that is needed most urgently, you stated that you heard something on your trip to the safe house that may be useful in helping us locate it."

"That's correct. I heard the repeated rustling of paper."

There was a short pause.

"I do hope that you are not trying to take us for fools Mr. Elliott."

"It's what the rustling signifies that is important. The psychopath who was driving me there always wrote down the directions for anywhere out of the ordinary that he was taking me and kept them on his lap. I couldn't see what he was doing because of the blindfold on this occasion, but my ears told me that he was doing what he always does and referring to the directions as he drove along. He's nearly veered off the road more than once in the past through trying to read and drive at the same time. He'd always have a courtesy light switched on in the car at night so that he could read them. As the police now have him in custody, albeit still unconscious from what I understood from them yesterday, you should search his trouser pockets to see if he still has the directions. You could check his jacket pockets as well and if the directions are in neither of those items of clothing you should check the Bentley when you retrieve it. They might still be in the car."

Mr. One raised his eyebrows in surprise at the usefulness of the information and exchanged a relieved glance with Gus. He said,

"You have just done yourself a very big favour Mr. Elliott. If you will both excuse me for ten minutes I will phone through that information to the relevant people and they will get on to it straight away."

He was in fact gone for forty-five minutes, during which Gus carried on the interrogation. When Mr. One returned he said,

"I've just been told your Bentley has been found Mr. Elliott, although you won't be very pleased about the location of the discovery. The KGB officer who stole it appears to have driven it to the edge of a deserted pier and then pushed it into the Thames."

"Oh. The upholstery and carpets will smell forever and a day. I think I will be leaving that behind when I vanish into my new identity."

"Indeed, you would need to dispose of it anyway. Even if we gave it a new number plate for you and had it re-sprayed, it is too like the old you and would make you that bit more noticeable wherever you choose to go."

"If it could be cleaned and then sold, I would appreciate that. Presumably the proceeds will be forwarded to my new identity?"

Mr. One looked decidedly impatient at this latest request but kept his cool. He said,

"I will see if that can be arranged at an appropriate moment, but let's not get ahead of ourselves – you do need to deliver everything we ask of you before we can get into that kind of detail. Now, to more pressing matters. The information that you've just given us was exactly the kind of thing that we need and if our discussions continue in a similar vein, you can be assured that we will honour our deal with you. We will be leaving within the next hour or so, but at seven o'clock this evening you will be released into MI5's custody and a car will pick you up and take you to a safe house. Our people will interrogate you for several days until we are sure that we have all the information that we need. After that, if I am satisfied with the results, arrangements for your new identity will be made and you can look forward to a new life."

"Are all charges to be dropped as you promised?"

"Yes, but again on condition that you cooperate fully. I have just spent half an hour on the phone to the chief constable so that the necessary arrangements can begin to be put in place. The needs of national security can move mountains when necessary. Should you not deliver on your side of the deal the mountains will be moved back again."

The Foreign Office man looked both relieved and edgy, a combination of emotions that was occasioned by his deep fear of the KGB finding out that he was still alive. Mr. One turned to Gus and said,

"What are the results of the interrogation that you continued while I was out of the room?"

"Quite promising, although the safe house team will want to delve rather more deeply into the issues we've discussed so far. Mr. Elliott's KGB codename was Jacob. At various times he has been under the direct control of Colonel Zaliatev, with several underlings keeping a close eye on him as well, including the gentleman currently in a coma and Irina Lashkanocova. He was required to provide regular summaries of key information passing between our Washington embassy and the Foreign Office, but that was the relatively mundane part of his role. He was told that he would be given a major task for which he was especially qualified, given his contacts in the US administration. That turned out to be a requirement to act as a credible supplier of the forged documents we found at his house to his US contacts. It was hoped that the documents would cause a major rupture in US-UK relations. It was at that point that he attempted to flee, but was intercepted by Lashkanocova. He'd tried to escape from the Soviets' grip once before and had been thrown into a KGB interrogation cell and warned that if he tried it a second time he would be executed. Lashkanocova drove him to a disused mineshaft to kill him, but made a botch of it and he managed to escape, at which point he fell into the hands of the police."

Mr. One said,

"That's a useful start. The team that will interrogate you over the next few days will want to know a lot more about these things Mr. Elliott, but while I'm here I'd like to know how you fell under the control of Colonel Zaliatev. I assume he found some reason to blackmail you."

"That is a not unreasonable assumption."

"Would you please tell me what that issue was and how he became aware of it?"

"If you don't mind, I would prefer to keep the precise nature of the issue confidential, but I can give you every other detail so that you can see fully how he operated in this instance. When I was much younger, I did something by accident that was of a deeply serious nature in its consequences. It was witnessed by an individual whom I paid off to keep it secret. The individual concerned did not turn out to be trustworthy and at a later stage sold the information to the Soviets. I should add that my actions did not in any way relate to national security. Zaliatev then used that information to force me to do the various things that I described to your colleague."

There was a knock at the door and a sergeant entered with the news that there was an urgent phone call for Mr. One, who hurried off to deal with it. When he returned, he was in full military march mode, quickly grabbing his coat off the back of his chair and saying,

"I'm delighted to say that the directions you told us about have been found. We will have to leave you Mr. Elliott, but as I promised, you will be released at seven o'clock this evening and taken to a safe house. Thank you for your cooperation and I will deliver on my promises as soon as you have satisfied our interrogators that they have all that we need to know. Good afternoon."

With that he swept out of the room with Gus hot on his heels. As they hurried down the corridor Gus said,

"Do you actually intend to keep your promises, Angus? It's highly unusual to agree to wipe clean such a dirty slate."

"The circumstances are highly unusual, given the need to retrieve your cousin from Zaliatev's grasp as well as deal with all of the other issues, so my preparedness to promise him things is far greater than would normally be the case. If I didn't honour my promises, what would you think of me, Augustus?"

"Irrespective of Elliott's gross idiocy in getting himself into so many messes, I would lose all respect for you and cease working for MI5. If our word on such matters cannot be trusted we are no better than our friends in the KGB."

"Indeed, my thoughts exactly. Murky though our business may be, there is still a need to uphold basic standards. The man has given us the best lead we've had so far on the possible location of Miss Emersly and we need to move quickly. I've organised a team to come down from London and meet up with us. All being well, if the safe house is indeed where she's being held, we should have your cousin in our custody by the end of today."

CHAPTER THIRTEEN

Julia was fast asleep in bed when her guard came in. He shook her roughly and told her to stand up. She did so slowly, not simply because her injured ankle was still sore, but as a result of her determination to show defiance to her captors whenever the opportunity presented itself. The guard took a ring of keys off his trouser belt and bent down to unlock the chain around her good ankle. Her eyes wandered onto the heavy washing jug that sat in the ceramic bowl on her battered old bedside table. Normally it had been kept on the dressing table on the other side of the room, out of her reach except for when she was unchained to have a daily wash. It had found its way onto her bedside table purely by accident during the morning. The guard had come into the room to take a photograph of her to be used at the meeting with Gus. He had given her a newspaper to hold to show the date on which she could be proved to be alive. He'd also been told to make her surroundings look as homely as possible to suggest that she was being well looked after. The room was so bare that it was difficult for him to find anything 'homely'. The bright red blanket on her bed was at least cheery looking and he had been given a state-of-the-art colour print film to provide a first-class photograph, so he had made her sit on the bed in order to fill the picture with what little vivid colour there was available. The only other homely items in the room were the jug and washbasin, so he had moved those items onto her bedside table to make it clear that she had access to bathing facilities. He'd absentmindedly left them there afterwards. Seeing her opportunity now, she had no hesitation. She grabbed the stoneware jug and gave him a cracking blow on the head with it before he had time to react. He slumped onto the floor at her feet. The key was already in the padlock that held the chain round her ankle, so she simply bent down, turned it and released her foot. She then tore off his trouser belt and used it to tie his hands behind his back. To make it even harder for him to try and come after her, she pulled his trousers down around his ankles and then bound them round and round with the chain before locking the padlock.

After having grabbed his key ring and his car key, she limped over to the open door and proceeded downstairs. It was going to be a challenge to drive his car with such a swollen ankle and quite daunting, given that she had never before driven in her life, but if she could just make it to the nearest phone box and ring for the police that would be enough. She could then stay where she was until they came to pick her up and arrest her guard. She was in the middle of imagining being able to go back to her apartment in London and be reunited with all of her friends when a female voice from inside the kitchen downstairs shouted something in Russian. Her blood froze. She had nothing with her that she could use as a weapon and had had no idea that another KGB officer had arrived while she'd been asleep. She attempted to turn around and hobble back upstairs to see if the guard had his gun on him, but the woman appeared at the bottom of the stairs. It was Irina Lashkanocova, her head covered by a hood as required by the Colonel. Seeing that Julia was unaccompanied she pulled out her gun and told her to stop where she was. She said,

"Where's your guard? He was supposed to bring you downstairs. What have you done to him?"

Julia was terrified, but decided that saying nothing was the best policy. Irina said,

"Move, upstairs, back into your room, let us see just what it is you've been up to."

When they entered the bedroom Irina cursed in Russian and told her to untie the guard and remove the chains and padlock. He was in the process of coming round. As he began to stir, Irina walked over to Julia, stared acidly at her through the eye slits in her hood, then knocked her unconscious with a single blow. She wasn't going to risk the same kind of surprise that Jacob had sprung on her and wanted this troublesome prisoner very firmly neutralised.

Less than twenty miles away, two cars and a van were speeding towards the safe house. The van contained what Mr. One liked to refer to as his critical operations support team, or COST for short. Not everything was going to plan, however. They suddenly found themselves held up by a flock of sheep. The flock had spotted a half open field gate, one that ramblers had not closed properly earlier in the day. The animals had played follow my leader out onto the road and were milling around, with some chewing the grass on the verges while others gathered confusedly in the centre of the single carriageway. Gus found himself part of an impromptu gang of shepherds as they frantically manoeuvred the animals out of the way. As they piled back into the vehicles Mr. One said,

"That's all we need. We're supposed to be on a high-speed rescue mission and we find ourselves in a scene from the dratted Archers."

As soon as the safe house came into view all the vehicles turned their headlights off. They parked twenty yards away from the entrance. There only appeared to be one light on in the house, in an upstairs room. The six-man core of the critical operations support team split into three sub-teams of two, with one pair going to the front door, one to the rear and the other two standing by the windows at either side of the front door. An excellent but rather incongruous imitation of an owl followed, at which point all hell broke loose. The front and rear teams burst into the house simultaneously and the pair by the windows followed the front team in, covering them from behind. The two-man crew from the second car had hidden themselves either side of the entrance gate while Gus and Mr. One stood watching from the side of the road, guns at the ready. The COST members shouted to each other as they moved through the house and then suddenly there was silence. A couple of minutes later they filed out through the front door and Gus and Mr. One went over to enquire what they'd found. The team leader said,

"The birds have flown I'm afraid. There's not a sign of anybody and there are no vehicles front or rear. We'll check the grounds to make sure there are no outhouses where anybody could be imprisoned, no underground facilities, tunnels etc. You never know with the KGB."

Gus and Mr. One went into the house to investigate. As they looked around the kitchen Gus said,

"The kettle's still warm, there's a piece of half-eaten fresh toast on the plate over there and today's newspaper is in the waste bin. There's been somebody here today and certainly up until a few minutes ago. Had it not been for those blasted sheep we might have caught them in time. Shall we have a look upstairs?"

They hurried up the polished wooden staircase and entered the first room they came to. Gus said,

"This is where they've been keeping her, this is the one we saw from outside with the light on. That looks like an ankle chain. It looks like there's been some kind of a scuffle – put all of the broken pieces of stoneware on the floor together and you'd get a jug. It must have weighed a ton."

"It looks like your cousin must have put up some kind of resistance before being taken away."

"That would be par for the course, she's a very feisty lady."

"I wonder why they left the light on – do you think they might intend

144

bringing her back after she's been wherever they've taken her, or whether someone from the KGB will be coming back to stay here until the next prisoner arrives?"

"I suspect that they left in a great hurry and simply forgot to turn it off. You could leave an operative hiding in situ for a day or two just in case somebody does return, but I suspect they're worried that their man in the hospital might recover and talk and have taken pre-emptive action by moving Julia elsewhere. Either that, or we've got a leak somewhere along the line and they've been forewarned that we were on the way. My gut feeling is that they've no intention of returning. This house will be sold as a result of it being no longer possible to guarantee its security."

Mr. One nodded and they began to search the room to see if Julia had managed to leave any clues as to where she might be taken. After ten minutes of forensically close investigation Gus said,

"Good old Julia. She was here alright. She's simply written her Christian name to minimise the chances of her handiwork being spotted by her captors, but she's left it for us to see. There's nothing else though, no clues that might help us."

He showed Mr. One where her name was faintly scrawled onto the paintwork behind the bedhead.

Mr. One said,

"Yes, I see. At least that's something. Other than that, it looks like she's vanished into thin air old chap. Tiresome as it is, we need to start from scratch and try and find out where they are most likely to have moved her. I think I need to have another chat with our Foreign Office friend and see if he can remember any conversation he had or overheard that might provide a clue as to where additional safe houses might be."

"What about my meeting with the KGB tomorrow – are you still happy for that to go ahead?"

"Yes, continue with that as if nothing had happened and make no mention of our visit here. I'll conduct a further interrogation of Mr. Elliott-Jacob first thing tomorrow morning. We'll speak when you get back from your meeting with the Colonel. If I find out anything of use it would be ideal if I could act on it while he and his cronies are tied up with you. Keep him talking for as long as you can."

Jacob had been moved to a safe house in Margate. Mr. One arrived at six-thirty the following morning. The room that was used for interrogations had a spectacular view of the sea, although it was too early for it to be visible. Some of MI5's more rough and ready interrogators had used the view to remind uncooperative individuals of one of the hazards of the seaside – the fact that careless people ran the risk of falling into the water and drowning. Mr. One got straight down to business.

"The information you gave us about the piece of paper with the directions on it was excellent. It's not often that we get a KGB operative who is stupid enough to leave such things on his person. Unfortunately, the woman we were looking for had been moved on by the time we got to the location. I'd like you to think back very hard through your time with these people to see if you at any time overheard even the slightest clue as to where other safe houses might be located."

Jacob nodded, thought for a couple of minutes and then said,

"There was nothing in what any of them said that suggested the location of other safe houses. They were quite careful in that regard. But there is something that's been bugging me off and on. When my interrogation by Zaliatev finished I was drugged and brought back to England. I don't know what it was they used, but I have vague, blurry memories of coming round every now and again before being given another injection and sent back to sleep. When I finally woke up properly, I was in my own bed at home. But I have a recurring memory of waking up somewhere before that, somewhere where I think I could hear a man speaking in English. The problem is it's pretty much of a dream-like memory. I remember a face appearing above me a little while after I heard the voice and then my consciousness fading again. They must have given me another dose of the drug."

"If the individual who was speaking English was the man who would become your chauffeur-guard, then you may well have been in a holding location from where he picked you up for the final leg of your journey back home. It would make sense if that was another safe house, probably located somewhere in the countryside, like the last one, to minimise the chances of such covert transfers of custody being observed. Was there anything else that you remember hearing other than the voice, something that might give us even the faintest clue as to a possible location?"

Jacob thought deeply for a minute or two. He said,

"It's all so hazy, but I do have a vague memory of something like the noise of an aircraft's engines. If it was a plane, it must have been quite low because I think it drowned out the Englishman's voice in the room. I just have this blurry and uncertain memory of some kind of plane-like roar. Is that of any use?"

"That could well be of enormous use. It makes sense for the KGB to have a safe house near to an airport that they use for special operations, such as your return to England. They probably hired a private plane to bring you back and then removed you in a crate or some such to avoid detection. If I was to hazard a guess, I would think we may be looking for a house in the countryside within a short distance from Blackbushe Airport in Hampshire. We've noticed KGB activity there before and it takes private aircraft as well as standard airline business. I suspect your vaguely remembered episode may well have been real and not a dream. We'll work out a search radius based on your description of the level of noise from the aircraft and start hunting within it. Well done Mr. Elliott, you may well have solved the puzzle for us."

Simultaneously, in the safe house in question, Julia was just coming round after being out stone cold for hours. Initially, everything was blurred and she had a violent headache. As her vision cleared and she tried to register her new surroundings, she heard the scrape of a chair and realised there was a large, hooded guard sitting opposite her bed. As she stared blinkingly at him, he got up and waddled over to the open door, shouting something in Russian to unseen companions. A clatter of shoes ascending a bare wooden staircase told her that she had visitors on the way. Moments later Irina burst into the room, followed by a second hefty guard. Both were hooded. She checked Julia's pulse and then, satisfied with what she found, grabbed her chin in her hand and yanked her head round so that she was looking directly into her eyes. She said,

"If you weren't such a tradeable commodity, you'd be dead by now after what you did yesterday. But if you try any more funny business I will hurt you really badly and you will only be available for return as damaged goods. Do you understand?"

Julia pretended to pass out rather than give her bullying companion the satisfaction of a reply. Irina slapped her hard across her face, forcing her eyes open with shock.

"Don't try and play dead with me you over-privileged little bitch. Let me introduce you to your new friends. Instead of one guard as before, you now have two and they have very short tempers and big muscles. You've lost the right to a room with a view because of your behaviour, so you'll no longer know when it's dark or light outside and you will never hear the little tweety birds for the rest of your captivity. Whenever you are unchained for the purposes of washing, the guard unchaining you will be accompanied by a second guard, with a gun trained on your head. You will be fed enough to keep you alive, but no more. You've lost the right to anything fancy. What a shame for someone who has been used to having so much – no more fine tea and cakes from Fortnum and Mason for you, my lady. You'll no doubt be keeping your fingers crossed that the negotiating parties will agree terms for your release, while I'll be keeping mine crossed that they won't. If the parties agree we will hand you over to the KGB who will hand you to the British."

"I thought you were the KGB."

"Well you thought wrong," Irina lied. "They will pay us for you if the British will give them what they want in return. You are the pig we are trying to sell on the street market, you are no more than that to us. If the deal falls through it will be my personal delight to execute you – like a pig. I think that's everything – is there anything else you would like to ask me? No? How disappointing. Do have a lovely time during the remainder of your stay with us."

Irina nodded to the guards and they left the room. Beneath her hood she smiled with her characteristic psychopathic false sweetness, flicked out the light and locked the door behind her.

Julia shouted a loud curse after them. As her splitting headache kicked her thoughts in all directions, she forced them to focus on a single, simple determination. She would survive, whatever they threw at her.

The story of why she'd been moved to her new destination was a classic case of incompetence in the collection of intelligence. In the morning of the previous day, the KGB spy who'd been sent to keep an eye on the Dogsbody situation at the hospital overheard a conversation that alarmed him. Dogsbody was being treated in a small ward with two other seriously injured patients in it. There was no way the KGB man could get into the ward because, at MI5's request, the police had increased the number of officers stationed outside it to two. He'd disguised himself as a hospital porter so that he would have a credible excuse for passing regularly by the ward, pushing various pieces of medical equipment. As he was going past during the mid-morning, two consultants came out of the ward in deep conversation and started to walk in front of the trolley he was pushing. He heard one of them say that,

"It's looking much better for him now. He's showing signs of brain function that are quite promising. If he continues with this rate of progress we may well be able to get him talking again soon. Then it's a matter of seeing how much he can remember."

The conversation had sent the spy scuttling away to the nearest public telephone box that he could find, from which he sent a coded message that would reach Zaliatev within twenty minutes. It was on the basis of that message that the Colonel decided to close down the safe house that Dogsbody knew about in case he gave away its location, should MI5 soon be able to interrogate him. The irony was that the medics had been talking about an entirely different patient. Dogsbody remained as sealed in his coma as before.

Unbeknown to Zaliatev, the hunt for the new safe house was already underway by the mid-morning of the next day. Mr. One had rapidly assembled his critical operations support team to search within the radius suggested by Jacob's new information and they began sweeping through it, looking for isolated buildings out in the country that might fit the bill. They were systematic in their use of local knowledge, questioning farmers and others liable to be out and about in the countryside enough to pick up on such things, to see whether they'd noticed any dwellings where the owners or tenants seemed to keep themselves to themselves, or whether they'd noticed any unusual comings and goings in the area. As in many such exercises, initially there were dead ends and time-consuming red herrings to follow up, with little in the way of real progress.

Things seemed to look up at around one o'clock when an elderly farmer was sure that he'd seen precisely what they were looking for behind a clump of trees at the end of the country lane bordering his land. The critical operations support team moved in quickly and within fifteen minutes of them having been told of the situation regarding the house behind the trees they had it under their full control. The lonely old woman who lived there made them all a nice cup of tea and then they all left, with their tails between their legs. Mr. One instructed them to be rather more mindful of the need to do a proper reconnaissance of a property before next deciding to move in.

By three o'clock in the afternoon they'd nearly worked their way around half of the search radius and Mr. One was becoming pessimistic. Then a farmer told one of the search teams about a cottage that he'd rented on a long-term basis to what he'd been told was a Swiss lawyer and his family who'd wanted it as an English holiday retreat. It was situated half a mile away from the farm, on a rarely used track and the family had requested complete privacy. The cottage was hidden from view by trees and the rent was paid every month directly into his bank account.

A reconnaissance team was sent to check it out discreetly. After half an hour they reported back that there appeared to be two extremely burly males in the house and a van and a car parked outside it. One of the males had been heard shouting something to the other in what sounded like Russian while outside the cottage. Despite speaking the language, the team leader hadn't been able to make out what was being said because the words were soon drowned out by a low flying aircraft. The noise of the plane very much suggested that, like the location Jacob had described, the cottage was directly under a flight path from the nearby airfield. That clinched it. Mr. One gave the order for the COST operatives to move in as soon as darkness fell. Until then they were to remain concealed from view.

At around four in the afternoon a woman came out of the house, got into the car and drove off down the track. A car was despatched to follow her when she turned onto the country lane at the end. She'd spotted the tail within less than a minute and pressed the accelerator hard down onto the floor. She left her pursuers far behind and used her advantage to swing the car through an open farm gate and hide it behind the wall. Once they had gone flying past, she drove out onto the road again and, seeing their tail lights disappearing into the distance straight ahead, took the first left turn that she came to and headed at speed to a village signposted as being half a mile away. When she got there, she found that there was a telephone box opposite the pub. She stopped to call the cottage guards and warn them that British Counter-Espionage appeared to be onto them. Having left detailed instructions on what to do, Irina jumped back in the car, turned round and headed back towards the cottage.

The episode with Jacob had very nearly been the end of her career. She was terrified now that she was about to lose her prisoner to the British, together with the two guards and that would most certainly buy her ticket back to Moscow. It would result in a demotion so far down the ranks that she may well be wielding a lavatory brush instead of a pistol by the end of the week.

When she neared the cottage she turned off her engine and headlights and, taking advantage of the downward incline of the track, coasted silently along for fifty yards or so. She parked the vehicle on the grass verge at the side of the track, about eighty yards from the cottage whose lights she could now see, ready for a quick getaway should she survive what was to follow. She opened the car boot quietly and removed a sub-machine gun which was ready loaded with ammunition. She took off her leather soled shoes and replaced them with soft-soled canvas shoes to facilitate silent movement. She then advanced stealthily towards the cottage, making full use of the cover of hedges and trees as she did so. She managed to get within twenty yards of the building without being spotted and was close enough to the MI5 team to hear them whispering. The last of dusk had now faded and the order was given for the critical operations support team to advance on the building. She could just see one or two of them as they were momentarily illuminated by the light from the cottage windows. When she'd rung earlier, she'd instructed the guards to switch on every light in the building so that she could see what was going on outside. The COST had almost reached the front door when Irina opened fire, spraying the air with a hail of bullets. The highly experienced team took immediate evasive action and only one was injured, but she had achieved her goal of creating sufficient deadly distraction for the escape plan to be carried through. She had provided cover for the guards to exit via a window at the side of the building and head off across the fields without being spotted. The burliest of the two had Julia slung over his shoulders as if she were as light as a blanket. As return fire cracked and rippled towards her, Irina jumped through a gap in the hedge that ran parallel to the track and sprinted along the field until she reached another gap just in front of her car. Peering back down the track, she could see that the cottage was now illuminated by multiple spotlights and could hear all of the commotion that told her that MI5 had burst in and were in the process of finding that, yet again, the birds had flown. Seeing no-one coming after her, she jumped in the car, swung it round and sped off down the track and back onto the lane at the end, unnoticed in all of the confusion. She turned left again at the same junction as before and then carried on until she reached the village from which she'd rung with her warning earlier. The guards had been told to cut across the fields until they got to where she was waiting, outside the telephone box. They couldn't miss the location of the village, given that it was the only street-lit settlement visible from the cottage.

As it hurried across the fields towards the village, the little escape party was not faring quite as well as Irina had hoped. The guards and their prisoner slipped and slid into a very full drainage ditch only three minutes into their flight and emerged soaked and frozen stiff. Unable to use any torches for fear of revealing their position, they tripped over everything that they possibly could and the more they ploughed on, the less lightweight Julia became for the increasingly weary hulk who was carrying her. Then the really bad news came. Their pursuers had brought dogs with them and these were now on their case. They could hear their barking as the animals hurtled forwards on their trail and they could see an array of flashlights belonging to the accompanying search party.

As her head bounced along on the back of her rapidly tiring captor, Julia allowed herself the luxury of hope. She smiled, a weary, battered shadow of her normal smile, but a smile nonetheless. Playfully, she waved her handcuffed hands welcomingly at the dogs she couldn't yet see, but could hear getting closer and closer and closer …

Not everyone was quite as welcoming of the pursuers however. Hearing all of the commotion, Irina reloaded the machine gun and headed out into the fields behind the village, determined to pin down the MI5 team long enough for the escape party to make it to her car. She was driven by a deep inner frustration and fury that things could go so wrong and was determined to fight as if she were five instead of one. As she stood ready for action on what she presumed to be muddy ground, her nose was offended considerably by an unappealing scent rising up from beneath her feet. Her fiery mood was not improved in the slightest when she realised that she was standing on an extremely large and malodorous cow pat.

The English countryside, it seemed, had made its own comment on titanic clashes between civilisations and ideologies.

CHAPTER FOURTEEN

Gus arrived at Lesnes Abbey ruins fifteen minutes before he was due to meet the as yet unnamed KGB negotiator. He had come with a fully loaded gun and an expectation that anything might happen. As he entered the abbey grounds, he noted half a dozen goons stationed at various strategic points. That told him straight away that he would be meeting Zaliatev himself. It was a quiet time of day in a quiet time of the year as far as visitors to the site were concerned and other than himself and the Colonel's minders, he couldn't see anyone else. He walked casually among the ruins, pretending to take an interest in various of the few remaining walls and ground stones. None of the minders acknowledged his presence or seemed interested in giving him a clue as to where Zaliatev might be, so he assumed it was intended to be something akin to a treasure hunt – find the Colonel and win a prize, a chance to talk about the fate of Julia. He decided that it would be a process of elimination – behind which of the walls would he find the fabled master spy, unless, of course, the great man hadn't yet arrived. He walked through a small gateway in one of the few substantial stretches of ancient stone and there he was, the Colonel, seated on a bench, watching a couple of crows as they hopped and cawed their way across the grass, hunting for things that were entirely their secret. He looked across at Gus and the two men contemplated each other in silence like gunfighters from an old Hollywood cowboy movie, waiting to see who would draw first. It was the Colonel who made the first move.

"Mr. Benedict, how nice of you to come. I have heard so much about you. It is my very great pleasure to meet such an English gentleman. Will you join me on this very basic but quite comfortable bench? Its austerity seems quite in harmony with the monastic surroundings."

Gus smiled wryly and nodded, sitting at the other end of the bench to his host. He said,

"I'm honoured to have the company of the most enigmatic figure in Soviet espionage. I suspect that you know rather more about me than I of you."

The Colonel laughed softly.

"You may well be right, but this is an opportunity for you to even the score. I have to confess, if everything that is in our files about you is true then I find you as enigmatic as you find me. Perhaps we can use this conversation to see if we can solve the puzzle that each presents to the other?"

"What is it about me that you find so puzzling?" Gus asked.

"It is more a question of what I don't find puzzling, there is so much that is unusual. You are not at all what I would expect to see in a British gentleman spy. On the surface you have all the usual attributes, the wealthy family background, the privilege, the public school education and the Oxbridge university pedigree. All of that is what I would expect to find. But then there is all of the money that you give to the English poor, the people in your grand bourgeois state who do not benefit from the capitalist economy, or that feeble little attempt at making British society less lop-sided, what you people call the welfare state. And it is not a small amount of money that you give. Your little cover operation that conceals your MI5 identity, your private detective agency for the very rich – that is the original goose that laid the golden egg and much of that egg you freely give away to those who need it. You seem to me to be in the tradition of the great benefactors of your country, the Robert Owens and the Titus Salts. You see, I have taken the trouble to read the history books of this old piratical society of yours and to look for the good within it as well as the bad, for traditions and beliefs that we wicked communists might be able to exploit. And were I looking for someone who was the inheritor of these charitable traditions, someone whom it might be possible to lure into support of the communist cause, then that someone would be you. Yet here you are, an intelligence operative of the British state, fighting the good fight for capitalism against the egalitarian doctrine of communism that is much closer to your personal beliefs than capitalism. That is the first great puzzle that I see. How do you explain yourself?"

Gus smiled mischievously, saying,

"If you are talking of strange things, Colonel, then the fact that you sound like my mother is the strangest thing of all."

"The very grand Lady Honoria – do I really sound like her?"

"She already thinks I'm a communist."

"And what are you, where do these contradictory beliefs and loyalties of yours sit within the bitter struggles between the great ideologies of east and west?"

"They sit in a place of their own – rejecting the way that the individual is swallowed up into a collective anonymity within Soviet communism and rejecting equally firmly the way that, under western capitalism, the right to individual wealth can be a means of collecting into very few pockets the money that is needed to enable everyone within society to have a decent and humane standard of living. There are no 'isms' that fully represent my views, Colonel. As I have said to my mother and others, I am interested only in fairness. You can call me a philanthropist if you like, but not a communist or a capitalist."

"How very unusual and how frank an answer. So, if you are entirely unconvertible to communism, do you think I might be convertible to your form of capitalism? Because, like it or not, it is the capitalist system that you rely on to provide the money that you then redistribute to the poor."

"It depends on precisely what it is that you believe, Colonel. I am different underneath to what I appear on the surface, as you have said yourself. Is the same true of you?"

Zaliatev smiled.

"I do enjoy playing chess Mr. Benedict and I suspect that you are an excellent player yourself. My answer is the answer of all good communists and that is that I believe everything that the Party believes in and that I will fight for it with my dying breath."

"That is the Party line and I would expect a KGB man to say no less. But underneath all of that, within the privacy of your head, does a man of your intelligence really believe all of the robotic drivel that Party apparatchiks and bureaucrats churn out?"

The Colonel smiled wryly.

"As a good communist I believe unreservedly in the collective wisdom of the people, as represented by those who have been elected to govern our great communist society."

"Your words say one thing and your face another, Colonel."

"Really? Perhaps there are several layers of meaning in everything we communicate to each other Mr. Benedict, some real perhaps, some imaginary. I would argue that what you are saying about me is imaginary while you would say it is real. In this out of the way place, this historic spot where confessions of doubt, heresy and wrongdoing were heard by monks and priests so very long ago, who is to say which of us is right and which wrong? Perhaps we might both be right."

Interesting though this preamble to their negotiations might be, Gus's main priority was Julia and part of him was anxious to start discussing her straightaway. However, he was mindful also of Mr. One's instruction to spin out the meeting for as long as possible to help give him time to try and launch a rescue mission while the Colonel's attention was otherwise engaged. The Colonel seemed willing to oblige with his curious anxiety for a game of intellectual chess, so Gus decided it was his duty to comply with Mr. One's request. He said,

"Tell me, Colonel, if the Soviet Union had been the product of a right-wing revolution instead of one on the left, would you still be in the same job?"

"By indirections you would like to find directions out Mr. Benedict, how very Shakespearean of you. I suspect it would depend on whom I looked up to most, the Soviet Union or a particular political ideology. If it were the Soviet Union, then I would serve whoever most seemed to protect its interests at any particular time. I cannot imagine a situation in which the Communist Party would not protect them, can you?"

"By the smile on your face, Colonel, I might imagine that you could, but that you would only tell me so through your facial expression and your tone of voice, not by your words."

"That is indeed a possibility, but then I might smile at everyone, even at the point of their deaths, and I might delight in creating the impression of ambiguities where none in fact exist. So perhaps you've uncovered my secret, or perhaps you know nothing at all. So much of life is an illusion Mr. Benedict, so much an imagining or simply a lie. Who knows for sure what anything is, or what anyone really believes? That is a neat summary of some of your Western philosophers is it not? Or maybe my humble origins make me ill-equipped to interpret what they say. But let me turn the tables – a much more interesting question than what beliefs drive me is what drives the good Mr. Benedict? What is it that persuades this rich Englishman to be so generous towards his fellow men? If he is not a communist or a socialist, is he driven instead by some form of religious belief? Is he trying to save his immortal soul through acts of great charity? The evidence would suggest not. Our research has been so meticulous that if he had been even an occasional churchgoer that fact would have been picked up. So could it be that this puzzling character simply cares about his fellow human beings and helps them out of sheer generosity? What a fine fellow he would be if this were true, someone that a simple follower of a great ideology like me could admire and even feel inspired by. Look at him, he does no small amount of what pages and pages of our doctrine say should be done with the force of the state to back it up, and he does it without anybody or anything in heaven or on earth to tell him this is what he should or must be doing. He does it entirely of his own volition. If the world were full of Mr. Benedicts, all like him, what a truly wonderful place it would be."

Gus smiled and said,

"With such heavy irony to precede it I can't wait to see what the punchline is, Colonel. You're going to tell me that in reality I'm a champagne socialist I suspect, given that I still hang on to the good life for myself as well as engaging in what you call 'generosity' towards others."

"I might call a man who tried to conceal such an apparent contradiction in his behaviours some kind of hypocrite or whatever if I saw evidence that he was publicising his generosity for some advantage while living the high life in private. But Mr. Benedict doesn't publicise his benevolence at all. On the contrary, he hides his light under the proverbial bushel. So I would say simply that he likes to be generous whilst also enjoying some of the riches he is sharing. A not entirely perfect but an honest man perhaps. Such a man would be seen as quite admirable by many I think, in a world where there is so little to truly admire. Indeed, you have been quite frustrating for me Mr. Benedict. I've looked very hard for weaknesses that I hoped I might be able to exploit, things that might enable me to compromise and neutralise you and stop you from getting in the way of some of Moscow's activities which you most annoyingly have helped frustrate over the last year or two, but I have found none. None until now that is. Then I discovered that someone very dear to you had been abducted and that I was in a position to help you free her. I realised then that this great generosity of spirit that you have could be used against you, because you would pay a very great price to help this poor imprisoned soul, this traditional damsel in distress, a woman who could even lose her life if I don't use my considerable power to intervene on your behalf. So that is the purpose of this little meeting today, to ask if you would like me to help you free your dear Julia. I have been allowed to meet her by her abductors by the way."

Given that Gus was by now aware that the KGB were the real abductors as a result of the information provided by Jacob, the Colonel's fictional version of events was wasted on him. However, he decided that he would have to play along with it if he was not to reveal the fact that Jacob/Elliott was still alive and kicking and in MI5's custody. He said,

"And who might these mysterious abductors be?"

"Well, I suppose we must go through these formalities. It's a bit like a Viennese waltz, isn't it? We are almost dancing partners. You ask me a question you know I will be unable to answer without putting your cousin's life at risk. I tell you that I am unable to answer it. You say that you need to see some proof that the party under discussion is alive. I show you it – here it is, a photograph taken yesterday of your beloved Julia in the rudest of health. You ask me what price is being asked for her return. I tell you. You are non-committal and say you will need to discuss it with your superiors. I say that's fine, but set you a deadline for an answer. You then send me your answer, either indirectly or in person and, if it is favourable, we negotiate the time and place of the release and make the arrangements for you to pay the price that is being asked."

"You've given me the photograph, Colonel, but you haven't given me the price."

"It is because of the price that I asked you to sit down Mr. Benedict. I wouldn't like you to fall over when you see its magnitude. And it is because there are in fact two prices that I asked you to come alone."

"If the price is too high, Colonel, then much as I might love my cousin, my superiors will not pay it. That's my next dance move. Now it's time for yours."

"The first price that I'm asking is only moderately burdensome. Your people caught two of ours in a neat little trap two months ago and you have them squirreled away somewhere for interrogation. You will know one of them as Sergei Ramalov. We need him back urgently for reasons that needn't concern British intelligence and the formal price for your cousin's release is his return to us. That is the price that you will convey to your superiors."

"And the second price, presumably that is one that I don't convey to my superiors?"

"Precisely so. The second price is the return of our agent that you have in hospital custody. I'm told that he is improving and may soon be able to speak. You will understand that I need him back before that happens. Your superiors will not be prepared to meet both these wishes, so you must meet this second wish for me without their knowledge."

"You know I can't do that, so I'm puzzled as to why you're even asking."

"I'm asking because I know that you can in fact do it. It is the only way you can get your dear cousin back because I am not prepared to help if you refuse. At the moment there are two guards on the ward where our man is being held. That has made it impossible for us to rescue him. You need to create a little window of opportunity for us to do what we need to do. We pride ourselves in helping those foreign nationals who have worked for us when they fall into enemy hands. We have a comfortable little flat waiting for this man so that he can begin a new life in the USSR. That is his reward for his loyal service and I intend him to have it."

"I'm sure you do, Colonel, but in order for him to have it you will have to find your own way of smuggling him past the guards. What you demand is not in my power, even if I wanted to do what you ask."

"Then we have had a pointless meeting Mr Benedict. I'm afraid that both of my conditions will need to be met before I'm prepared to make the deal that will release your cousin. I don't like anything that is pointless but, I must confess, I rather like you, so what I'm going to suggest is this. You go back to your superiors and convey to them the first part of my asking price. You then have one day in which to think in more detail about the second part. You are a very clever fellow, Mr. Benedict, so I am sure that you can dream up a way of doing what I ask without exposing yourself to any risk. If after one day you still refuse to do what I ask all negotiations will be over and I will tell your cousin's kidnappers that they have an asset that has no retail value. They are quite ruthless and you will probably never see her again."

"I think, Colonel, that there would be considerable consequences if anything were to happen to Julia. Whatever your convenient fiction about third-party abductors, MI5 has concluded that all the available evidence suggests that she is in KGB custody, which means that you are directly responsible for her safety. I'll convey your first price to my superiors and on wiser reflection you may choose to accept that as sufficient payment for Julia's release, but your second price is not something that I will be worrying about."

"MI5 can think what it likes about the identity of the abductors, but I can deal only in facts Mr. Benedict. I'm afraid my position on the two prices will not and cannot change. You have one day."

Gus said,

"Tell me, Colonel, you are a man who began your career under Stalin and must have been part of the great purges – the executions of his opponents for little purpose other than the preservation of his oppressive dictatorship. I suspect you have been responsible for many deaths and you are, by unsubtle implication, threatening another one now, one of an entirely innocent person. When you lie in bed at night and contemplate the life you've lived and the value, or lack of it, of those things you do as part of your job, how do you rationalise all of the killing and threats to kill?"

Zaliatev's eyes narrowed and he took a deep breath. With a smile that was more menacing than friendly he said,

"Oh how the British elite love the moral high ground, even when it is quicksand beneath their feet. As your remaining empire dissolves before your eyes, you forget so quickly your history of oppression and dominance of peoples who didn't ask to be dominated. Let me assure you, Mr. Benedict, if a person was an individual of high moral value, someone who put the needs of those less well off than them above their own, I have always found ways and means of preserving them from lethal punishment, even when that put me at considerable risk during the Great Purge. You would expect a true communist to do no less, I think. It is equally a shame that I have found so few people who have met this basic standard of human decency and if the needs of the state require it, I have shed few tears when

I have had to order the demise of those who don't. I have spoken with your cousin and she shares nothing of your concern for the English poor. So when I look at her, I think, why should I expend any effort saving her life unless she has some value in a trade with the British? If you and your superiors choose to reject our terms then the fate of your dear relative is entirely on your head, not ours."

"Who was it who said that those who set themselves up as judge and jury should always be afraid of those who in turn will judge them? And before you criticise the imperial excesses of past British governments you might do well to remember your country's recent invasion of Hungary and its continuing subjugation of Eastern Europe. It has been extremely interesting meeting you Colonel. Good afternoon."

With that Gus rose, tipped his hat, unsmilingly, and then casually walked back through the arch, past the assorted goons and out of the abbey grounds.

The Colonel sat in deep thought for a few minutes. The meeting had not gone according to his expectations and despite having the upper hand, a human 'asset' that he knew Benedict desperately wanted back, he had not managed to control the negotiations in the way that he had intended. That told him one thing, that the British had high hopes of being able to rescue Benedict's cousin without any help from him. He knew by now that the house where Julia had first been held had been raided by British Counter-Espionage shortly after he had moved her on. As he was unaware that Jacob had survived, that made him suspect that Dogsbody must already have talked, given that he had direct knowledge of where that house was. As far as the Colonel knew, Dogsbody didn't have any idea of the location of the house in which Julia was now being held, so in theory there should be no danger of her being found, unless Irina and the guards had made some kind of horrendous error that had left a clue as to where she was being taken. That possibility was one that started to worry him seriously when he remembered the deficiencies in his subordinate's handling of the Jacob situation. She was due to check in at six pm and he decided that he would instruct her to move Julia to a third location, just in case. He assumed that the very fact that Gus had turned up for the meeting meant that the British were not yet in possession of the location details of the latest safe house, so it should be okay to leave the prisoner where she was for a few more hours. But he did not want to go beyond that, given Gus's confident manner during their discussions, which suggested that MI5 were expecting a breakthrough within the next twenty-four hours.

Zaliatev got up and rejoined his minders. He wouldn't have put it past Gus to have set up an attempt to kidnap him, which would have turned the tables neatly and given the British a powerful lever to force the KGB to release Julia. His team were stretched across the abbey grounds as they walked back towards their waiting vehicles, each primed to expect some kind of special operation. Gus, however, was as good as his word. He had come alone and nothing happened to the Colonel or his team. The situation facing those guarding Julia was very different, however, as the Colonel would discover shortly.

CHAPTER FIFTEEN

As the hue and cry of the chase got ever closer, Irina waited for the escaping guards to come near so that she could ensure her gunfire was aimed solely at the pursuing British. Suddenly a super-bright flare was fired into the sky above the mayhem and she could see that the two KGB men were only about three hundred yards away. What she could also see made her furious. In order to facilitate their escape from the hotly pursuing hounds they had dropped Julia and were now fleeing without the hostage. The dogs were almost at their heels and she judged that they would be taken prisoner before they reached her. Had they still been carrying Julia she would have started firing at the pursuers and the dogs to try and help the little party to make it into the back of her car and escape. She was so incensed by the fact that they had chosen to release the hostage without her permission, however, that she was minded now to kill them. With typical coldness she reasoned that if they were so concerned to protect their own skins that they would freely throw away a major negotiating asset, then they would also be likely to crack easily under interrogation. Within the psychopathic workings of her mind that conclusion could have only one result. She pressed the trigger on her machine gun and sprayed them with bullets before turning her attention to their pursuers. The MI5 men hit the ground as soon as the first shots spat from her gun and immediately started returning fire. She threw herself down behind a stone cattle trough and, to her horror, descended face first into a pile of dung. If anything, her misfortune made her even more angrily determined to survive. Holding the machine gun above the top of the trough she continued spraying bullets until the light from the flare faded. She then used the return of darkness to make a high-speed dash back to her car and dived into the driver's seat, with bullets ripping and zipping through the metal of the vehicle's body and only narrowly missing her. Driven now entirely by adrenalin, she started the car and accelerated away so fast that smoke billowed out from under her tyres. She hurtled like a madwoman down a succession of single-track country roads that would have left her with no chance should she have met something coming the other way.

Finally, she made it out onto a major road back to London and didn't stop until she was certain that no-one was following her. Pulling into a layby, she was conscious that both she and the car were richly aromatic thanks to the animal ordure that was sticking to her like glue. In addition to being contaminated by the dung, the car had now become a liability – several locals had given it admiring glances while she had been parked in the village. They would have been able to give a good description of it to the MI5 men and one of them might even have remembered part or all of her number plate. The fact that it was now also riddled with bullet holes meant that she would automatically come to police attention should she not part company with it rapidly. For reasons unknown, whenever Irina had the need to dispose of a vehicle, she always chose pushing it into a suitable depth of water as her default option. Having quickly consulted her map, she headed for a quiet stretch of the Thames. On arrival, she parked the car facing directly onto a three-foot drop from the riverbank into the water. Then, with the handbrake released, she pushed the vehicle slowly over the edge. It at least would be given a bath. She now had to walk the remaining three miles back to her flat and take a bath herself, removing the stench of a day that had gone so disastrously wrong that she didn't even dare begin to contemplate how the Colonel would react.

At the same time as Irina was speeding away from her MI5 pursuers, Julia was being lifted out of one of the three drainage ditches that cut through the muddy fields between the safe house and the village. She'd been tossed in as if she were an unwanted sack of potatoes and was shivering violently from the icy water that she'd thought would be her final resting place. Being handcuffed and with her ankles bound tightly, she'd found it a nightmarish struggle to try and wriggle herself upright and push her head above the five feet of filthy standing water. As she lay gasping at the side of the ditch while two of her rescuers unbound her ankles and shot the chain on her handcuffs to smithereens, Mr. One strode over. He said,

"Ah, Miss Emersly I presume. Your cousin will be greatly relieved to know that you are safe."

She managed to pull herself up to a sitting position, and, while still shivering, surveyed Mr. One with an arch eye. He was slightly startled by her powers of rapid recovery, particularly considering the fact that she had just been half drowned. She coughed and spluttered a little and then, with characteristic dark humour, said,

"I've been a little tied up for the last few days, but you can tell my dear cousin that my diary seems to be free for the rest of the week. Where is the wretch? I was expecting him to ride to my rescue on a white charger and carry me back to London as his exceedingly fruity damson in distress."

"Augustus has been engaged in a parallel attempt to rescue you today, one that we didn't need in the end. As soon as we've cleaned up here, I'll give him a ring to let him know that you're safe."

"Well, you can tell him that he owes his cousin a slap-up meal and a bottle of champers. He was supposed to rescue me from my lonely prison tower on day one, not wait until I'd been chucked into a ditch. Oh God, I'm cold – by the way, did your chaps blow that horrible mad harridan to kingdom come or did she simply disappear in a puff of diabolical smoke?"

"We have someone in pursuit, but that's all I can tell you at the moment."

"Well, never mind, I'm sure there's a very hot seat waiting for her in hell whenever her number is finally up. I could do with a hot seat myself at the moment, my btm's absolutely freezing."

Mr. One now fully appreciated what Gus meant when he described his cousin as 'feisty'.

After Julia had been examined, patched up and discharged from hospital, she underwent two days of questioning by MI5 and the police. As soon as that finished, Gus granted her wish that he should take her out for a slap-up lunch. It was late afternoon by the time he got back to his office. Alice said,

"Ah, the man himself. It's ten to four and you have a ten to five."

"And after translation from double Dutch that means?"

"My favourite chap is coming to see you in exactly one hour."

"And which of Alice Harding's many favourite chaps is this one?"

"Don't be mischievous, Gussie boots, it doesn't suit your complexion. You know very well who I mean."

Mr. One arrived, as always, precisely on the dot. Indeed, Alice had once said that if ever he was late, she would ring the Royal Observatory and tell them that Greenwich Mean Time was up the creek. She was trying to educate him about the virtues of acknowledging the existence of the 'lower ranks' by giving him a beaming great smile whenever he arrived or left, which was having a positively destabilising effect on his facial muscles. Smiles were not a normal manoeuvre for Mr. One's lips and the consequence was that the most he could usually muster in return was a half-smile, sometimes accompanied by a slight rippling of his facial muscles as a bonus. But Alice regarded even these incomplete gestures as a one hundred per cent improvement on the grim and dismissive formality with which she had repeatedly been met on their first acquaintance.

Throwing his coat over the back of his usual chair in Gus's office he said,

"I trust your lunch with your cousin went well Augustus?"

"Exceptionally so Angus. That woman's as tough as a triple armoured tank. She's spent days in captivity, seen her lover lying dead on the ground – murdered – been knocked senseless twice, thrown into a ditch and half-drowned and yet the way she chattered through lunch you'd have thought she was just back from her holidays. That's not to say she isn't grieving for Michaels, she is. She's dealing with it by distracting herself from the memory of what happened by talking, talking, talking – my God, how my cousin can talk."

"Your family is made of strong stuff Augustus – your own war record demonstrates that fact several times over. Now, I've got another visit to make after this one, so you'll forgive me if I get straight down to business. As you'll know from your own conversations with your cousin, at no point did any of her abductors admit to being KGB and we know obviously how Zaliatev tried to build a narrative about her being held by a third party, with himself as simply an intermediary. Even by the usual standards of Soviet misinformation that claim is risible, but he did go to considerable lengths to make it difficult to disprove. Very deliberately, there were no forms of identification in or on the clothing of the two kidnappers who were killed during the rescue operation, and there was nothing within either house where Miss Emersly had been held to indicate any links with the Soviets. She never saw the faces of the people in charge because either she was blindfolded or they were wearing a hood when she encountered them. The mastermind behind the abduction was extremely meticulous about such things, so, in short, we have no visual or documentary proof that the KGB was behind it. As you know, Miss Emersly didn't see the actual killing of Michaels, but on the basis of what Mr. Elliott has now told us there's no doubt in my mind that the Colonel was behind both the assassination and the abduction. That shows just how far he was prepared to go to protect the mole that ironically, of course, we now have in our custody."

"It might be worth seeing if the Home Secretary would agree that Elliott has now given us enough evidence to kick Zaliatev out of the country."

"Well, yes and no. I can understand your preference to see the back of him after the way that Miss Emersly was treated and he crossed several lines at once with the assassination of Michaels. However, he knows that he can't get away with another killing like that on British soil and the advantage of dealing with the devil one knows is that we have finally had the time to build sufficient familiarity with his modus operandi to start countering his KGB mischief effectively. With the successes of our recent operations we've made considerable progress in pushing him back into his box and if we had his replacement to deal with, we'd have to start learning from scratch about the new bod's ways of operating. With the capture of Elliott we're in a position to obtain significant insights into Zaliatev's ways of plotting and thinking and with our freeing of your cousin we've deprived him of a means of forcing the release of KGB people whom we need to hold onto. That leaves just two things on our immediate 'To do' list. First, we need to find out who that scurrilous tabloid journalist Chabler has been gathering information about so that we can begin to identify any remaining moles or moles-to-be. He's very clearly on Zaliatev's payroll. Second, we need to pay another visit to our friend Elliott. He has been cooperating well with our interrogation team and says he is now ready to make the disclosure of truly major information that he promised when we first met him. Apparently, he will only make the disclosure to us, so I will be picking you up from Chez Benedict at seven am sharp tomorrow."

Mr. One was as good as his word, arriving at seven am precisely as promised. When they were shown into the room in the Margate safe house where Jacob/Elliott was waiting for them two hours later, Gus was struck by how nervous he looked. All of the faux cocky self-confidence of their previous encounters had gone. As they sat down on the other side of the table to him Jacob said,

"Before I give you anything I need you to restate your absolute guarantee that you will honour the promise you made to meet my conditions and give me a new identity and immunity from any prosecution."

Mr. One said,

"That's entirely dependent on the precise nature of what you have to tell us Mr. Elliott."

"That's not good enough – I need more. What I've got for you is gold."

"If gold it is then you have my guarantee. You've been very cooperative with our people during your interrogations so far, so I have high hopes that you mean what you say when you tell us that this information is of critical importance. But I would rather like to hear what it is that you have for us."

"OK. It's about the Ministry of Defence. The people who kept a close eye on me were careless in the topics of their conversation when they thought I wasn't around. When that mad woman was present one evening, I heard her telling the half-wit who drove me everywhere that one of his next jobs after me would be keeping an eye on a Ministry of Defence mole. She said he'd been getting a bit stroppy and needed a firm guiding hand. She said the mole was the key to the Soviets finding out about proposed alterations to NATO's defensive battle plans, so it was vital that he should be forced to deliver. It sounded like she's his handler on behalf of Zaliatev."

Gus said,

"If this was to be one of his next jobs after you did that mean that they intended disposing of you even before you fell foul of Lashkanocova?"

"It sounded rather like it."

"Interesting. Did she say anything that might provide a clue as to who this mole might be?"

"Well, whoever he is he's got major problems funding repairs to his ancestral home. She said something about that having been the key to the KGB's ability to recruit him, although she didn't elaborate."

Mr. One's eyes lit up. He said,

"Now that is gold Mr. Elliott. Is there anything else that you can tell us?"

"There is one final revelation of at least equal significance, but that will have to wait until I have in my hands my new identity, passport and everything that goes with them."

"Very well. All of that is in progress. When everything is complete, we shall expect to be given full details of this final revelation. Once you have provided them to us, we will hand over immediately all of the documentation that you need."

As Gus and Mr. One were driven back to London they ruminated on what they'd been told. Mr. One said,

"We need to find out who within the MoD's senior civil servants has direct access to the defensive battle plans and who from that select group has a large house in need of serious repair. Then we need to put him under surveillance to get the necessary proof of treachery. We also need round the clock surveillance of Lashkanocova. If we can find out how precisely she is picking up the intel from the mole she may lead us straight to him."

"Presumably it would help if we picked up our journalist friend, Mr. Chabler, and brought him in for a nice cosy little chat about the precise nature of the treachery he is engaged in on behalf of the Colonel? That in itself might give us the likely identity of the mole."

"My thoughts exactly. I'll arrange to have him hoovered up off the street when he sets off for work tomorrow."

When Frank Chabler was brought in for questioning early the following morning, he did not look a happy man. He was complaining about the absence of his hat, which had been dislodged and left behind during the struggle to get him into a car. His thickly Brylcreemed hair, pointed nose and angular eyebrows blended well with his sharp-as-three-knives suit, making him resemble a second-hand car dealer at the most disreputable end of the market. His mock cockney accent struggled a little to remain consistent as he raged through an imaginative range of expletives. Try as he might, he couldn't free his arms from the grip of the two exceedingly muscular heavies who had been charged with the task of bringing him in and he was propelled forcefully into the interview room where Gus and Mr. One were already waiting. As soon as he was pushed down into a chair he attempted to jump up and run past his captors to make his escape. The very large hand that grabbed his collar forced him to do an about-turn and re-inserted him into his chair. With the assistance of its fellow hand, it removed his tie and used it to lash one of his ankles to a chair leg. He let fly with another batch of expletives, but as no-one seemed to take any notice, he finally seemed to run out of energy and sank into silence. He sat glowering at his interrogators, who seemed more interested in chatting to each other than him. Finally, Mr. One engaged him eyeball to eyeball and the questioning began.

By the end of the day both Gus and Mr. One were thoroughly fed up with their unwilling guest. It seemed that he had denied everything bar his own existence and had made reference to rights that were more numerous than those contained in all of the legal conventions in history. He had refused to be cowed by threats of him being charged with treason and seemed immune to any pressure or sanction that his two experienced inquisitors could dream up. They were treated several times to accounts of his alleged wartime heroics and were told that they were worse than any tyrant he'd fought against. Despite being 'accidentally' locked in the interrogation room overnight he proved even more defiant and bombastic the following morning and by eleven-thirty both Gus and Mr. One had run out of all patience with him. Leaving him locked in the room with a cup of water and a stale sandwich, they retreated to Mr. One's office and sank exhaustedly into a couple of comforting, well-padded chairs. Mr. One said,

"The man's a nightmare. No wonder no newspaper will have him on their premises for longer than it takes him to file his freelance kiss-and-tell nonsense. What on earth do we do to get him to talk Augustus? He's so belligerent and bolshie I can't think of any threat that will have an immediate impact on his thick little skull. We could try pressuring him by handing him over to the police on a charge of being complicit in a blackmail operation run by a foreign power, or some such – I'm not sure what the precise legal formulation would be – but he'd pretty soon rumble the fact that we just don't have the evidence to make it stand up. One of my men has been through his flat with a fine-toothed comb while he's been our guest, but he's been very careful to make sure that there's nothing incriminating on the premises. He's simultaneously the best and the worst lead we've got."

The glum look on Gus's face was suddenly replaced by a mischievous grin. He said,

"Might I make a suggestion that could considerably speed matters up?"

"I'm listening, Augustus."

"I think the solution to our problems with Mr. Chabler might lie with Tasty Harry. He provides me with information without charge in recognition of my having helped his family in the past, as you know, but the services of his that I'm thinking of hiring are of a more complex nature than normal and will be subject to a fee."

"What precise services are we talking about Augustus?"

"He is very good in the persuasiveness department. If anyone can persuade someone as difficult as Mr. Chabler to reveal just who it is that Zaliatev has been paying him to gather information on it's Tasty."

"When you refer to 'persuasiveness' are we talking about legal or illegal practices?"

"What Harry is good at is persuading people he is about to use highly illegal methods and being so convincing that he doesn't need to use them at all – the people being questioned generally find him so credible that they decide that spilling the beans is very much in their best interests."

"I see. I'm trusting that you will keep a sharp eye on what happens to ensure that we don't have any embarrassment on our hands."

"On a good day I would almost say that Tasty is a gentle giant," Gus said with a mischievous glint in his eye.

"And what about the bad days?"

"They're a little less predictable. I try not to use him on those days."

"How certain can I be of getting results for my money?"

"With the care and imagination that Harry will put into the matter, I would think that you can be at least eighty per cent certain of him delivering what you want."

"Very well. If you let me know how much you think Mr. Tasty will require for his services, I'll tell you whether my budget can cover it. I shall not enquire too closely about the finer points of his methods as long as they do not include actual physical torture."

"Excellent. If I move very quickly, I know just where he'll be for his lunch today. He's very much a creature of habit."

Gus caught up with Tasty at his favourite fish and chip restaurant half an hour later. There was someone else sitting at his table, an anxious looking middle-aged man in an ill-fitting suit. Tasty did not look in a happy mood and appeared to be reading the Riot Act to him. When he saw Gus approaching his face changed in an instant.

"Gus me old mate," he boomed, "good to see you. Come and take a seat, Mr. Forgetful here is just leaving, aren't you? If you wouldn't mind clearing your plates and taking them to Elsie over there that would be much appreciated."

Mr. Forgetful peered round at Gus with terrified eyes and hastily scrambled to his feet, gathering up his plates and tea mug so quickly that he nearly lost control of them. He then hurried towards the waitress, looking back more than once as if he thought the devil might be on his tail.

"Don't forget what you need to do Mr. F," Tasty shouted after him, "it can be quite tricky trying to hobble around town with one leg."

As Gus sat down in the chair of the recently departed, he said,

"Given that your friend very clearly has two legs at the moment I assume that is what might be described as a gentle warning?"

Tasty roared with his characteristic deep bass laugh.

"You are a one Gus me old mate. Let's just say our friend has a bit of an unreliable memory with regard to things he owes. As a man of kindness and charity, I was just helping him to remember some of them. To what do I owe the pleasure of your company?"

"I was wondering if you might be prepared to use those same skills to help a person of interest to us remember some vital information we need from him very quickly. We've had nearly twelve hours of fruitless conversation with him, but he has been determined to keep shtum. We're releasing him back into the big bad world at five o'clock this afternoon. Should you be available, I wondered if you would be prepared to scoop him up with one of your sizeable hands and take him somewhere for some rather more persuasive questioning – for a suitable and very unofficial fee of course. We don't want any physical harm to come to him, we would just like you to do what you're so very good at and that is convince him that terrible things are about to befall him if he doesn't start cooperating."

"Ah, now this goes a little beyond the agreed services that I can offer you for free in eternal gratitude for your past kindnesses. You wouldn't happen to have a little brown envelope that I could take a peek at would you?"

"I certainly do. It's under my hat."

Tasty raised his eyebrows archly, lifted the hat off the table and grabbed the thick envelope stuffed with five-pound notes, saying,

"Wonderful, instead of a bunny I pull a wodge of fivers out of a hat. I might make the Magic Circle yet."

Having counted the contents under the table the big man said,

"That would seem to be in order me old mate. I'd normally require quite a bit more, but given our history there's an automatic discount. Who is your tongue-tied friend and what do you need me to find out?"

"He's a rogue tabloid journalist who is being used by our Soviet chums to dig up the dirt on people. I need the names of all the people that he's investigated so that we can close down the Soviet operation. As always, I'm relying on you keeping everything that you hear to yourself."

"My lips are sealed and my memory of anything I hear will be even shorter than that of Mr. Forgetful. Here's what I'll do. You tell me where to find this gentleman and what he looks like and at the appointed hour I will assist him into a waiting motor vehicle. He will be chauffeured to Sid Sowsnan's meat storage warehouse in Brixton, where a variety of delightful experiences will be offered to him should his tongue remain tied. I'll tell Sid to expect you, so if you motor up there for around five fifteen or so you can linger in the shadows ready to make a note of all you hear. When we've finished chatting with the gent we'll give him a free lift to the docks, where we'll drop him into the water on the end of a line and then pull him out again with fishes in his pockets. We'll tell him that if ever he lets his Soviet friends know they've been rumbled he'll take a second, one-way dip into the water with a concrete block round his ankles. No significant violence will actually happen to him, as per your instructions, but I'll do me very best theatricals to persuade him that it will if he's not prepared to be Mr. Chatty. Does that sound alright me old mate?"

"Absolutely perfect Tasty. As ever, you are a master of your craft. We, of course, never had this meeting."

"The only person who was ever here was Mr. Forgetful me old china and being as forgetful as him I've already forgotten everything that we've talked about in the chat we haven't had."

Gus laughed as he put his hat on, ready to leave. He passed a photograph across the table to Tasty and said,

"That's our man. We'll release him from a car right outside your favourite pub at five pm, if that's acceptable. You can bung him straight into your vehicle as soon as we've departed and I'll drop in at the meat warehouse at five fifteen, as you suggest."

"Sounds like a plan to me, Gus me old china, I'll see you then."

Gus arrived at the meat warehouse at the agreed time and was shown up to the second floor by one of Tasty's helpers, a man whose arms seemed as thick as most men's thighs. Gus secreted himself in the shadows in sight of the action. Tasty nodded to him and grinned wryly before returning his attention to Frank Chabler, who was hanging upside down with his bare feet tied to a large meat hook. He sounded more disgruntled than ever. He screamed,

"I'll have you for this, you'll be headlines in every newspaper in the land – MI5 torture chamber, exposed!"

"MI5? We're nothing to do with them me old china. We just get information for people who want it from geezers who aren't very chatty.

There's someone who's paid me to get information from you, so aren't you a lucky duck? Now, here's how it's going to work. I'm going to ask you some questions and if you answer them fully and correctly, you'll be home in time for your supper with all your toes attached and in full working order. Should you be a little tongue tied, then it'll be my pleasure to assist you in the chattiness department. I often find that the tongue and the left big toe are connected, so if you refuse to answer the first question in full, I'll use these very sharp bolt cutters here to slice that little piggie off. I usually find geezers become ever so amazingly chatty once I've done that. Should you still find it difficult to have a little chinwag with me, I'll snip your right big toe off as well, which should restore a nice sense of balance and stop you toppling over."

Tasty looked across at Gus and winked. He continued,

"Should you still have problems wagging the old tongue in the required manner, we then move on to the rest of your toes and so on. Your head's the last bit we get to, but I've only ever had one punter where we've had to lop that off as well. He wasn't at all chatty after that, but at least the client who'd paid me felt he'd got his money's worth."

Chabler's eyes looked as though they were going to spin round and round in their sockets. Tasty continued,

"Now, to start the ball rolling, I'm going to ask you what dirt the Soviet gent you've been working for told you to dig up and then I want you to list all the names of the people he asked you to investigate. If I think you've missed even half of a detail then it's off with your left big piggie. That's fair enough, isn't it?"

Chabler emitted a noise that was more akin to a terrified squawk than anything else. Tasty continued,

"So, off you go, quick as you please – and you'll need to shout because I'm deaf in one ear."

Chabler started to whimper. Tasty slipped the open jaw of the bolt cutters around the base of his prisoner's left big toe, as if ready to begin slicing through it. He said,

"I'm sorry, I didn't catch that. Have another go. Get it right and I can put the bolt cutters back on the table. Get it wrong and off the toe goes, just like a chicken leg."

"The Russian geezer will kill me if I say anything."

"He's nowhere near this gaff, so he's hardly going to hear what you say me old mate, whereas I'm standing right beside you, just about to slice your toe off and pop it in the old meat grinder so we don't leave any mess behind. Come on, one final chance for good luck, spit it out."

Tasty tightened the grip of the cutters just enough for them to slightly indent the skin, as if ready to begin slicing. It worked.

"Alright, alright, hold your horses, I'll tell you everything."

"That's a good boy, your mother would be proud of you Frankie Chabler. Off you go then – and no porky pies if you and your toe want to remain a happy couple."

"He wanted me to get the dirt on three Defence Ministry officials – Charles Fossett, Henry Crudley-Walpole and Sir John Waterman-Blythe. Fossett was on the edge of bankruptcy after a divorce settlement and had been raising cash by taking bribes to help an arms manufacturer get contracts they wouldn't normally have been considered for. His stately pile of a house was falling down around his ears and he needed money quick before it was too late to save the dump. I got hold of the hard evidence. Crudley-Walpole had been relatively penniless before he married the daughter of a banker and was in severe danger of losing all the wealth she'd shared with him should anyone find out that he was having it off with her sister. I got the photos that show in graphic detail what he was up to. Waterman-Blythe has some very strange sexual appetites and I got the photos to prove it. That's everything I swear."

Tasty looked across at Gus who had just finished scribbling down all the details. Gus smiled and gave a thumbs up sign. Tasty said,

"I said you were a lucky duck Frankie boy and lucky duck you are."

As he was speaking, he cut through the rope from which Chabler was suspended. His prisoner dropped onto the hard floor with a loud yell.

"Well, granted, that bit wasn't so lucky. I meant to grab hold of your ankles before you dropped, but there you go, aren't I a butterfingers? Now, I've just got to take you for a quick bath in the Thames and then it's back home for you – you can sit in front of the fire with a nice cup of cocoa and a cream bun. Lovely."

"What do you mean 'a quick bath in the Thames'? You promised me nothing would happen if I told you everything."

By this time Tasty was dragging him back to the car, with the terrified journalist's ankles tucked under the big man's left arm while Chabler's once sharp suit collected all of the grime from the warehouse floor as he was pulled along. Tasty said,

"Nothing fatal will happen to you Frankie boy, I'm a man of my word. We're just going to give you a little bath and then you can dry out nicely by the fire when you get back home."

Gus heard the prisoner whimpering again as Tasty, his helper and Chabler disappeared from view. As he made his own way out of the building, he wondered whether Tasty had been making things up when he said he'd once lopped a man's head off. On the balance of probabilities, he concluded that it was just a piece of terrifying make-believe, part of the skilful theatrical performance that had been put on for the purposes of extracting the required information. But nevertheless, it was never possible to be entirely sure where fiction ended and facts began in the dark underworld that his larger-than-life friend inhabited. Gus shuddered a little as he got back in his car.

CHAPTER SIXTEEN

As Irina stood in the cold, echoing corridor outside Zaliatev's intimidatingly large office she felt very much like the pupil about to be expelled from school for theft or some equally disreputable offence. Her only game plan was to defend herself vigorously for now and then try and shift most of the responsibility for the Jacob and Julia disasters to the Colonel when the interrogators began what she knew would be a gruelling ordeal back in Moscow. She was certain that she would be sent back home in disgrace as the scapegoat for recent setbacks. She was already beginning to try and dream up ways of manufacturing false evidence in her favour when the door of the anteroom finally opened and a flunkey summoned her into the great man's presence.

The extent of her fall from grace was emphasised by the fact that, prior to the Jacob and Julia failures, she'd had virtually guaranteed access to the Colonel, without any need for an appointment or an administrative go-between. She'd certainly never been required to stand in the corridor before.

Normally, she would have been invited to sit opposite the Colonel's desk, but the chair had been moved right to the back of the room, very deliberately. She was instructed to stand to attention and to explain herself. Zaliatev was at his most distant and cold. He said,

"We have discussed the errors you made during the Jacob operation on a previous occasion. Today, I would like you to explain your failures in the handling of the secure detention of Benedict's cousin, someone who should have been a prime negotiating asset for us, but who was rescued with embarrassing speed and ease by the British. Do you have anything to say that might be relevant in your defence?"

Irina was, if nothing else, an accomplished natural actor and it was almost as if the gears in her head could be heard whirring and clicking into place as a sudden adrenalin rush pushed her straight into thespian mode. She had given considerable thought to what she would say in this moment and the words now tripped forcefully off her tongue as if they were scripted for a courtroom movie. They were almost the whole truth. The fate of the safe house guards was a little different to what actually happened, but Irina was a talented creator of alternative realities. She said,

"I can say categorically that the failure was not mine, Colonel. On the contrary, I did everything as instructed and by the book. I moved the prisoner to the second safe house as soon as you told me to and no indication of where she was going was left in the previous safe house. When the British surrounded the second location, I provided cover fire to enable the guards to escape with the prisoner and to follow a specified route to where I had a car waiting for their evacuation. The British had deployed an elite team, however, and the guards were not able to make it to the car. I then had to avoid capture and escape from the scene, which I did, disposing of the car as I did so. I followed all the protocols."

Zaliatev stood looking out of the window as she spoke, hands clasped behind his back in military mode. He turned round to face her with eyes of ice and an ominously accusatory tone in his voice. He said,

"If you didn't leave any clues as to where the prisoner was being taken, how is it that the British were able to find the location so quickly? Nobody other than you, me and the guards knew she was going there."

"There are three possible answers to that question, Colonel. First, that your telephone communication to me was intercepted and its contents leaked to the British. Given that the message was in code, that means that it was most likely intercepted by someone on our own side who knew how to decipher it. They could be a double agent and, as such, they simply passed the information over to their British handlers. The second answer is much simpler. There are several people on our staff who have access to the list of UK safe houses. Any one of those could be a double agent who immediately gave the information to the British when asked. MI5 then simply had to work its way around the various houses until they found the one where the prisoner was being held. The third answer is that the British have been following our operatives as a matter of course and have observed visits to one or more of the safe houses and have made a note of their existence. In hunting for the prisoner, they used their own list of known safe houses and got lucky."

Zaliatev by now had walked round to her side of the desk and stood towering over her. Looking down into her eyes, he said, almost with a hiss,

"All very interesting and almost plausible comrade. But we have only your word that nothing was left in the first safe house that would have enabled the British to guess where the prisoner was going, as they presumably would have removed such evidence and taken it with them."

"There was nothing to leave for them to find, Colonel. Your coded message was delivered over the telephone, as you will remember, and I had no need to write it down, given that I decoded it in my head and already knew where the safe house was."

"Did you really? We only commissioned it six weeks ago and you have had no previous dealings there."

"I do my homework, Colonel and keep up to date with things. I noticed that it had been added to the existing list, to which I, like you, have access."

The actress within Irina enabled her to keep outwardly calm, but inside she felt almost as if she were back in the field, being pursued by the British, with bullets flying everywhere. Zaliatev smiled, a stillborn gesture, full of menace rather than warmth. He said,

"Really? Most busy people would not check the safe house list unless they were intending to make use of it immediately. I can see no credible reason why you might have consulted it when you had no need to do so. How do we know that you're not the double agent to whom you refer? Recent events make it distinctly possible that you are. You could have encouraged Jacob to try and escape and then used that as an excuse to kill him and bring our operation against the Americans and the British to a sudden end. As far as the most recent debacle is concerned, you could have tipped off the British yourself to save them having to pay the heavy price that I set for the prisoner's release. It seems remarkable that you have been at the dead centre of two recent operations that have failed, one after another, failures that have protected British interests at the expense of ours. It seems remarkable also that while both of the guards from the safe house were killed by the British, you were allowed to escape. How very convenient, wouldn't you agree?"

"My record as a loyal member of the Communist Party of the Soviet Union is impeccable and beyond reproach, Colonel. Even if that is ignored, to have engineered the failure of two of our operations so closely together would not only have been remarkably stupid in terms of creating grounds for suspicion, but it would quite possibly result in my return to Moscow under a cloud. Such a person would hardly be of much further use to the British and they are not fools, so they would have organised things rather more intelligently than that. I do not see a single shred of evidence that suggests that I have been anything other than completely loyal to the Party and to you."

"That is for me to decide, not you comrade. For the moment you will retain your rank, but your performance will be reviewed on a weekly basis and there will be an inquiry into the causes of the recent failures that you have been involved in. You will retain your responsibilities, but until the inquiry is complete, you will be shadowed in all dealings with foreign entities, including the British defence ministry mole that you have been handling. Igor Rebenski will perform this role and you should liaise with him in all external dealings and ensure that you keep a detailed and witnessed record of all of your actions. Is that clear?"

"Yes Colonel."

"Good. You may now leave comrade."

As she started to walk away, he said,

"Oh, and while I remember, your existing office has had an extra desk moved in while we have been speaking. Comrade Rebenski will be sharing with you henceforth."

The unsettling implications of this last announcement could hardly be missed by Irina. Formally, she had retained her rank, for the moment at least. But in reality, she had been effectively demoted, now having to share both her office and her every action of any importance with a man who she knew to be one rank below her. While theoretically his role would last only as long as it took for the inquiry to reach its conclusions, there was a clear danger that she might be being used to train him up as her replacement and that she would be fully and formally demoted and sent back to Moscow as soon as he was fully up to speed with all of the details of her job. Her mind was in a state of some disarray as she tried to grapple with the complexities of her new situation.

The Colonel sat back and relaxed in the comfort of his leather desk chair. Once 'the accused' had left, a man with a face like death incarnate emerged from the little side room that joined onto the main office. The two men nodded at each other and the guest, a senior counter-espionage investigator from Moscow, drew up the chair that had been denied to Irina and sat down. The Colonel said,

"Did you find that little performance convincing?"

"I have heard many such self-justifications in the past. It is surprising how soon they melt away in the Lubyanka."

"Indeed. So we proceed as planned and give her enough rope to hang herself with?"

"Given the evidence that you have shown me it should be only a matter of time before we are able to reel this one in and send her back home for processing."

The Colonel nodded, his emotionless face concealing a deep sense of relief that the Moscow man appeared to have accepted his version of events. His thoughts about Irina were complex. While her utter ruthlessness was a weapon that initially he'd felt could be powerfully deployed against British interests, he'd quickly come to realise that it was also a potential danger to him when combined with her obvious ambition. He was certain that, should she sense any weakness in his position, she would begin exploring the possibilities of undermining it further in the hope that she might be able to replace him. She very much saw herself as the next generation, waiting for its chance. It seemed that the only value guiding her actions was her own self-interest. He had no regard for her as a person therefore, the value-free were ten a penny. He viewed her as useful only for as long as she could advance his strategic objectives regarding the British. He didn't seriously believe that she was a double agent, but the Jacob and Julia failures meant that he was in urgent need of a scapegoat to cover his own back. She seemed to be the obvious candidate for the role. He had no qualms about this because he was certain that he was dealing with an individual who had no conscience about anything at all. In eliminating her, he would be doing both himself and humanity a favour, removing one more poisonous apple from the tree of life. He knew that she would resist his efforts with some vigour but, as a keen follower of chess, he to a degree relished the challenge.

At the same time as the Colonel was grilling Irina, Gus was sitting in a snug private room at Mr. One's favourite watering hole, The Proud Hussar, caressing a pint of extraordinarily good best bitter. The thick ancient oak door that sealed the room was as effective as a brick wall in its soundproofing abilities. Mr. One was in revelatory mode. He said,

"We've checked out the three Ministry of Defence people whom Chabler confessed to having investigated and there's only one who stands out as a likely employee of our friend, the Colonel. Waterman-Blythe does indeed have some very strange sexual habits, but he's rather proud of them from what we can tell, even to the point of bragging about them. He is an extremely odd individual, but a man with no shame is not someone whom it is easy to blackmail. Crudley-Walpole had indeed been in mortal fear of his very rich wife finding out about his extra-marital shenanigans, but his fear has been somewhat lessened by the fact that it turns out his dearly beloved knew about them anyway and started divorce proceedings against him three weeks ago. I don't think that the KGB is going to be very successful in trying to blackmail him into becoming a mole now, given the circumstances. Charles Fossett is another story, however. Our investigations show that he has indeed been taking substantial bribes in return for helping one arms manufacturer in particular secure contracts that it should not even have been in the running for. His rather grand ancestral home has been in need of massive repairs if it is not to collapse and taking very substantial bribes as a way of funding these seemed a rather too tempting prospect for our man. Should he have been exposed by the KGB he would have lost everything – his MoD job and the opportunity to solicit bribes that it offers would have vanished and his very palatial home would have been replaced by a prison cell. I think he is our most likely candidate, given both Elliott's reference to a man with a house in dire need of repair and the fact that Chabler has given our Soviet friends the full details of his skulduggery."

"Do we have any evidence of instances where he could have been passing secrets?"

"Not as yet. What we do have is twenty-four-hour surveillance in place on both him and the Soviet intelligence officer whom Elliott identified as the MoD mole handler, Irina whatever-her-name is."

"Lashkanocova," Gus said, helpfully.

"Indeed. I think I shall just refer to her as L in future to avoid having to wrestle with such a complex name on top of everything else."

"You are aware that she changes her appearance more often than a flea leaps in a day. She has a wig for every occasion."

"Yes, I know. Young Montgomery is the main chap on the job and he's noticed that she changes significant items of clothing as well, further adding to the difficulty of spotting her when she's out and about. Being an exceedingly bright spark, he's observed that she has a signature eccentricity in her walk, a swagger in the way she leads with her left foot. It never varies. She could dress like the Queen of Sheba, or wear a wig that made her look like Marilyn Monroe, but the swagger would give her away to Montgomery. Best man we've got for the job. I've put Hales and Waterswood on alternating shifts to follow the good Mr. Fossett."

Hales was at that precise moment following the Ministry of Defence suspect as he set off on a lunchtime excursion. Fossett was a portly middle-aged man with an appropriately crooked nose, the result of a car accident. He walked like a guided missile, whizzing and hurtling through the busy throngs in a manner that was totally unexpected, given his girth. Journey's end was a shabby looking Georgian terraced house down an anonymous looking side street. Having checked that he wasn't being followed and completely failing to spot the skilful Hales in the process, he pushed an envelope through the letter box and then spun around on his heels and headed back the way he had come at the same vigorous pace as before. When he'd gone, Hales waited for fifteen minutes to see if anyone approached the house and when they didn't, did so himself. A cursory examination of the building from the pavement suggested that it had been unoccupied for some time. He rang the doorbell and when he didn't get a reply, peered through the letterbox. The envelope that Fossett had pushed through was sitting on the floor, untouched. Using the appropriate tool from his key ring, he picked the lock and, after checking that nobody was watching him, slipped inside. Having investigated the contents of Fossett's secret communication, he then microfilmed them and replaced the envelope with a spare that he always carried in his boy-scoutish 'be prepared for everything' kit that he kept in his briefcase. He stepped back outside again, pulling the door closed as he did so. Checking to see that, as far as he could tell, he hadn't been observed, he then hurried back out onto the main road and called a taxi. Within less than an hour the microfilm was on Mr. One's desk.

Approximately one hour later, Montgomery spotted Irina leaving the Soviet embassy in a cream jacket and skirt, as opposed to the long black dress and matching coat that she had worn when entering the building in the morning. She had also changed her wig from a blonde to a brunette model. Once again, it was her characteristic walk that gave her away. She was followed out by a man of about thirty with an angular, stone-chiselled face and a piercing dead-eyed gaze. With his over-sized black hat looking as though it was constantly in danger of slipping forwards onto his nose, he followed her at a distance of twenty yards or so. Montgomery followed them both on the other side of the road.

The pursuit of Irina ended at the same terraced house that Hales had followed Fossett to. Hales had arranged for a car to keep watch on the house after his visit earlier in the day. Parked fifty yards further down the street, Montgomery recognised it immediately, but the fact that it looked unoccupied and derelict, with two flat tyres and its back bumper hanging off, persuaded Irina that it was an irrelevance. With a series of moves that were so quick they seemed like an illusionist's trick, she unlocked the front door, pocketed the envelope that had been left for her and closed and secured the door again. Like Fossett, she scanned the faces of the few people around. Her eyes focussed on those of the man from the embassy who had been following her and she glared at him briefly, before doing an about-turn and heading back the way she had come. Her shadow followed immediately, remaining, as before, twenty yards behind. Fifty yards behind him, Montgomery followed also, a participant in the strangest of formation dances. The hidden occupants of the derelict car contented themselves with having secured detailed photographic evidence of the pick-up and left him to it.

By late afternoon Mr. One was back in his office, staring at the reports filed by Hales, Montgomery and the observers in the car. He had already viewed the contents of the microfilm that Hales had left for him to examine. He looked across at Gus and shook his head sadly. He said,

"According to his record, Fossett distinguished himself repeatedly during the war. His quick thinking is credited with saving a flight of six Spitfire pilots from certain death by surprising their attackers from the rear and he has more medals than most people have coins in their pockets. Yet here he is, throwing everything away, having corruptly enabled a sub-standard arms manufacturer to win contracts for which it is completely unsuited and ending up being blackmailed by the KGB as a consequence."

"A shame it may be, Angus, but whatever his past heroics the man is now a crook and a traitor and the fact that he comes from traditional landed gentry stock doesn't make him any better than the lowliest of petty criminals."

"You're right of course, Augustus. I suppose he's just another mole we need to pull out of his burrow by the scruff of his neck. I've sent Montgomery and Hale to pick him up for questioning when he sets off home in about ten minutes or so."

What Mr. One didn't know was that Fossett might have lost sight of Fossett the hero, but he hadn't forgotten the skills of Fossett the military man. He had anticipated being caught right from the start and had an escape route ready planned. When the two MI5 men 'assisted' him into a car as he left his office building at five, he pretended to be fully cooperative and sat silently between them on the back seat as he was driven to his reckoning. What neither of the intelligence men knew – and should have checked – was that he was armed. He waited until the car became stuck at a set of traffic lights in a quiet part of the city and then whisked the gun out, shooting each man in the thigh, before pushing the screaming Montgomery out onto the tarmac so that he could make good his escape down a side road. He was heading for a small rented garage in Clapham, where he had a car registered in the name of a man long dead, with two suitcases full of clothes, a considerable amount of Swiss francs and two false passports in the boot.

Gus was still in Mr. One's office when the news of what had happened came in. Mr. One cursed, an unusual occurrence with him. He said,

"I can't believe it – two of our most intelligent people on the job and neither of them seems to have thought to check the man for a weapon. Now how on earth are we going to find him before the Soviets spirit him out of the country?"

"I don't think he'll go to them."

"What? Why on earth not? He knows we're onto him now, so they're his only option – if he wants to stay out of prison that is."

"From what I've read about him in the file you showed me earlier he's not going to want to live out the rest of his days in a small apartment in a society that is the complete opposite of what he believes in. He likes big houses, fast cars, lots of money and fine dining."

"So where is a chap like him going to run to then?"

"Well, he's a much-decorated pilot is he not, so my guess would be to an airfield. We need to find out pretty damned quickly if he has access to a small plane and if so, where."

"If you're right, by the time we've done that he'll have flown out of the country."

"The arms manufacturer he's been taking bribes from, my guess is that they're in the aircraft business, is that right?"

"Not as such, but they do have a small airfield about sixty miles from London. They inherited it with the factory site when they bought it, it's all in the file about them. He may well have access to a company owned private plane as part of the deal he has with them. How stupid of me for not thinking of that. I'll get on to the police straight away."

"No, that's not necessarily a good idea. He'll spot them a mile off and do another runner. If you get your driver to bring a car round to the front we could try and intercept him ourselves."

Jenkins, Mr. One's driver, covered the sixty miles at such a speed that Gus was convinced his hair would have turned grey the next time he looked in a mirror. The airfield was enclosed within a high perimeter fence that had only one padlocked gate through which it could be entered. There was a security lodge by the gate, but nobody was in it. There was a single medium sized hangar, which was not open, together with a small control tower that was unoccupied. There was a large warehouse building about two hundred yards away from the airfield and Mr. One told the driver to park around the rear side of it so that they would be able to see anyone arriving at the gate and surprise them. He said,

"It all looks very deserted, Augustus, I hope that your hunch is the right one."

"Well, there's a risk I could be wrong, but Fossett has been in a position to demand the biggest and best of deals from this company and I can't see him resisting the temptation to demand access to a company plane for his own use from time to time. I suspect that he has keys to the gate and the hangar. If a plane's inside he's got the ideal means of instant escape."

"The key word is 'if', is it not? If there isn't one inside then we're wasting our time."

"I do believe we're about to find out."

A pair of sports car headlights were approaching at some speed. The Jaguar XK120 screeched to a halt in front of the gates and Fossett jumped out to open the padlock. Mr. One said,

"Well I never. Your instincts are always impeccably correct, Augustus. Time to put your foot down Jenkins."

Jenkins obliged, the tyres of the deceptively sedate looking black saloon screeching so loudly that Fossett dropped the key just as he was about to slot it into the padlock. He whipped his pistol out of his pocket and took direct aim at the approaching car's windscreen as it hurtled

182

towards him. Unfortunately for Jenkins, he caught the bullet straight between the eyes. With no living foot to hit the brake pedal the killing turned out to be the means of Fossett's own demise. Frozen in the glare of the car's headlights, like a proverbial rabbit, he was smashed against the gate with bone-crushing force. There was a loud scream and then silence, the vehicle's engine having cut out. As the minutes passed, nothing moved in the dark shadows cast by the airfield's perimeter lights. Somewhere in the surrounding undergrowth, a wildcat howled.

CHAPTER SEVENTEEN

The news of Fossett's death sent shockwaves rippling through the high command of the KGB's London operation. One failure, in the form of Jacob's loss, would have been unfortunate; two, in the shape of Julia being rescued by MI5, would have been damaging; but three, occasioned by the untimely end of their prized MoD mole, was nothing short of calamitous. Irina could feel the blood freezing in her veins when she heard what had happened. Her shadow, Rebenski, greeted her with a cold formality when she arrived in her newly shared office at eight-thirty the next morning. His eyes suggested he was watching a dead woman walking.

The Colonel's heart skipped a beat when he was informed of the disaster. He could sense the grinding wheels of two imaginary motorised steel blocks as they slowly but inexorably rolled ever closer, one on either side of him, ready to crush his bones under the weight of his section's failures. His UK operation was being dealt body blow after body blow and he was seemingly unable to do anything about it. If he didn't act dramatically and quickly, he would be left holding the unwanted baby, a man who had been transformed almost overnight from being one of the most feared and successful of the KGB's old brigade into a failed has-been, ripe for recall to Moscow and, at best, being forcibly retired early. At worst, he could be investigated for possible culpability in the failures and maybe even charged with treason. He needed someone else to be guilty and he needed a narrative built around that person to make this credible – and he needed these things fast. Mikhail Grimlinski, the visiting counter-espionage investigator from Moscow, looked at him the same way that Rebenski had looked at Irina when he walked into the Colonel's office, unannounced, at nine am. That sent all of the survival bells ringing inside Zaliatev's head and his formidable mind swung into gear. He looked his visitor straight in the eye, with a determination and menace that were eloquent communicators of the fact that he was still very much on top of the job. He said,

"Good morning comrade. We have a traitor in our midst and it is my intention to have that individual in your custody by tomorrow evening at the latest."

"There is clearly something going badly wrong, Colonel. Are we talking about the same person today that we were yesterday?"

"We are. I have this morning set in train crucial actions that will have trapped her and established her guilt beyond all doubt before she has time to even begin to suspect that she has been discovered."

"I'm glad to know that, Colonel. May I ask what these might be?"

"You shall see shortly, comrade. You will be my guest of honour when a traitor is unmasked."

In reality, the Colonel had still to manufacture the necessary incriminating evidence. He was deeply experienced in such matters and as soon as he could delicately eject the investigator from his office his creative powers would be unleashed. For Irina, that was the very worst of outcomes that she could have expected from this situation.

At half past nine she was startled when Zaliatev walked into her office, without knocking. His face was a picture of darkness. He walked over to Rebenski and tossed an envelope onto his desk. He said,

"That is the list of all our safe houses in the UK. There are two new additions at the bottom, together with two deletions of the addresses that have become known to the British, courtesy of carelessness by some within this office. We have a person of interest that we need to hide in one of the new addresses for a week or so. I want you to go with Yuri and Sergei to bed him in and make absolutely certain that there is no foreign surveillance on the house. It's the last one on the list. We're picking him up at two o'clock this afternoon. You'll find summary details of him in the envelope. You can look at them afterwards. I want you to come with me now – in five minutes I'm briefing all of those involved on the extra security measures that will be needed to protect this asset. Lock that envelope in your desk and don't let it leave this office, I don't want any more leaks."

Rebenski did as instructed. As the two departed the Colonel turned back and gave Irina a look that would have caused the fiercest bull to whimper. He said,

"I want you in my office at four o'clock precisely this afternoon. The inquiry that is being conducted into recent reversals needs a statement from you concerning your latest failure. They want to know how the identity of the Ministry of Defence mole could have been leaked to the

British. They will then consider your explanation and you will know your fate by five o'clock today. The inquiry is being chaired by a specialist in such matters from Moscow, so you would be advised to be open and honest in your every answer."

He slammed the door behind him, leaving Irina shaking and feeling physically sick. She was certain now that the combined weight of all three of the recent disasters was going to be dropped onto her shoulders from a very great height. The mention of the man from Moscow was designed to communicate that fact to her, to intimidate her before she even set foot in the room. She had been chosen to be the scapegoat that saved the Colonel's career and the fall she would need to take would be so hard it might even kill her. She had a deep fear that a charge of treason was being cooked up and that the fate that awaited her in the Lubyanka would be a bullet in the back of her head. She ran rapidly through all of the options for saving her skin and there seemed to be only one that had any prospect of success. She would have to defect and do it straight away. She had a significant amount of information that was tradeable and she could add to that by using her peerless lock-picking skills and making a note of the contents of the envelope that the Colonel had been so keen to see hidden away.

After having quickly selected a suitable pick she checked the corridor to make sure there was no sign of anybody outside and then hurried over to Rebenski's desk. The lock was easy to open, but she needed to be careful about the envelope. She put on a pair of gloves to avoid leaving fingerprints and then lifted it delicately out of the drawer. It was unsealed, but that did not mean that the contents could be removed without the fact that they had been disturbed being detected. If it had been left there as a trap, one of several possible means of detecting that it had been opened would have been almost invisibly attached to either it or the document, or both. She held the envelope up to the light from the window and delicately prised apart the document within it. She could see no easily breakable threads between the four pages of typescript or other ways of monitoring its handling. The knowledge that someone could come into the office at any minute was acting like a steel pressure band inside her head and she knew that she would have to take a risk and presume that there were no other little traps that she hadn't spotted. She pulled the document out of the envelope, grabbed a piece of paper and a pen and made a quick note of the two new safe house addresses, including the one where the high value asset was to be located. She translated all of the details into her own code in case she was arrested with the information on her. Having noted also the name of the asset, together with several key, marketable details about him, she delicately reinserted the document into the envelope and put it back in the drawer, in exactly the same place. If there was to be a reasonable chance of the asset still being hidden in the chosen safe house after she defected then it would need to look like she hadn't had access to the document, so her efforts in this regard were highly important. The information concerning his whereabouts would be a useful add-on to the information that she had to trade with the British. She re-locked the drawer and heaved a sigh of relief.

Grabbing a blonde wig out of her collection, she pulled it on, then took her dress off and replaced it with a white blouse, beige jacket and matching beige skirt that she had never before used. They had been kept for circumstances in which she would need to leave the building in clothes that had not previously been logged by anyone watching her. Pulling a matching shoulder bag off the top shelf of the cupboard within which she kept her collection of 'theatrical costumery', she hurried over to the door and stuck her head out to survey the corridor once more. Seeing and hearing no-one, she made her way quickly from the KGB suite at the top of the embassy to a fire escape at the rear. Having deactivated an alarm that would have alerted everyone in the building to the fact that an entrance or exit had been improperly breached, she slipped out of the fire exit and headed off in search of a taxi.

At the same moment that she left her office, Zaliatev turned to Grimlinski and said,

"And there we have it, a traitor caught red handed in the process of copying highly secret information for transmission to an enemy."

The two men were standing in the office next to Irina's. They had watched her open the desk and the envelope within it through a couple of well-hidden spy viewers that had been inserted into holes drilled in the wall joining the two offices. Grimlinski said,

"A very simple but highly effective trap Colonel. I presume that the details of the new safe houses and the supposed person of interest are all fake?"

"Indeed comrade, the last thing I would wish is that she should be given any genuine new information to try and trade. She has done quite enough damage already."

"Good. Now we must see where she runs and whom it is she's been passing her information to. I have stationed four men within sight of the embassy as you suggested. They have instructions to follow her wherever she goes and to seize her as soon as she meets with whichever of our British friends turns out to be her handler. That meeting will be the final, clinching evidence of her treason. By the end of today we should have enough evidence in place to send her back to Moscow in leg irons, figuratively speaking of course."

He smiled, a gesture that was a rare visitor to his face and one that was never tinged with kindness.

Irina, meanwhile, had spotted the first of the tails, who had hailed and jumped into the taxi that was now following hers. She told the driver of her taxi to take her to a derelict old dockland warehouse that she had used previously for various purposes. Once there she ran into the crumbling three storey building and hid within the shadows. The second taxi arrived within seconds and after paying the driver, her tail stood for a few moments trying to guess which of the old buildings in the vicinity she might have gone into. He didn't get time to make a decision. A single gunshot rang out and he dropped dead onto the ground. There was so much noise from machinery and the shouting of dockers several hundred yards further down the river front that the sound of the revolver passed unnoticed by anyone other than the gulls that it sent scurrying up into the air. She hurried out from her hiding place to check her handiwork. Her victim stared blindly up at her, with a bullet placed squarely between his eyes. After checking that there was no-one in sight to watch her, she grabbed his ankles and heaved him quickly into the derelict warehouse. She manoeuvred him into the darkest of corners and covered him with some old sacks that were lying around on the floor. She then hurried out of the building and out onto the road that ran behind it, in search of the nearest bus stop.

Four hundred yards further down the same road, two additional tails were nearing meltdown while they waited for a lorry to be moved. It had broken down while reversing into a warehouse. The vehicle was so large that it completely blocked the road and pavement. The driver finally managed to re-start the truck's engine, just in time for them to see Irina, with her distinctive walk, disappearing around a corner in the distance. They had been part of Grimlinski's 'belt and braces' team, the second and third tails that were to follow the first in case anything went wrong. They'd hired a Ford for the day rather than risk her recognising an embassy car. With the lorry finally out of the way, the KGB driver now put his foot right down on the accelerator so that they could catch up with their quarry before she disappeared from sight and they became the targets of Grimlinski's wrath for losing her. When they rounded the corner, they were just in time to see her jumping onto a bus. Keeping as much distance as they could from it to try and avoid arousing her suspicions, they followed it for ten stops before Irina jumped off and headed down a deserted narrow side street. The vehicle continued its pursuit, keeping even further back this time, with the tail in the passenger seat jumping out and hurrying ahead to follow her on foot. The street opened onto a major road at the end and he only just made it in time to see her stepping onto another bus that was going to Mayfair. He beckoned wildly to the driver to catch up and they then began following the bus. She alighted in a bustling New Bond Street and had disappeared by the time the tail in the passenger seat had jumped out to follow her. He began searching desperately within the crowds, trying to get a glimpse of where she might have gone.

Irina, meanwhile, was hiding in plain sight within a telephone box, with her back to the outside world. She knew that what the KGB regarded as Gus's cover operation, the detective agency, functioned as a normal commercial business and she soon found its number in the much-thumbed telephone directory. He was the one person in British intelligence whom she knew directly and had actually met, so he was her automatic choice as the contact through whom she would try and set up her defection. Alice was more than a little startled by the voice at the other end of the phone when Irina rang.

"I need to speak to Benedict, now. Tell him it is a matter of life and death. My name is Irina and he has met me before with regard to his cousin."

Normally, she would never identify herself over a public telephone line, or say anything about the business that she worked in. But this was not a normal situation and she needed to move quickly.

Thirty minutes later Mr. One burst into Gus's outer office like a tornado, although it was rare to see a tornado with one arm in a sling, the result of the car crash when Jenkins and Fossett had been killed. Alice very literally jumped in her seat as the door burst open and the human whirlwind powered through, straight into Gus's inner sanctum, flinging the door to behind him without a word. She muttered "Good God Almighty," while ruminating on the fact that all of her attempts to improve One's social graces had come to naught.

"Augustus," he said breathlessly, "I decided to come as soon as I got your message. This could be monumentally important. Give me the full gist of what's going on."

"Basically, it appears that Zaliatev's number two wants to defect. Her situation is so desperate she was prepared to tell me more than one might ever expect over a telephone line because she needs to be evacuated urgently. She's in the process of being framed for a string of recent KGB failures and fears that she will meet her maker in the basement of the Lubyanka with a bullet in the back of her head. If we will give her an absolute guarantee of a new identity and a safe location well out of the KGB's reach, she will spill the beans on pretty well everything she knows as the price for her rescue. She has been his number two for some time and has had access to a whole raft of policies and operations that will be of immense interest to us and our allies."

"So basically, I need to put the choreography in place to facilitate her crossing of the lines."

"To an extent, but not entirely."

"I don't understand."

"She's doing much of it herself. In the first instance she will only meet someone from MI5 whom she knows personally and there is only one individual who fits the bill – yours truly. She doesn't want anyone else to know where she is in case there is leakage somewhere along the line and a KGB hitman gets there before us. I'm meeting her at nine o'clock this evening and if I can provide a signed, written guarantee of what she wants, she will hand over immediately some crucial information as an initial down payment, with far more to follow. All you need do is provide me with the address of a safe house where I can take her that will have the necessary levels of protection in place and organise the signed guarantee that I will take with me."

"I'm surprised that a signed guarantee is so important to her, she'll know only too well that such things can be valueless."

"Startling as it may sound, she tells me that Zaliatev's briefing notes on me state that I am a man of absolute integrity. I don't think that's meant as a compliment, I believe that has been noted simply because it is useful to the KGB to know whose word actually means anything when they have to do a deal with their enemies. This is one such deal and she believes, rightly or wrongly, that I will not be so unethical as to convey a guarantee of her safety that I know to be worthless."

"Quite remarkable, especially when all of the information we now have on this woman shows her to be absolutely ruthless and totally without ethics when dealing with others. She even machine gunned to death two of her own men during the operation that rescued your cousin."

"Indeed. The situation is rich with irony."

"It's her utterly ruthless nature that makes me more than a little worried about your safety Augustus. This could easily be some kind of set-up – maybe she intends killing you as a demonstration to her superiors that she is most certainly not working for, or with, the British."

"That's always a possibility, but there's a risk in everything we do is there not Angus? What we're being offered is the biggest of prizes in terms of intelligence gains and such things do not come without the danger that they are simply traps of a lethal nature."

"I think I will need to organise suitable back-up for you, just in case."

"That would be a bad idea I'm afraid. She's chosen a location for the meeting where it is virtually impossible for anyone else to be present without her spotting them. I did also give her my word that I would not reveal the chosen location to anyone else."

"And your word is your bond, etc. Yes, I appreciate that Augustus, but I don't think you should believe yourself obligated by such a guarantee when you're dealing with a person whose ethics seem to be interchangeable with those of the angel of darkness."

"How very biblical of you Angus. No, I'm afraid that's the way things are. If I give my word, I keep it. Full stop."

On the other side of the lines, Grimlinski appeared to be in imminent danger of involuntarily launching into space as an incandescent human Sputnik. He stormed into Zaliatev's office, saying,

"Unbelievable! Absolutely unbelievable! The clowns have lost her! Two of them followed her as far as Mayfair and then she gave them the slip, as if she were a ghost, and the other one that managed to stick with her for the first part of her journey has disappeared off the face of the earth. Nobody knows where he is and the only conclusion that I can draw is that she has either knocked him senseless – if he had any sense to have knocked out of him, which I doubt – or killed him. As you know, there should have been a fourth man available, but it turns out that he had the runs and ran into an embassy toilet instead of after the target. You couldn't make it up!"

"She is highly dangerous and well skilled in the art of disposing of tails comrade. I assume that you've called in help from another team and briefed them so that they can extend the search to a wider area?"

"Of course, but they're even more incompetent than the others. Nobody has seen hide nor hair of her. I'd never have chosen these two teams to do the job had I been made aware of their mediocrity. If this had been an operation in Moscow we'd have such a tight grip on her movements that she wouldn't be able to sneeze without us knowing. Here, they've lost her for good, I think. She clearly intends to defect and there's nothing now that we can do to stop her."

"When the stakes are so high one should never give up comrade. The fact that she was last seen in Mayfair is interesting. I think maybe that the best strategy now is not to try and follow her, but to follow the person whom I think she will most likely contact. Tell your men to keep looking and I will try an alternative approach that may yet stop her in her tracks."

Terrified for her life though she might be, Irina was nevertheless managing to get a certain amount of satisfaction from running rings around the teams trying to find her. When she had finished her phone call to Gus, she pulled a lightweight black coat out of her shoulder bag and slipped it on over her jacket and skirt, covering them completely. She then took another wig out of the bag. After swapping that with the one that she had initially fled in, she exited the telephone box looking a completely different woman. Only her trademark walking oddity gave her away, but, as she blended into the throngs of people flowing down the street, such a thing was much less easy to spot.

She had chosen to meet Gus in a location she had used once before for clandestine purposes. It was a courtyard garden at the rear of a substantial Georgian house in Camberwell. The house had been mothballed following the death of the owner, Lady Jane McMattersly, and had been suggested as a meeting place by a contact when she had bought information off him three months earlier. The lock on the gate in the high wall that surrounded the garden was easily picked and she slipped inside two hours prior to the meeting with Gus. The adjoining properties were commercial and unoccupied at night, so there was no-one to observe or overhear her. There was a bench under the colonnade that ran along the rear of the house from where she could see if anyone came in through the gate. A trellis that lined much of the outer wall of the garden provided a convenient climbing frame which she ascended periodically to see if there was any sign of unwanted presences within the narrow street that ran past the rear of the house. The plain, unfussed architecture of the more modern buildings on the opposite side of the street made it difficult for anyone to hide without being spotted. There were no recessed doorways, porticos or other convenient places for someone of ill intent to lurk in the shadows. She was as certain as she could be that she hadn't been followed and that there was nobody within the near vicinity of the walled garden other than herself.

At three minutes to nine a car drew up outside the rear wall of the garden. Irina retreated deep into the shadows of the colonnade and held her breath, her gun at the ready. The gate creaked open and the silhouette of a man appeared, slightly illuminated by the mediocre street lighting. He walked slowly into the middle of the garden. He had a cigarette in his mouth and a lighter in his right hand, which he raised slowly and flicked on in order to light the cigarette. Irina could then see that it was Gus. She walked slowly out of the shadows, her gun all the time pointed at him and said,

"Do you have the guarantee?"

"I do. I'm going to put my hand inside my jacket to remove it, OK? Here it is. Use my lighter so that you can read it."

She took it from him and did as advised, all the time keeping one eye on him. Apparently satisfied, she put it in her coat pocket and pulled out an envelope. She held it out and said,

"Here is the first down payment on my new life."

A single gunshot rang out and she collapsed at Gus's feet. Her head was at an angle that just caught the faint light from the nearest streetlamp and he could see that she had been shot in the side of the skull. He made as if to grab his gun and run for cover, but his right arm was still a little stiff as a result of the recent car crash in which Jenkins and Fossett had been killed and he couldn't move as quickly as usual. A familiar voice said, sharply,

"Stay right where you are Mr. Benedict and don't move."

There was a slight gap where the gate had not closed properly and through which the fatal shot had been fired. It was through that the Colonel's voice came. He said,

"What a perfect opportunity to shoot you both and then have your body disappeared along with hers so that nobody would ever know precisely what had happened to you. That would certainly be one problem less for me, given all the damage you have done to my plans over the last couple of years. Would you shoot you if you were me do you think?"

"Only if I pulled a gun on you," Gus said.

There was a slight pause and then the Colonel said,

"That is the right answer. People without principles I have no hesitation in despatching into the afterlife, if such a thing indeed exists. But the one thing I do admire in you Mr. Benedict is that you are actually a man of strong principle – such a rarity in my experience. My one remaining principle is that I do not kill those who stand for some kind of decency unless it is absolutely unavoidable. That which is rare in our profession can too easily become extinct. On that sole basis you will live to fight another day, as they say. Do give my best wishes to your cousin by the way."

"How did you know we would be here?"

"For that I have you to thank, Mr. Benedict. I was sure you would be her contact, so I simply followed you. A colleague once described me as a ghost in terms of my tailing skills. I honestly believe there is not a person that I have followed that has been aware of the fact, so you can take some comfort in that. You have not been careless, just a little outclassed for once, I suppose. It is only fair that I should turn the tables and frustrate your purposes instead of the other way round don't you think? Who knows, I might yet be able to make a habit of it. Keeping you alive may give me that satisfaction."

"I assume that your people will be doing the housekeeping?"

"Indeed. The body will have disappeared within the hour. Now I must disappear I'm afraid. Throw your gun across to me please and then her bag and the envelope that she was about to give you."

Gus did as instructed. The Colonel picked the three items up, putting the gun and envelope in his pocket. He said,

"Thank you. Now, in the usual way of these things, please count to one hundred and then get in your car and drive away. Until we meet again."

Gus could just see through the slightly open gate as Zaliatev doffed his hat in imitation of his parting gesture at their previous meeting. Then he was gone.

Gus knelt down and checked Irina's pulse, just for formality's sake. It was perfectly obvious that she was dead. Her face looked as devoid of life as it was of the principles that so obsessed the Colonel. It was beautiful yet vacuous. He wondered how many people she had killed without thought or remorse before meeting her own untimely end. He remembered Angus telling him how she had shot her own men during Julia's rescue. Then he walked slowly out to his car, a leaden feeling of anti-climax and failure in his mission weighing him down.

He didn't know quite what to feel about the dead spy in the garden. He had seen so many dead bodies in the war and the experience had left him with an ingrained acceptance of the inevitability of death as a frequent occurrence. But he still couldn't avoid a certain sadness at her demise. It was as much occasioned by the sudden ending of a self-serving, ruthless life as it would have been by that of someone whom he had felt a degree of affection towards. With people like Irina, he despaired at the futility of their existence, a wasting of their short time on the planet that could have been put to so much better use. One life only, gone in an instant, with nothing of any worth to show for it. Everything and everyone sacrificed for the great career that had in the end simply been her passport to oblivion. He thought of the men with the body bag who would be arriving shortly and her final disappearance into an incinerator, ending as a puff of smoke that nobody other than her cremators would notice. Some new life that she had bought for herself, some end to the great career.

He drove off into the darkness.

CHAPTER EIGHTEEN

It was a bleak and bleary day, with patches of early morning mist floating across the road from time to time. Mr. One's newly repaired car sped through the Kent countryside towards Margate and the safe house where Jacob was coming to the end of his various interrogations. Both Gus and One were in a sombre mood as they reflected on the fact that their last outing in the vehicle had ended with the driver, Jenkins, being shot and killed. Both men sensed what the other was thinking and, in an effort to cheer things up a little, Mr. One said,

"Three out of four is not a bad average."

Gus's mind took a second or two to switch from the memory of that fateful night to One's remark. He said,

"Three out of four what precisely Angus?"

"Successes at the expense of our KGB friends. We turned Elliott and got him to supply a barrowload of information without his former masters even knowing that he was still alive. We rescued your cousin without losing any men, while they lost two of theirs – and then we put an end to Fossett's career as a traitor, although in a rather more terminal fashion than we anticipated. We've only been outsmarted by them once recently, with regard to that female agent. I'd say that's pretty good going."

"It's certainly better than a kick in the pants as they say, Angus, although I really should have brought the Irina woman in safely. I should have spotted that I was being tailed – leading Zaliatev straight to what should have been our biggest intelligence coup for years was unforgivable."

"It's regrettable, certainly, Augustus, but while we're getting experienced in blocking his operations, we haven't got any better at tracking his movements. That man is the best in the business in terms of

195

his ability to avoid detection. Each time we've worked out how to keep tabs on him he changes his modus operandi and we lose track of him again. Spotting his meeting with the hack journalist Frank Chabler was one of the few successes we've had in tailing him. A man with his skills would have been able to follow either of us without being spotted. Had it been me instead of you I doubt that I would have fared any better. The woman would still be dead. The choice of how she was going to come in ultimately was hers and that's where the responsibility should lie, I'm afraid. If she'd have picked a public venue and agreed to us being there in strength, she'd probably still be alive and we'd be spending this week doing a deal and interrogating her."

"Possibly so, although Zaliatev may still have put a sniper in place. He wanted her dead at any price I think."

"Well yes, indeed. I think we've just got to accept that it's win some, lose some. We've won on far more occasions than he would wish and maybe we should just be happy with that. Perhaps we might spend our time more usefully by planning for our final meeting with Mr. Elliott, or Mr. Jacob as the Colonel refers to him apparently."

"OK."

"Elliott has said that he will now give us the additional key information that he promised during our last meeting, providing that he is satisfied with the guarantee of immunity from prosecution agreement that I've brought with me, together with the passport and other details of his new identity. He'll be looking to you as well as me to confirm that it's all kosher. He may or may not accept my reassurances, but you have a natural ability to persuade people that what is promised will be delivered."

"Presumably you're going to wait and see if his allegedly major revelation is all it's claimed to be before you activate the guarantee?"

"Indeed. But I'd also like to probe him a bit further, just to make sure that he isn't sitting on any more information as useful insurance for a rainy day. I'd prefer to secure a full disclosure of what he knows, if I can."

"So you want to make him sweat a little before reaching a decision on whether now is the right time to give him all of what he wants?"

"Correct. I'll only agree to the guarantee being activated at the point where I'm as certain as I can be that he's told us everything he knows."

The safe house was a dark, old building with a steep, echoing staircase that led up to a musty, shadow filled landing. Jacob was waiting in a room that looked out to the sea, which lay in a calm stupor between the beach and the horizon, a grey reflection of a depressingly dull sky. He turned to greet them as they entered, his face bearing all the washed-out signs of a man who had been subjected to continuous interrogation over several days. Mr. One nodded as he entered and gestured to Jacob to sit down at the table in the middle of the room. One laid all of the paperwork out in front of him once he had sat down, an enticing little pile of desperately wanted documents within inches of the man whose future depended on them. Jacob eyed them nervously, a man who was almost over the line into a new life, a re-start in a new identity, free from the need to continuously look over his shoulder. Mr. One said,

"Perhaps I should begin by thanking you for your cooperation so far, Mr. Elliott. You've given us a significant amount of valuable information and it all checks out. I believe you have an additional piece of information of truly major import – something that you wish to tell only us – and that you are now prepared to disclose it."

"I need to see the immunity from prosecution guarantee and the new identity details that I asked for as the price of my cooperation first."

"I don't have any problem with that. I've brought everything that you asked for with me. Please, take a look for yourself."

Mr. One pushed the relevant documentation and passport over to Jacob's side of the table. The anxious looking recipient examined them carefully. He said,

"OK, so these are mine now I presume?"

"Providing I'm happy with what you have to tell us."

"I don't see how you could be anything less than satisfied. That Russian woman should have been rather more careful to check my whereabouts within the house before she discussed confidential matters with the psychopath, or other psychopath to be more accurate. They were both off the scale in that respect. Shortly before my ill-fated escape attempt, I overheard her telling him that once I had completed my mission and he'd sorted out the stroppy MoD mole, his next job would be a prominent government minister. The individual concerned had engaged in some seriously scandalous behaviour that would not only cause him to be sacked if it became known, but would also lead to his public humiliation. He'd been made aware that the KGB had a full dossier on his activities and had been told that he had a simple choice. He could either be their servant, providing full information on everything of interest that was discussed in the cabinet, or he could refuse. If he did stand up to their blackmail, they would leak the full details of everything they had on him to the British press. From what she said it was pretty certain that he would cave in to their blackmail. Once he did, the psycho's job would be pretty much the same as it had been with me. He would be taken onto the minister's domestic staff and would bully him back into compliance every time he tried to escape from his obligations to Moscow."

"Do you have the name of this minister?"

"I have his name and the details of the scandalous behaviour that she mentioned. I will only give you them if you both confirm that the deal I requested has been granted and that all of these documents are now mine. I have no more information that I can give you, so your final confirmation of the deal is essential. I refuse to be kept waiting any longer."

"If you have the information that you claim to have and it checks out, then you have your deal. But you need to give us the information that you have first."

Jacob paused for a moment and then said,

"I can see all of the documentation in front of me, but I need your absolute word that it will all be activated – that there will be no danger that the passport will bounce at the border, or that the guarantee of immunity will turn out to be worthless."

Mr. One turned to Gus, who said,

"My understanding is that if this information is as significant as you claim and you have passed over to us all of the other information that you have, then your deal will indeed be honoured in full. I wouldn't say that if I didn't have confidence that my colleague would keep his word."

Jacob scrutinised Gus's face. He was utterly weary and his only thought was that the man looked honest and on that necessarily thin, impressionistic basis he decided he would have to take a risk and do what was being asked of him. He had run out of cards that he could deal. Desperately hoping that he was not about to be double crossed, he grabbed a pen and a piece of scrap paper that was lying on the table and proceeded to write something. He then passed the paper across the table to Mr. One. One picked it up casually and read its contents. He then folded it and put it in his wallet. He said,

"The name is familiar and the seriously scandalous misbehaviour is familiar, but the fact that Zaliatev has that information and is using it for blackmail purposes is new. That is an extremely valuable revelation Mr. Elliott. You don't happen to know how he got hold of the details?"

"She mentioned a journalist, Frank somebody or other, I can't remember his surname. She told the psycho that he'd been asking too much money for his services and that he should pay him a visit to help him lower his expectations for future jobs."

Mr. One nodded and said,

"We need to be certain that what you've now told us is everything you know Mr. Elliott. You'll understand that we don't want to be wasting time in pursuit of loose ends."

"The only reason I know what I know is because that arrogant bitch was so contemptuous of me that she almost assumed I didn't exist as a sentient being. It was because of her carelessness that I heard what I did. I didn't have access to anything beyond what she said. If I'd have tried to look for any documents that she might have brought with her on her visits to the house, or anything like that, she would have killed me as quickly as she might have sneezed."

Mr. One sat back in his chair and thought for a few moments, drumming his fingers on the table while he did so. He looked across at Gus and then said,

"My colleague and I are just going to have a little chat if you wouldn't mind waiting outside the room for a minute or two Mr. Elliott."

Once the door was safely closed behind Jacob, Mr. One turned to Gus and said,

"I know I said earlier that I was going to grill this character until he was burned to a crisp, but what he says makes sense. I really do believe we can trust him on this one, what do you think?"

"You said you already have much of the same information about the minister in question, so given that what our friend has told you corresponds with all of that it would seem reasonable to assume that his additional information about Zaliatev's attempts at blackmail is reliable as well. That will enable you to close down a potential truly major information leak and in itself justifies any decision to give him his deal. I'm inclined to believe what he says about not knowing anything else and every minute longer we keep on talking to him is simply more time for the Colonel's man in the cabinet to give away secrets."

"OK, I'll tell Mr. Elliott that he has his deal as soon as we catch our alleged ministerial mole attempting to betray a government secret. The passport and everything else will be activated at that point. I'll get a trap set up, providing the PM agrees and we should have a twenty-four-hour surveillance team in place by close of play this afternoon. I'd like you to spend a few minutes with Elliott going over the details of his transition into a new identity, new life, what he needs to be careful about, all that kind of stuff. While you're doing that, I'll start making the phone calls regarding our cabinet mole. I'll need to get the PM fully on board before I can get anything moving. Given the high stakes in terms of possible serious leaks I don't think he'll get in the way."

"That sounds like a reasonable plan. Shall we tell our friend his good news?"

They called Jacob back into the room and told him to sit down. Mr. One attempted a convivial smile, but the unfamiliarity of the gesture meant the end result looked more like a grimace. He said,

"We were going to give you a rather tougher time Mr. Elliott, but I think that I can judge when a man is telling the truth and when he's not. What you have just told us would seem to me to be sufficiently credible for us to bring matters to a swift conclusion, not least because I need to set matters in train regarding our ministerial friend straight away. You have your deal, providing that we can catch the alleged ministerial mole in the act and by so doing prove your information to be accurate. Arrangements will be made to get you out of this country within four days of this happening and my people will arrange for your financial assets to be untraceably routed to your new identity. If all goes well you will be able to start your life again sooner rather than later – and hopefully not make quite such a mess of it next time around. Good morning."

Jacob looked startled by the sudden, albeit conditional, granting of what he'd been desperately hoping for since his first encounter with the MI5 pair. The door banged to behind Mr. One within little more than a second of his final words. Jacob said,

"I presume that dramatic exit means there's no room for negotiating about the time I'm expected to wait before I can begin my new life?"

Gus said,

"Indeed. Sorry about that old man, but you needn't worry, sooner or later the deal you've just been given will be honoured in full, subject to the conditions stated."

"But what if this idiot of a minister doesn't give in to the blackmail, or if he's too clever for them to catch him? What happens to my deal then?"

"With the level of surveillance he's going to be under we'll know if he hiccups, so any attempt to pass secrets to the KGB isn't going to be missed. And if he is brave enough to reject any blackmail demands that are made, our surveillance team will pick that up and we will probably suggest that he pretends to change his mind before the KGB have time to spill the beans on his sexual shenanigans. We can then use him to feed false information to the Soviets. That would be an excellent outcome from our point of view. So, one way or another, if your information about Zaliatev's blackmail operation is both honest and correct, as I'm sure it is, we'll be able to verify it and you will get your deal."

"I feel like I've been here forever, as if there's no way out, no route back into some kind of normal life. The strain of waiting is beginning to drive me mad, I'm sure of it."

"Well at least you're alive and kicking old man, not everyone you've encountered during your adventures is in the same happy state."

Simultaneously, in the Soviet embassy in London, Comrade Grimlinski was just completing his investigation of Colonel Zaliatev, a deeply secret operation that its subject had not been informed about. The comrade had been happy to accept that Irina was a double agent and fully endorsed her execution and disappearance, but his ultra-suspicious mind had become convinced that the Colonel had been using her as a distraction from his own double dealings. As a result of a routine, random bugging operation he had known for some time that Zaliatev had long lost his respect for most aspects of Soviet communism. That was all he needed to make him question why such a man should remain one hundred per cent loyal to a communist power. The recent string of failed operations for which Irina had been solely blamed could not have been simply the result of one person's treachery, he felt. When his investigations had revealed that the Colonel had held a secret, one-to-one meeting with Gus at Lesnes Abbey, his suspicions had been doubly aroused. There was no record of what had passed between them. Then, the shadow he had instructed to discreetly follow the Colonel had come up with some dynamite news. His quarry's skills at throwing tails off the scent were so great that he had nearly always lost him, but on one crucial occasion he had managed to stay in place. He had seen Zaliatev shooting Irina and then noted how he held a calm and apparently business-like conversation with Gus, even though he was too far away to hear what exactly was said. He had seen the Colonel walk away without any sign of a confrontation with the English agent and then observed Gus drive away shortly afterwards. To Grimlinski, that was the clincher. Irina clearly had known something that was dangerous for each man and had been eliminated with the consent of both. That could only mean they were in league and that the Colonel was playing some kind of a double game in which he was in partnership with the Englishman. Within Grimlinski's fevered, paranoiac imagination, there was a missing link to be uncovered and when he found that he would be able to nail the Colonel as a second and much bigger traitor. He was beginning to form a clear view of what he thought he was looking at. The Colonel's game was simple but ingenious. He would appear to be the ultra-loyal and diligent KGB officer by conducting operations which would cause significant damage to the West. However, since he was in some way in league with people like Gus, he would use the treacherous Irina to make the operations fail, without her being aware of her status as a pawn in his wider game plan. That would protect Western interests while making it look as though he was the good communist whose work was being undermined by a Soviet double agent. Irina would then pay the price and the fact that he had caught and executed her would again make him seem like the supremely loyal and dedicated communist that he wasn't. And now the final pieces of the jigsaw seemed to be falling into place. The Colonel had, on the previous day, triumphantly shared with him the details of his successful blackmail operation which would turn a top British cabinet minister into a Soviet spy, leaking crucial details directly from discussions involving the Prime Minister to the KGB. He had said that the new high-ranking mole was being activated the following morning. Grimlinski now expected there to be yet another reason why this crucial intelligence breakthrough would be thwarted before it could bear any significant fruit and that, for him, would be the clincher in establishing the Colonel's guilt. A fourth failure in a row would be just too great a coincidence and there would no longer be Irina to hide behind. As far as Grimlinski could see, the operation could only be sabotaged if the Colonel himself betrayed it to the British, given that he seemed to have kept it so close to his chest. He was unaware of how much the Colonel had told Irina and how Jacob in turn had overheard her discussing the details with Dogsbody. As soon as the expected failure occurred, with the exposure of the minister concerned, the comrade would personally deal with the Colonel in the same way that Irina had been dealt with. Going through all the rigmarole of bringing him before a Tribunal would be too risky. Zaliatev was such a convincing liar that he might wriggle free without being found guilty and then he would in turn be plotting the death of Grimlinski, and the comrade knew only too well that he would not survive once he was on the Colonel's list of 'things to do'. No, there was only one safe and viable course of action. He would need to do the job himself. It would be simply a matter of deciding between a surprise bullet in the back of the head, if he could catch the Colonel off guard, a long-range execution with a sniper's rifle, or ripping him to shreds with a machine gun. Comrade Grimlinski was extremely proud of his sniper skills, but a close-range killing, using either a pistol or a machine gun, would require less preparation work. He decided that he would sleep on the matter.

Back in Margate, Gus was in the process of winding down the meeting with Jacob while Mr. One was busy over the telephone, setting the trap that would catch the ministerial mole. Gus had an agenda that had not had any prior discussion with Mr. One. It was the direct result of the deep background investigation that he had been asked to do as part of the process of evaluating the reliability of the information Jacob was offering in pursuit of his 'deal'. He had been mulling over the pros and cons of proceeding with it during the journey over and had now decided that ethically there was only one course of action. Whether Mr. One would agree was another question, but he would cross that bridge when he came to it. He said,

"Now, before I go, I need to run through the protocols and advisories regarding your proposed new life so you don't make any errors that would reveal your location, or the fact that you are still alive. There are many advantages to being thought to be dead Mr. Elliott, as I'm sure you appreciate. But before I do any of that, there's a significant issue we need to deal with. We're giving you immunity from prosecution, as you requested, and that immunity includes the crime that first made you vulnerable to blackmail by the KGB."

"The details of which I will be keeping to myself, as agreed."

"When our people check your past there's nothing that can be kept to yourself, Mr. Elliott. We did uncover the fact that you accidentally killed a pedestrian while clearly drunk and tried to pay off a witness to make sure that you were never prosecuted."

"Oh. I see. That's a nightmare I prefer not to be reminded of."

"That may be the case, but the young man's family has found the death of their son much less easy to forget than you have. It ruined his parents' lives and his mother has never got over it. I know that because it was my sad job to investigate that part of your past."

"It's not something I can ever excuse myself for, I know that."

"I'm sure that's the case, but there's rather more that you can do than simply feel guilty about something for which you have no intention of ever paying the lawful penalty."

"Such as?"

"You're a wealthy man, Mr. Elliott and we will be very kindly arranging for your money to follow you into your new life. The young man's parents are anything but wealthy. His father developed a drinking problem after the death and lost his job as a result. They've been living in poverty ever since. You can change their circumstances very radically by sending them a substantial sum, a gift in memory of their son from an anonymous donor. How does that idea grab you?"

Jacob looked lost and confused, like a child being led through a secret garden that previously he'd found too frightening to enter. He said,

"How much do you have in mind?"

Gus took a piece of paper out of his pocket and wrote down a sum. He then passed it to Jacob who visibly blanched. He said,

"That's a quarter of my entire wealth."

"Think of it as something equivalent to a court award of damages, something that in your case is both punitive and compensatory. There is nothing that can ever bring their child back to them, but you can buy them out of some of the consequences of having lost him. You can pay their debts, give them the money to buy a decent house and compensate them for the wages that the father lost as a result of the state your crime left him in. The fact that someone visibly cares might even be a great comfort to them, who knows. What do you think?"

"Can we at least negotiate about the sum?"

"No, it's take it or leave it. You'll still get your deal if you reject my suggestion, it's just that you might have a problem or two persuading us to rescue you should the cover of your new identity be blown. You'll remember how your last attempt to escape into a new identity ended. The next time you end up in a Soviet prison you won't come out alive again, that I can guarantee. So if you can't bring yourself to think of your little payment as an act of recompense, perhaps you might consider it as insurance."

"That's moral blackmail. I don't get it, what's in it for MI5 if I pay these people off?"

"Let's just say that some of us don't particularly like being accomplices to serious law breakers. If we give you a deal that includes immunity for this particular act, we'd like to think we'd ensured that you at the very least compensated the victim's family. It's as simple as that."

"And if I don't pay up, you might just accidentally leak my new identity and my whereabouts to the KGB, is that the undercurrent I can sense here?"

"Did I say that? I don't remember doing so. Leaks are always possible, but we could take extra measures to make sure that your new identity and location are as leakproof as possible. Or we could decide not to, that is a possibility, who knows?"

"So I am in fact being given no alternative. You're just burying your threat between the lines. What if I were to pay half of this amount? That would be more affordable and the parents would still be comfortably off as a result."

"I've given you a figure that provides the family with some sort of justice Mr. Elliott. That is the figure that will make you worth fully protecting from our point of view. Unless you tell me otherwise, I'll arrange for the amount to be deducted from the funds that are transferred to the account that you will hold in your new name, once your deal has gone through. Do you tell me otherwise?"

Jacob stared at the wall morosely. He said,

"Do what the hell you like, you clearly intend to. Just make sure that the rest of my deal is honoured."

"Oh, it most certainly will be. This impressive evidence of your remorse will work very much in your favour. As soon as I know that the payment has been made, you'll be given a code and contact details to use in the event of you fearing that your identity has been compromised. I will also ensure that your details are only ever available to my colleague and I and the head of MI5. There will be no possibility of a leak."

Gus had long experience of setting up new identities and he was well versed in the art of making them secure. He spent the next half hour explaining in detail to Jacob how he could best protect himself once established in his new life, while never letting him forget that all his efforts would be in vain if MI5's in-house protection of his new name and location were to in any way become 'insecure'. When he'd finished, he went downstairs and found Mr. One completing a series of phone calls to

London. As a freelance MI5 operative, Gus knew very well that, despite his long experience and seniority arising from his past roles when a full member of the service, he had no authority to force Jacob into the kind of payment that he was now confident would be made. He had taken a risk and calculated that when he told Mr. One what he'd done and why, One would be in sufficient sympathy with the reasoning behind it to give it the official, binding authority that only he could provide. But Gus had no guarantee of this. When he confessed what he'd been up to he was not disappointed. One smiled wryly and said,

"How very Augustus Benedict. I think your role in this arrangement will be one of those things I keep in my head and not on paper, but in this instance your Robin Hood instincts have my full support. I don't feel as uneasy as you about Elliott having avoided a prison sentence for his inexcusable crimes. The fact that his actions caused him to fall into the hands of KGB blackmailers, who then incarcerated him in one of their delightful interrogation cells after he tried to escape from their clutches, would seem to be a severe punishment in itself. I'm sure that he had a far worse experience being drugged and terrified out of his wits by them than he would ever have had during several years in a British prison. But he did cause catastrophic damage to the young man's family and I'm very comfortable with the idea that he should compensate them for the pain he caused. I will make the necessary arrangements for the compensation to be extracted from his wealth and sent to them, anonymously of course. I will need to confirm with him that he consents to this arrangement, but from what you tell me there should be no problem in that regard. Now, before we accidentally turn MI5 into a thoroughly moral enterprise, let me tell you what's happening with regard to our somewhat compromised ministerial friend."

Mr. One explained the nature of the trap that had been set for the minister in question. He'd had authorisation from the Prime Minister and all of the necessary surveillance manpower would be in place by late afternoon. If the ministerial mole tried to pass a secret he would be caught immediately. It was now just a matter of awaiting developments. He said,

"All in all, this has been a very successful day, Augustus. Our friend Elliott's revelation was of far greater importance than I anticipated. I'm heading back to London now if you'd care to join me."

"No, thank you Angus, I'd appreciate a brisk, brain-clearing stroll down the promenade if you don't mind. I'll catch the train back afterwards."

"Your wish is my command, Augustus. I'll see you tomorrow afternoon. In case you've forgotten, we've got a meeting about Zaliatev at three."

Gus took his time strolling down Margate promenade, letting the brisk breeze and the scent of the sea fill his mind with thoughts of faraway places, of oceans he'd crossed in the past on the way to missions where he'd believed he had a greater chance of being killed than surviving. The Zaliatev operations had an echo of that. They had hit closer to home than most other recent missions, with the threat that had been posed to his cousin's life and the moment after Irina's execution when the Colonel had weighed in the balance the pros and cons of adding Gus to his list of kills. His cousin had survived and, yet again, so had he, but such near misses naturally made him want to reassess whether his continued commitment to the security services was worth the risks to himself and his wider family, or whether it might be time to settle for a quieter life and restrict his activities purely to his private detective agency.

He bought a cup of tea from a dowdy, windswept stall where he was the only customer on this out of season day and sat down on a bench facing the lapping tide, with its aroma of fresh seaweed. As he let the familiar soothing brown liquid bathe his lips while the cup warmed his cold hands, two things struck him, almost simultaneously. First, how even the deeply flawed, self-serving Jacob had needed the trust that Gus seemed to generate before he would make his final and most important disclosure. Second, the Colonel's startling and unsolicited revelation that he had one remaining principle, a determination not to kill "those who stand for some kind of decency unless it is absolutely unavoidable". He remembered Zaliatev's exact words as if they had been burnt into his brain, "That which is rare in our profession can too easily become extinct. On that sole basis you will live to fight another day ..." The more he thought about it the more he was confounded by this extraordinary reason for Zaliatev not shooting him along with Irina when he had the chance. There would have been no witnesses and the two bodies would have been 'disappeared' in the same incinerator. The same man who had been coldly ruthless in his execution of her had passed over an opportunity to simultaneously eliminate an enemy agent who had been causing him problems he could well do without because he admired Gus's 'decency'. There seemed to be a puzzling contradiction between the hard-boiled executioner and his act of mercy. As Gus sipped the cup of bland but soothing tea, he contemplated the significance of these two examples of his apparent indispensability within the moral quagmire of the intelligence business. He wondered if they were sufficient reasons for him continuing to do what Mr. One had frequently told him was a job that had been tailor made for him by the Almighty. Gus was deeply sceptical about the existence of an Almighty and suspected that if such a being did exist it might be equally sceptical about a doubting Thomas such as him. So, One's assurance on its own was not a clinching argument in his inner debates about his future. But maybe Jacob and Zaliatev had unwittingly provided the additional reasons he needed to keep going.

While Gus was contemplating all of this, the trap that was being set up to ensnare the ministerial mole was being finalised. It caught its man two days later. The would-be traitor had ordered a lunchtime bowl of soup and a coffee at a small but smart restaurant only a fifteen-minute walk from Westminster. He had booked a table by one of the windows and, on departing, had left a small but thick envelope on the floor, carefully concealed behind the long red velvet curtains. The Soviet embassy man who came to collect it five minutes later was well known by sight to one of the surveillance team. He had booked the same table. When he exited the restaurant half an hour later with the envelope safely installed in his inside jacket pocket, he found himself being jostled by a group of four men who were apparently having some sort of an argument. Their shouting grew intense and he was pushed out of the way as three of them chased after the fourth and they all ran off into the distance. It suddenly occurred to the embassy man that he should check his inner jacket pocket and when he did so his worst fears were confirmed. The envelope had disappeared.

When news of this incident reached Grimlinski's ears he concluded that he was now in the endgame. The final piece of the jigsaw slotted into place at teatime on the same day. It was announced that the minister in question had resigned with immediate effect, "to spend more time with his family". For the comrade, these two events meant one thing. Only he and the Colonel had known about the envelope drop and as he hadn't leaked any information about it the informant must have been the Colonel himself. The collector had known none of the details of the operation, other than the fact that he was required to do a pick-up of an envelope containing unspecified information. The Colonel had once again sabotaged his own operation, probably via his contacts with Gus. He had set up a spectacular KGB coup with the recruitment of the minister, making himself look like the ultimate Party loyalist. He had then protected his Western friends from the consequences of his actions by betraying the mole before the first secret could be picked up. Previously, he had used Irina to do his dirty work, now presumably he would find another subordinate to take the blame. It was just a matter of time before he announced who this would be. Grimlinski wasn't prepared to wait for that to happen. He decided that he now had all the evidence he needed to execute the Colonel. It was just a matter of working out how this could best be done without leaving any trail that might lead back to him.

By the following day he had the answer. When Gus was sitting having a mid-morning pot of tea at his favourite café he was surprised when the waitress gave him a small envelope that she said had been left by a smartly dressed young man with a foreign accent. On opening it, he found it to be an invitation to meet from an unnamed individual who seemed most likely to be the Colonel. It said, "Yesterday's resignation has caused unusually severe difficulties with my superiors. We may be able to collaborate on something that would take the pressure off me and give you something of significant value in return. If you're interested meet me at nine o'clock tonight at the walled garden, the scene of our previous 'fatal encounter'. Come alone or everything is off."

Gus was both intrigued and deeply suspicious. The fact that the letter made reference to the walled garden and the 'fatal encounter' made it highly likely that it was from Zaliatev. After some consideration of the matter, he decided he would take no risks. Using his MI5-derived authority he was able to persuade the head of the insurance brokers whose offices looked down on the garden from the other side of the street to let him use one of the firm's top floor windows as a surveillance post from six o'clock onwards. From there he would be able to see exactly what was going on in the street and whether the Colonel arrived alone or with company.

Zaliatev, meanwhile, had received a message of his own. On his way into the embassy for a meeting with Grimlinski about the latest failed operation, he was surprised when a young woman approached him with an envelope that she said she'd been paid to give him. She knew nothing about the man who had paid her, other than that he was a 'banker type', well spoken, well dressed and impeccably polite. The Colonel at first feared an assassination attempt and his finger was on the trigger of the pistol in his coat pocket from the moment she addressed him. Cautiously, he took the envelope and pocketed it, before hurrying on to the embassy. Once inside he found a typed message that said, "If yesterday's events caused you serious problems with your superiors in Moscow, we could discreetly collaborate on something that might take the pressure off, something that is of significant mutual benefit to both them and the UK. I've convinced my superiors that it is very much in UK interests to offer this assistance, given the significant intelligence benefits that they will derive from it, so I have their full support in this. If you're interested, meet me at nine o'clock tonight at the scene of our previous 'fatal encounter', the walled garden in Camberwell. Come alone or everything is off."

The Colonel was as suspicious as Gus had been after reading his own message. But he was indeed under severe pressure as a result of the latest operational failure and ultimately, he decided, beggars couldn't be choosers. It looked as if the invite was almost certainly from the Englishman, given the reference to the last place they had met. Maybe Gus felt he owed the Colonel something after he had spared his life, maybe there was a real possibility that what was being offered would give the Colonel a lifeline if, as he anticipated, questions would shortly start to be asked in Moscow about whether he was over the hill. He would be extremely cautious in case it was some kind of a set-up, but in the current circumstances he couldn't afford to ignore any opportunity to improve his drastically declining operational success rate. He would go along an hour before the meeting time and scout out the situation before deciding whether or not to enter the walled garden.

By seven o'clock in the evening Gus was spending his time trying to guess the age of the various buildings opposite his top floor surveillance post as a means of keeping his eyes focussed on the street, in which nothing seemed to be happening. Then, at seven-fifteen, there was unexpected activity. A car appeared, a black Ford Consul. It drove slowly down the otherwise deathly quiet street and paused outside the gate leading into the walled garden, before driving off into the distance. Ten minutes later, it reappeared and went through the same routine again. Fifteen minutes later, it came by a third time. This time it stopped about eight yards from the gate. A shadowy figure stepped out. Gus was both alarmed and perplexed. The man was thickset and unfamiliar. He was certainly not the Colonel. The sash window was open nine inches so that Gus could hear what was going on outside. It was just enough for him to be able to stick his head slightly out and watch as the man picked the front door lock of a building on the opposite side of the street to the garden, a few yards further down from where Gus was hiding. As soon as he had the door open, he signalled to the car, which drove off while he slipped inside. Gus decided to see if anyone else turned up. He had another fifteen minutes or so to wait. At approximately eight o'clock he saw another man emerge from a side road thirty yards down the street. This time he was familiar. It was most definitely Zaliatev. He walked slowly and cautiously towards the garden gate, which, unlike the last time, was unlocked and then peered in. Apparently satisfied that the garden was unoccupied, he stood surveying the surrounding properties for a few moments and then walked back the way he had come. Gus had noted earlier that, unlike the street he was watching from, the side road had numerous shadowy porticos within which it was possible to hide. He assumed that the Colonel had concealed himself in one of those at the very top of the road in order to scrutinise anyone who passed up and down the adjoining street before the appointed hour of nine pm. Assuming that the unknown man who had broken into a nearby building was engaged in the same activity, there were now three individuals watching the street.

At nine pm precisely the Colonel emerged from his hiding place and walked cautiously back down towards the garden gate, all the time checking every angle and shadow in the buildings around him. Evidently satisfied that he was alone, he slipped into the garden and disappeared from sight. Had the third individual not appeared earlier on, Gus would have gone straight down to meet the KGB man. However, he now had a problem. He'd noted that no signals had passed between the Colonel and the house where the third individual was concealed, so assumed that the two were nothing to do with each other. Clearly the intended meeting between Gus and the KGB man could well be some kind of a third-party set-up with the two men as the stooges, which would be a danger potentially to both of them, or somebody had learned of its details and was there to snoop, which equally could be problematic. Gus decided that the wisest and safest strategy was to stay exactly where he was and see what happened.

In the building a few doors down from Gus, Grimlinski was watching carefully. With no sign of the Englishman by ten past nine he decided that he clearly hadn't taken the bait, but the Colonel at least had. That was all the proof his paranoiac mind needed that the two men were in league and had carefully planned the succession of recent failures of KGB operations. Originally, he had intended to surprise and kill both of them, but now he would have to make do with just the Colonel, which would at least solve the main part of the problem he was dealing with, a previously undetected double agent within the KGB's London operation. He had carefully oiled the front door after breaking in so that there would be no tell-tale squeaks or creaks when he opened it. He delicately and slowly prised it open and after checking that all was clear outside, stepped out onto the pavement, his rubber soled shoes making no sound. He crossed rapidly to the other side of the street and then, staying in the shadows as far as he could, started to move towards the garden. Gus could just see the outline of a submachine gun in his hands. He was as sure as he could be that it was a Soviet weapon of early 1950s' vintage, making it almost certain that the Colonel was being stalked by one of his own people. He now had to make a split-second decision as to whether he would simply observe the outcome of an internal KGB dispute or whether he should return the favour that the Colonel had done for him in sparing his life during their previous meeting. The key determinant in his decision was of a practical as much as an ethical nature. He hurtled down the staircase and flung open the front door just as Grimlinski slipped into the garden. He shouted a warning to the Colonel and then took cover behind the side of the door frame, his pistol at the ready. Taken by surprise, Grimlinski paused just long enough to miss the faint movement in the shadows at the back of the garden that preceded Zaliatev taking aim with two perfectly placed shots. A short burst of machine gun fire preceded them, but the bullets went nowhere near their intended target. The comrade was dead before he hit the ground, a crumpled heap, his eyes staring sightlessly at the night sky.

The sound of the gunfire brought the Ford Consul out of its hiding place two side roads further down and it pulled up outside the garden gate. As the driver got out Gus could see that he too was armed with a submachine gun. With little more than a second's thought he took careful aim and shot Grimlinski's sidekick in the right leg, almost at the same time as another shot rang out. The Colonel was rather less humane, having aimed straight between the hitman's eyes. There was a clatter as the second machine gun hit the pavement, this time without being fired at all.

Zaliatev emerged from the garden and after examining the corpse, looked across the road towards where Gus was standing. He said,

"I do believe we were both intended to be dead by now Mr. Benedict. It is most unusual for our counter-espionage people to make such a mess of things, but then they didn't account properly for you. May I ask why you decided to save my life when you had been wise enough to stay out of the trap that was so uncivilly set for us?"

Gus smiled wryly and said,

"Last time we met, very curiously, you said you wouldn't kill me because I had a degree of 'decency'. Be that as it may, to think decency is a virtue worth preserving you must have at least some of it yourself, buried deep within that ice cold, murderous exterior. If I'd let you be killed, they'd have replaced you with an Irina think-alike and that would have left me with the depressing prospect of wrestling with an enemy with no decency at all. So, you could say either that I opted for the lesser of two evils, or that I 'did the decent thing'."

Zaliatev laughed appreciatively. He said,

"It is a long time since I can remember liking anybody Mr. Benedict, but I think I could almost manage it with you, even though it is MI5's successes that have occasioned me this unwanted excitement tonight. You will understand that I can't say any more on the matter than that, or comment on the identities of our deceased friends. I presume your people will deal with the tidying up before the police arrive to confuse matters. Given the high-ranking status of one of them, I think the mysterious disappearance of these two gentlemen would be the least problematic outcome for both your political masters and me."

"Great minds think alike Colonel. If you would care to skedaddle into the night, I will arrange for a team of 'street cleaners' and 'gardeners' to do the necessary."

Zaliatev nodded, briefly smiled and then walked swiftly back the way he'd come. He doffed his hat as he left, a gently ironic gesture which Gus reciprocated.

As the Colonel hurried back to his car, parked two side roads further down, he felt a sense of euphoria, something that he hadn't experienced for a long time. Partially, it was the simple result of having survived a determined assassination attempt. But it was bolstered by the knowledge that had there been enough credible evidence to accuse him of any wrongdoing, an officer of his rank would first have been hauled before a Tribunal or some suchlike back in Moscow. Grimlinski's botched assassination attempt, with no prior Tribunal or hint of what was coming, was testimony to the fact that he had no hard evidence and most probably had been acting in isolation, with only a subordinate officer in the know. The fact that such proof of wrongdoing was clearly missing gave the Colonel the space to manufacture his own evidence about serious security breaches being directly traceable to Grimlinski. Once two or three days had passed without any sign of the comrade, the Colonel would of course launch an immediate operation to find him. After no trace had been found, he would report back to Moscow that it looked likely that the comrade had defected to the West and had been spirited away to a new identity in a hidden location. That serious embarrassment for Counter-Espionage should be enough to keep them off his back for some time. For the Colonel, the thought of this 'liberation' added an extra spring to his step.

But there were other undercurrents at work within his notably refreshed state of mind. He hadn't been joking when he'd originally told Gus that he'd spared his life because of his 'decency'. Ever since his communist and religious belief systems had come crashing down in the wake of the Hitler-Stalin Pact, and his somewhat late conversion to the view that the purges during the Stalin years had been unjustified in terms of their scale and the motives behind them, he had found that looking for decency was like trying to find humility in a roomful of egotists. He'd rarely felt he'd encountered it in any credible form within the KGB or amongst its political masters, or in any of the governments and intelligence services that he'd spied on, but, for him, Gus was a genuine exception to the general rule. He had little sympathy with the Englishman's commitment to a capitalist power, but he had noted two things about the man that had impressed him: his fairness and trustworthiness. It was all in the dossier that had been compiled about him as a routine matter of course. This was a wealthy man who didn't just keep his money to himself, but gave sizeable chunks of it away to the less fortunate: ex-soldiers who had fallen on hard times, women who had too little to feed their children properly. Zaliatev still had a faint hope for a resurrection of a genuine form of communism, or some equivalent egalitarian system, at some time in the probably distant future. But after his experience during the Stalin years, he had believed that a large obstacle would always stand in the way of that dream: the corruptibility of human nature. To find someone who was genuinely a philanthropist in such a hard-edged profession as the intelligence business was therefore not only a surprise, but the match that re-lit the faint flame of the Colonel's long-lost hope for a fairer world, one in which the poverty that had sat like a noose around the neck of his own family would be eliminated. He had been unimpressed by those Western politicians he had encountered who laid claim to egalitarian views, rightly or wrongly believing them to be shallowly based. But Gus's beliefs were matched by his actions in every respect that he could find. It didn't mean that he and Gus would become bosom buddies: Zaliatev still believed that, despite the failings of Soviet communism, the West was the greater evil and should be weakened and undermined in all the ways possible. That would always keep him and Gus on opposite sides of the fence. But it did mean that he could respect the man, a compliment that he extended to hardly anyone, communist, socialist or capitalist, high or low ranking, male or female. In some curious way, within the complex mix of disillusionment and residual beliefs that populated the Colonel's tortured mind, Gus was a one-man statement of the fact that decency was still possible within even the most secret and lethal arms of governance. The fact that such a man had saved his life had genuinely moved the hard-bitten KGB veteran.

Gus, meanwhile, had dragged the body of the second hitman into the walled garden, out of sight of any randomly passing policemen. As he stood waiting for the clean-up team to arrive, he found himself looking down into Grimlinski's dead, staring eyes, as he had done with those of Irina. It was a clear night and they seemed to be peering deep into the heart of the universe above, as if they were looking for the deceased KGB man's future place or purpose. To Gus, who found it difficult to believe in an afterlife, there was nothing for them to find. The moment that the comrade had entered the garden with the intent of killing the Colonel was the point at which he had cut off his own access to what finite future remained for him. Looking up into the infinite array of galaxies above, Gus wondered how he would feel when his own luck ran out and he lay on his back somewhere, looking at the same view for the last time in the short interval before someone put a final bullet between his eyes. Would all of his scepticism suddenly disappear and would the fear that he may be wrong in his doubt lead him to make a last-minute declaration of belief in a creator, heaven, hell and all of that litany of religious faith? He smiled to himself as he wondered if the Colonel's judgement that he was a 'decent' man would be enough to squeeze him through the proverbial pearly gates. His train of idle thought was interrupted by the sound of the clean-up team's van arriving in the street outside. He bent down and closed the eyes of the two deceased Soviets. He had no prayers to say on their behalf, but he wished the dead no ill.

After sorting out the procedurals with the team, he left them to it and wandered back across the street to the insurance brokers' offices. He shut and locked the front door, posting the keys through the letterbox. As he watched the bodies being loaded into the back of the van the fact that, had things gone differently, they could have been his and the Colonel's corpses, fully hit home. He wondered if he had done the right thing in saving Zaliatev from Grimlinski's bullets. He was, after all, a ruthless operator who had held Gus's favourite cousin as a hostage. But he was also the man who had chosen not to kill Gus when he had the chance of doing so without any British witnesses, and had made that choice on what, for him, seemed quite extraordinary grounds. In saving the Colonel, it might be considered that Gus had merely returned the favour. But equally, he thought, a man who at least had spared his life on the basis of a principle rather than expediency had some genuine worth, what those of a religious disposition might regard as a chance of redemption. For that reason in particular, perhaps, he had made the right decision in warning Zaliatev about the assassin. But there was also a strong argument that his intervention in an internal KGB dogfight had best served the practical interests of MI5. The point he had made to the Colonel about 'better the devil you know' was in no way frivolous. His replacement would very likely have been in the Irina mould and operators like her would have been entirely treacherous opponents to deal with. Compared with her, the Colonel at least had some recognisable principles, ruthless though he may be.

With all of that resolved in his mind he decided that a quiet drink in his club was called for. Turning up the collar of his coat against the bleak chill of the night air, he walked off down the street, a man grateful still to be in the land of the living, leaving behind those who would have had him dead.

CHAPTER NINETEEN

Zaliatev arrived back at his apartment block in a reflective mood. During the drive home he had been ruminating about the various possible acts of treachery that he could invent, manufacture evidence for and then lay firmly at the door of the recently deceased Grimlinski. He was still deep in thought as he got out of the car. As always, his radar eyes checked out everything around him: all the other parked cars, all the shadows and crevices within the external structure of the ornate 1930s' apartment block, the ornamental hedges that were just high enough to conceal an attacker and the top of the building, in case a gunman had positioned himself there. Even though the block was occupied entirely by Soviet embassy staff, his experience earlier in the evening had proved that he was at risk from some of his own people as much as anyone else. Seeing nothing of concern, he locked the car door and headed towards the entrance.

As he travelled up to his apartment in the teak panelled lift, his mind switched back to Gus and the unexpected intervention that had saved his life. Had it not been for the Englishman's warning he might now be dead. It had been a long time since he had been so near his own demise and it made him think back to the religious upbringing of his childhood and the emphasis that was laid on the importance of a death that was free from sin. He had committed so many sins in his life that he wondered how long it would take to confess them all. He wondered also whether he might ever regain his faith in an almighty deity, a merciful being who would explain to him why the murderousness of the Stalin years and the horrors of the Nazi invasion of the Soviet Union had been allowed to happen. He knew that he too had been corrupted by all of the viciousness that he'd witnessed and had his own roll call of the dead to answer for. The weight of his own inevitable death suddenly seemed to sit heavily on his shoulders and made him fearful in a way he hadn't been for many years. What if he were wrong and there really was some kind of life beyond death, a heaven and a hell and all of those same things that Gus had briefly contemplated earlier? While they had not troubled Gus for more than a few moments, the legacy of the Colonel's lost religious values meant that such thoughts haunted and taunted him, suggesting the grim possibility of an eternity spent in the hell that until tonight he'd almost forgotten about, a place of darkness and torment that his traditional Catholic upbringing had burnt into his consciousness as a young boy. As he walked down the corridor towards his apartment, he was visibly sweating with all the long-forgotten fear that such thoughts were dredging up from the memories of his childhood.

His mind switched back to more immediate priorities as he reached his door. As always, he meticulously checked all the little means that he used to reveal whether or not anyone had picked the lock and sneaked into his apartment, planting false evidence against him, or waiting to assassinate him. In particular, the hairs lightly glued across the top and bottom of the door and its frame were still in place. Reassured, he turned the key in the lock and entered. He had gone no more than a foot or so inside when he felt a sharp pain in his abdomen. It didn't make any sense. He experienced severe indigestion from time to time, but he had never had a pain there before and never anything so intense. It stopped him in his tracks and he had to lean on the little side table near the door for support. He then felt a second even more severe pain in his back and he realised that he was being stabbed. As he descended to the floor, his fingers gripping the table edge and then letting go amidst the intensity of the pain, he was vaguely conscious of a figure standing above him. He recognised the man as someone whom he'd noticed talking to Grimlinski a couple of days ago, a hard-faced, shaven-headed thug who had only recently arrived from Moscow. He must have been waiting somewhere in the corridor outside to sneak up behind his victim. He was smiling as the Colonel looked up at him, too much in shock even to reach for his gun. Punching Zaliatev in the face, he sent his head cracking hard against the highly polished floorboards. He said,

"How so very long I've been wanting to do that to you."

As Zaliatev groaned, his nose bleeding badly, his assailant continued,

"Those who live by the sword die by the sword Colonel, isn't that old saying so very true? I've cut you in just the right places to give you a long and painful death. You won't remember my father, but you took him from our house when I was a child and he died in the Lubyanka because of you. When I joined the service, I always dreamed of a time like this and now, miraculously, it's here. You must tell me, these moments before death that you are experiencing in the same way that you made my father experience

216

them – what are they like? Do you see the whole of your worthless life flashing before your eyes? Are you desperately trying to make some amends for all the deaths you've caused, pleading for your soul to some god or other? How does it feel, how does it really feel when it's happening to you and not someone you've butchered?"

The light was fading within Zaliatev's mind. He was trying to focus on his past and his future simultaneously: where, if anywhere, he might be about to go; whether it would be to the hell he had so feared a few moments ago as a result of all his past actions; whether there was anything that could be done to stop himself going there; but he was finding it difficult to make his thoughts stick. They were sliding out of his grip, slowing down, disintegrating, then nothing. He slipped into unconsciousness as the hitman watched with undisguised satisfaction.

Putting his knife back in its sheath, the assassin hurried outside and wheeled in a large laundry basket that had been in the corridor, waiting for its cargo. He pulled a tarpaulin out of it and used it to wrap Zaliatev. He then hauled up the Colonel's limp body with some difficulty and managed to bundle it into the basket. He wheeled the contraption out of the room and into the lift, exiting from the building thereafter via the service door at the rear. He hurried over to his nearby car and deposited the body in the boot. Then he drove off at some speed. He smiled to himself as the phrase 'how the mighty have fallen' came to mind. In the Colonel's case, he had fallen into the car boot.

In a sense, Zaliatev was about to become a corpse at the hands of a corpse. Grimlinski had trusted only two men with the details of the illicit operation to kill the Colonel and, if they were lucky, Gus as well. One had died outside the walled garden along with his boss. But Grimlinski was a man who believed in the importance of a 'belt and braces' approach. In case the Colonel got the better of him and escaped, he'd positioned a second man at his apartment block, someone who'd been feeding his growing paranoia about Zaliatev being some kind of a double agent since he'd arrived from Moscow. It was an easy task, executed in the knowledge that the thorough seeding of a few doubts and rumours would quickly lead to a universe of conspiracy theories growing within the comrade's fevered mind. This sower of untruth was an up-and-coming young officer whom Grimlinski regarded almost as a son and the 'son' in turn seemed to regard his powerful mentor almost like a father. Fathers and sons, a combination the Colonel hadn't reckoned with.

Just over an hour later the assassin's car drove down a long, muddy track, deep into a wooded area of the countryside fifty miles or so from London. Once he had found a spot that met with his requirements, he stopped and tipped the tarpaulin-wrapped Colonel out onto the ground.

Taking a spade out of the car boot, he rapidly dug a shallow grave. Then, with no ceremony at all, he reached down to push the tarpaulin and its contents into the freshly dug hole. He was totally unprepared for what followed. Six gunshots rang out, shattering the silence of the wood. The gravedigger was blasted backwards by the impact of the bullets and dropped heavily into the mud with a sickly squelch. The loosely wrapped tarpaulin, from which gunsmoke wafted upwards, began to wriggle. What Grimlinski's man had omitted to do was to check for and remove the Colonel's gun. He had carelessly assumed his victim to be so far gone that such basic checks were hardly necessary and he had paid the ultimate price for his naivety. What he had also failed to realise was that Zaliatev's experience during the Second World War had made him a highly skilled survivalist. He was an expert in wound management and the stemming of bleeding. In addition, the assassin's supposedly lethal stab wounds had not been precisely enough directed to guarantee death. They were the work of an apprentice rather than a master. While the Colonel had lost consciousness following the attack in his apartment, the ice cold of the car boot and the violent jolting about due to the hitman's erratic driving, had woken him sufficiently to be able to rip his clothing and use it to make emergency bandages and then, through various means, stop the bleeding, externally at least. Now, despite feeling desperately weak, he managed to drag himself out of the tarpaulin, over to the car and, after an agonising struggle, into the driver's seat. Fighting all the time to stay conscious, he managed to start the engine and then turn the car around. Very slowly, he managed to drive back down the long muddy track and out onto the road. He then headed off, looking for the nearest village where he could crawl to a front door and ask the occupants to ring for a doctor and an ambulance.

As a man whose childhood memories had earlier resurrected a terror of a death beyond which damnation might lie as much as salvation, the Colonel was now determined to hang onto his life. He was acutely aware how close 'the spy who breathed fear' had come to breathing his last. Almost involuntarily, he found himself praying for his own survival, forgiveness, all kinds of long forgotten things. He wasn't even sure whom he was praying to – the God of the Catholic or Russian Orthodox Church, or some less well-defined being, a deity made up of various vague and woolly ideas about what a merciful creator might look like. As he drew up outside a house in the first village that he came to, his innate cynicism fought back against this apparent resurfacing of religious faith. He wondered if his sudden abandonment of long-term atheism would last beyond a successful trip to the operating theatre, should he survive. There was no-one more cynical about the Colonel than the man himself.

In the middle of the afternoon two days later, Gus was surprised when

Alice handed him a brief, cryptic message. She said,

"I've just had a rather odd phone call from a man with a hint of a Russian accent. He was struggling for breath a little and there were background noises that made it sound very much like he was in a hospital. He told me to write this down and pass it on to you and then hung up."

Gus looked at the message, which said, "There is some additional tidying up to do. You will find some more surplus material in the woods three miles south of Little Bellinghurst, about 2,000 yards from the road, down a track on your left."

After notifying Angus, he was picked up from the office by a two-man team within half an hour and driven straight down to the notified location. It didn't take them long to find the bizarre woodland scene, with a bloodstained tarpaulin minus its contents, a freshly dug grave and a corpse who was a Soviet 'diplomat', if the contents of his wallet were to be believed. The positioning and spread of the blood on the tarpaulin suggested strongly that it had held someone with serious wounds that were rather different to those of the dead man. Whoever it was appeared, in a biblical sense, to have picked up his bed and walked - or slithered - towards the car whose tyre tracks were clearly visible in the mud. Gus rapidly concluded that the missing injured party was most probably the Colonel, which would fit in with the weakness that Alice had noticed in the voice of the telephone caller. His suspicions appeared to be confirmed two days later when Angus informed him that inquiries had unearthed a hospital admission with serious knife wounds that looked likely to have been Zaliatev. The victim had been found in Little Bellinghurst several days earlier and taken straight to a London hospital. The police had interviewed a man who fitted the Colonel's description to a tee, and were sold a story about a robbery with violence. They were having problems in taking the matter further because the victim had discharged himself and vanished into the ether.

That was the last Gus saw or heard about the Colonel for some time. Routine MI5 monitoring reports noted that his apartment had been taken on by somebody new and there were no sightings of him anywhere near the embassy. There were no reports of him having left the country, but equally there was no evidence of him being anywhere within it. Then, twelve months after their last encounter, Gus was told that MI6 believed they had sighted the KGB man in several different overseas locations, but every time they tried to follow him, he disappeared into thin air. Nobody had been able to get close enough to confirm that it actually was him and he was too agile a moving target for anyone to get a decent surveillance photograph of his face. It was not known if he was still working for the KGB or whether he'd decided that it would be safer to disappear into a new identity and a new life after the attempts to assassinate him. When telling Gus about the most recent sighting, Mr. One said,

"Apparently our friend has been nicknamed 'The Ghost' by our SIS colleagues."

Smiling wryly, Gus said,

"How very like the Colonel, first he manages a miraculous woodland resurrection and then he masquerades as an ethereal spirit. At least he's not haunting our patch."

Two weeks after Zaliatev's mysterious disappearance, Jacob entered into his new identity in Switzerland, his long-awaited 'life after death'. It was somewhat soured by his becoming increasingly paranoiac that, somehow or other, the KGB would discover he was in fact still alive. He was to spend the remaining fifteen years of his life forever looking over his shoulder, fearful of the same 'ghost'.

The family of the young student that Jacob had killed had a rather more satisfactory 'life after death' thanks to the money that Gus had ensured was diverted to them to fund a new house and a future free of the poverty that had followed their son's demise.

For all his faults, that was something of which the Colonel would most certainly have approved.

Ghost or no ghost, Gus was convinced that somewhere, sometime in the future, their paths would cross again …

OTHER MYSTERIES BY P.J. ANDERSON AVAILABLE FROM
Nine Lives Original Books

The Spy with an Angel's Eyes: an Augustus Benedict Cold War spy novel

"The characters spring embodied from the page, even those with bit parts ... and the turns of plot are satisfyingly unexpected." A.B., a former book editor and previously of the Financial Times.

Some of Britain's gentleman spies were die hard patriots and traditionalists, a very few were traitors and one was so exotic that nobody knew quite how to describe him. His name was Augustus Benedict – a man with a razor-sharp mind and a knack for uncovering the truth at the heart of the most deeply buried secrets, an incurable lover of formidable women and a secret philanthropist with a curious side-line as a twentieth century Robin Hood. When a series of unexplained killings of British and Russian spies in and around Cold War London drew the CIA, the British intelligence services and the KGB into a dangerous blame game that could have spun out of control at any moment, Benedict was brought in to help get to the truth of what was going on. The CIA flew in Jennifer Marquis, one of its top operatives, to conduct its half of the investigation. Marquis and Benedict were ex-lovers. When the two were reunited in the race to find who was behind the killings, the sparks began to fly in every sense of the word. Mixed in with everything else were the most dangerous men in the British criminal underworld and they were in no mood to take any prisoners. Not everyone who began the investigation would live to see its end ...

Nine Lives Original Books has published two other of P.J. Anderson's mysteries. *'A Man Twice Dead: an almost perfect crime'* at first appears to be very much in the vein of traditional whodunnits. But as the story unwinds, it becomes apparent that something a little different is going on. *'The Ghost Fabler'* is a hidden gem which contains several compelling ghost stories, themselves woven within another ghost story, which in turn merges into a chilling tale of the macabre ...

A Man Twice Dead: an almost perfect crime.

For A.B., a former book editor, 'A Man Twice Dead', "... fizzes with inventiveness and ingenuity." For Delwyn Swingewood, it is, "... a country house murder mystery with a difference."

Country house murder mysteries are, of course, a fiction, unless a vengeful and brilliant mind decides to create a real one to right a wrong – and kill those who he, or she, presumes to be killers. What better way of playing with them, gradually rooting them out and then imposing the ultimate penalty? The assassin makes his victims the centre of a real-life plot, inspired by the whodunnit novels of the past, one which is perfectly executed, until … In real life, of course, not everything goes to plan. It seems that, in the end, only the unexpected is to be expected …

The Ghost Fabler: supernatural tales told within a chilling tale of the macabre

Who is the icily charming 'Mr. Green' and what is the real nature of his influence over powerful American business mogul Sebastian Engel? Why is he so determined to force traditional Irish storyteller Christine O'Donnell to work for him and why does he threaten the children she tutors? Can she turn detective and discover what his real purposes are and save both herself and the children? This is a unique and genuinely chilling book, a web of traditional ghost stories woven within a Faustian tale of evil at its most deadly and ambiguous. "Well, what can I say – what a creation …. It's like walking across Morecambe Bay without a guide: put a foot wrong and you don't know what you'll step into. Evil is to the side, at the front, behind, below, above … I do not remember breathing as I read the final chapter." A.B., a former book editor and previously of the Financial Times.

Printed in Great Britain
by Amazon

23910042R00131